No Good Deed

GOES UNPUNISHED

No Good Deed Goes Unpunished

A Novel by

Mike Chase

authorHOUSE®

AuthorHouse™
1663 Liberty Drive
Bloomington, IN 47403
www.authorhouse.com
Phone: 1-800-839-8640

Published by AuthorHouse 01/28/2013

ISBN: 978-1-4817-0135-8 (sc)
ISBN: 978-1-4817-0136-5 (hc)
ISBN: 978-1-4817-0137-2 (e)

Library of Congress Control Number: 2012924008

CHAPTER ONE

Walking Mark Wright through his gutted and gravel strewn basement, I explained the various plumbing and electrical issues I'd encountered during the demolition. Having completed many different remodeling projects at his hundred year old farmhouse over the previous ten years, he readily accepted my estimates on the fixes needed, giving me the go ahead on all of them.

After we headed upstairs, his wife Sandy told us about the threatening weather report being scrolled across the screen below 'Survivor'. As the television blinked out and the house went dark, Mark said, "There it goes again. I usually give it an hour then fire up the generator." Grabbing a flashlight off the top of the refrigerator, he opened it up and asked, "Bud light or Heineken?"

A large boom of thunder shook the house just then and I politely declined his usually accepted offer of a beer at the end of my work day. After going over a few of the remodeling details with Sandy, I said, "Should be here about eight thirty tomorrow. You all have a nice evening." Mark said, "You too, Mitch. See you tomorrow."

Thunder rumbled and distant lightning illuminated the darkening sky as I headed towards my van around quarter after eight. Lightning began streaking across the horizon soon after leaving the Wright's basement refinishing job, fifty miles north of my home in Orion, Missouri, thirty miles west of St. Louis.

My ears were still ringing from jack hammering trenches in the basement floor to install drain piping for a new bathroom as I called my wife Andrea. She was used to me working late, especially on jobs this far away, but if I was going to be home after nine the call was required.

She answered on the fifth ring. “So, what’s up? How late are you gonna be tonight?”

Well, used to it and liking it are different things.

“I’m headed home now. Can you check out the weather? It looks like I’m heading into a hell of a storm.”

I figured she was already ensconced on Facebook. After a bit of grumbling about having to close down her chat session she asked, “When are going to get an iphone?”

This came up nearly every time she had to use her computer or iphone for my information, especially if she was in a juicy conversation on Facebook. Somewhat of a dinosaur in the technological sense, I’d been promising to upgrade for months. My year old flip phone was a bit battered but still working and I had never taken the time or money to switch.

I said, “I’ll get one tomorrow,” then told her of the impressive lightning display I was witnessing as she got on the weather web site. Cloud to cloud lightning is rare in the Midwest. I was awed by the display, elaborating on it as she interrupted me and asked, “Where are you now?”

"I just passed the entrance to Logan." This being a conservation area she said, "That doesn't tell me anything. How far north of Heron are you?"

"About fifteen miles."

"Well, you're headed into a doozy of a downpour and they have a tornado warning for Lincoln County. The area around Heron is solid red. Be careful."

I glibly said, "You know careful is my middle name."

I heard her mumble, "Whatever" then she said, "Yeah, right."

Trying to sound offended I said, "What do you mean? I'm always careful . . . . I'll be home about nine . . . . love you."

"Love you too, but I'm still not buying it. Get me a bottle of merlot at Walgreens, okay?"

"Sure will. Anything else?"

"No, that oughta do it. Just drive safe. Bye."

"Bye"

Hanging up, I began planning the next day's activities. I'd found a slight crack in the cast iron tee for the upstairs toilet after taking down the existing paneling and ceiling. The correct way to fix the problem would be to cut it out and replace it with PVC pipe. This would require removing the toilet and cutting into the upstairs bathroom wall. Mark had agreed to this procedure as opposed to patching the crack. Thinking of the materials and time I would need for this latest curve to my already tight schedule, I pulled onto southbound Route 61.

Traffic was light, one of the benefits of working odd hours. Cruising along at sixty five as Bruce belted out 'Jungle Land' on the CD player, the little daylight remaining vanished as quickly as if someone threw a switch.

The first drops to hit the windshield were huge, splattering out to plate size before I could get my wipers turned on. Within a few seconds the roof of my two ton cargo van sounded like someone was playing the drums on it, quarter size hailstones smashing into my windshield for brief seconds at an amazing clip. Coming out of the hail there was a brief lull, only an occasional large drop falling, but descending into the Cuivre River valley the rain began coming down in torrents. Visibility dropping to next to nothing, and remembering Andrea's request, I slowed down to forty something for the deluge.

My wipers were having a hard time keeping up as a black Mustang flew by me through the slanting sheets of rain. Shaking my head a bit as I mumbled "Crazy," the rapidly fading tail lights swerved wildly as they swung into the right hand lane on the approach to the bridge. In a blink, the tail lights vanished off the right side of 61 just before the beginning of the guard rail.

The delay between perception and action chewed up some distance before I began hitting the brakes as hard as I dared. Hydroplaning as I pulled onto the shoulder and fighting the vans inclination to slew off the road, the rapidly nearing guard rail gave me another frightful consideration. I jammed on the brakes harder, the back of the van sliding towards the slope. The end of the guard rail was only five feet away when I finally stopped. Blowing out my held breath, I grabbed my phone and dialed 911.

The operator answered, "911. What is your emergency?"

Scared by the near miss, I shouted into the phone, "A CAR JUST WENT INTO THE CUIVRE RIVER!"

"Calm down sir . . . . tell me what happened and where you are."

Realizing how loudly I'd spoken, I took a deep breath then more calmly said, "I just saw a car go over the side on the north end of the southbound bridge over the Cuivre on Route 61."

"Can you see the car now?"

"Wait a second, I'm gonna have to get out to look for it."

I opened the door and was instantly drenched. After running hunched over to the edge of the hill, the top of the car was barely visible about two hundred feet ahead. The normally benign Cuivre had been over bank full on my trip north in the morning, and was now spreading over the fields of the valley. Gazing through curtains of rain, the car appeared to be moving slowly towards the river through the dark water covering a field.

"I can see it. It's floating towards the river!"

I glanced towards the road to see if anyone else was stopping, but apparently the downpour had ensured the other drivers' oblivion of the sudden event.

"What is your name?"

As I thought, "What the hell does that matter?" another look at the floating car confirmed that it was indeed headed towards the deeper riverbed. Realizing that if it reached the concrete slope below the bridge it could be swept downstream, I began jogging along the shoulder outside the guard rail, nearly yelling into the phone, "My name is Mitch Cones. I'm gonna see if I can get to the car. Send somebody here quick!"

I was the only person that might get there in time to save the passengers, if indeed they weren't dead already, since there was no sign of anyone trying to escape from the car. The 911 operator was asking, "Is that spelled C . . . O . . ." as I plopped the phone down next to the guard rail.

CHAPTER TWO

Looking back at the flooded field, the car was straight out from me and about fifty feet away from the bottom of the twenty foot tall bridge embankment. About half out of the water and bobbing up and down a bit it was spinning in the current but still moving towards the river. Weeds sticking out of the water convinced me it couldn't be that deep, and the car was only a short distance away. Even after this mental downplay of the inherent danger I mumbled, "What the hell am I doing?" as I took my first hurried step downhill.

My feet totally slipped out from under me and landing on my butt I was already rushing towards the water below. Grabbing instinctively at the slick grass to slow my descent to no avail, I quickly slid down the steep slope and splashed into the water. My feet hit bottom just as my head was going under. Thrashing my arms, I was able to right myself after a few panicky seconds and begin swimming across the ditch.

The water felt warmer than the rain that had been pelting me since I'd left the van. After I made my first few controlled strokes I felt for bottom. Finding it, I hurried up the slope of the ditch, half swimming and half walking. Gaining the top I looked for the car. I expected it to be fairly close but it was twenty yards away, bumping towards the river.

I cursed myself for not going farther down the shoulder before I headed into the water, or leading it, something a good wing shooter should always do. Coming out of the neck deep drainage ditch I pushed through some saplings and weeds, bouncing through waist high water as I rushed towards the car.

The clinging mud of a plowed field beyond the weeds began sucking off my tennis shoes and I quickly lost them both, but in a short while I reached the passenger door. The forward momentum of the car was increasing as I grabbed hold of the handle and looked inside. There was only one person visible, sprawled face up across the front seats.

Water was just creeping above the seat inside but window level outside the car. Knocking hard on the window trying to arouse the apparently female and unconscious occupant and seeing no response, I knew I was going to have to get the door open fast before she might drown as the water rushed in.

Upon forcing the door open against the weight of the water by putting a foot on the car and pulling, the muddy flow poured in and filled the interior up to the dash, the whole car sinking and slowing. The force of the water against the door suddenly pushed it all the way open, swinging the car in line with the current as I struggled to keep from slipping below it.

Finally getting my footing and climbing into the car, I frantically grabbed at her hair and pulled her head above the water. Using my body to push hers into a sitting position and then cradling her with my left arm, I pushed aside the long dark hair covering her face to determine if she was alive. She felt limp in my arms as the flashes of lightning reflecting off the water revealed a long gash in her forehead streaming blood over her face.

My own survival had crossed my mind as I slid into the quagmire and if the current had been too strong I might have aborted my rescue attempt after the first plunge. Deciding not to risk my neck any further for a corpse I yelled, "ARE YOU ALIVE?" and got no response.

For a second, I debated just dropping her and getting the hell out. Instead, I grabbed her somewhat roughly by the neck with my right hand to try to feel for a pulse.

At the pressure from my fingertips she began gagging and sputtering out water and I knew she was at least still alive. Saying, "Can you hear me?" after releasing my pressure, she started coughing and shaking. As I grabbed her around the shoulders to keep her from slipping back below the water her eyes flew open. Pushing me away with unexpected force, she screamed, "LEMA GOO!" I screamed back at her, "WE HAVE TO GET OUT OF HERE!"

She was pulling away in a panic, her hands flailing at me, but a second later she seemed to suddenly understand her predicament. She quit struggling against me and took a deep breath, expelling it with a loud rasp. I yelled, "COME ON, WE GOTTA GO," grabbed her arm, and pulled her towards the door.

Luckily the current was still holding the door open as I let go of her and jumped back into the nearly four foot deep water. Turning around to grab her she was groping under the water and I yelled, "WE DON'T HAVE TIME FOR THAT!" The current was pulling her away from me as I yanked on her arm. She was pulling back for a second, as if she didn't want to get out, then her resistance suddenly quit and we both tumbled into the flooded weeds outside as she spilled out of the car. Trying to grab hold of her and stand up at the same time, I slipped, letting go of her to get my head above water and take a breath. Finally regaining my footing I pulled her up by both arms and shouted, "YOU OKAY?"

Her eyes were looking at me but her head was kind of rolling around. She coughed a few times then sputtered out, "Uh . . . d . . . d . . . d . . . dass."

She was a tall woman, maybe even taller than my five-ten. Grabbing her by both shoulders I looked at her and yelled, "HOLD ONTO ME!" Her eyes were looking right at me then they closed and she collapsed. As she fell, her arms sliding down my waist as her head hit my chest, I frantically tried to get a hold on her. Gaining a bit of one as I slipped in the muck, I pulled her back up in a few seconds. Yelling, "YOU OKAY?" again she nodded, barely, then feebly said, "Yas."

Not sure if I could manage it if she passed out I yelled, "I'M GONNA GET YOU OUT OF HERE BUT YOU GOTTA STAY AWAKE."

She sputtered and coughed, weaving sideways a bit. I pulled her back to upright as I yelled "CAN YOU HEAR ME?"

The blood was streaming into her eyes and she made an attempt to wipe it out before saying, "Uss."

Close enough by me considering.

Wrapping my left arm around her we began plodding ahead against the steady current. The rain was coming down as hard as I'd ever seen it fall, thunder boomed nearly constantly and the nearby lightning made me want to get out of the water as quick as possible. She started babbling incoherent bursts of words but between the thunder, wind, and splashes from the deluge I couldn't understand, and really didn't care, what she was saying at that point.

Bearing straight away from the river we soon reached the edge of the corn, sinking in six inches or so with each step. She swayed back and forth like a drunk, and each step was a chore as I pulled her along by the shoulders with her stumbling and mumbling through the muck and dirty brown water covering the corn sprouts. I sure didn't want to get in a conversation, at least not until we got out of the water, but she got louder all the way.

Saying "Right" and "Yeah, okay" to her incoherent babbling, we slowly made our way about eighty yards before attempting to cross the ditch. The water was below my waist and I figured with average slope we'd be fine. Pushing through the weeds next to the ditch again, the water deepened as flashing lights began reflecting off the water. I felt her tense in my grasp as she straightened up a little and asked semi-clearly, "You . . . yo goat it?"

I said, "Yeah, I got it," thinking she was talking about being able to cross the ditch.

Sirens were screaming as she stammered out, "You . . . you . . ." Distracted but still plowing ahead, my right foot hit nothing but water. Turned towards her, I fell off the eroded bank into the ditch, pulling her with me.

For maybe ten seconds we were swimming, or rather I was swimming and pulling her along with me. After a bit of initial panic, the years of swimming lessons kicked in. I grabbed her around the shoulders and towed her till I felt ground underneath my feet then struggled up the slope through the water, her limp in my arms once again.

With us mostly out I slipped, dropping her as I slid all the way back in. She wasn't moving, except sliding downhill, as I scrambled back next to her lying face down. Having a hard time keeping both of us from slipping back in the water, I started smacking her on the back to make her cough up the water she'd swallowed. Trying to remember steps of my long ago CPR lessons I was pulling her over to begin trying when she began coughing up water and shaking once again. A few seconds later a light blazed on us, blue and red flashes back lighting two patrolmen as they headed our way.

CHAPTER THREE

After they scrambled down the bank one shouted, "Anybody else out there?" He grabbed my arm and pulled me uphill, slipping close to the water himself in the process.

As he let go of me I said, "No, I don't think so," then he turned to help his partner with her as she continued retching.

They pulled her to a kneeling position and his partner said, "Can you breathe?"

Continuing coughing, she waved her arm and choked out, "I . . . cough, cough . . . okay."

They could tell by the blood streaking down her face that she wasn't okay. As I clung to weeds to maintain my newfound position on Terra firma, the one closest to me shouted, "Are you hurt?"

I said, "No, just help her. I'm all right," even though that wasn't quite how I felt. I slipped my way behind them as they struggled to get her up the slippery slope. Sinking to my knees upon reaching the level shoulder and exhaling a large sigh of relief, I watched the cops set her down on the back seat of their squad car.

The flashing lights of a second police car were pulling to a stop behind the first and the wail of an ambulance siren was coming down the hill. The officers were toweling the blood off her face as I stood up and walked towards their car.

She was saying something to them I didn't catch as I came into their view. On seeing me she pushed them away and leaned out, looking up at me as I came to the side of the cruiser. Blood from her forehead began coursing down her face again, the rivulets mixing with raindrops and meandering off her chin.

Considering the events of the past twenty minutes, her look was totally unexpected. She was staring intently into my face with a seemingly malevolent glare, the flashes of light radiating off the cruisers roof casting her face in a macabre blue and red glow and enhancing the affect.

The cops were asking her if she was hurting anywhere else, but she just stared at me with that quixotic look and didn't say a word. The sight and her expression sent a cold chill through me as her gaze didn't waver. Assuming she must be in shock, I moved back a few feet as paramedics rushed past me.

As the paramedics began checking her out the rain suited trooper from the second car was being given a quick, hushed rundown on the details by the first two cops. Turning towards me he said, "Don't go anywhere."

Thinking, "Where am I going to go?" I watched the three cops escort the woman as the paramedics helped her towards the ambulance. After spending a couple minutes, I assumed asking her questions, the three of them walked back towards the first cruiser. I was sitting in the open back seat as the trooper walked up to me and and asked, "You got I.D.?" I pulled out my drenched wallet, digging for my license as he asked, "Can you tell us what happened here?"

Handing him my license I said, "Sure" then he said, "Watch your legs," shutting the door after I pulled them inside the car.

The single trooper, whose name tag read, "Trooper Gabe Richards" got into the other side of the back seat while the first two jumped into the front seat. Gabe again asked, "What happened here?"

In as few words as possible I explained the whole ordeal to them. Officer Ted Briley, the cop in the front passenger seat whose name tag I'd seen, interrupted me once and asked, "Where's your shoes?" After telling about them being sucked off by the mud in the cornfield, I finished my account of the rescue.

Gabe then asked if I knew the woman. I thought the answer to that was obvious, but I just said, "No, like I said she had just passed me and I saw her go off the road."

"If you don't know her, why'd you jump into the water to save her?" asked the driver, who hadn't said anything yet.

I thought, "That's a hell of a thing to say," but I wasn't really sure of the reason myself so I replied, "It just seemed like the thing to do at the time, I guess."

They kind of exchanged glances, then Gabe asked, "Is that your van?" pointing at it parked twenty feet or so in front of us.

"Yeaaah"

"Do you think you could drive to the station to give a statement?"

"What about my shoes?"

I knew you weren't supposed to drive without shoes but Gabe just said, "I don't think we're going to be able to find them."

Not quite sure how to respond to that, I decided not to answer and looked out towards the river. A news van and another two cop cars had pulled up in the past few minutes. The new arrivals were wandering along the shoulder, mostly shining spotlights and staring towards the dark water below. Gabe asked, "Where was her car the last time you saw it?"

"About a hundred yards ahead of us and maybe thirty feet from the bank."

The cops all got out of the car, but Gabe told me to stay inside. I watched them walk along the edge of the shoulder with most of the group outside towards the river, spreading out and shining their spotlights in slow arcs onto the water below as they got near the bridge. After about five minutes they came back and the first two quickly jumped into the front seat. Gabe opened up my door and asked, "Where is her car?"

Considering my story this struck me as a strange question, assuming he would know it may not be visible anymore. I said, "Probably floating down the river. When we left it was almost under water and heading that way."

He seemed satisfied with that and shut the door, then walked over to the group of cops who had gathered at the edge of the road. After a minute the later arrivals began heading back to their cars and pulling out, turning off their flashing lights as they did.

Officer Briley got out of the front seat as a lady reporter with an umbrella and a plastic wrapped microphone walked up to the car. She held the microphone up to him and he began pointing around, first at my van then into the flood below, then into the back seat towards me. The rain pounding on the roof kept me from hearing what he was saying but from her look towards me, I could tell he'd told her what I'd done. She pointed at me and Briley opened up his door and asked, "Would you like to talk to the news?" as he jumped back in the front seat.

I guess it hit me then that I would be portrayed as some kind of a hero. I thought about the moment when I'd almost left her in the car and decided I didn't want to talk to any reporters just then. At that moment I was too played out, muddy, and pent up in my thoughts about the recent events and the woman's sullen glare to care about my possible five minutes of fame.

Opening the door and looking at her, I leaned out a bit from the cruiser and said, "No," then closed the door. The driver turned around and faced me as he asked, "Why don't you want to talk to her?"

I said, "I don't really feel like it." and he just shrugged and seemed to accept my explanation.

Pointing towards the spot I asked, "Can I go and pick up my phone? I threw it down up there by the guard rail."

Briley asked, "Why'd you just throw it down?"

"I didn't want to go swimming with it."

After a bit he said, “They don’t work too well after you go swimming with them, do they? I’ll help you find it.”

We got out of the car and began walking towards the spot where I’d slid down the hill. The reporter was standing behind my van and I assumed she was taking down my plate numbers to find out my identity. I quickly found my phone but had no screen when I opened it up. I shut it off, this not being the first phone I’d gotten wet. Sometimes they worked afterwards and sometimes they didn’t, but I knew the best thing was to just shut them off till they dried.

Having watched the procedure Briley said, “I guess you don’t have to go swimming with them. Is this where you went down the hill?”

Pointing at the spot I said, “Yeah, the car was right out there.” Following my finger with the beam towards the now nondescript patch of water, he then shined his flashlight on the slope revealing a faint trail where the grass had been beaten down by my slide.

Seemingly amazed Briley said, “Looks like you had a hell of a ride there.”

“It wasn’t no fun.”

“I’d bet it wasn’t.”

He followed me back to my van. The lady reporter tried to stick the microphone into my face saying, “Sir, we’d just like to hear about your rescue of the woman.”

Briley said to her, "He doesn't want to talk to you." Coming around to the drivers' side with me he asked, "You sure you're okay to drive?" as I opened the door.

I replied, "Yeah, I'm sure" as I got in. I shut the door and rolled down the window, noticing him checking out the inside of my van, tools from front to back in the cargo bed. There was some paperwork lying on the front passenger seat and he seemed to be trying to read it as I bent down and pulled off my muddy socks, but he didn't say anything about my lack of shoes. Looking back at him he was eyeing me strangely, then just said, "Could you please follow us back to the station in Heron?"

Because the look he'd given me had seemed friendly, and he'd said 'please', I thought it was my prerogative. As I started the van to get some heat going my body told me I didn't want to go to the station, but my mind told me I shouldn't refuse. Delaying my response as I dried my drenched phone off with a napkin left over from lunch I asked, "Do you got a phone I can call my wife with?"

Already well past nine and our recent conversation coming to mind, I knew she'd be worried and the sooner I called her the better. He hesitated a few seconds, then dug his phone out from under his rain slicker and said, "Keep it quick" as he handed me his phone.

Leaving the window open, I dried off the phone a bit on the passenger seat and called Andrea's cell. She picked up on the first ring and I said, "Honey, it's me."

After a second she said, "What's up? Where are you calling from?"

"I just saved some woman's life and . . ."

"Yeah, right."

This bugged me so I said sternly, "Just listen to me for a minute, would ya'?"

She said, "Okay" and didn't interrupt me again as I gave my explanation non stop.

"I'm talking on a cop's phone and he's standing in the rain outside my van so I'm gonna make this quick. A woman drove her car into the Cuivre and I pulled her out of it. I have to go to the Heron police station and give a report on what happened. I'll get home when I can."

After a few seconds she surprisingly asked, "Why'd you do that?"

Not wanting to even go into that I said, "I'm still trying to figure that out."

"Where's the station?"

"I don't know. I'm following the cops there."

"I'll look it up. I'll be there in forty five minutes."

"You don't have to do that. I'll be home in an hour or two."

"I'm coming. Are you hurt?"

"Nah, just cold n' wet. If you're coming, bring me some dry clothes and shoes."

"Okay, anything else?"

"No, that oughta do it."

"I love you, but next time, don't be so stupid."

"What next time? I'll see you in a bit. Bye."

More than a little peeved at her for calling me stupid, I hung up then handed the phone back to Briley. After saying, "Follow us," he sprinted towards his car, already pulled up in front of me and blocking the right lane with lights flashing. Flashing my lights to let them know I was ready to go, I swung out onto 61 slowly. Following behind them till they got off at the Heron exit I wondered why they didn't turn off their flashing lights, regretting my 'decision' to give a statement.

CHAPTER FOUR

Pulling into the station, the two news vans in the parking lot kind of surprised me. The rescue story must have gotten out even without a statement from me, and this was confirmed when reporters headed towards my van after I parked. "Must be a slow night" I thought.

The cops got out of their car telling the journalists to back off as I exited the van. They began shouting questions anyways, and cameras were flashing as the cops hustled me into the front door.

The driver, Officer Ben Duncan, was pulled to the side by three men as we entered the front. A tall cop in a worn leather coat faced us saying, "Ted, take him up to the desk and read him his rights."

My rights? "What the hell you gotta do that for?" came out of my mouth before I could think. This certainly wasn't starting off on a good note.

The cop who'd said it answered, "It's just standard procedure in any investigation. Don't read anything into it."

Somewhat placated by his statement I followed Ted to the front desk. He read me my rights rather loudly as the other three talked in hushed tones, their words inaudible though I tried to listen.

Epaulets on his shoulders denoting rank, the only uniformed one in the bunch walked towards me after the unheard whisperings and eyed me over. He seemed to scowl at me for a few seconds then said to Briley, "Take him back to One."

The gist of my treatment so far made me regret agreeing to subject myself to it. Assuming I'd had the choice, I followed Briley to an interrogation room at the back of the station. Entering the room I asked, "What the hell's going on? I thought I was just coming here to give a statement?"

He held his hands out as if he didn't have, or, wasn't willing to reveal the answer then said in a nice tone, "Just give your statement then. You want a coffee or something?"

Increasingly perplexed, I requested a towel and some coffee and he left the room to get it. Coming back in less than a minute he said, "I don't know if I'd have done it." as he handed me the towel and coffee.

He was the only one that had seen the true perspective of the situation as I'd taken the plunge. Assuming he was talking about heading into the water, I took his comment as a compliment. I said, "Aw, sure you would've" while thinking, "Now there's an honest cop".

The three cops that had diverted Duncan at the door came into the room. The uniform said, "We got it Ted" and Briley left the room. As the obviously ranking officer turned towards me I wondered if he always looked mean or what, a virtual snarl still plastered on his face. He said, "Mr. Cones, I'm Captain Harold Smythe. Could you take a seat?" pointing towards the lone chair at the back of the table.

Perturbed about his apparent animosity, I sat down and tried to quell my mounting anger. The other two took the chairs on the opposite side, Smythe remaining standing as I met his condemning gaze with my own.

Perhaps seeing the anger building in my face the suit on the left tried to deflect it by saying, “Mr. Cones, can I call you Mitch?” in a friendly tone.

“Yeah, I guess you can call me whatever.”

My response obviously wasn’t what he’d expected. He gave me a look I didn’t quite decipher, then he continued by saying, “Mitch, I’m Detective Bill Curtouis and this is Detective Sergeant James O’Brien,” pointing at the cop in the leather jacket. “First off, we’d like you to tell us exactly what happened out there tonight. Could you speak into the microphone and tell us everything you remember?”

Trying to get this over as quickly as possible, I realized that the most complete story would be the best to accomplish this desire. They could take my statement then I’d call Andrea and tell her I was already leaving and she could turn around. Sounded like a plan, anyways.

After taking a few more sips of coffee while I envisioned a quick departure I repeated my story in a lot more detail than I’d told the cops at the scene, starting when I left the job and finishing at the point when Briley said, “Follow us.” I told them everything she’d said that I could remember including her, “You got it?” query, and that I was wondering why she hadn’t said anything to me afterwards. At the end I said, “I guess that’s about it” and immediately Smythe asked me to repeat it again.

Their somewhat skeptical looks as I had told my tale again seemed totally out of place considering the facts and my conversations with the officers at the scene. Smythe especially was looking at me like he didn't believe me, or maybe even that I was some sort of criminal. This made me rather indignant, if not just plain pissed off. I said, "No, I won't repeat it again. Just listen to the tape!"

All three kind of jumped back at my refusal, then Smythe said, "We just want to be sure of the facts because we didn't find any trace of her car. For all we know now, there wasn't even a car of hers involved."

"Why don't you just ask her?"

"We would, but she hasn't said a word since they got her in the ambulance, and she never said anything about another car or you saving her."

I assumed that meant she wasn't unconscious or unable to talk. The look she'd given me while standing outside the cruiser flashed through my head, but I said, "Maybe she's just in shock."

"It doesn't appear so, and I'm wondering why she would just clam up if your story is true."

The "if" really got me pissed. I took a deep breath to regain my composure and said, "Everything I told you is true . . . . Listen to the 911 tape. Why would I call 911 if it wasn't true. Your officers saw me climbing out of the water with her . . . AND she was talking to them after they put her in their car . . . . Call up the Wrights. They'll tell you I just left there and that I didn't have a woman with me when I did."

"We'll do that, but it seems that she must have some reason for keeping quiet, don't you think?"

"I sure don't know what that reason might be. I didn't understand anything she said to me other than what I've told you."

"Wellll" he drawled, "it seems the name she gave us doesn't come up in our search of DMV records. Did she tell you her name or did you happen to get her plates?"

I looked at him like he was crazy and said, "Wellll, no, I didn't think to introduce myself or dive under the water to get her plates. I was kind of busy with other things."

I guess he caught my sarcasm because next he said, "Don't give me that attitude!"

I said "You obviously don't believe me after I risked my life out there tonight to help a stranger. In my place, wouldn't you get an attitude!"

"Since we don't know who she is, we can't be sure she's a stranger to you. Officer Duncan said she gave you a funny look while she was sitting in the car. And, according to him, she never said thanks or anything to you . . . . even though you were standing right in front of her. Why do you suppose that is, if you'd just saved her life like you say, unless maybe you were the one that put her in the water in the first place?"

Duncan must have also noticed the strange look she gave me. Looking at him in consternated amazement at this accusation I said, "Beats me. I've been thinking that was kind of odd myself but I sure as hell didn't PUT her in the water. Talk to officer Briley.

He saw where I slid down the hill. Why would I drag her along the guard rail where anybody driving by could have seen us if I was trying to drown her or whatever you're thinking?"

"Maybe she was running away from you and that's where you caught up to her and you both slid down the hill there."

I couldn't even begin to understand his twisted logic and shaking my head in disgust I said, "What the hell is wrong with you?"

O'Brien, who reminded me of an older Sam Elliot had been sitting there just listening up to this point. He cleared his throat and in a deep gravel voice said, "It seems somebody must be hiding something. I've never seen someone just plain refuse to talk after their life was just saved. Most times they can't shut up. Nobody saw a car in the water and no other cars were there when officers Duncan and Briley showed up. Why didn't you try to flag someone down to help or something?"

I thought of the cars splashing by me as I ran down the shoulder and said, "I was the only one that saw her car go off the road because there weren't any other cars around and you couldn't see shit through the rain as hard as it was falling. Do you think people would have stopped for a guy waving his arms on the highway on a night like this?"

He seemed to consider all this for a moment, then said, "I guess maybe not."

"Like I told you, the car was heading for the river. I knew if I didn't try it might be gone before anyone else could get there, and it WAS gone by the time they did. Are you even looking for it?"

O'Brien cleared his throat again, then said, "We'll send some boats to the scene and will probably send out divers in the morning if you're sure she wasn't with you to begin with. Are you sure about that?"

I stared at him and felt the small hairs on the back of my neck tingling. I'm usually slow to anger, but this was starting to really get to me and I snapped out, "What, you think we just decided to go swimming? And if I was trying to kill her why wouldn't she say that to anybody? She sure had the chance!"

He must have seen the improbability of that finally, because he said, "We just don't want to risk people out there looking for a car that isn't there. I believe you've been telling the truth but we need to know for sure before we do that, you understand? We can't be sure now when she might start talking, so we have to take your word about it. You see why we need the truth, don't you?"

I saw his point, but it still didn't sit well with me about their tactics. I said, "I understand about all that but I've told you nothing BUT the truth. The car is in the river, although I think you're probably going to have a hard time finding it. It could be anywhere by now."

Seeming to look off into space for a second, he turned back to me and said, "That's what I'm worried about."

Since they seemed to finally believe me I asked, "Is my wife here yet?"

Smythe said, "You can talk to her when we're through." as if he was being magnanimous about it.

I'd had about enough of him at that point. I'd gone there thinking they would be patting me on the back for my actions. Instead, it seemed they wanted to pin something on me. Smythe's comment made me want to just get the hell out of there.

Turning towards Smythe, I spat out, "Are you charging me with something or what? This is fucking ridiculous!"

He said, "Calm down. No, we're not charging you with anything, at least not until we talk to the woman. We just want to know who she is and what happened out there," as if everything I'd said had gone in one ear and out the other. "Why didn't you want to talk to the reporters at the scene or out front? Most people would be glad to be known as a hero!"

I saw his reasoning, wishing I'd just stayed at the scene and hammed it up for the reporter, but decided right then I wasn't going to talk to Smythe anymore after all the bullshit he'd been putting out. I stared at O'Brien saying, "I didn't know that I'd be treated like this or I WOULD have talked to her. I want to talk to my wife. Am I free to go?"

The three cops in the room looked at each other, and with a shrug O'Brien said "You know we can keep you for twenty four hours, don't you?"

The thought that they might do that to be sure, or maybe just for spite, made me hold back the first reply that popped into my mind. Trying to keep my temper I toned it down and said, "Yeah, I know that, but if you do that, I'm going to talk to the news and anybody else that will listen and tell them how you treated me here tonight, and I'm going to press charges against you for unlawful detainment. When the real truth comes out you're gonna look like a bunch of idiots." I guess I didn't tone it down that much after all.

I thought I'd just ensured my accommodations for the night and was truly surprised when after a few seconds O'Brien said, "Mr. Cones, we're just doing our jobs here. If everything you told us is true, and I believe it is, I can understand how you'd be upset right now. Sure you're free to go, but we're going to want to talk to you again. What's your phone numbers, your wife's number and while you're at it can I get the Wright's number too?"

I gave him the numbers then got up and left the room, followed closely by the trio of interrogators. Rounding the corner into the front room, I practically ran into Andrea waiting at the front desk. The parking lot was still lit up with the lights of news vehicles, but I was glad they at least hadn't been allowed in the lobby.

Giving her a quick hug as I saw her look of worry, I said "Let's get out of here." I caught Smythe staring at us with a chagrined look on his face. He shook his head and turned towards O'Brien saying, "Tell them they can come inside," as he gestured towards the parking lot.

O'Brien hadn't moved as Andrea started asking a stream of questions. Not wanting to have an audience while I told her about the strange aftermath I turned us towards the door saying, "I'll tell you all about it when we get home."

Smythe came up behind us and said, "Mrs. Cones, could we talk to you for a minute?"

This just kind of blew the roof off the feelings of relief I'd been having since seeing Andrea. Spinning around and facing him I snapped, "What do you need to talk to her about? She wasn't there!"

Knowing he had no right to force her to talk he just said, "Well, I guess it can wait till later." Then he glanced out the window saying, "Do you want to talk to them now?" as he gestured at the news media outside.

I surely didn't and said, "Not after what you just put me through."

"Shall we release your name to them?"

I doubted that would make a difference after seeing the first reporter taking down my plates, but decided to say no anyway. Then I asked, "Could you at least get us out of the parking lot without being mobbed?"

Andrea was bewildered by the exchange and kept looking at me for some answers to her befuddlement. She had logically assumed that I would be getting thanked rather than interrogated for over an hour.

Smythe said, "We'll be in touch tomorrow," then turned to the detectives and said "Let's get them out of here."

O'Brien said, "Mrs. Cones, would you like an umbrella?"

She seemed surprised by the offer but said, "I sure would. Thank you." as he handed her one.

Leaving the building, the rain was pouring down even harder than when I'd entered it. Our police escort told the group of umbrella holding reporters outside, "Make way, let us through" as they shouted questions, obviously still hoping for a statement from me.

Andrea was looking totally perplexed and I could tell she didn't want to wait till we got home for some answers as she said, "Let's just take my car. We can come back tomorrow and pick up the van."

I asked O'Brien if it was okay to leave my van there that night. He said, "Sure, that's fine. You're really not supposed to drive without shoes anyway."

CHAPTER FIVE

We got in Andrea's Lesabre and headed towards home. I half expected a convoy to follow us out of the parking lot, but none of the reporters' cars or vans did. Andrea pulled back out onto southbound 61, then turned and asked, "Why were you so mad at that cop?"

Still somewhat steaming and not wanting to snap at her I said, "Let me get out of these wet clothes then I'll tell you all about it."

I'd always hated the feeling of wearing wet jeans, and I'd been itching, cold and uncomfortable since sitting in the cruiser. After taking out my wallet and emptying my front pockets of the large assortment of screw gun bits, change and junk that had accumulated throughout the day, I began stripping off my wet clothes. Putting them in the plastic grocery bag Andrea had brought my dry clothes in, I threw the bag on the back seat floor, toweled off a bit, and donned my dry duds.

Feeling somewhat comfortable finally, I began my tale of the rescue and subsequent interrogation. First, I tried to explain to her, and maybe myself also, what I'd been thinking when I'd gone into the river. Best I could come with was it just seemed like the timing of the events had thrust me onto the stage, so to speak, and my part was already set. Some inner voice told me if I just watched the car float away I'd always feel like I choked when the pressure was on, having to wonder what if, and no amount of rationalization later would be able to prevent it. It's amazing how quickly the mind can think, and this sudden conviction had compelled me to grab my part by the horns.

"You're just lucky you didn't get gored by those horns. So if you saved her, why were you so mad at the cops? What did they say to you?"

"Nobody else ever saw her car and she quit talking right after the cops showed up. That Captain Smythe basically accused me of making up the whole story, and it fucking pissed me off. Said I must have had her with me or at least knew her, cause she gave me a look like she wanted to kill me when the cops were trying to clean her up . . . . They couldn't believe she'd act like that if I'd just saved her."

We had a good marriage, and I had never been unfaithful to her in any way since the day we met. By her words, she'd been cheated on and burned by her first two husbands and I'd had to deal with their faults, as well as my own, in order to gain her trust. Perhaps the fact that the cops seemed suspicious of me, or maybe just her innate distrust of men, made her ask, "Did you know her?"

I certainly wasn't expecting that question from her. The fact that she'd even asked made me bark out, "What? Hell no. I didn't even get that ungrateful bitch's name. They're gonna search for her car in the morning, and I sure hope they find it so they'll know I wasn't just making up the whole damn thing. If that woman had just said anything, really, I wouldn't even have to worry about it."

I replayed the whole sequence of events in my head as Andrea kept asking questions. As I told her all the details, more questions than answers were forming in my head. Why had she been driving so fast in a blinding rain? What had she been talking about when she asked me if I had "it". Why had she started screaming at me when she came to in the car? I hadn't seen it as anything other than panic at the time, but her silence made me think it was instinctive. Why had she given me that hateful look? Since Duncan had also noted it, I was sure I didn't just imagine it. Why hadn't she thanked me in any way for what I'd done? Why had she gone totally quiet soon after being rescued? Why wouldn't she even give her real name? Why had Smythe been such a prick and seemed to want to blame the whole thing on me?

The woman had appeared to be somewhere in her early thirties to me, but between the rain, the blood and the mud I couldn't have bet on that. My first inclination was to assume she was a wanted criminal of some type, but the more I thought about her scream and the momentary panic she'd had when she came to, the more I discounted that explanation as the only reason for her actions.

As I was lost in this reverie of thought, Andrea's phone rang and startled the hell out of me. We were almost home as she answered "Hello," then quickly passed the phone to me. I knew before the caller spoke that it must be the cops because no one ever called us this late.

"Hello"

Smythe said, "Mr. Cones?"

I thought, "Who else would it be?" but just said, "Yeah, it's me."

"Mr. Cones, this is Captain Smythe. I'm at the hospital with the woman you rescued."

At least he said that, so I assumed she had started talking. "How is she?"

"Well, the cut on her forehead is pretty bad, but we think she'll be okay. She doesn't appear to have any other injuries except a few bumps and bruises."

"That's great."

"The reason I'm calling is that she has requested to see you. Do you think you could come to the hospital and talk to her?"

"Now?"

"Well . . . . yes . . . now, if you would. We'd appreciate it."

Thinking, "Then I don't want to do it" I said, "Can't it wait till tomorrow?"

"Her request to talk to you is the only thing she's said, and we're hoping to clear up this incident as quickly as possible. I think that might be in YOUR best interests too."

Obviously until she started talking or they found her car, Smythe wasn't going to let me off the hook. We were pulling into the driveway and all I wanted to do was take a shower and go to bed. Thinking about the only other way I might clear myself of this quickly I asked, "Did you find her car yet?" without much hope of an affirmative answer.

The rain had not let up since I'd left work and the river would be rising. When we'd made our escape from the car, it had only been about fifty yards from the concrete embankments below the bridge. Once it got there the swollen river would surely push it downstream, at least until it hung up on something. Soon after we'd left it it must have been pushed into the ditch by the current, totally submerged and invisible to anyone at the scene.

He said "There is still no sign of it. We'll be sending boats out tomorrow to try to find it but with the way it's looking outside, we called off the search till then. If it's there, we may not find it until the river goes back down."

"Great" I thought, there's that "if" again, then said, "I'm at home now. If it's so important, I'll clean up a bit and head back there. Where's the hospital?"

Andrea said immediately, "You're not going back there tonight in this kind of weather. Tell him you'll go to the hospital tomorrow morning."

I knew I would have a fight on my hands with her if I insisted on going, especially after she had asked me if I did know her. To leave now might make her think I really did, and that was the last thing I wanted. At the same time, the woman's request to talk to me had piqued my curiosity, to say the least, and I wanted some answers myself.

Smythe had been giving me directions to the hospital as I was weighing my decision. He was asking, "How long will it take you to get here?" as I made up my mind and decided it wasn't worth a fight with Andrea to go.

"I'm sorry, but it will have to wait till tomorrow. I can be there by eight."

Smythe didn't say anything for a few seconds. Finally, after blowing out what sounded like an exasperated sigh he replied, "Well, I guess you've had a long night already. Someone will be waiting for you in the lobby. Just ask at the desk when you get there."

I said, "I'll be sure to do that. Thanks for calling," rather sarcastically then hung up the phone.

Andrea turned to me and asked, "Why did they want you to go to the hospital?"

"It seems that the woman wants to talk to me. She probably just wants to thank me for saving her."

Even as I said it, something told me that probably wasn't the reason. She could have easily done that after I saved her, but hadn't. I suddenly thought about how calmly she'd asked me, "You got it?" If indeed she had been in shock as her actions and stunted, incomprehensible monologue till then seemed to indicate, how had she pulled out that lucid question from her delirium? She hadn't given me anything, so maybe she meant, "Do you understand it?"

I wished I'd been able to hear more of her rambling discourse as Andrea asked, "Is she talking to the police yet?"

I didn't want to lie about it, but knew that if I told her the woman would only talk to me her suspicions would only increase. I said, "Yeah, she's started talking." I felt bad about the half truth, but really didn't want any more conflict at the moment.

We went inside and after Andrea asked me if I was hungry I said, "No, I just want to take a shower and crawl into bed. I'm beat," whether more from a long day at work, the rescue, or the interrogation I couldn't be sure. After a quick shower, I tried to get to sleep. Andrea had drifted off while I was in the shower, and an hour later I finally did the same, dramatic images of the evening playing on my eyelids every time I closed my eyes.

CHAPTER SIX

I awoke the next morning at about six as Clyde, one of our golden retrievers, began whining to be let out. We have a doggy door but he's a night barker, scared of his own moon shadow, so unless we were gone we always closed it at night. For a second, the events of the previous night seemed like part of the nightmare I'd had and the feeling of being dragged into a vortex persisted after I opened my eyes. Shaking my head to wake up, the events of a few hours ago suddenly came rushing back at me.

As I sat up in bed, Andrea rolled over and put her arm around my waist. Sleepily she said, "Good morning." Stroking her arm, I said, "Good morning to you too." She sat up and gave me a kiss, then said, "How'd you sleep? You were tossing and turning all night."

Thinking about my nightmare I gave her a hug, then said, "Tell you the truth, like shit. Dreamed I was drowning in this big whirlpool with a bunch of other people."

She said, "That's hardly surprising after last night. I still can't believe you did that. Well, at least you got to wake up in our bed."

The possible bad consequences of my rescue attempt had not been in my mind at the moment I stepped off the shoulder, but now they came flooding into my brain. I tried to shake off those dark thoughts and concentrate on my agenda for the day.

After letting the dogs outside and grabbing us a cup of coffee, I took a long hot shower. As I emerged from the bathroom Andrea said, "I'm going to take off work today and go to the hospital with you."

Thinking about my white lie of the previous night I realized if we both went there and the woman would only talk to me still, my fib might come out. That would certainly stir up the suspicion pot, even though I'd never deserved it. Those little white lies always seem to have a way of coming back at you.

"You don't have to do that. I'll probably just be there for a few minutes then I'm going to work from there. You can just drop me off at the station."

Andrea wouldn't have it and said, "I'm going. You need to take off today too. You might cut your arm off if you try to work after what happened last night!"

She was being a little dramatic, but knowing when she got like this there was no changing her mind all I could think to say was, "Yeah, you're probably right."

I might have tried a different tack, but just then the home phone on her night stand rang. Andrea picked it up and said, "Hello?"

I knew by her quick glance that they were asking for me so I asked, "Who is it?"

"It's the police."

Feeling a sense of dread, I grabbed the phone. I heard a voice say, "Is this Mitch Cones?"

"Yes"

"Mr. Cones, this is detective Curtouis. Has anyone contacted you since you talked to Captain Smythe last night?"

"No, besides my wife, you're the only person I've talked to since then. Why do you ask?"

He paused for a good five seconds as if to weigh his next question. "Are you sure the woman you rescued hasn't made contact with you?"

Huh? As far as I knew, she didn't even know my name. Even though she had asked to see me the chance that she might try to call me didn't seem reasonable. Besides, they probably had someone watching her at the hospital, so how could she have called me without them knowing? All this was swirling through my brain as I answered "No, like I told you, I haven't talked to anyone since Captain Smythe."

His next statement was already in my head before he said it. "The woman disappeared from the hospital last night. We thought she might have tried to contact you since she asked to see you last night. Could you check your phones to see if she might have done that?"

I looked at the answering machine and Andrea's cell phone and said, "I don't see anything"

"Are you sure? Right now, you're our only lead as to who she might be."

"How am I a lead? I already told you guys a hundred times that I don't know who she is. If you needed to know so badly, why didn't you just fingerprint her or something?"

"We were going to do just that this morning but she disappeared before six."

As his statement hit home, I realized that my situation was only getting worse. If they couldn't find her or her car, my culpability for being a villain of some sort would greatly increase.

"Wasn't somebody watching her? How could she just walk out without anyone seeing her?"

"She was sedated to help her sleep and pretty banged up. We had no reason to believe that she would try to leave. There was an officer in the hall and she was on the second floor. It seems she escaped through the window, but right now we don't know how she could have done that. We need you to drive back up here, or if you'd like, we can send a car to pick you up."

Andrea had been staring at me with an increasingly worried look throughout the conversation. I thought about everything I'd just heard and felt the swirling vortex of my dream take hold in more substantial form.

"I'll be there in about an hour."

"Thank you, Mr. Cones. We'll be looking for you then."

He hung up and I grabbed the remote to turn on the news. On the second channel I hit, footage of my face taken as I'd leaned out the car to say "No" to the reporter was on and the commentator was saying, ". . . . last night around eight thirty. A passing driver apparently pulled the woman to safety. The woman and the driver have not been identified. Divers are searching for her car as we speak. We'll take you to Jane Lawrence at the scene."

I was thinking, "That was weird," because of the timing of catching my own face on TV for the first time, when the view on the screen changed. A comely blond news reporter was standing beside the guard rail near where I'd thrown my phone down. The rain had stopped, but the sky behind her was an almost solid black mass. A lightning bolt flashed as she started speaking.

"This is Jane Lawrence at the scene of last night's dramatic accident and rescue. I am standing above the Cuivre River, where, as you can see, divers are attempting to locate the car that plunged into these raging waters around eight thirty last night."

The camera panned down to show four boats searching the flood waters on the north side of the embankment. Some, seemingly manned by civilians, were using long poles to probe the bottom and in the actual police boat you could see assorted scuba gear and men talking into microphones. The water appeared to be much higher up the bank than it had been when I left there. I immediately thought, "They're not going to find it there."

By now the normally tranquil North Cuivre, barely floatable in a canoe during the summer, was close to a mile wide at that point. Even when the water had only been up to my waist I could feel its' inexorable penchant to take anything not attached downstream. I thought, "Hell, it could be halfway to the Mississippi by now," thirty five river miles away.

Jane said, "We are trying to piece together this bizarre episode, but as of now, all we know is that after receiving a 911 call from the unidentified motorist of a car going into the river at this spot at eight thirty two last evening, police responded to the scene. The first officers on the scene helped a man and woman out of the water below, and he told the officers he had rescued the woman from her car. The man declined to comment to the reporters at the scene or at the police station after the incident. The woman was injured and in shock and was transported to Mercy General Hospital in Heron, Missouri. We'll fill you in on further details as they become available."

I said to Andrea, "They barely helped me out of the water," as Jane listened for a few seconds to her headset. She turned her face back to the camera and said, "This is just coming in. The woman disappeared from the hospital last night, some time between four and six this morning. Police still haven't determined her name and are trying to locate her. If anyone has seen this woman, or knows who she is, please contact the Heron police department or your local law enforcement agency."

They had put up a picture of her on the screen. It showed her sitting up in a hospital bed, clean and dry, but showing some big bruises and a puffy six inch bandage across her forehead. I looked closely at the picture and figured I wouldn't have even recognized her from the evening before. She looked closer to forty than the early thirties I had figured, but that might have been just due to her battered appearance. She seemed defiant in the photo, as if she was mad at the photographer, and I thought in spades, "This woman is trouble."

I had told Andrea about the disappearance of the woman as I'd turned on the TV, even though she'd probably gathered that from my conversation with Curtouis. I began dreading the return trip to the station, knowing I couldn't tell them anything I hadn't already and they might be even more suspicious after the escape of the woman. Also, they probably weren't going to find her car, at least not quickly, the only other corroboration of my story. In short, I was screwed, and began trying to cover my ass. Even when you're totally in the right, you still have to do it sometimes.

Calling up the Wrights to tell them I wouldn't be able to make it there today, Mr. Wright surprisingly answered on the start of the second ring. Like most of my customers, I'd done many projects for them over the years and we were friends, at least of sorts. I knew their schedules and seven o'clock was an hour before they usually got up. Mark asked why I couldn't make it, and I told him quickly about the previous night's events. If nothing else, he could tell the cops I'd left there without a woman.

After telling him about it he asked, "That was really you who saved that woman? We just saw it on the news. A Captain Smythe from Heron called us at eleven thirty last night and asked if you had been working here until after eight, but he didn't say why he was asking."

"Yeah that was me. You told them I was there until after eight, didn't you?"

"I sure did because he seemed pretty concerned about the exact time. He also asked a lot of other questions about you and I told him you were one of the most straight up guys I've ever met. They don't think you were doing anything wrong, do they?"

"I'm not sure what they think after this morning . . . . It's kind of . . . uh . . . complicated right now . . . I have to go to the police station and . . . I . . . I'm not sure when I can make it back over there. I'll call you and let you know after I clear up this mess."

"You just do what you got to and we'll see you when you can, okay?"

At least this isn't going to be a problem there I thought, as I said, "Thanks a lot. I'll get back over there as soon as I can."

"Thanks for calling. I'll see you later and you can tell me all about it."

CHAPTER SEVEN

Andrea and I headed to the door to go back to Heron, and on opening it found two news vans parked out front. I thought, "Here we go again." as we stepped out on the front porch. How they found me I didn't know but I guessed, "That's their job," like the Heron cops of the night before.

Reporters with their entourages were exiting the vans as we walked down the steps towards Andrea's car. They came up on the driveway and the first to speak said, "Mr. Cones, can we talk to you for a minute?"

I remembered my threat to the cops, but since they hadn't detained me, I felt no urge to become a spectacle of interest. Suddenly becoming angry for their gall in being at my house after refusing to talk to them last night, I flashed a perturbed look at them and said, "No, I don't have anything to say."

Obviously, they weren't about to take no for an answer, because the questions just started flowing.

"Did you know the woman?"

"Do you know where she is?"

"Why don't you want to talk?"

"What made you dive into the river to save her?"

We just hurried into the car and I started it up. They were practically draping themselves across the car as I put it in reverse and slowly backed out of the driveway. I didn't want to hit them, but figured it would be their fault if I did.

Some of the neighbors were standing outside watching, probably since the news vans had first pulled up. I shifted into drive after backing out, and a reporter stood right in front of the car, backed up by a cameraman. "Man, these guys don't give up!" I said to Andrea as I inched my way forward. They moved to the side and finally I was able to get going.

Andrea looked at me and asked, "How long do you think THIS will go on?"

I surely didn't know, having never been in this situation before. I replied, "Hopefully not long. Maybe they'll find her and quit bugging me."

We arrived at the station and I was surprised to see no sign of the press there. After walking inside and telling the desk clerk who I was, she told us to take a seat and someone would be with us soon. We hadn't even sat down yet when Detective O'Brien came out of the back and walked towards us. He said, "Thanks for coming. I'm sorry about the way it went last night, but I just have a few more questions for you."

I thought, "Yeah, probably a whole day's worth." but replied, "I'll be glad to help you any way I can, but I already told you everything that happened."

"I'll try to make this quick as possible, but after her disappearance, we think there's a lot more to this than meets the eye, wouldn't you agree?"

I certainly agreed with that statement, but didn't want to give him any more encouragement to keep me there all day, so I just said, "I guess it looks that way."

He then turned to Andrea, saying, "Mrs. Cones, I need to talk to your husband. Could you just take a seat in the waiting room? I promise I won't keep him long."

I knew she didn't want to do that, but surprisingly she only said, "I'll be waiting for you," kissed me then headed towards the bank of chairs.

O'Brien turned back to me and said, "Could you come with me, please?" and before I could answer, began walking to the back of the station. I followed him and was soon seated in the same chair as the night before. O'Brien said, "Would you like some coffee?" and I thought, "This is starting to sound too familiar," basically that same question having been the prelude to their "accusations" of the preceding evening.

I said, "No, let's get this over with." and folded my hands on the tabletop.

O'Brien sat down across from me and said, "Mr. Cones, can I call you Mitch?"

"Sure, that's my name."

He looked at me sideways for a second then said, "Mitch, I've listened to the 911 call, the tape of your interview and I've read the reports given by the officers at the scene. We talked to the Wrights to confirm you'd been there, and on face value, everything points to the conclusion that it's just like you say it happened. Had she not escaped, because right now we think that's what we should call her disappearance, we would probably not have any further questions for you. Oh, by the way, everyone thinks that was a very brave thing you did, even though we probably didn't say that well enough in our interview last night."

I thought, "You didn't say that at all," but just stared at him and said, "That's okay."

"Now, you've stated that you saw her car headed towards the river and decided to try to save her yourself, is that correct?" I just nodded then he said, "How did you know it was a woman in the car?"

After the fact of course I knew it was a woman, but he was trying to mince my words and catch me in some sort of lie it seemed. I felt my blood beginning to boil again and said, "Of course I didn't know who was in the car at the time I headed towards it. I probably said it was a woman because that's what it was. I didn't mean I already knew it was a woman before I reached the car."

Thinking about my statement for a while, he said, "Well . . . . that sounds reasonable . . . . You also said she only babbled as you made your way out of the water. Besides the few things you told us she said, are you sure you can't remember anything else she said while she was "babbling"?"

If she hadn't been asking me if I understood her then maybe "it" meant something out of her car, and I sure wouldn't have gone back for her purse or whatever the hell she was talking about. Other than that, I didn't catch any words that I could be even reasonably sure of. I said as much to O'Brien then he said, "What about other words you may have thought you heard?"

I knew that nothing else she'd said had been clear enough to understand and said, "That's all I remember her saying. She wasn't talking too good but she kept talking anyways."

"Why didn't you ask her what she was talking about?"

"Like I said, I started to, but we went under water as I was. Besides, it really didn't seem too important at the time. Whatever she was talking about, I didn't have and I wasn't going to try to find it at that point. It was all I could do just to get her and me out of the river."

Without hesitation, he said, "That was a hell of a thing to do at that. Now let's talk about when you were standing in front of her as the officers were cleaning her up. Officer Duncan says she kind of pushed them away and just stared at you. She didn't say anything at all, and we find this kind of strange since you had saved her life just moments before. He also said, not only did she not say anything, but if looks could kill, you'd have dropped dead on the spot, his words not mine." He paused for affect and stared at me closely.

Her accusing look at me had certainly seemed out of place with the situation and I had replayed it in my head many times since. It now seemed clear that she was thinking I had "it." I hadn't been searched, so it seemed logical that she hadn't accused me of anything in her brief dialogue with the officers at the scene. That pointed to the conclusion that whatever "it" was, she didn't want them knowing about. The fact that she had a head injury might negate some of the importance of her actions at the time, but her silence and hateful stare had not seemed like the actions of a delusional or confused mind. There must have been something of grave importance to her in the car to be concentrating on that instead of being thankful she was alive.

I suddenly was certain that she had escaped so quickly because she was worried the police would find "it."

O'Brien had been staring at me intently as I'd mulled all this over in my head, and after telling him my thoughts, I said "Maybe she was just out of her head or something, but she sure seemed to be trying to say something to me. She might have been just asking me if I understood what she'd been saying when she asked me, "Do you got it", but I sure as hell don't know was going through her mind when she gave me that look."

"It does seem strange. And you are sure that she didn't give you anything, and besides her, you took nothing out of the car?"

"Yes, I'm sure. I'm not a thief, and I didn't even look around the car other than to make sure she was the only one inside."

"Mitch, nobody is trying to call you a thief. I'm just curious about what could have been so important to her. You didn't see anything in the car that might have caused her to react the way she did?"

"I'm curious too, but that don't mean I know what she was talking about. Like I told you last night, the car filled up as soon as I opened the door. Whatever was in the car, I wouldn't have seen anyways. It was dark and that water was brown as mud. Have they found her car yet?" After watching the news, I was pretty sure they hadn't, but wanted to get off the talk about "it".

"Not the last I heard."

"I was watching the news this morning, and it seems they should be looking downstream more. The spot they were looking is about where it was when we left the car. I'm sure it probably got swept under the bridge pretty soon after we left it."

"They've been looking as far as a half mile or so downstream, but with the amount of water flowing it could be anywhere. We'd probably call it off for now, except for her disappearance. With what you just told me, the key to that disappearance is probably in her car, if it didn't get washed away, don't you think?"

"I'd be surprised if anything's still inside the car. That current was pretty strong and the door was open when we left it."

He just shook his head in agreement and said, "Yeah, you're probably right about that."

A thought hit me and I asked, "Do you know if they showed her face on the news last night?"

"Yeah, channel seven got film of her as she was entering the hospital, and they had a piece about it on the eleven o'clock news."

"What about the face shot they showed this morning. Was that on last night?"

"No, we only released that when she disappeared."

"Well, someone could have figured out that was her, maybe, last night, and that someone helped her get out of the hospital."

"Tell you the truth, that's the way it looks right now, but I really can't say anything more about it. If you happen to remember anything else she may have said, please let us know. Other than that, I'm pretty sure I have all I need from you. You can go now, and thanks again for coming in. Hopefully she or her car will turn up, and we can figure this out when she does."

As we'd been talking I'd remembered the look on her face in the picture flashed on the TV screen. I suddenly had a bad feeling about the whole thing. I asked as I stood up, "Do you think she'll try to find me?"

He said, "No, I doubt it," but the look on his face didn't match his statement. This made me even more sure that she probably would if she could.

"Did anyone tell her my name?"

He glanced through the reports sitting on the table in front of him for awhile. Then he looked up rather sheepishly at me and said, "Uh . . . It seems that she asked that last night when she was asking to see you. The officer gave her your name because, of course, at the time we had no way of knowing she would disappear. She told him she just wanted to thank you, and that seemed . . . . logical at the time. We'll probably find her soon and you won't have anything to worry about."

I thought, "It was probably that prick Smythe," that gave her my name as I asked, "Why do you think it's going to be so easy to find her when you don't even know how she could have escaped?" Obviously, she had a big reason for escaping from the hospital and someone was helping her.

"We know how she escaped, but I can't give you any details right now."

My premonition of her being trouble came back to me, but now the trouble was pointed straight at me. I said, "Do you think we should be worried if you don't find her?" No matter what his reply, I knew I would be worried.

He thought about it a little too long before replying, "Nah, we think she's probably just wanted for something and will get as far away from here as possible. We're running her fingerprints through AFIS and hope to get a match soon. Besides, even with your name, she probably wouldn't want to find you anyway."

He might as well have said, "We know she'll come gunning for you!" for all the comfort I got from his statement. I hated to admit it to myself, but Officer Duncan had hit it on the mark about her gaze at me, and I knew it. I figured they wouldn't give us protection even if I asked, but thought I may as well anyway. I said "Do you think we could get someone to keep an eye on our house or something. If I tell my wife about everything, she probably won't be able to sleep, and I sure won't get much either."

I guess the implications of everything we'd just discussed were beginning to hit him too, because instead of a flat out refusal of my request, he replied, "I don't think you need to worry, but I'll talk to the Orion P.D. and see if they can do some drive bys for the next few days."

I said, "Thanks" and started leaving the room. He came up behind me and put his hand on my shoulder. I turned to face him and he asked, "Do you have any guns in the house?" Apparently he didn't really believe his last statement.

"Yeah, I got a shotgun and a rifle for hunting."

He seemed genuinely concerned as he said, "I think . . . . just to be safe . . . . you might want to keep them handy till this is resolved."

I said "I was already thinking that," then turned and walked back to the waiting room, feeling much worse about the whole situation than when I'd arrived.

CHAPTER EIGHT

Andrea was reading a magazine as I came out and threw it down when she saw me. She got up and hurried towards me, asking, "What took so long? He said it wouldn't take this long." Almost an hour had gone by and from the look on her face I could tell she had been getting impatient. Glancing at O'Brien, she looked back at me, anxiety replacing boredom in her expression. His poker face must have been absent because she'd caught some of the same look of concern I'd seen at the end of our interview. In a voice that went up a few decibels she asked, "What did he tell you in there?"

I quickly debated with myself whether I should give her the true gist of our conversation or not, but knew that to sugarcoat it wouldn't be fair to her. She could be in danger as much as I, and to not tell her might put her in even more. At the same time, I didn't want her to think we had a target painted on us, because I wasn't really sure of that either.

This dilemma didn't resolve itself quickly enough for me to answer her before she said, "They haven't caught her yet have they?"

"No, they haven't. They think someone may have helped her, but it's probably just a matter of time till they find her." I knew this was kind of a cop out, so I quickly added, "They're gonna have the Orion police keep an eye on the house till they do."

Instead of her being reassured by my statement, she seemed to be taken aback that it might be necessary for them to do so. She shrilly demanded, "Why would they have to watch the house? You said you didn't even know her. Why would she want to come to our house?"

I knew I would have to tell her everything we'd talked about, and she wouldn't like it one bit. I said, "Let's just sit down for a minute and I'll tell you all about it" as I took her arm and headed to the bank of chairs.

O'Brien followed us out and said, "I'm sure she won't try to do anything to either of you. She's probably long gone from this area, but we still don't know how she got away."

Andrea's mouth dropped open at that, and O'Brien tried to recover from his gaff by saying, "I don't think she's dangerous," although how he could know that wasn't lost on Andrea or me.

She immediately said, "How do you know? Do you even know who she is?"

O'Brien got a pained look as he stammered, "Well . . . no . . . we don't know who she is just yet, but we're working on that."

"You mean . . . . you had her for six hours and you don't even know her name?"

Knowing he couldn't answer that to her satisfaction, he tried to change the subject by stating, "We had no reason to think she'd try to escape. She wasn't being charged with anything, and she had no I. D., which we assumed had been in the car. Because of her recent trauma and her head injury, we thought maybe she was just confused and that she would start talking today. We are taking prints and DNA from the hospital. If she's in the system, we should have some answers to that at anytime now."

This still didn't placate Andrea enough, because she asked, "What if she's not in the system?"

Most of my cop show watching, in fact almost all, had occurred after I met Andrea at age forty three. She'd probably seen every episode of "Law and Order", her favorite, at least two times. Probably like most cop show junkies, she always tried to figure out who did it before they let you know on the show. She also knew about law enforcement's difficulties establishing identity in cases where the person didn't have a record.

The admission by O'Brien that they still didn't know who she was had gotten her into a tizzy, and O'Brien just stared at the floor. He knew as well as her that if she hadn't ever been arrested there was a good chance that her identity wouldn't be revealed by DNA or fingerprints. O'Brien looked up at her and said, "We can get you some police protection if you're worried about her."

I guess this alleviated her anger, because she said, "I sure hope it don't come down to that, but we'll take it," in a much calmer voice.

I wasn't sure at that point that we needed police protection, but I really wasn't sure that we didn't. Wondering about the intrusion into our lives, I asked O'Brien, "How does that work?" The absurdity of needing protection from a woman whose life I'd saved wasn't lost on me, yet the fact was I was feeling kind of apprehensive as I thought of her accusing, hateful eyes.

O'Brien answered, "I'll have to check with Orion, but considering the circumstances, I think they'll park someone outside. If they won't, I'll make sure we can get someone to do it, at least for the next few days. She'll probably be found by then."

Andrea appeared to be satisfied with this, because she said, "That would be great."

Wanting to be rid of the place once again I asked, "Do you think we can go home now?"

"Yeah, I'll call you in an hour or so and let you know about the setup."

"Let me see if my phone's working. I left it off since yesterday." Digging it out of my pocket and turning it on, the screen came up and it appeared fine. "It looks all right. Call my number to see if it rings."

"You haven't had it on since last night?" he asked as he dialed my number.

"No, it was all wet and I turned it off." My phone rang and I hit answer and said into the phone. "I didn't have any screen after I found it."

After saying into his phone, "I can hear you loud and clear." he hung up, then said, "See if anybody tried to call you."

After checking, I said, “No, nobody’s tried to call. If she does, believe me I’ll let you know.”

Even with all this talk about police protection, my first urge was to get out of there and try to go back to our normal life. I was kind of ashamed at the thought that I might be scared of this woman, having never been truly ‘scared’ of a woman before. That thought made me ask, “What time do you think they can be there?”

“We can get someone there by this evening.” Suddenly I felt embarrassed for asking for police protection. My embarrassment didn’t outweigh my or Andrea’s concern, but it was close.

CHAPTER NINE

We both thanked him and went out to our cars. This time I asked her if she was okay to drive and she said, "I don't think we're in trouble on the road." I flashed back to the moment when I saw the Mustang catapult off 61, but said, "I think we'll be fine. I'll follow you." .

We headed home and she called me as soon as we pulled back onto 61. "Do you think we should go home? Let's go eat somewhere and wait till they can get someone over there." I knew then that she was really worried about the possibilities of the woman or her accomplices being dangerous and even perhaps vengeful. I had tried to sound calm and unafraid, but fear has a way of creeping into the eyes and speech of people who feel it.

"Where were you thinking?"

"Let's go to Ethyl's. We haven't been there in awhile."

I was starving at that point, having gone without supper the night before. We never ate a real breakfast, except on weekends when we both were home. My stomach was roiling, although hunger was only part of it. A good meal was what I needed, and Ethyl's always had it. I said, "That sounds good. I'll see you there."

I'd never been much of a phone talker, always keeping my conversations to a minimum, especially if I knew we would talk in person soon. Her fear was evident by her next statement, “I’m not sure we should go home till they find her.”

I thought of my own fears, but dismissed them after thinking about the expense and hassles of not returning home. Why should I be afraid? She hadn’t said anything to me that should make me feel that way. Yeah, she’d escaped from the hospital, but why would she want to hurt me or Andrea?

The line from an old song, “Paranoia will destroy ya.” Came to me. I didn’t want to scare her with my dark thoughts so I said, “I don’t think we should worry about it.”

Andrea was silent for awhile then said, “I don’t want to go home. That woman must be a criminal or a psycho or something. I sure as hell don’t want to run into her when we open the door, do you?”

The mention of a face to face encounter made me shiver. The thought that she might try to find me, for now I was almost sure of the possibility at least, had drifted in and out of my thoughts since figuring out the logical reason for her enmity. I was trying to tell myself that there was no reason to worry, if only because she was a woman, but the truth was peace of mind had already lost the fight.

I had never, to my knowledge, had any true enemies. The years had gone by with a general good will towards man and all that implies. Though certainly not gregarious, my acceptance of the wide spread nature of human attitudes and experiences had allowed me to adopt a live and let live policy since childhood. Believing that all people had the right to their own opinions, my apolitical stance had engendered relatively few conflicts. Yeah, I’d had my share of arguments with girlfriends, wives, fellow workers, employees, drunks in bars, and the occasional stranger for things that I'd blown off within a short time, if I even worried about them after the fact.

This felt different, for never had I sensed the degree of hostility towards me that emanated from the eyes of the woman. The whole concept of true hatred was foreign to me. Yet, thinking again about her piercing stare, that is what I believed she felt for me as I had stood in front of her. I was lost in this train of thought when Andrea said, "Did you hear me?"

I snapped out of my reverie and realized I hadn't spoken for awhile. Between the traffic and the train of thought I had gone almost two miles without even thinking of answering. I said, "Yeah, but I don't think that's gonna happen. Let's just go eat and not worry about it."

"Okay, but you're going to have to go home and check it out before I head back there."

"I'll go home after lunch and call you when she isn't there. Let's not get all worked up about something that ain't gonna happen." This was one of my standard replies to her worries about the general precariousness of life, but even as I said it, I felt another shiver go down my spine.

We went to Ethyl's and had a really good brunch. I tried not to think about anything relating to the woman after I said to Andrea as we entered the place, "Let's just have a nice breakfast and not talk about that woman." She did well with this request, minus a few comments, until we'd paid the check and were heading for the door. Before we reached it she asked, "Where to now?"

I had assumed her fears about going home were only temporary, and that doing so wouldn't be a problem for her after a chance to get thoughts of the woman out of our heads. This obviously wasn't the case and I didn't want to push going home until she felt safe about it. I said, "Let's check into a motel room somewhere. I'll go home and get us some clothes and you'll see that we don't have to worry about that lady."

"I won't worry when they get her. I saw her on TV and she looked pretty mean."

When we got to her car, Andrea turned to me and threw her arms around me. We had been married three years and this wasn't the norm, even after a nice meal out. My somewhat sporadic work habits, aloofness at times, addiction to the outdoors, our increasing age or whatever might be to blame for our lessening closeness in the past year or so, but I forgot about it all as she pressed into me. She practically purred, "You don't want to go home, do you?" kissing me firmly after she said it.

Surprised by her sudden fawning, I gave what I was receiving and we made out in the parking lot like two teenagers. Coming unglued at the lips after a minute or so, I said in my best sultry voice, "I'm all yours. Where would you like to go, madame?"

I didn't necessarily need to go home, but I also had been thinking if I didn't, I would be giving in to my fears. Afraid of maybe acting like a big scaredy cat as we'd had our lunch, the perception didn't sit well with my own image of myself. Even though the memory of her stare wouldn't leave me, I'd decided that we shouldn't live our lives based on a premonition, or whatever it was that I'd been feeling.

We decided to stay at the Embassy Suites in the new convention center in St. Charles, about ten miles east. Detective O'Brien called as we were kissing goodbye. Andrea stood next to me listening as I answered and told him we wouldn't be going home that night, and he needn't worry about having anyone outside. I asked him if there was any further news on the woman or her car.

"No, we haven't come up with a thing. Give me a call before you head home and I'll give you the latest."

"If you do come up with something important, would you please give me a call?"

"I sure will. You take care of yourself till then."

"I always try. Thanks a lot. I'll talk to you later."

We were only putting off the inevitable return home, but the hundred dollar price of the room seemed a paltry price for Andrea's peace of mind, even if it was only a temporary respite. Our two golden retrievers, Bonnie and Clyde, had a full food dispenser, a two gallon bucket of water and an open doggie door. We had left them home overnight many times, but my thoughts were about them and the doggy door as we checked in paying cash, sans luggage, and headed to the room.

Andrea threw her arms around me as I shut the door. I kissed her passionately for a while, then picked her up in a bear hug and backed us towards the bed. Fervently tearing each other's clothes off, our urgent desires kept us from contemplating the future for the next hour. Strangely exhilarated, the intensity of our passion reminded me of our first night together. I'd known then that I was in love for the first time in pushing twenty years, though I'd fooled myself a few times in the interim. Finally exhausted, we snuggled and took a nap, uncharacteristically locked in each others arms as we slept.

On waking, I felt alive and energetic, my fears greatly abated. Andrea woke up as I got out of bed, saying, "Maybe we need a little more excitement all the time. I think you've been holding out on me lately."

I bent down and kissed her hard, then said, "I was thinking the same thing." We took a shower together for the first time in a couple years, the sparks still flowing freely between us.

Five hours after checking in as we got dressed again, Andrea said, "I haven't called anybody yet. You think it'd be okay to tell everybody about all this?"

She's a talker, and spent countless hours on the phone and Facebook discussing mundane aspects of everyday life with her sisters and friends. Surprised by her ability to not discuss this extensively already, I said, "Well, that isn't like you. You must be chomping at the bit."

She said with a smile, "Don't call me a horse. I'm just going to call a couple people."

"Yeah, right. I'm getting hungry again, so keep it down to twenty and I'll be happy."

She waved my statement off, and then she called everyone she knew it seemed, telling them I was the one who rescued the lady and about our situation now. I called my parents and a couple of friends, but after talking to my fishing buddy Fred Akers I was tired of telling the story and began watching TV for any news about the woman or her car. Unlike Andrea, I didn't elaborate about our recent fears, especially to my parents, because I was increasingly becoming unsure of their validity.

I couldn't find any coverage of the story and figured maybe they would have some on the evening news. We decided to go down to old town St. Charles and browse the shops. We wandered the cobblestone streets and bought a few nicknacks, then had dinner at Alexander's, an old favorite, located in a building dating to the early 1800's.

At about ten we returned to the hotel. After checking out the news and finding nothing about the woman, I said, "See, it must not be that big a deal if they don't even have a story about it tonight."

"I hope you're right."

We again made love that night more passionately than in quite a while and fell asleep in each other's arms, not talking about the future or the events of the past day.

Waking the next morning at seven thirty I looked over at Andrea, still sleeping, and a smile crossed my face as I thought about our session of the night before. My thoughts turned to the woman, but I hadn't had any nightmares like the previous night and I took this as a good sign. After rising out of bed and starting the in room coffee maker, I turned on the news. There was a brief piece, mainly reiterating the police's request for information on the woman.

As I was coming out of the bathroom, Andrea woke up and smiled at me with a mischievous look. She said, "Come back to bed. I'm going to take off work again." as she pulled back the covers to let me in. My ears stayed on the news even while the rest of my mind and body didn't, but nothing was said that interrupted us.

At about ten thirty we left the hotel after a wonderful breakfast. Andrea had agreed to go home if I went in and checked it out first. Feeling practically carefree compared to the day before, only as a last second consideration I told her to park down the street till I came out of the house once we'd gotten there.

I called O'Brien's number, and after he said, "O'Brien here", I said, "Detective, this is Mitch Cones. We're heading home now and should be there in twenty minutes or so. I'll call you if there's any problem."

"Would you like to have an officer check it out first?"

"No, that's alright. I think it will be okay. Thanks anyway."

"Well, if you have any trouble, give me a call. Would you still like to have someone outside tonight?"

"I'll talk to the wife, but if everything's okay at home, I don't think that will be necessary."

"If you think so. Give me a call and let me know so I can set it up if you change your mind."

"I will. Since you haven't said anything, I assume there's no word of the woman."

"No. We didn't get any hits from her blood or fingerprints, so she hasn't been arrested. That fact might give your wife some ease about her."

"I hope so. Tell you what, I'll call you either way after I talk to her again. She seems pretty calm today, but she might still be a bit uneasy about all this. I'll let you know about the protection then."

"Okay, Mitch, please do."

CHAPTER TEN

A few minutes later, I parked two houses down on the street, Andrea pulling up in front of me. I got out and walked to the side of her car, saying, "I'll be right back out."

My fear had abated to the point where I was feeling silly about having had it in the first place. I walked through the yard and looked in the translucent sidelight window. Usually, but not always, the dogs are waiting with tails wagging on the landing of our split level after hearing either of our cars pull up. I didn't see them, but figured they weren't there because we had parked down the street. I was almost putting the key in the door lock, then thought maybe I should go around back and check it out before I just walked in.

Going back through the yard, I saw Andrea miming through her windshield, "What's wrong?"

Heading to the side of her car, I said, "Probably nothing. I didn't see the dogs. I think I'll go around back and check it out first." She looked suddenly worried, so I said, "I'll be right back," again.

A strange anxiety built itself in my mind as I went around the side to the gate of our six foot privacy fence and opened it. We have a dog run on the opposite side of the yard, and the dogs can only go there or on the deck. Looking up on the deck and not seeing them, alarm bells began ringing in my brain because they always hear the gate open if they are out back. I debated just shutting the gate for a half second and getting out of there, but didn't, thinking maybe they had gone to the front door since I'd been there. I chastised myself for my fear, but it wouldn't go away.

Heart pounding, I headed to the steps at the end of the deck and began climbing them. After two steps I could see down the forty foot length of the deck, and Bonnie was sprawled by the back steps, blood plastered on her golden coat. I cried out in anguish, jumped up the last steps and quickly opened the gate to run to her. Still holding it, the reality of the situation hit me full force. Someone had killed her, and that someone could be anywhere right now, including in the house. I turned around and took the ten steps in two strides, running to the front of the house.

Andrea saw me coming, and her eyes flew open wide as I yelled, "GET OUTTA HERE!", waving my arms towards the street. She started up her car and threw it in drive, slamming to a stop as she reached me, still running down the street. I jumped in and yelled, "GO GO GO." I was shaking all over and she was yelling, "WHAT HAPPENED, WHAT'S WRONG?" as she stomped on the gas and headed down our residential street, hitting forty in no time and careening out onto the main street at the next corner without stopping at the stop sign.

I stammered out, "B . . . B . . . BONNIE'S DEAD!"

Stunned and speechless, she was already hitting seventy on the forty mile per hour main drag as I yelled, "SLOW DOWN," feeling we were out of danger for the moment, except from her driving, since she was still flooring the pedal.

As she slowed a bit she yelled, "DID YOU SEE HER?"

I coughed out, "Somebody shot her. She was dead on the deck."

Andrea cried out, "OH MY GOD," and began choking out sobs as I yanked out my phone and dialed 911 for the second time in my life.

The operator answered, "911. What is your emergency?"

"My name's Mitch Cones. Somebody shot our dog at 802 Hawthorn in Orion," only speaking calmer than the other night because of my recent experience with talking to a 911 operator. I couldn't imagine this as a coincidence and knew my statement wouldn't come close to portraying the urgency of the situation.

She started asking calmly, "Where are you at right . . . ," but I cut her off and yelled, "I THINK THERE'S SOMEONE IN THE HOUSE!"

"At 802 Hawthorn?"

"Yes, you need to get somebody there right away! This is a lot worse than a dog. Someone may be waiting inside for me."

Although I certainly didn't know that for sure, I figured that would hurry them up. She asked, "Where are you now?"

"We're heading down Tom Ginnever. I'm the guy that saved that woman that disappeared from the hospital in Heron yesterday. I think her or somebody she knows killed our dog when they came looking for me."

"Officers are on the way. Stay on the line until I can patch you into them. Find some place public and stay there."

I told Andrea, "Take a right and head to the police station." I figured that was about as safe as we could get.

The next thing I heard was some static, then a voice came on and said, "Mr. Cones, we are pulling up to your house. What exactly did you see there?"

I knew that any patrol officer wouldn't know all the terrible implications of the killing of our dog. How could they? Feeling that I should warn him about the very real danger he may be putting himself in, I said, "My dog was all bloody and looked dead when we came home. I saved the woman whose car went into the Cuivre a couple nights ago. She's disappeared and she might think I took something important out of her car. I'm sure she's behind this somehow and there might be someone still in the house waiting for me. I can't think of any other reason for someone wanting to kill my dog."

Crying into the phone after I said this, he waited a few seconds then asked, "Is the house open?"

"It was locked when we left but you can unlock it from the doggy door on the deck. Bonnie's back there."

"We're going around the back. I'm gonna let you go."

The operator came back on and said, "Mr. Cones, can you come down to the station?"

"We're already heading there. We'll be there in five minutes."

Hanging up, I pulled O'Brien's number off the phone and hit dial. He picked up on the second ring and I blurted out, "SOMEONE SHOT OUR DOG!"

"Is this Mitch?"

"Yeah, when we got home Bonnie was dead. I called 911 and an officer's there already. I know it was that bitch that did it."

After a few seconds of silence he said, "Damn . . . I'm awful sorry to here that. Did you go inside?"

"No, soon as I saw Bonnie we got the hell out of there."

"Where are you now?"

"Heading to the Orion police station."

"Good . . . . I'll call up Orion and fill them in. You just keep yourself together, okay?"

I let out a snort then said, "I can try. Let me know if you find her, would you?"

"I sure will. Good luck!"

CHAPTER ELEVEN

We arrived at the station and hurried inside. Andrea was crying and understandably very distraught, as was I. My nightmare kept popping into my head and began to seem all too real. Anger, sadness, bitterness and a resolve to somehow get even all swirled through my brain. All these conflicting emotions were hitting me as we hurried to the desk. I said to the front desk clerk, "I'm Mitch Cones. Have you heard from the officer at our house?"

The clerk didn't answer me, just called to the back and said, "The Cones are here."

Two uniformed cops came out and very morosely one said, "Mr. Cones, I'm Sergeant Dave Kelly. Can you come with us please?"

They hurried us past a room full of mostly empty desks. The few people there watched us as we went past, many with expressions that I read as pity on their faces. I took that as a very bad sign, and even before we had made it through the room I was asking, "What did they find at the house?"

Nobody answered me while they hustled us into yet another interrogation room, where two suits were already sitting behind the table. One of the suits said, "Why don't you both take a seat."

Kelly pulled back a chair for Andrea and we both sat down. As soon as we did, I asked again, "What did they find at the house?"

They all looked grim as one the suits cleared his throat and said, "My name is detective Joseph Sanchez. We just heard from the officers there. I'm afraid they found your other dog dead also. Someone broke in and your house was certainly searched for something. There was no one there but it appears whoever did this spent some time there. We've sent a team there already to investigate this. When was the last time you were there?"

Andrea had let out a wail at the mention of Clyde's death, and her wracking sobs were so loud I'd had a hard time hearing anything after she began. I had grabbed her in a tight grip around the shoulders and she was burying her face into my chest, but her wails only gained in pitch even so. A uniformed woman officer came in after the detective who hadn't spoken opened the door and said, "Maria, could you come in here and help Mrs. Cones?"

Tears were flowing freely down my cheeks also. The news wasn't unexpected, but hearing it as fact had made my stomach wrench. A burn of pure hatred to a degree I'd never felt before crept throughout my body. Officer Maria had gently helped Andrea up and was trying to console her as she led her out of the room. Sanchez asked again, "When did you leave your house?"

I tried to reply but only a choked gargle came out. They were both looking at me, but neither said anything until a few seconds later as I was trying to get my emotions in check enough to speak. The detective who hadn't introduced himself said, "Mr. Cones, I know this is a very hard thing to take. We are going to try our best to catch who did this, but we need some help from you to understand who might have WANTED to do this. They obviously weren't just burglars, because the officers who went in first said it didn't appear that any of the normal things burglars might take were missing. Your wife's jewelry was dumped out, and every room appears to have been searched, but in a more careful manner than the average grab and run burglar would do. We understand you are the man who rescued that lady from her car the other night, is that correct?"

I had gotten a partial hold on my wildly running thoughts, and after a couple sobbing coughs I replied, "Yeah, unfortunately that was me. I sure wish I'd let her drown."

They both looked at each other at that statement, then cocking his head up, Sanchez said, "Let's start with that. You didn't know the woman, did you?" They looked at me expectantly as I blew my nose and wiped the tears away, taking another ten seconds to speak.

"No, I'd never seen her before."

Sanchez then said, "And as far as you know, no one else would have reason to have wanted to hurt you or your family?"

"No, as far as I know, we don't have any enemies."

"What do you and your wife do for a living?"

"I'm a contractor and Andrea is an office manager. I'm sure this was done by the woman I saved or someone she knows. There just isn't any other explanation that makes sense. She escaped from the hospital and to do that she must be a criminal of some sort. After I saved her, she never thanked me, just gave me a look like she wanted to kill me. How's that strike you for gratitude?"

The other detective spoke up and said, "I'm detective George Pollitt. We got a call yesterday from a detective in Heron, and he mentioned that you might want some police protection but said he would get back to us on that. Why did you feel you might need it?"

"Let me try to help you understand why. I save some woman that I don't know then she looks like she wants to kill me right afterwards. She doesn't say anything to the cops. She gives them a wrong name and that's about it. She's injured, but within a few hours escapes from the hospital, probably through a second story window, without anyone seeing her leave. As I was saving her ass, she said, "Do you got it?" At first I thought she was talking about me getting us out of the river but maybe she meant something out of her car, and it was underwater by then and heading for the river.

Her ungrateful ass is the only thing I took from the car, but she was unconscious when I got to it. She must think I took something out of her car, and she or someone wants it back, obviously real bad. While I was talking to detective O'Brien he told me a cop told her my name, and the press was at the house yesterday morning even though I didn't agree to release my name to them. If they could find me then I figured she could. I asked O'Brien yesterday for protection mostly for my wife's sake, but now I don't know what to think. The whole thing is starting to seem like a nightmare."

Sanchez asked again, "And when were you at the house last?"

"We left the house yesterday morning a little after seven to go talk to detective O'Brien. We stayed at a hotel last night, mostly because my wife was worried about going home. We never went back there till this morning when I saw Bonnie, and got out of there as fast as we could. I'm thinking this was done by some pretty bad people. The fuckers even killed my dogs. Who the fuck does something like that?"

I had started crying again as I remembered Bonnie and Clyde, two of the nicest dogs you could want. Even though you hear about evil people on the news and they are on TV shows all the time, you don't really want to think that they are out there, but you know they are. Most of the time you don't think you'll ever run into people like that. I sure never had to my knowledge. Orion had been rated the third best city of its size in America to live in the previous year, and I knew this kind of thing didn't happen often here.

I thought about all this as I tried to get my rage and crying under control. Pollitt and Sanchez had been shaking their heads as if they agreed with my assessment of the situation. They both looked concerned and sympathetic as they waited for me to get a hold of myself once again. Maria had set a box of tissues on the table when she'd taken Andrea out and I had already gone through half a box.

Finally Sanchez spoke up and said, "Mr. Cones, we are going to keep you and your wife safe. You can count on that. We would like you to come to your house with us if you feel up to it. Do you think you could do that?"

I wasn't sure how I'd react on seeing what had been done there, but I wanted to see it anyway. Wondering about what to do with the bodies of my dogs, a dreaded task because I was the reason they had been killed, I answered, "Yeah, I can go there. What about Andrea? I don't think she should see it, and she probably won't want me to go. Can I go talk to her now?"

Pollit said, "Of course you can. Follow me and we'll see how she's doing."

He got up and beckoned me to follow him. We went into another room and Andrea was there looking like she was in shock, tears streaming down her face but no sounds coming out. She's a pretty tough girl, but this was just too much to take for anybody.

She saw us coming in and jumped up and hurried towards me, holding her arms out to hug me as she did. I gave her a long hug and kissed her on the forehead saying, "Everything's going to be fine," not that I felt that way at the time as she broke out into another wail.

The detectives just stood in the doorway for the next couple minutes until Andrea had slowed her wailing down to choking sobs, squeezing me tight the whole time. When I thought I could talk to her I said, "They want me to go to the house with them. You'll be safe here until I come back."

She pushed away from me a bit so her eyes were looking into mine, then stammered out, "Wha . . . what are we gonna do?"

That question could have lots of different answers and I didn't have any at that moment. "We'll figure it all out. I won't be gone too long. Just wait here and we'll come up with a plan when I get back. Do you think you'll be okay till then?"

Her insistence on not going home might well have saved our lives, since they had probably broken in during the night. I wasn't leaving if she said no, no matter what the detectives wanted me to do. My guilt was inching up with every sob from her as I remembered the moment I'd dropped the phone and headed to the

Mustang. In the blink of an eye, our world of relative tranquility had been shattered by my impulsive decision. The effects of this decision were only now beginning to manifest themselves, but I already knew it had changed our whole life.

She turned to look at the detectives in the doorway, seeming to search for words then finally imploring, "Make sure nothing happens to him." She looked back at me and kissed me, then said tearfully, "Just be careful for a change, okay. I'll be here waiting for you."

Following the detectives, we entered the lobby and O'Brien walked in the front door. Spotting me, he nodded at the detectives, then asked softly, "How are you doing, Mitch?"

I let out a snort at this ludicrous query, saying as I ignored his proffered hand, "Pretty shitty, although if we'd been home last night I'd probably be doing a lot worse."

Stepping back and disregarding my ambivalence, he said, "You might be. We sure didn't think anything like this was going to happen. Captain Smythe even told me to tell you he's sorry about the rough time he gave you, and I think that might be a first for him."

"That wouldn't surprise me."

He turned towards Sanchez and Pollitt, holding his hand out again and saying, "I'm detective James O'Brien from Heron. I talked to a Lieutenant Baker yesterday about having you do a few drive bys at Mitch's house. Just thought I'd see if there was anything I could do to help you guys."

Sanchez and Pollit shook his hand and introduced themselves then Sanchez said, “We were just heading over to Mitch’s house. Have you come up with anything on the woman he saved?”

“That’s kind of why I’m here. They just found her car in the river a few minutes after I talked to Mitch and are hauling it over to impound. I heard it’s amazing how much mud was already in it, but they should have it all checked out in an hour or so. It was registered to a Sarah May Willows of Minneapolis, Minnesota. We don’t think she was the driver, because in her drivers’ license picture she was a redhead and it doesn’t look like the woman who escaped from the hospital. She was clean, so the fingerprints aren’t going to help us much, but we called up there. They agreed to check her out, and we should know something pretty soon. We gave Mitch here a pretty hard time the other night, which he sure didn’t deserve by the looks of it now. What’s the story at his house?”

Sanchez told him about the break in and the state of the house, then said, “Why don’t you clarify what happened the other night with Lieutenant Baker. He’s in back and you can meet us at the house later if you’d like.”

O’Brien said, “I sure will. Keep Mitch here safe, would ya’?” tapping me on the shoulder as he headed towards the back. Sanchez said, “You can count on it. We’ll see you over there.” and began opening the front door.

CHAPTER TWELVE

I followed the two detectives outside and got into the back seat of their sedan. "Do you know where it is?" Sanchez was driving, and shaking his head slightly up and down he said, "Yeah, we know." in a very somber tone.

The police station is about three miles from our house and in a few minutes we had turned onto our street. The whole circle next to the house and the street in front was ablaze with flashing lights. A large crowd of people had gathered to watch the proceedings from the nearest corner, held back from the immediate area around the house by barricades that had been placed a hundred yards up the street from the house in both directions.

After getting waved through by a cop at the corner and threading our way through the barricades, we double parked out front. Two people in lab type coats went inside as more cops exited the cars parked out front There was yellow crime scene tape strung around the whole yard and many of the neighbors were hanging around outside. I wondered what they all must be thinking as I got out of the car, but had more pressing thoughts. I followed the detectives up the drive without casting them a glance.

When we got to the door a pretty lady in a lab coat handed us all a pair of foot booties, saying to me, "Please don't touch anything." Feeling like an unwanted guest in my own house, I put them on and we went inside.

The first thing I saw was all the books and pictures from the shelf at the bottom of the stairs, not thrown around but neatly stacked in front. The pictures had all been removed from the frames. Everywhere I looked it was the same. Kitchen cupboards, dressers, closets, bathroom cabinets and any place you might put something had been emptied, but fairly neatly stacked on the floors in front of them. The floor grates were all pulled up and lying next to their holes.

The only thing that appeared to be missing after I did a quick perusal of the house was our computer hard drive. I had expected it to look like a tornado had come through, but obviously whoever had done this didn't want to make much noise or miss something.

I was thinking, "They must have been here for hours." as Sanchez said to me, "It looks like these guys certainly were looking for something in particular. Do you see anything besides your computer missing?"

That struck me as strange, because if it was missing I wouldn't be able to see it, but I knew what he meant. It would be hard to tell what might be missing from the state of the place, but none of the other electronics, my guns, or other normal burglar targets seemed to be gone. I said, "It's kind of hard to tell, but besides the computer, I don't think so. Like I told you, I think they were looking for something they think I took out of that woman's car. It must have had something to do with a computer."

Remembering when I had my hand around her neck, Sanchez brought me out of my daydream by saying, "Whatever she was talking about must be valuable as hell to them. In my twenty years I've never seen this."

Assuming he was talking about the utter efficiency which it appeared had been used to ransack the place I walked to the open back door and glanced onto the deck. A blanket covered mound was lying to the side of the door and another where I'd seen Bonnie. I choked out a sob, knowing the one by the door must be Clyde and I hadn't seen him because of the furniture and hose reel blocking my view. Two men came up on the deck with a stretcher and put Bonnie on it, glancing at me and shaking their heads as they picked her up and headed off the deck. The shed out back was emptied also, everything in it spread out with the same meticulous precision as the house.

Turning to Sanchez, I said, "How long do you think they were in here." It had to be way more than one, and the fact was this had to have been done by very organized and professional thieves, not just your normal cat burglar types. I'd have felt better if all of it was missing or if the place had been the disaster I'd expected. This thought made me shudder as I realized that also meant they would not be the type to give up until they got what they wanted, and the killing of the dogs meant they would be utterly ruthless in getting it. Besides that, they probably thought I still had 'it' since they hadn't found us at home.

Sanchez seemed as amazed by the state of the house as I was. He finally answered my question by saying, "It looks like they must have been here all night. I'd say it's a damn good thing you didn't come home. I think we're dealing with some real dangerous people here."

I certainly had already come to those conclusions, but just said, "I think you're right."

Fingerprint technicians were dusting all the surfaces around the house, but I was sure they wouldn't find any prints that would help them. People like that wouldn't be stupid enough to leave prints at the scene. Picturing them as some kind of ninjas, I began thinking they would find me no matter what I did if they could do this as quickly and coldly as they had. This sure wasn't the work of a banged up woman. They probably didn't even have to shoot the dogs, because they had liked anybody who would pet them, their bark being far worse than their bite.

It looked like they had been shot where they lay, because both were in their favorite spots. That meant the dogs hadn't even heard them coming even though they'd always barked at the slightest noise out back.

Pollit came up to me and said, "I'm awfully sorry about your dogs. I have a golden too. The techs would like to fingerprint you and your wife to eliminate your prints. Has anyone else been in the house recently?"

I thought about it and said, "Only Andrea's daughter and our grandson. He's only two."

"Well we'd like her prints too, if you think she'll agree."

"Do you really think they left any prints? I kind of doubt that after seeing the way they searched the house."

"I doubt it too, but you never know. Any chance is better than none." I took that to mean he already had little hope they would find anything to tell them who had been in our house.

Looking out the front window, I saw uniformed officers talking to the neighbors outside. Our house is next to a corner with a circle, and you can see fifteen or so houses from our front window. Two cops were standing in the street and talking to the Dillard's, the young couple directly across from us. Another was talking to the lady who lives three houses away. She was shaking her head, either in a negative reply to their inquiries, or maybe, at the things people could do.

I'd begun thinking about what Andrea and I might do as soon as I'd realized what kind of people had done this. Looking at the scene in the street, I knew we wouldn't be coming back here soon, if ever, to resume our previously pedestrian lives. As Pollitt walked outside, Sanchez was talking to the tech guys and didn't appear to be getting any answers to his liking. Walking over to him, he turned towards me and I asked, "Can I take some clothes and stuff out of here?"

The clothes from the dressers and closets were piled up in tottering stacks on the stripped bed and the floor in front of the closet, probably after every pocket had been searched. Sanchez turned to the tech and said, "What about it?"

The tech said, "Yeah, but let me help you." He was holding two plastic evidence bags with a few strands of hair in them, but to me it looked like they were most likely just mine and Andrea's hair. He began walking towards the bedroom and said, "Just point out what you'd like and I'll grab them. We can't let you take much just yet, okay?"

"I understand. We've been in the same clothes since yesterday and I don't know when, if ever, we're going to feel comfortable enough to come back here."

"Yeah, after looking around here I don't think I'd want to come home either if it was my house. We're going to need some samples of hair and stuff from you and your wife, and anyone else that's been here within the past few days."

"Whatever you need."

I began pointing out some clothes, not that I really cared which clothes he grabbed as long as we had something to change into. As I pointed them out, he spent a few seconds checking out each item before putting them on a plastic sheet which he had spread on the floor.

It appeared they had already vacuumed the carpet, because the few bare spots looked cleaner than when we'd left. Looking in the bathroom, I asked, "What about some of that stuff?" pointing towards the pile of toiletries which had been dumped on the floor of the shower.

"We really don't want you to take anything which might hold a print just yet."

I thought, "If they can't get a print off anything else, they sure won't get one off a toothpaste tube." Suddenly thinking about my guns, I asked, "When do you think we could take anything we wanted out?"

"Probably tomorrow. Do you have any medicine or other things that you really need here? If you do, I'll dust them right away so you can take them with you."

Things that we really need? What are those? Looking at our possessions piled unceremoniously throughout the house, everything had felt tainted. Always knowing they had been touched by maybe the same hand that had killed my dogs, the invisible stain would never go away, it's smear on my conscience indelible. At that moment, if I could have afforded to, I'd have told him to burn it all when they were done.

"Mr. Cones? Did you say something?"

I had turned away from him and realized I'd been mumbling under my breath. Turning back towards him, I said, "Give me a second." as I tried to concentrate on his original question.

Andrea took a few different prescriptions, at least occasionally. My present state of mind might preclude my memory of her most recent ones so I said, "Maybe just the inhaler. Can you dust all the stuff that's not too old. I'm not sure exactly which ones she might want before we come back here."

"I can, but it might take awhile to sift through all this and find them. Are any necessary on a daily basis?"

"No, I don't think so. Not really." Not wanting to guess at it, I decided to call Andrea up at the station to ask her. As my hand reached for my phone a sudden jolt of thought hit me.

The burglars or the people they worked for had found me in no time and done this already. They had our computer, and that meant they had our whole families' names, addresses, and phone numbers, including ours. They might already be able to listen to our calls. Any technology is almost always available to those who can afford it, and they must have deep pockets to have put together a crew to do this so quickly.

We were lucky they hadn't found us last night, because that's what they had most likely hoped to do. Not finding us at home, they did the next best thing and searched the house, and might even have left someone here after searching to get us if we came home. Perhaps only our quick exit had prevented them from handing us the same fate that befell our dogs, at least after determining that I didn't have what they were looking for. Paying cash for the room last night might have kept us from a rude awakening. They could already be hunting down our family. My speculations about their abilities and resolve were spinning wildly upward and even as I said under my breath, "paranoia will destroy ya," the bigger part of me was thinking, "Better paranoid than dead."

Sanchez had been standing in the hall as I came out of the bedroom to call Andrea and watching me as I'd grabbed my phone. Thirty seconds later it was still in my hand. I hadn't moved, my survival instinct spinning wheels of thought about all the possibilities of their powers.

He walked towards me, still in a semi trance, and said, "What are you thinking?" I snapped out of it and explained the gist of my recent thoughts to him, maybe hoping him to say something like, "I doubt it" or even better, "I think you're just being dramatic," but he didn't. He just looked at me and said, "You haven't gotten any strange calls, have you?"

"No, besides a few family members wanting to hear about the rescue, nobody has called us today at all. Come to think of it, why haven't they called? I know they have our numbers. I'd think they would just ask me for whatever it is they are looking for. Do you think these guys are so bad they can't just ask?"

"After what I've seen here that wouldn't surprise me. I've dealt with all types of criminals, but I don't think I've ever dealt with this kind. This had to be done by some pretty motivated and skilled perps. We aren't finding anything we think we can use. Speaking of that, did you vacuum just before you left?"

My recent thoughts about the techs having vacuumed popped instantly into my head. My mouth kind of dropped open before I stammered out, "Na . . . no, I thought the lab guys did when I saw how clean the floor was. Our dogs shed, uh, I mean, they used to shed constantly and I noticed how clean the carpet looked in the bedroom. You think they even vacuumed before they left?"

He motioned for me to follow him into the living room. Our vacuum cleaner was standing there. We always left it in the office when we weren't using it. He walked to it and took out the canister that held the dirt and showed it to me. He said, "The lab guys noticed this right away," as he held it out for me to look. The inside was clean as a whistle. He replaced it then opened the empty filter compartment. "I think they took it and the contents of the canister with them. They must have vacuumed before they left, unless you think this is what it looked like."

"No, I know that's not what it looked like."

"We didn't think so."

My head was reeling even more with wild, or maybe not so wild, speculations. I suddenly thought about the dogs and said, "What about bullets from the dogs?" Sanchez shook his head and said, "The techs think they were strangled with a garrote of some type and then knifed, but certainly not shot. That may be the most telling evidence of the type we're dealing with. They won't know for sure until they do an autopsy on them."

I had anguished about the dogs since seeing Bonnie, but my own life seemed to be getting more precarious by the minute, and thoughts of their demise were being quickly replaced with thoughts of my own. The mention of an autopsy made me ask, "Will I be able to bury them?"

He looked somberly at me as he said, "Mitch, I think you have a lot more than that to worry about," shaking his head slowly then breathing out a long sigh afterwards.

Thinking of my beloved companions, for they were much more than just dogs to me, I started sobbing softly. Sanchez stood there and just watched for a few seconds, then said very softly, "Why don't we get you out of here." He put his hand on my shoulder, gently steering me towards the steps.

Exiting the front door, an officer called to him from across the driveway, "I think we have something." He beckoned at Sanchez to follow him, and Sanchez turned to me and said, "I'll be right back."

I immediately shot back, "I think I have the right to know too."

Motioning for me to follow him he said, "I guess you're right."

I followed him as the officer led us into the neighbor's yard where the normally house bound and feeble octogenarian that lived next door was still standing. The officer said, "Mr. Russell, could you tell the detective here what you saw?"

Kevin was staring at me and said, "Sorry to hear about your dogs, Mitch." Then he turned to Sanchez and said, "I heard some weird noises and I went out back and then I heard sounds in Mitch's back yard, maybe like somebody was climbing over their fence. About ten seconds later a car slammed its' brakes, and then it took off burning rubber. Sorry, but I didn't see the car. I was thinking about calling 911 till I saw all the cop cars pulling up."

CHAPTER THIRTEEN

Sanchez looked astonished, staring around the scene at the fifty or more spectators, and I felt a bit dizzy as I realized the implications of his story. Mine surely, and perhaps even Andrea's life would not have been worth a plug nickel, at least after they'd ascertained I didn't have what they were looking for.

Her lead foot had probably been the only thing that had saved us since I had to assume they took off trying to catch us. I wondered why the guy didn't come outside, but he must have not wanted possible witnesses to the scene that would have occurred, or maybe he'd been slacking off. I'd always thought the scene in 'Pulp Fiction' where John Travolta comes out of the bathroom to find Bruce Willis holding his gun couldn't happen in real life but I pictured it as I tried to comprehend why I'd been able to escape.

The way Mark described it we couldn't have been more than a minute ahead of them. Hell, for all I knew, they might have even tailed us to the police station, only breaking it off when they saw where we went, for I hadn't been worried about a tail at the time.

Sanchez grabbed me by the arm and said, very forcefully this time, "Mitch, I think I should get you out of here." He began trotting to his car, my arm clutched tightly in his hand. There were cops all around but if he was worried about my safety, my own like thoughts were not just paranoia. Letting go of me as I kept pace, I trotted alongside him and jumped into the back door that detective Pollitt had already opened. Pollitt slammed the door as soon as I was in and jumped in the front, his eyes searching Sanchez's for a clue to the hurry.

As Sanchez threw the car in drive and screeched towards the barricades he nearly yelled, "Did you hear that guy next door's story?"

"No, I went the other way and was just coming back when I saw you running to the car. What did he see?"

Sanchez looked visibly shaken up as he said, "I think he heard a killer jump the fence in back right after Mitch left and a car was waiting to pick him up!"

He turned a bit to glance at me in the back seat then said, "Mitch, we're going to put you in witness protection. You and your wife are in a lotta danger I think." as he turned on his grill lights and siren and began quickly weaving his way through the barricades. When we'd cleared the astonished looking spectators he gunned it and squealed around the next corner. Addressing Pollit again he spat out, "I don't know why Jonesy didn't come in and tell me about what the guy saw," shaking his head back and forth at his incredulity.

Pollitt said, "Shit, they must have had a whole crew in there to do what they did in one night. Leaving somebody there only makes sense. Mitch, do your neighbors and you know each other very good?"

We were halfway back to the station, Sanchez doing about forty five on a twenty five mile an hour street as I began to answer, "Not really, just enough to say hi and . . . .".

A flicker of movement caught my eye and I turned towards the passenger window, seeing a dark colored SUV racing at us from the side down a cross street. As we flew into the intersection with a two way stop for the cross street, I was trying to yell a warning as the SUV jammed on its brakes a second before impact, but it was too late to prevent the collision. The slam of the truck into the passenger front quarter panel spun us around and we began rolling as the passenger side wheels caught on the pavement.

None of us had put seat belts on in the heat of the moment. I slammed into the roof and back to the back seat as we completed a full 360, rocking halfway over again before the destroyed car came back down on its' tires amid the sounds of busting glass and screeching metal.

Coming to a stop fully cognizant and seemingly unhurt and knowing the collision had been intentional, I tried to get up as quickly as possible. The first thing I saw after pulling up off the seat was Sanchez slumped over the steering wheel, blood pouring out from all over his face. Pollit was shaking his head, drops of blood flying out and looking like he didn't know what hit us, which he didn't because he'd been looking at me as the truck had slammed into us. Looking out the busted windows I saw two men getting out of the back seat of the truck that rammed us, it having plowed into a tree across the street and about fifty yards down from where we'd stopped.

The one closest to us seemed injured and fell down as he got out but I quickly saw that he had a large black pistol in his hand. The line from 'Butch Cassidy and the Sundance Kid' came into my mind as I thought, "Who are these guys?"

I grabbed Pollitt by the shoulder and shouted, "WATCH OUT" as I saw the second guy come around the corner of the truck holding what looked like an Uzi and seeming unscathed. Expecting him to start blasting, I frantically dove for the door on the opposite side of him. Pushing hard on it with no luck, I looked back towards the gunmen's car and saw the Uzi guy begin running towards our car holding the machine pistol in front of him but not firing.

We had stopped halfway in a yard about sixty feet from the intersection, the drivers side facing the street we'd just come down. Grabbing the door handle again, I heard screeching brakes and looking out saw an Orion squad car sliding sideways towards the intersection we'd been slammed into while crossing.

As the Uzi toting man began crossing the street, Pollitt was pulling his gun up and swaying a bit began firing out the shattered window. I was expecting to hear the staccato sounds of a machine pistol start at any second, and all I could think to do was get as much metal and distance between me and the barrel as possible. In other words, I panicked.

The door wouldn't budge so I dove out the busted window, cutting my leg on the jagged glass remaining. Crumpling in a heap as my left shoulder made contact with the curb, I saw an officer jumping out of the squad car passenger door, pistol drawn.

The detectives' car was between him and the Uzi holder so he crouched down and made a dash towards the car, firing two shots as he ran. I heard the clatter of a gun hitting pavement and the wail of multiple sirens from every direction as a shotgun began booming. The driver of the squad car was firing as he advanced towards us, the sound of a large caliber pistol adding to the cacophony as the second gunman started firing towards the driver of the squad car. He got off two shots before his gun fell silent as the first running cop made it to the side of the car. He yelled, "STAY DOWN" as I looked over the trunk then he began shooting towards the gunmen's car.

I'd seen a second squad car racing around the corner of the intersection a hundred yards ahead of us and both the back seat gunmen face down and bloody in my brief glance, so I knew one of the guys in the front seat must be a threat. Pollitt and both patrolmen continued firing but quit within a few seconds as the cop beside me ran around the car and headed towards the gunmen's. The second squad car slid to a stop as I looked back over the trunk, watching all four cops advancing on the smashed gunmen's car with weapons aimed.

As they reached it one more shot rang out, and I saw a white cargo van slide to a halt a couple hundred yards from the cross street ahead of us and then slam into reverse and turn around, heading away from us as fast as it could. The cops all heard it and raised their guns towards it but it was out of range. One of them ran to the second squad car and began shouting into his mike as I stood up and limped towards the front door.

A very beat up looking Pollitt was shouting at Sanchez, "Joe, Joe, can you hear me," as I began tugging on the door. Sanchez moved his left arm and put it on the dash, pushing himself back in the seat as his eyelids fluttered against the blood.

Just then cop cars began screeching to stops from every direction. Sanchez was asking Pollit, "Wha' happened?" as three cops ran to the side of the car where I was still pulling on the door handle with no success. One said to me, "Are you shot?" as he looked at the blood soaking my pants above my right knee.

Glancing down I saw a three inch tear in my jeans and said, "I don't think so" as I felt my leg.

The other two had started pulling on the door and one said, "We got this. Why don't you sit down and let John take a look at that."

I sat down on the curb and suddenly felt like I was going to pass out. My body was bruised all over and all of my injuries started aching at once though I hadn't felt any pain till right then. John tore open my pant leg at the rip and there was a fairly deep gash just above my knee. He pressed on it for a few seconds then said, "Do you think you can hold down on this?" as he grabbed my hand and put it over the cut.

John stood up and helped the other two officers push the door open far enough to get Sanchez out of the front seat. His face was bleeding badly and his left leg looked broken as they gently pulled him out of the car and set him down on the lawn, but he was talking and asking slurred questions at least. As more cops began running up he looked at me holding my leg and grunted out, "Yer a dang'ous guy to be around," seemingly trying to force a smile but not succeeding.

Gurney toting paramedics ran up as Pollit came out the driver's side door. He looked a little better than Sanchez, but not much. He looked down at Sanchez and asked, "You gonna make it?", and Sanchez grunted out, "Gonna . . . . take a lot more . . . . 'an that to kill me" as they were loading him on the stretcher.

Another paramedic knelt down beside me and said, "Let me take a look at that." After a quick probe he said, "It doesn't look too bad." as he applied gauze to it and wrapped an ace bandage around my leg. They helped me up and put me on a stretcher anyway, and I surveyed the scene as they began hustling me back to the ambulance.

Twenty or more people were already in a whir of activity, mostly around the gunmen's car. In a brief look towards it as I'd sat down on the curb, I'd seen the first four cops pulling the seemingly injured driver out of his seat a lot more roughly than Sanchez had been extricated from his, pushed onto the ground and cuffed, then yanked back on his feet. The back seat gunmen were not moving as cops ran up to them and kicked away their guns before feeling them for a pulse.

Two uniformed officers got in the ambulance with me, their faces grim as they clutched shotguns and surveyed the scene outside. As the back door of the ambulance closed, I saw Pollitt being helped into the same ambulance they'd put Sanchez in. In a few seconds we began the trip to the hospital, a squad car leading and another following.

CHAPTER FOURTEEN

After being hustled in and getting ten stitches on my leg and another six on two other cuts, I asked one of the cops guarding me how the detectives were doing and he just stared at me with a stoic look. I guessed he was blaming me as another of them said, “Joe’s gonna make it, but he has a broken leg and lots of other injuries. He’s in intensive care but I heard he’s out of the woods. George is okay other than a bunch of cuts and bruises. How you guys all survived that wreck is beyond me.”

When the truck hit us, I had flashed back to another collision twelve years ago. At the time, I was a subcontractor installing furniture in new restaurants being built for a national chain. I had been in the back seat of my conversion van when it was hit broadside by a semi doing sixty, seeing its’ grill looming through the curtains a split second before impact. Pushed sideways and eventually coming to a stop in the ditch, the horrific and surreal scene was forever emblazoned into my memory.

Virtually unscathed myself, my employee and friend Ken and his girlfriend Justine, who had come along on the trip because she wanted to go to Branson, were both dead. That tragedy had weighed heavily on my conscience ever since, for it had been against my better judgment that I’d even allowed her to come along and if she hadn’t, I would have been driving. The anguish and guilt had never totally gone away, but since then, I’d felt I wasn’t destined to die in a car crash. Had I stayed in the car, my injuries from the rollover wouldn’t have been much worse.

Soon after, three suits came in and one said to the officers, "You guys can go get a coffee or something. We'll keep an eye on him." The speaker said, "Mr. Cones. How are you feeling?"

"I've felt a lot better, but I guess it could be a lot worse."

"Yeah, from what I saw of the car, I'd say it sure could've been. You've had a busy couple of days, haven't you?"

"A lot busier than I like."

He said, "I'm detective lieutenant John Usteff and this is detective Browning and detective Schmidt," pointing at each in turn.

I said, "Glad to meet you," as surprisingly they held out their hands to shake mine.

After this rather cordial introduction, Usteff said, "You realize those guys were trying to get YOU, don't you?" kind of cocking up his eyebrows as he said it.

Having come to that conclusion I said, "It seems they must have been, because they never fired at the car. I expected the guy with the machine gun to do that any second as he ran towards us."

"We assume they were under strict orders not to kill you. We think they just meant to cut you guys off and grab you out of the car, but Sanchez left your house in such a hurry they didn't have time to get set up before you got there."

I thought about the van and asked, "Did they catch the van that turned around?"

"Unfortunately, no. It wasn't seen after Officer Jones called it in, even though we tried to find it immediately after his call. It's a damn good thing he told McKay to follow you guys or we might not be talking to you now. We've put out an APB for it, but they didn't get the plates so we don't know if we'll find it. The guys in it probably ditched it soon after getting away, so we probably won't get them anyway. It seems you're attracting quite a lot of attention."

He was looking at me forebodingly as I replied, "Not the kind I like."

"Yeah, I don't think anybody would. I heard all about the other night. I know you already said you didn't take anything but her out of the car. Why do you think they're after you, if she really didn't give you anything?"

"The only thing I can figure is that she either thought I grabbed something before she came to, or she just told them that to get herself off the hook for taking it in the first place. I did say, "Yeah, I got it" to her, so she probably really thinks I do. Have they figured out how she escaped?"

He looked like he was trying to make up his mind whether to tell me or not for a few seconds, then said, "They found round marks up the side of the building. They used suction devices to climb to her room and a glass cutter to get in. There was no sign of a struggle and the officer in the hall didn't hear anything, so she either went with them willingly, was drugged, or was too scared of them to cry out. Anybody that would do all the things they've done has to be worth being scared of."

"You can say that again! What about the guys that rammed us. Have you figured out who they are."

He was shaking his head as he replied, "Only the driver survived, and he ain't sayin' nothin'. They had two tasers on them and a tranquilizer gun, probably to get you away without a fuss. None of them had anything to identify them on their persons or in the truck, which was stolen this morning. We've taken all their prints and DNA, but so far, we don't have squat on 'em. They all had more than five grand in cash in their pockets, so we think between all that they are professional hit men, certainly not the type you want after you."

He kind of arched his eyebrows again as he said it, staring at me as if to see my reaction. Maybe because I was getting used to being scared, an unfamiliar emotion for me until recently, I didn't shiver. I just couldn't seem to feel anything other than hatred and a desire for revenge, though I knew my chances of getting it were slim to nonexistent.

I'd never been a violent person, having only been in a few fist fights, all in my youth. Pushing fifty now, I'd thought for many years that I wouldn't ever use violence again as the means to an end. It felt strange to be really glad that three of them were dead, something I'd never thought before about any particular person. Somehow though, I knew that wasn't quite the same as pulling the trigger, even though I'd never imagined I'd feel the longing to do so.

Today had changed me though. My naivety and innocence was over. A good deed had turned into pain and misery, and I didn't know where or how it might end. My mind reeling with a kaleidoscope of images, I began to think I could kill anybody involved and feel less remorse than I felt for killing the deer and other game I'd hunted. These people couldn't even be human, at least not in the sense of having a conscience, the main difference between humans and animals as I saw it. That made them fair game.

The detectives had been watching me, my demeanor gradually hardening as I envisioned my capacity to exact revenge. Browning spoke up and said, "Don't even think about it."

Snapping out of my reverie, I said, "Think about what?"

"Believe me I've seen that look before. We are going to put you and your wife in protective custody till this is finished. The best thing for you to do now is concentrate on her and the fact that you're still alive. Leave the rest up to us. We have a score to settle with them ourselves."

"And what do you mean by protective custody? How does that work?"

It seemed like a year ago that I'd asked O'Brien the same thing, but I knew Browning's idea of protective custody was not going to be an occasional drive by the house. Usteff said, "We are taking you to a safe house when we leave here. Your wife will be brought there tonight also. You will not be able to call anyone or have any kind of contact with people you know. It's for their sake as well as yours. We will contact your wife's job and let them know about her being gone indefinitely, and I understand that you are self employed."

"How about my family? They took my computer and our whole families' names and addresses were in it. Do you think they would do anything to them?"

"We are reporting that you were killed in the crash, but they seem to have lots of eyes and ears around and that might not fly. Whatever it is they're looking for, you can bet it's worth a bundle, but most times the kind of people that might have ordered this won't take pointless risks. What they might do in the future is anybody's guess right now, but let's just worry about what you're gonna have to do. I don't think these guys want anybody but you."

I'd pictured them as ninjas when I was at the house and had no illusions as to what type of people it would take to do that alone. If they weren't worried about being cop killers, then they sure weren't going to think twice about killing me. I said, "I know these guys aren't my friends."

Schmidt let out a stunted chuckle at that and said, "You can bet your ass on that."

This stark confirmation of my thoughts suddenly made me switch my focus to my new reality as I asked, "So how long do you think we'll have to be in protective custody?"

Usteff shrugged and held his hands out saying, "There's no way to tell. It might be a day and it might be years, although if it came down to that, we'd place you in federal protection. They're set up for that a lot better than we are. We usually just keep guys for a few days that are waiting to testify in court cases."

My voice raising I asked, "You mean we wouldn't be able to even talk to our families for years, maybe? Are you even going to tell them about all this?"

Holding his hands up as he tried to supplicate my anxieties he said, "I only said it might be years, and we're already doing that. Your wife had the family list sent over from her office, and we're trying to contact everyone on the list. We're telling them what we can about the situation, but also about our attempts to make you out as dead so they won't worry if they see it on the news. We haven't gotten around to all the details, but we're probably going to have to stage a fake funeral for you."

I knew the norm about the American justice system, including that apprehension and trials, especially major ones, can take years sometimes. This just kept getting worse. I asked, "And from what you know now, what do you think are the chances you're even going to catch these people?"

Usteff pursed his lips together and shook his head back and forth, always a bad sign. "Hopefully we'll figure out who did this soon, but right now I'd have to say this is probably going to take a while. Once they're all convicted you might be able to go home."

"Might?"

"To tell you the truth Mitch, unless the guy in the hospital talks, and he probably won't, we might never know who actually ordered it. I doubt those guys even knew who was really paying them to do it. They didn't leave anything at your house and they didn't have anything on them that we could tie to somebody else. And just because they're murderers don't mean they'll rat out their buddies if they even know who they are, so we're starting with shit here. We don't take 'em lightly when they go after cops, but unless we find that van or the guys that were in it even better, this ain't gonna be easy. I know that isn't what you wanted to hear, but that's about the gist of it."

"What if I don't want to go into witness protection?"

Their mouths all kind of dropped at that. After what I perceived as a derisive snort, Browning said, “Weren’t you listening? These guys tried to grab you in broad daylight out of a cop car less than a mile from the station, and that shows they’re either real stupid, or that what they think you have is worth dying for. Whatever that is, you can bet they got paid a pretty penny to attempt that like they did and I’m not talking about the few bucks they had on ’em.”

Seeing no real hope, I asked, “So if I go in witness protection, what’s to say everything will be just fine?”

Usteff looked right at me and said, “We can’t promise everything is going to be just fine. Far as you’re concerned, it probably won’t ever be. We can only try to keep you and your loved ones out of harms way.”

His earnest gaze gave me no doubt as to his sincerity. The illusion of returning to a life of semi-tranquil bliss was just that. It was time to move on. Think like a detective. I asked, “What makes you think this all boils down to money?”

“We’ve considered that this was the work of zealots for some cause or another, but the equipment and coordination of their attempts to grab you makes me think this was more likely financially motivated. I went to your house before we came over here, and from the looks of it and their botched attempt today, I’d say they’re willing to do damn near anything.”

“Anything to get back something I don’t have? That doesn’t sound right if all’s they’re worried about is money.”

Schmidt looked at me like I was a dummy saying, "Whether you have it or don't won't mean shit to them if they catch you. After the trouble you put 'em through, you're a dead man. These kind of guys don't play by any rules but their own. They'd squash you like a bug and only worry about whether they got any guts on their shoes. Do you get the picture? If you don't take our help here, you probably won't last a week. Shit, you might not even make it home. Think about your wife if you're not going to think about yourself. You want these guys to get hold of her?"

I didn't know what to think, and that was the trouble. Today had been one of the worst of my life, but I knew it could get worse. The thought of giving up our whole lives because of me being brave, or stupid, was just too hard to wrap my churning brain around.

Andrea was a lot closer to her family than I was to mine, if only because all six of her siblings lived close. My twenty three year old daughter, Morgan, was doing humanitarian work in India and my twenty six year old daughter, Patricia, was a research scientist working in Africa. I guess the stupid gene doesn't always get passed down. I wasn't sure how far my adversaries tentacles could reach but I felt a bit better knowing that at least my girls weren't in town. Hell, they might have gotten snatched by now if they were. The rest of my family was scattered around the country, but I might have put them in danger already.

"If we go in protection, what's to keep them from hurting our families anyway?"

Browning said, "If they think you're dead or you can't be found, then they can't use them for leverage to get what they want, which you don't have anyway. Unless you want to maybe listen or watch while they torture or kill your loved ones, I think you better take our advice."

I began crying and thinking about the dogs. I'd gotten them killed and that might just be the beginning. The whirlpool just kept spinning down and down and the bottom wasn't even in sight.

"Where is my wife now? I'd like to talk to her. Does she know about what happened?"

Schmidt said, "I think even if we didn't tell her she'd have figured it out when the station emptied. They heard the gunfire from there. She is still there and we've let her know you're okay. We can't bring her down here because it's too risky and we just don't have the kind of manpower we need in this situation. Hell, this is the worst thing that's ever happened in this town, at least since I've been on the force. You can talk to her on my phone. Just keep it to telling her you're okay and don't go into any details about what we've talked about here."

CHAPTER FIFTEEN

He took his phone out and dialed the number saying, "This is Schmidt. Could you put Mrs. Cones on?" After a minute, he said, "Mrs. Cones? This is Detective Avery Schmidt. I'm going to put your husband on."

I was thinking about when I'd been about to call her as he handed me the phone. Not sure what to say, after a few seconds of listening to silence I slowly said, "Honey, I'm alright . . . . Can you hear me?"

"I knew I should have said no," she began, heaving sobs as soon as it came out.

After listening for a few seconds longer I asked, "Honey, are you okay?" realizing how utterly inane that question was as soon as I said it.

Suddenly vociferous, she retorted, "Am I okay? Of course I'm not okay. Why the fuck you would you even ask that?"

She hardly ever said fuck. Having met in our forties, she was already well aware that the gulf between how the sexes think can be wide as the Pacific, but that didn't stop her from always trying to get me over from China. I could tell she hadn't known whether to worry about me or be pissed at me, one usually following the other. I usually tried not to give her reason to worry about me, but I didn't have a clue about what to say that might placate her in this situation. "I'm sorry about all this," my standard reply when I'd screwed up, was all I could come up with.

"Sorry, is that all you can say. I don't think sorry is going to cut it this time."

I started realizing that she was well into the pissed stage, worry having gotten off the boat already since she knew I was okay. "Honey, could you please try to settle down. This isn't getting us anywhere. How was I supposed to know this kind of shit was gonna happen?"

I guessed she was trying to calm herself down, because she didn't say anything for a good ten seconds. When she finally began speaking, her voice had taken on a metallic tone. "We aren't ever gonna get over this. Them people aren't ever gonna leave us alone. You finally did it. Why couldn't you think of us instead of everybody else for a change?"

She'd said that to me many times about jobs I'd done for less than they were worth. I almost said, "I'm sorry" again, but caught myself in time. "If I could take it all back, I would, but I can't. We're going to need each other even more from now on, so let's not fight about what's already happened."

I could hardly blame her for her rant but knew that wasn't getting us anywhere. They'd told me not to talk about the possible immediate future, so I was at a total loss for words as I listened to her weeping into the phone.

After a minute, her crying had subsided to sniffles. Hoping her jag was over I said, "I'm not even going to try to tell you this is all going to be fine. Right now, I don't have a clue. All's I know is that whatever happens, I want us to be together. I love you and wouldn't blame you if you wanted to get as far away from me as possible, but I sure hope you don't."

I waited for agonizing seconds before I heard her reply. "Mitch, you know I love you too, but I just don't know if I can take this. I don't want to live every day wondering when someone's going to knock on our door and shoot you or even worse. I don't know if I can put my family in this kind of danger. What if they grab Willy," our grandson by her daughter and the most loved thing in her life by a long shot, "because of this? How could I live with myself if that happened, knowing I could have prevented it. I've put up with a lot of crap from people over the years, but I don't think I can put up with this. I'm sorry, but that's just the way I feel."

She had begun crying again as she said it, and so had I. I hadn't cried in years until yesterday, no, that was just this morning, but it seemed like it was becoming a regular thing. How to answer her blunt statement was totally beyond me at the moment. I'd lost my dogs, my possessions and house were defiled, my life was virtually gone, if not in the physical sense, and now it seemed I was going to lose my wife because of my stupid decision to jump into that quagmire. The old adage, "Life isn't fair" didn't even begin to cover the scope of this. Lamenting wasn't going to help me, but that was all I had.

Though in reality all this had started because of a good deed that fact had become lost in the tumultuous events of today. It didn't even matter. The end of our relationship, perhaps even our lives, could be on the near horizon. I heaved a deep sigh as I realized nothing I could say could possibly make her feel any better about the situation I'd gotten us into. She was right about it all, and even I had to concede that. Although we'd never been close to a divorce this could certainly become, if it wasn't already, the proverbial straw. Hell, this wasn't a straw, it was a redwood.

Her points had hit home like a William Tell arrow. I realized I couldn't even ask her to change her mind because if something did happen afterwards, I wouldn't be able to live with it either. I thought about what Sanchez had said after the shootout, and I certainly was and maybe always would be dangerous to be around. I was so choked up it felt like I was going to strangle and I couldn't seem to get a hold of myself enough to talk. I'd always abhorred self pity, but it was hard to avoid at that moment.

CHAPTER SIXTEEN

The detectives had been watching me throughout the conversation and seemed anxious for me to end the call. I finally put the phone back up to my ear and said, "Andrea, just know that I'll always love you." then hung up. I handed the phone back to Schmidt and sat down on the bed, bawling my eyes out. The detectives just hung back and didn't say a word. Finally, I guess Browning couldn't take it anymore because he went out in the hall and yelled, "Could we get somebody in here?"

He scooted down the hall to look for a nurse or somebody to help me, although I don't know what they could have done at that point to relieve my anguish. A nurse came in, and although she couldn't possibly know why I was so distraught, put her arm around me. Saying, "Let's just give you something to calm you down." she left my side to head to a cabinet for some tranquilizers or something.

Seeing her coming back with a syringe, I stood up and said in a very tremulous voice, "You ain't sticking that fucking thing in me."

She jumped back at my words and looked at the detectives for a reason for my outburst. Usteff walked over next to me and tried to put a hand on my shoulder, but I pushed it away before he even made it there. He put his hand back down and said, "Mitch, I think you should let her give it to you."

I glared at him as if he was the cause of my sorrow and spat out, "I don't fuckin' care what you think. She ain't stickin' that in me."

I had always hated needles but that wasn't the cause of my seemingly hysterical outburst. My sorrow had quickly built into an overwhelming rage. I just wanted to tear out of there and start hunting them myself. If they thought they were bad ass, I'd show them what bad ass was all about and they could take fucking notes. At that moment I didn't give a rat's ass about what might happen to me as long as I could see them bastards squeal under my hands as I choked the life out of them and kicked them in the balls for good measure. Remembering that my guns were still at the house and thinking about how I might get more, I headed for the door.

All three detectives grabbed me and wrestled me back towards the bed, me screaming, "LET ME GO!" and trying to shake their grasp by swinging my arms at them the whole time.

They held me down on the bed as a whole flock of nurses and doctors rushed into the room. A doctor yelled at the nurse as she was getting ready to stick me, "What have got there?"

"One milligram of Ativan."

"Make it one milligram sodium pent."

As the sedative kicked in, my thrashing subsided and the last thing I heard was Schmidt saying, "Them fuckers better be glad they weren't in front of him just now," as my conscious faded to black.

In the last hours of my sedative induced day plus slumber, I had a nightmare that was more vivid than any I could ever remember. Although I'd had one the other night, I'd never been prone to them. I had, till the last few hours anyway, just chalked that one up to the harrowing water rescue, that seeming to fit the type of nightmare I'd had.

As my conscious woke up enough to begin dreaming, there was a sailboat floating on the horizon of a totally calm sea. I was swimming towards it, but couldn't seem to get any closer. I kept yelling at it but nobody could hear me as I watched people laughing and talking. Kicking harder to get closer to the boat, the water started turning into a viscous fluid. I looked back at the boat and saw Andrea looking at me, standing alone by the rail as the other people just kept partying on. She was reaching out to me as if she saw me and wanted to hurry me on, but I couldn't make any headway against the ever thickening slop I was stroking through. Finally, a man walked over to the rail and saw me too.

I was thinking, "Now they'll turn the boat around," as I watched him turn to the side. Instead of him moving towards the tiller, he turned towards Andrea and his face turned black. With one quick heave, he picked her up and threw her in the water, almost the consistency of peanut butter. I kept thrashing my arms but to no avail. I could see Andrea slowly sinking into the muck as I put my hands on top of it and slowly forced my way straight up and out of it. Andrea was still sinking as I got on my feet on top of the water, the consistency of Jell-O by now, and began bouncing towards her as I rushed to save her. The boat was sailing away on a sudden breeze and the merriment of the passengers was louder than ever as she disappeared under the surface. I got there a second too late and began clawing at the surface, but by now it was hard as concrete. I scratched at the surface till my fingers were bloody stumps, but I couldn't reach her or see her.

CHAPTER SEVENTEEN

As I opened my eyes and began to wake up, I realized my arms were pinned down by something. Looking down at them, I saw the straps and wondered why I had them on. I felt like I should go back to sleep so I could wake back up in my own bed, for this surely must be another dream.

Closing my eyes to do that, someone began saying, "Can you hear me" and I wondered why they wouldn't let me go back to sleep. They must be very rude.

"Mitch, we need you to wake up." I lurched upright in the bed until the straps stopped me, blinking my eyes and shaking my head to clear my grogginess. The room was full of people and I was bewildered by their presence until I started remembering the past day. Usteff asked me, "Are you with us?"

I was breathing hard and trying to get my thoughts in focus as he said, "They had to sedate you. Are you settled down enough to talk?"

My lips and gums were sticking to each other and my mouth was parched. Spotting a pitcher of water sitting on a cabinet, I croaked out, "Could I get a drink?" He poured me a cup and asked, "Can I take these straps off you?" I said, "Yeah, I'm feeling much calmer. I promise I won't freak out again." as I began vaguely remembering my tantrum.

He unbuckled the right arm strap and handed me the cup. As he did, I noticed he had a black eye at the same moment I saw the cuts on my knuckles. Taking the cup, I drained it in one long drink then said, "I'm sorry about my temper tantrum. I don't normally act like that."

He felt his eye as he said, "Well, you sure got a mean right cross. It took all three of us to get you down on the bed. And before you even think it, we sure aren't pressing any charges or even mad about it ourselves."

I looked around the room at the other detectives and believed him. O'Brien was standing in the doorway, and when he saw me notice him he said, "Good to see you're still alive. I know this won't help much, but the department wanted to do something."

He handed me a large envelope and walked to the other side of the bed, undoing the left arm strap. I opened up the envelope and pulled out a sympathy card which had been signed by ten or so people. The drugs were wearing off and total recall was setting in. I began tearing up and set the card down.

My brain was churning, yet I realized the first thing I had to do was convince them I would be rational so I could get out of here. Whatever sympathy they may have for me wouldn't change the facts. Before speaking, I vowed to myself to not say anything they could construe as being vengeful or irrational.

"How is Andrea? Is she here?"

Usteff said, "She has been taken to a safe house. Someone called her phone and said this would all end if you give them what they want. We got the call taped and we've had your number under wire since you were sedated yesterday. We tried tracing the call but didn't have any luck. They didn't say what they were talking about, and we're sure you don't know either. You are still sure about that?"

"Yeah, I'm sure. Whatever it is I'd give it back to them in a heartbeat to end this."

"I'm sure you would. We'd like to move you as soon as possible. We will tell you what's happened in the last day as soon as we get there, so just be patient. Do you think you're ready to go?"

I had to use the bathroom and felt mighty grubby, so I said, "I sure am. Let me just clean up first."

He handed me the clothes I'd picked out at the house. After a shower, mostly spent inspecting my severely bruised shoulder and many other injuries, I put on Levis, a Boundary Waters sweatshirt and my old but comfortable ostrich skin boots. Usteff told me to lay down on a gurney and not move or talk, then covered me up with a sheet from head to toe and wheeled me to an ambulance parked at a loading dock.

As they closed the back door, Usteff helped me put on a vest then said, "Stay down on the gurney till we tell you otherwise."

Donning a vest himself and an ambulance driver's uniform, he got behind the wheel. Three SWAT team looking guys got in the back, all wearing body armor and carrying a multitude of weapons. None of them said a word as the door opened and we started out of the garage, but they all seemed to tense up as we headed into the street. I began wondering what had happened while I was out, this seeming to be a much more dangerous trip than I had even expected.

CHAPTER EIGHTEEN

We headed north out of town, the sun setting on a cloudless sky as we pulled onto a gravel road after about thirty minutes. Usteff said, "You can stretch now if you want to."

I sat up and looked out the windshield as we crossed a small bridge. After winding through the forested creek bottom, we started uphill through close cropped pastures. A ranch style farmhouse with dormers stood on top of a hill with sweeping vistas of countryside all around. There were only empty pastures for a few hundred yards in every direction from the farmhouse, and no other houses were within sight. A single row of mature white pine trees ran along the north and west sides of the barnyard.

The barn door opened and the ambulance pulled inside, the door closing quickly after we entered. We all got out of the ambulance and walked over to a table covered with an array of electronic gear and automatic weapons. The two men who'd been sitting in chairs in front of the table stood up and eyed me over. The men who had opened the door were peering through slits as one of the men standing in front of me spoke into a mike and said, "Are we still clear?" Three people responded in turn, all saying it was clear.

The speaker, a broad shouldered man in his thirties, stared at me for another few seconds. His face held no smile as he started speaking without further ado.

"Mr. Cones, I'm special agent Michael Hart with Homeland Security. It appears you stumbled, or rather dove into a rat's nest the other day. The woman you rescued was driving the car of a Sarah May Willows of Minneapolis. We are sure that she wasn't Sarah, but still haven't identified her. Sarah's house was searched and blood was found there, but no body. Her house looked almost like your house, so either she or the woman you rescued must have something that these guys want back.

Sarah is . . . . at least she was, the girlfriend of a professional soldier or what you'd probably call a mercenary by the name of Hank Sloan. He spent time in Angola and the Congo back in the nineties, and in 2001 the FBI raided an apartment in Minneapolis on a tip that he was staying there.

His whereabouts haven't been known since then, but he's been on our radar since coming up as a suspect in the hijacking of a military shipment in Turkey about four years ago. The perps in that were highly skilled and left no survivors and the contents were never recovered.

We have ID'ed two of the men killed in the shootout as professional soldiers who were in the same areas as Sloan in the nineties, and probably are in cahoots with him. To bring them here must have taken quite a reason, because one of them was a Frenchman by the name of Raoul Villiard and the other was an Algerian by the name of Tomas Abboutti. Villiard was a Lieutenant and Abboutti was a Sergeant in the Foreign Legion twenty years ago till they both got honorably discharged and stayed in Africa. In their business, the private sector pays a lot more. I'm telling you all this so you have no doubts about the need for all these precautions."

Questions that had been forming on the ride there dropped out of my head as I took this all in. "How many others are out there that you think might be in cahoots with Sloan?"

I got the dummy look again, but at least Hart quickly tried to hide it. Looking at me very seriously suddenly, he said "With the right motivation, Sloan could probably pick from hundreds of this type. He was good at what he did, by all accounts we can find, but we think he's probably got somebody else calling the shots on this. He has never been known to operate in the U.S. before."

"So . . . . what now? Do I have to stay here until you find Sloan?"

"We are going to put you in federal witness protection, but you will be here for at least a few days. The place is comfortable and you will have at least eight agents staying here with you for the duration of your stay. This place is a well guarded secret and you will be safe here."

"Is my wife here?"

"Yes, she's in the house. I want to ask you a few questions, and then you can see your wife. Is there anything, even the smallest detail that you omitted in your statements to the police about the events of Monday night?"

I told him about her reaction as she came to, and that I hadn't thought much about it at the time because I did have my hands on her neck and thought she just freaked out. I told him her exact words to me as we began crossing the ditch, "You got it" before we both went under water.

"And you're sure she didn't give you anything?"

"No. I checked, but I didn't have anything that she might have given me. She was talking a lot and I think she was trying to tell me something, but I couldn't hear shit between the rain and the thunder. Even when I could hear her it was mumbo jumbo. I figured she was asking if I understood "what she'd been saying."

Hart asked me some more questions, but nothing else could be said that I hadn't already told the cops. I asked, "What about our families. My daughter is in Uganda right now. Has she been told about this and is she getting out of there?"

Hart said, "We sent a plane to pick up both Morgan and Patricia and they are headed for the states as we speak. Your funeral is scheduled for Friday and they will be there. We didn't tell them you are alive yet because we want all appearances to be believable, since we think these guys will be watching. As soon as the funeral is over, we'll tell them I'm sorry we had to do that, but it really is for their safety. The rest of your family will be here also and hopefully they've been briefed enough to make it believable.

The news has been running stories about you being killed and we hope they are buying it, but the fact is we don't know how deep this goes. If Sloan was involved in the hijacking, then we're talking about some really bad scenarios here. The shipment had some pretty bad stuff on it, but even I don't know exactly what it was. This is turning into a national emergency as we speak, and homeland security upgraded the threat to amber yesterday after we figured out who was probably involved. Like I said, you dove into a real rat's nest."

The thought hit me as I was listening and I asked, "What if they knew I didn't have "it' and don't have any clue about what "it" might be. Would they leave us alone then?"

"I'm not sure whether that would make any difference now. They obviously think you have it."

Even as I'd said it, Hart's expression had convinced me of the answer. My thoughts on the ride here had mostly been about how I could insulate everyone I knew from this. Now that I knew a little more about my pursuers, I realized that I couldn't be sure of anything. I might as well accept the fact that my life was now wrapped up in this beyond repair. The track of my thoughts, normally about the comparatively mundane 'perplexities' of my job and life, must change to the new reality, thoughts of me and my family staying alive.

The thought that my family might be in peril now because of me was totally unacceptable, but what could I do about it now? Nothing. I trusted the cops to do what they could, but the scope of this was unfathomable, even to them it seemed.

Living in fear and never seeing our families again was something I knew Andrea and I couldn't abide. Where did that leave us? Everything he'd said just made me realize all the more I could never go back to my life, at least not the one I'd had till three days ago. My funeral was tomorrow, so that certainly meant I had started a new life, a new beginning. A beginning of what? Of living in fear, of isolation from my family, of Andrea missing hers because of me? What kind of life would that be?

While making a stab at pondering these disturbing thoughts, one of the agents held out his hand. Shaking mine, he then said, "Mr. Cones, I'm agent Tyler Frost. I assure you everything has been taken care of that we could possibly do. Your wife has talked to her daughter twice in the last hour. This place is as safe as it gets, at least around here."

Frost seemed to be studying me as he let go of my hand. I thought of my promise to myself to stay rational, but couldn't seem to wrap my thoughts around his assurances. Even the best protection could be penetrated, and every assurance in the book of our safety didn't make it so or change the objective of my pursuers. I'd had a good life till then, in my estimation, and going into seclusion didn't figure into how I wanted to live the rest of it.

An alternative formed in my head, and I said, "What if they thought I would give them what they want? Would that keep them from wanting to kill us?"

Frost looked at me for a moment, his countenance darkening as he said, "I thought you didn't know what that was."

"I don't, but what if they thought I did? It might at least draw them out and end this sooner."

Frost seemed to think about this for a few seconds, finally saying, "That doesn't play into your funeral tomorrow. We want them to think you're dead. That will keep them away from your family, at least we hope so."

"What do you think is the worst case scenario for what would cause them to react the way they did? Are we talking about terrorism, perhaps hundreds or maybe thousands of people dying? Or are we talking about some kind of a heist, a robbery or something? I don't know that I could hide out here if a bunch more people might die because of me."

Frost said, "If that ends up being the case, it won't be because of you. They would have done it anyways. Whatever that woman took must be important to their plans, but without knowing what that was, we can only guess. We still don't know who she was, but we know she wasn't Sarah. We just got a positive ID that a body found floating in the Mississippi up by Minneapolis was her a few minutes ago. Her fingerprints don't match the woman you rescued. Nothing in the car was suspicious, but whatever it is could have easily been washed out. We just don't know what to expect now."

Shaking my head distractedly, I asked, "Why do you think they didn't just call me and ask for it back? I could have saved them a lot of trouble."

"Well, we've talked about that a lot, and the only thing we can figure is that they have to kill you whether you give it to them or not, but they can't kill you till they know for sure whether you do have it."

I mulled this dark and disquieting answer over for a while, not seeing any hope for a normal future, no matter how I took his statement. Finally giving in to the inevitability of choosing between dying and cloistering I asked, "Where do you think we will be safest once you move us from here?"

"We will probably have to move you around for awhile, but eventually somewhere in the west. Depending on what comes up in the future, we might have to seclude you in the Rockies somewhere."

I thought, "Well that's better than New Jersey" then suddenly wondering if they had told her about all this I asked, "Can I see Andrea now?"

Hart said, "In a minute. Mitch, I know they had to sedate you yesterday. Considering the circumstances, I'm not going to hold that against you. I just need to know that you won't do anything like that again. You're going to have to trust us. We're doing everything possible here, and we can't have you thinking about taking matters into your own hands."

"I'm not gonna say I haven't thought about somehow getting even, but I won't have another episode like yesterday. I just kind of lost it. I won't act like that again."

Hart looked at me for awhile before replying, "I hope not. Whatever this is all about, you did what everybody'd like to think they'd do in that situation. This isn't your fault."

Thinking about what he said, some of my guilt was assuaged, but not nearly enough. Worried about Andrea's state of mind, and how she was feeling about us, I asked, "Do you think I could see Andrea now?" Hart said, "Sure, we'll take you to her. Follow me."

CHAPTER NINETEEN

He headed to the front corner of the barn as a four foot square of floor began rising up. Concrete stairs led down from the opening. Following Hart, Frost and Usteff, I descended the stairs and began walking down a well lit tunnel with concrete walls. About thirty feet in a heavy steel door opened as we approached it and silently shut after we went through.

I said to Usteff, "This is quite a place you got here." He said, "Yeah, I was pretty amazed when I saw it yesterday. The house is built like a bunker. All the walls are concrete and the glass will stop anything short of an artillery round. They gave me the grand tour and said this has been here for twenty years and only been used a few times. You should be safe here for as long as it takes."

We climbed a set of steel stairs and a four inch thick steel door swung silently open as we reached the landing at the top. We emerged into the kitchen and Andrea was sitting at the kitchen table, two agents standing by the counter with coffee cups.

As I began rushing towards her, she stood up. Her face didn't brighten and her moves seemed mechanical as she stepped towards me. I had tried to absorb all the information that Hart had given me, but seeing Andrea made the present the only thing I could think of as I tried wrapping my arms around her to comfort her obviously distraught psyche.

She wouldn't allow it, pulling back from my grasp as her eyes looked directly into mine without a hint of compassion. She said, "Did you hear what kind of people broke in our house?"

My thoughts went straight back to our dilemma and I said, "I heard, but we WILL get through this. We're safe here for the time being, and this will end, I promise you."

She stepped back from me and shrilly said, "How do you know? For all we know they could be outside right now."

One of the cops said, "Mrs. Cones, you already know this is a safe place and we have Willy and Jody in a safe place. You can talk to them again if you're still worried." as he held out a strange looking phone towards her.

She seemed to somewhat calm down immediately, saying in a slowly rising crescendo as she turned towards him, "I'm sorry. I know you're doing all you can, but I TOLD him to be careful that night. He NEVER listens to me, just FUCKING does whatever he damn well pleases!"

Turning back to me, the blood welling to her cheeks as she stared at me with her face and mouth trembling, she suddenly barked vehemently, "This is all your fault, you and your macho bullshit. You just always gotta do things your own way don't you, and never once stop and think about us. How you feel now, Mr. TOUGH guy?"

Shrinking back from her lambaste, her livid, nearly unrecognizable face spewing spittle on me, I realized seeing me again had made her react the way she did. The disturbing words she'd said over the phone during our last conversation seemed endearing compared to this vitriolic tongue lashing, and I knew in that instant that I'd lost her forever. She hated me for putting her and perhaps everyone she knew into this situation.

The agents seemed more shocked than I at her tirade. All of them seemed unsure about how to handle this. Usteff finally spoke up as he stepped between us. "Mrs. Cones . . . . Andrea . . . . you shouldn't blame Mitch for all this. I understand that you're very upset right now, and believe me, anybody would be, but he's really not who you should be blaming. I know for a fact that he loves you dearly, and that he's certainly no happier about this than you. Let's just try and get through this as best we can, because there isn't any going back to the way it was."

Her face still trembling, she stared at him angrily. Her mouth opened a few times and she looked like she was ready to start on him. Instead, she threw her hands on top of her head, violently shaking it back and forth for a few seconds as if trying to exorcize a demon within. As she calmed down a bit, her hands slowly sunk to her face and she began crying into them. Usteff finally moved towards her and gently put his hands on her shoulders saying, "There now . . . it's okay . . . just get it all out," Andrea's head sinking into his chest and her sobbing wracking her whole body with spasms.

Horror stricken by her scathing, vicious rebuke, I'd slowly recoiled from it till my back hit the counter. Eyes wide open and mouth agape, the decimation of my dwindling hopes for an even somewhat tolerable resolution was complete. Watching my loathing wife being consoled by another man for despair she felt because of me, a knot the size of a baseball formed in my throat. I stood there dumbfounded, no words capable of adequately expressing the dejection I felt. I'd thought my spirits had hit rock bottom well before this, but that was only a ledge on the way down.

The stunned agents only watched as Usteff held Andrea tight, her spasms settling into a slight quiver as her jag spent. She looked up at him finally and said, "I . . . I'm sa . . . sa . . . sorry. I . . . I need to sit down." He helped her sit down, and as he stepped away, her gaze fell upon me. Her quivering cheeks were streaked with tracks from her tears and makeup, but her hard eyes were unyielding. Staring at me fixedly without showing any sign of remorse for her condemnation, she shook her head once then turned away from me as if the sight of my face reviled her.

It felt like a cruel joke was being played on me, a lookalike actress playing Andrea's part without researching her character. I just could not reconcile the actress with the real life character, because I didn't want to give credence to the script. My desire to cajole her or beg her or whatever it took to make her change her mind flickered out as she calmly requested water in a surprisingly even, civil tone.

Speechless, I could only watch as Andrea took a few swallows from the bottle handed to her by one of the agents. After making an effort to push her hair out of her face and wiping her tears with a Kleenex she asked Usteff, in an even more friendly tone, "When we leave here, can I be put in separate protective custody?"

Seemingly taken aback for a moment by her emotionally neutral, pragmatic question, he blurted out angrily, "Why . . . no, how could you want to do that? I don't think you really mean that, and if you do, I don't think you're considering everything."

As Usteff looked at her with consternation, seeming to be searching for something further to add, she said calmly, "I think I AM considering everything. Can I be put in separate custody or not?"

Hart walked over and stood next to her, his disbelief at the recent events still plain to see. "Mrs. Cones, why don't you give this some thought while you're here? We aren't going to discuss this further right now, but if you still feel the same way in a few days, we will discuss it then, okay?"

She actually smiled at him as she said, "I can wait till then. I'd like to go to my room and clean up a bit. Could you please have his clothes put somewhere else?" Standing up without a backwards glance, she walked over to the trash can by the refrigerator and threw the empty water bottle in.

Usteff moved over and stood in front of her as she turned towards the door between the kitchen and the rest of the house. Obviously flustered, he said, "Let me just say for the record that I think you're wrong about this."

CHAPTER TWENTY

As he finished his sentence, a crackle sound came out of the radios of the agents. Frost jumped up and said, "What was that?" A voice from the next room replied, "I don't know." Frost said into his mike, "Two, did you hear that?" He seemed to be listening as a louder pop sound followed immediately by a loud squealing began coming from all their radios. Frost yelled, "They're here!" but from the reactions of the other agents, I knew they had already figured that out.

Frost was practically screaming, "Hal, do you have a visual?" as a ponytailed guy in a Hawaiian shirt came in from the room off the kitchen, cocking a submachine gun as he said, "IT'S ALL DOWN!"

As he finished speaking a boom came from outside. Spinning quickly towards the kitchen window, I saw fragments of the barn doors raining down as trails of light streaked into the gaping maw. Frost and Hart jostled me aside to look out as three loud bangs accompanied by bright flashes came from inside the barn.

Someone inside began firing out as three dark clad figures raced towards the barn. The closest man went down as the other two began firing their machine pistols, not slowing down or quitting firing as they disappeared into the smoke. In mere seconds they came back out and spread out in cover fire positions as two other black figures ran towards the house through the smoke that was pouring from the barn.

Already running to the door that led into the mud room off the kitchen Hart shouted, "They're coming!" I turned from the window as Usteff grabbed Andrea and pulled her onto the floor behind the island in the kitchen. Usteff ran into the front room and shouted, "There's a Humvee coming up the drive!" as the running men threw themselves down in front of the concrete back porch. Hart seemed to be deciding whether to open the door or not as one of the men outside yelled, "SEND OUT MITCH CONES OR WE'LL BLOW UP THIS WHOLE HOUSE!"

I'd seen them pretty well as they had raced towards the house carrying large rucksacks, presumably filled with explosives. The flood lights had been shot out during the first few seconds of the attack, but I had seen that both men were dressed in black and appeared to have blackened faces.

Usteff said from the front room as he blazed away, "Four are behind the Humvee," as Hart finally opened the door leading into the mud room. Looking towards him, I saw that the door to the porch had a continuous large hinge and steel plating on the backside.

The steady chatter of automatic weapons being fired from the dormers began echoing through the house. Hart yelled, "I can't see the guys behind the porch!" as he gazed through what looked like a high mail slot next to the back door. There was a peephole in the solid door and he moved over to that and looked out, then immediately stuck the barrel of his machine pistol through the slot and began spraying bullets into the yard.

Looking out the back window again two four wheelers veered behind the burning barn for cover as Hart's clip emptied.

Hearing Hart changing clips, I looked over at him just as he stuck the barrel out the slot again. Before he even got off a shot a bullet slammed into his gun barrel and Hart's left hand seemed to explode as the misshapen round caught him on the ricochet. A salvo of rounds was hitting around the firing port and in a split second after Hart's hand exploded he was hit again as his gun clattered on the floor. I saw him jerk with the shot and as he was spinning down to the floor two large booms rocked the attic and dust and smoke billowed through the house.

The stream of gunfire from the attic quit immediately and an eerie silence fell over the house as the cloud settled. In a few seconds a voice called out, "MITCH CONES. COME OUT OF THE HOUSE NOW. YOU HAVE THIRTY SECONDS OR EVERYONE INSIDE IS GOING TO DIE."

I looked over towards Hart and Frost was kneeling over him, then he turned and looked at me, shaking his head in a negative way. I wasn't sure if he meant not to go out or that Hart was dead as I glanced towards Andrea, curled up in a tight ball against the kitchen cabinets with her hands over her ears and her eyes squeezed shut.

The whole sequence of events from the first crackle on the radio till now had occurred in less than two minutes. The only agent I could still see or hear was Frost as he got up and said, "I think they mean it."

My mind was reeling but I still had a concept of time and I knew the thirty seconds was about to expire. I yelled, "THIS IS MITCH CONES. I'M COMING OUT!"

Andrea heard me and opened her eyes, but she appeared to be in shock and just stared at me. I looked at her for few seconds knowing this would be the last time, then walked to the back door in a single minded stupor.

CHAPTER TWENTY ONE

Frost was watching me but didn't say a word as I grabbed the steel lever on the door and opened it a crack. Looking out at the porch, I spoke through the crack and said, "I'M GONNA COME OUT. I'M NOT ARMED."

Two dark figures rose slightly up with weapons trained on the door, the four wheelers racing towards them as one said, "Come out now with your hands out."

I sensed Frost coming up beside me and saw him start to stick his pistol out the firing port. I grabbed the barrel and looked at him, shaking my head back and forth. With my hand still around the barrel I said, "I'm comin' out." I turned towards Frost and mimed, "There's no other way." as I pulled the door open just enough to slide through.

As Frost shut the door behind me, I held my hands out in front of me and said, "Here I am. Just take me."

One of them was already jumping onto the porch towards me. As his rifle butt began swinging towards my face I actually had time to think "It sucks that this is the last thing I'm going to see!" as the other yelled, "HAKIM. STOP!" Shrinking backwards to avoid the blow, the butt glanced off my temple and I crashed to the concrete floor of the porch.

The blow dazed me, but didn't knock me out. Feeling many hands grabbing me, I writhed a bit but was quickly thrown onto the back of one of the four wheelers. A plastic zip tie was quickly strapped around my hands and then another through the first and the strap on the seat. At the same time, both my ankles were zip tied around the vertical struts for the foot rests.

The last one had just been snapped into place when the driver jumped on and the idling machine took off. The other very silent ATV followed quickly behind us as we raced around the back of the now fully engulfed barn.

The overwhelming certainty that I was going to die soon came to me but I couldn't seem to care as we raced away from the drive leading to the farmhouse. They hadn't bothered putting a mask on me or in any way hiding their faces, other than the camo paint.

I could hear shooting and far off sirens coming from the direction of the road as we sped down the first hill and through a cut fence. The driver seemed to have no trouble negotiating all the turns at high speed as we flew through pastures, crop fields and wooded ravines with no headlights.

The straps were cutting into my boots and wrists with every bounce and brush was whacking me in the face as we cut through some woods and then splashed through a stream bed, water drenching me. I had kept listening for the sound of an explosion, thinking they might blow up the house even though they had me, but it never came.

The water from the cold stream brought me out of the daze I'd been in and I looked up at the sky. I suddenly had an overwhelming desire to know which way we were headed. Many years of studying the cosmos in remote areas where you can actually see millions of stars had made me fairly adept at picking out direction based on their constellations. After coming out of the stream bed we went through another cut fence and into a large hilly pasture. I looked up and the Big Dipper told we were headed almost straight north as the driver gunned it up the steep hill.

The sudden burst of speed bit the straps deeply into my wrists and then suddenly they were swinging up and over my head. Arching backwards, the zip ties around my ankles strained against the sudden burden of being the only thing holding me on the four wheeler. If not for them, I surely would have tumbled backwards off the bike.

We crested the hill at about thirty miles an hour, becoming airborne momentarily. As we landed heading down my hands and body involuntarily flew forward. My wrists were still strapped together but as they flew forward they went over the head of the driver. He must have felt my arms connect with his shoulders and my body slam into him, hitting the front brake hard, because when we hit the ground again a split second later, the front tires dug and the back tires cart wheeled over.

The straps around my ankles dug deep into my boots then broke and we were flying through the air. I heard a large crash followed immediately by the sensation of my arms being pulled out of their sockets. I landed squarely on my back and the driver slammed into the ground between my out stretched legs, my strapped wrists still around his neck. The straps bit into his and my flesh deeply, and my left arm finally popped out of its socket as his weight and momentum pulled me forward.

The bike behind us was flying through the air to our right as we completed another somersault or two and came to rest.

Simultaneously, I heard a loud crash and then the sounds of a man moaning loudly soon after as I realized I was alive. I had come free from the driver on the last bounce and my adrenalin rush cut off the pain momentarily as I prepared to stand up. All I could think about was getting as far away from them as possible.

I pushed myself off the ground and almost fainted from the pain. The backs of my wrists were steadily dripping blood, my left shoulder was shooting waves of pain throughout my body, but my legs were at least working, the pain from them being overshadowed by all the rest. I glanced at the driver as I finally stood up, intending to start running or at least trying to, but realized quickly he was no threat. His neck was nearly severed and his head lay at a right angle to his body.

The other driver had quit moaning, the sudden quiet in stark contrast to the violent sounds of the past few seconds as I glanced towards him and prepared to 'sprint' away. He wasn't moving as I staggered a few steps towards him, hoping to see that he was dead also. Seeing the glint of his machine pistol lying off to his side, the strap still around his back, he made a lurch to push himself up.

I'd seen what looked like a Colt .45 automatic in a leg holster on the now dead driver. I looked back down at his grotesque body and saw it was still in the holster. Stumbling back towards him, I tried to bend down quickly and unsnap the holster, but fell towards the body instead as my wobbly knees gave way. Pain from my shoulder shot through my whole body as I crumpled on top of his bloody corpse. Pushing up with my right hand, I rolled off him, crying out as I did.

Breathing hard as I tried to get myself turned over, I heard the other thug begin stirring and groaning. Pushing down on the ground with my right hand, I brought myself to my knees and shaking severely managed to get the snap off the leg holster and bring the gun out. I had hardly ever fired a pistol in my life, but I fumbled with the gun and flipped the safety off as I saw the other guy trying to get up.

The gun felt very heavy as I raised it up and pointed it towards the now rising second driver. He wasn't looking at me, appearing punch drunk as he stumbled and rolled a few feet down the hill, putting him about forty feet away from me.

I had almost fired before he fell. Lining up another shot at his mostly hidden body, I wondered how far we were from the pick-up point they must have for transferring me off the ATV. I decided not to shoot unless I had to, and began painfully standing up while trying to keep the gun trained. Holding the pistol as steady as possible, I advanced towards the groaning figure as he tried to push himself up again. I closed the distance quickly and stood behind him in a few seconds, debating whether to shoot him or not.

He was on all fours facing down the hill away from me. I tried to use my left hand to help steady the gun, but the instant pain made me grunt. Rolling over, he tried to get his machine pistol off his back on seeing me. I just started pulling the trigger, and the first shot hit between his legs as he brought his gun around his back and began lining up. My second and third shots found their mark, his stomach and right shoulder gushing blood as the force of the impacts knocked him onto his back.

The whole corner of his shoulder appeared to be missing as he unsuccessfully tried to squirm away for a second, pushing himself with his feet as he stared at me with an astonished look in his eyes and face. Taking another step closer, I shot him between his eyes from five feet away. Slowly collapsing to my knees, I dropped the pistol, the act of firing it having pushed me close to blacking out from the pain.

I felt like just lying down and letting go. What would it matter? This crazy world could go on without me, and everybody I cared about would be better off for it. Only anger at the way I was going out impelled me finally to give a shit about my continued tenure on this planet. I wasn't going to go out lying down.

"Get your ass up, Mitch." I feverishly looked all around for the speaker. Seeing no one, I looked down at the corpse in front of me. I knew he didn't say it, but the sight shocked me into action.

More of his buddies could be anywhere, and would come running if they had heard the shooting. Suddenly rejuvenated in purpose, I pushed myself up and grabbed the pistol again, tucking it into my pants after flipping the safety back on. Yanking on the machine pistol, I tried to pull the strap over his head, but shooting lances of pain shot throughout my body as it caught on his left armpit. I let go of it and stood up, trying to fight the veil of blackness pressing on me again.

After a few seconds of heavy breathing, more like grunting, I stooped over and pulled the strap around his arm. Looking at the unfamiliar weapon, I heard the sound of a vehicle coming from the north.

He had a sheath knife snapped on his webbing belt. Bending over, I set the gun down and gave a pull at the knife. It unsnapped more easily than I'd assumed, and I almost fell backwards as it came free. Catching my balance, I stuck it in my pants next to the pistol and picked up the machine pistol.

The closest woods were about a hundred yards away from me to the east. Stumbling towards them, the faint light of headlights coming my way began dancing across the taller plants scattered through the roughly knee high grass, and I realized I wasn't going to make the trees before the lights might be full upon me.

I'd made it about fifty yards before I plopped myself down behind the thickest clump close to me. Clutching the machine pistol in my right hand, I rested the front stock on the ground, pointing it in the general direction that the still unseen vehicle was coming from. I found a lever that I hoped was the safety and clicked it forward. The pistol was digging into my stomach, so I pulled it out and laid it down in front of me. Propping up the machine pistol again, strange headlights came over a rise in the field a hundred yards away. They had some kind of slits and I remembered old war movies I'd seen them in as they disappeared into a depression in the hill.

They seemed to be on a beeline for the bikes. I figured the guys in the truck must have some kind of tracking device on them or knew the exact route by which the ATVs were supposed to come. Thinking about ammo, I hoped it didn't come down to that, because the guys in the truck probably had plenty.

The black truck slammed to a stop about twenty feet away from the second drivers turned over ATV, almost running over his corpse. Two guys jumped out of the bed and dropped to the ground as they saw the bloody body. The guys in front were getting out and someone said, "Get down. Frank's been shot." They dropped to the ground also and one of them said, "See anybody else?" The other guy said, "No, but Frank's gun is gone."

My finger was resting on the trigger, but I couldn't see anybody as I heard the rustling sounds of men crawling through the grass. I tried to listen for the sounds coming closer, but they seemed to be fading away. "FUCK!" was the next word I heard, coming from somewhere near the spot where my driver had met his gruesome end. "JORGE'S DEAD AND CONES IS GONE!" one of them called out in a loud whisper.

I was trying to quit breathing hard as the night got deathly quiet. The drops of sweat from my brow and blood from my wrists hitting the grass in front of me seemed like Congo drums as I tried to become part of the landscape. If they spotted me the only thing I could do was try to take as many with me as possible, knowing I had little chance of surviving a shootout with at least four trained and unhurt killers and I sure as hell wasn't going to outrun them. Giving up never even crossed my mind as I heard some whispering and figured they were deciding whether to look for me or get the hell out of there, sincerely hoping they would take the second option.

The passenger door of the truck opened and a spotlight shined down the other side of the slope at first but quickly began revolving to my position. The clump of grass which I had felt semi safe behind in the darkness seemed like a wisp of smoke as the powerful beam glanced over me and amazingly continued its' sweep. The holder of the beam had almost completed a full circle when the faint sounds of a helicopter began to pulse the air.

In the same instant I heard the rotors, the beam switched off and I heard, "Grab Jorge and Frank and throw them in the truck.

I'll find Cones." I thought, "You stupid fucker, you're dead." as my finger almost squeezed the trigger, though I couldn't see the speaker. The plastic cuffs on my wrists might not keep me from killing this terrorist boss or whatever he was, but I debated whether to try to cut them off right now or keep the gun trained on the truck. I had clear shots at the men loading up the bodies, despite the moonless night, but knew there was small chance of getting them all.

All my senses had kicked into overdrive as soon as I dropped to the ground, or maybe before that. The terror of my situation, combined with my pain, began to creep into my psyche in the short seconds it took for three guys to throw the bodies in the back. The adrenaline wasn't working and everything began to hurt as I lay there immobile, wishing the truck away no matter what I had to do after.

The sound of rotors had diminished in the interim. I knew they had probably landed at the farmhouse, some two miles or so distant by my calculations. The truck finally started up and within seconds had wheeled around, luckily away from me, heading back the way it came from without headlights.

CHAPTER TWENTY TWO

I saw a lone figure standing where the truck had been, a vague outline of his upper torso silhouetted in the star light. The waves of pain seemed to diminish as I watched him stand there for maybe thirty seconds and not move a muscle. If I had known the machine pistol would shoot, I would have let out a burst as soon as the truck's engine faded from hearing. The uncertainty about its' mechanisms kept me from shooting, wondering whether I needed to chamber a round as I'd seen in the movies but not daring to make the sound that would require.

The dark figure turned on a black light penlight and began searching the ground around where Frank's body had been. After another half minute, I heard a slight "Ah". The dim, blue light walked straight towards me, and I almost pulled the trigger again as it shot into the pasture behind me. It suddenly clicked off and the silhouette disappeared from view in the same instant.

The "Ah" sound I'd heard had seemed like something Edison or Bell might have said when they solved the equations of their obsessions, sure that this finally was the right answer. I knew instinctively that he had seen my blood trail and was going to follow it. The possible added fire power of the machine pistol began to seem insignificant compared to the proven Colt. I slowly lowered the machine pistol onto the grass and picked up the Colt, flipping the safety forward as I strained to hear in the silence. A faint rustle came from directly in front of me, but I still couldn't see my stalker.

Another while went by without a sound. I was regretting not taking a shot at the last sound when suddenly a swath of grass about ten feet in front of me parted. Seeing the outline of a face, I moved the gun barely an inch and shot three times before the gun emptied.

Dropping the Colt quickly on hearing the first click, I grabbed at the machine pistol, fumbling to get my bloody and throbbing hands in the right position to aim and fire the gun. Expecting him to start firing back at any second, I pulled the trigger on the machine pistol as soon as I had it lined up.

It just made a soft click, making me mighty glad I'd picked up the Colt. Dropping the machine pistol on its' side, I feverishly tried to pull back on the bolt, this proving to be very difficult with my hands strapped and slippery and pain shooting through my whole body. After a futile few seconds of the gun just sliding back towards me, I heard a wheezing sound coming from my stalker. I pushed the machine pistol ahead of me and used my head to keep it from sliding backwards as I finally chambered a round, the pain of the movement causing me to cry out loudly.

The strange wheezing sound was continuous now. No other sound but occasional crickets and frogs could be heard as I finally pointed the gun back towards the killer's position. If I heard a single sound that sounded like him trying to get up, I was going to empty the gun in his direction, but the wheezing stopped and stillness fell.

I lay there frozen in position for another few seconds before inching my way forward through the small but thick clump that had hidden me. I saw an inert form clearly as soon as I'd crawled a couple feet. Trying to keep the gun on him, I stood up slowly and hobbled towards him.

He was laying face down and the back of his neck had a large hole in it with frothy, pinkish looking blood running off both sides. Pulling out the knife I'd taken off Frank, I slowly lowered myself down right next to him. Laying the knife on the ground in front of me, I unsnapped the sheath and propped it between my knees with the blade facing out. Squeezing my knees tightly together, I cut off the zip tie with a quick pull against the blade. My left arm flopped to my side uncontrollably, the jolt of contact with the ground excruciating.

I screamed out in agony and fell back onto the grass, writhing in pain. As I tried to control my volume by pressing my lips tightly together I heard a quiet beep. A voice said softly, "That you?" I looked towards the source, seeing a hand held radio strapped on my latest victim's belt, half buried under his side. Forcing myself back into a sitting position, I slid it off his belt and stared at it. The urge to tell them about killing him hit me hard but I fought it back, seeing this as my first opportunity to gather some information.

Scrounging through his pockets with my right hand, I pulled out a large roll of cash, a pen knife, a Zippo lighter, and a pack of cigarettes, but no wallet. Kicking his corpse to roll it over, I unbuckled his webbing belt and tried to pull it off him. The first stabs of pain made me keep pushing the body over with my feet till I had freed it. Taking a swallow of some type of energy drink from the metal flask on it, I surveyed the other contents. There was an empty sheath, two pouches with spare clips, and a pistol in a snapped holster. Scooting towards his outstretched hands, I saw a large Bowie knife lying mostly buried in the grass. Expecting to find another gun of some sort, I actually chuckled a bit, well in my mind at least, as I realized he'd brought a knife to a gunfight.

Grabbing all the stuff I'd gathered, I stuffed it in my pockets and clumsily strapped the belt around my waist after laying down on it. I wasn't sure if the truck would come back, but decided to get out of there. After climbing to the top of the hill, I looked back north. The radio beeped softly again and a voice said, "Jay, you there."

I didn't want the sound to give me away so I turned off the receive button. Suddenly wondering if they could somehow track me by the radio, I threw it in the grass and scanned the pasture looking for the truck to reappear. A few seconds went by, then a faint motor sound, but no light, began coming into the field from the ravine a quarter mile or so north. I said, "Shit!" and began lurching down the hill, trying to go as fast as possible without falling over.

Reaching the woods, I went through the fence cut and ran about twenty yards to the left. Slowly lowering myself down behind a large tree next to the fence, gasping and wheezing with pain and exertion, I debated my options. Laying there catching my breath and trying to stifle my sounds, I looked for the best way to run. A couple minutes had elapsed before I pushed myself back up, intending to follow the trail the four wheelers had blazed back to the farmhouse. Glancing towards the field before I began the next trek, I saw a blue light at the top of the hill a hundred yards away.

Dropping back down quickly but not taking my eyes off the hillside, the light shut off and three amorphous forms were silhouetted in the skyline for a second. They disappeared as they began coming down the hill through the tall grass and occasional saplings on the steep slope.

My wrists were steadily dripping blood on the ground in front of me, the amount more than many deer had left as I'd trailed them to their final rests. There was no sign of the three for a minute or so then I heard the barely audible sounds of voices. A half moon was just beginning to rise, and faint light began filtering through the trees into the field, brightening slowly as the moon ascended.

I was about thirty yards away from the creek crossing and suddenly the sound of soft splashes could be barely heard over the brook's constant melody. The slightly louder sounds of men creeping over the gravel next to the stream soon after convinced me I hadn't imagined the splashes. I scooted around the tree to face the direction of the sounds and propped the machine pistol in front of me again, resting it on a large root. I flipped the safety off and prepared to fire, assuming these guys to be more bad guys.

The brush was thick along the stream bank, but sparse through the woods between the stream and the fence, ensuring clear shots at them as they came out of the creek bed and moved towards the field to hook up with their cohorts. The sounds stopped, and as seconds stretched by, I figured they were peering over the lip of the creek bed. The murmur of a subdued voice caught my ear then silence fell again. Leaving the gun lying, I pushed myself up a bit and looked around the tree trunk into the field again. Seeing a vague, shadowy form at the bottom of the hill but no lights, I slowly picked up the machine pistol. Figuring it was only a matter of minutes, or maybe even seconds, till they joined up with the guys in the creek bed and trailed me to the tree, I decided to open the ball myself and at least go down fighting.

As quietly as possible I scooted towards the other side of the tree and propped the machine pistol up once again. The killers had bunched up as they neared the fence cut, their heads and shoulders now stark in the moonlight as they seemed to be conferring. They split up a bit and began moving forward as I drew a bead. They were at thirty yards as I cut loose with the machine pistol, aiming at the guy closest to me. The previously still night erupted with gunfire. I held the trigger down trying to sweep the gun with one hand, but had little control over its' jerking movements as spasms assailed me.

Hearing and actually feeling the whiff of bullets flying over me from both groups, I hugged the ground between the large, protruding roots of the maple tree, wondering if I had any ammo left. To my surprise, the two groups were still firing at each other, but after a few seconds the firing stopped. I'd assumed the sounds I'd heard in the field had been these two groups talking, but if they were firing at each other, then the guys in the creek had to be cops.

Taking a gamble on that reckoning, I yelled, "This is Cones" and immediately saw a man rise up from the grass in the field and make a crouching run towards me. I turned towards him and pulled the trigger, hearing only a soft click. As he neared the barbed wire fence, I made what surely would have been a futile grab at the pistol on my belt, seeing the guy begin to stagger from the impact of bullets as I brought the pistol out. Completing his death dance, he fell across the fence, blood showering me from his many hits.

Frost yelled out, "Cones" and I shouted, "Over here." Four guys jumped over the creek bank and two ran towards me low while another two ran to the edge of the woods and crouched behind trees, looking for further targets.

Frost threw himself down on the ground next to me as the other cop stood up and peered around the tree at the field. Frost grabbed the arm of the gunman splayed over the fence, throwing it back down in a second and asking, "How many were out there?"

"Just three, I think. I killed three more over top of the hill."

He looked at me incredulously, but just asked, "Are you hit?" as he noticed the blood on my face and arm.

"No, that blood is his, but my left shoulder's all fucked up."

"Do you think you'll be okay for a minute? We have to check on the other two."

"Could you show me how to use this pistol?"

Grabbing the pistol he nearly whispered, "This is a Berretta nine mil. You just check for ammo like this," popping out the clip and looking at it then slamming it back in, "make sure a round is in the chamber by pulling back on this slide," as he cocked the gun, "make sure the safety is off," as he pushed the safety off, "and pull the trigger." He handed me the gun after pushing the safety back on saying, "We got two more guys over there," pointing at the barely visible crouching other cops, "so be sure who you fire at."

I said, "I will" as I pointed the pistol and aimed over the barrel at the field in front of us. The other cop had been in cover fire position as this quick instructional lesson had transpired. No sounds could be heard coming from the field as he spoke softly into a head mike, "This is Blue. See anybody?" I couldn't hear the reply but he next said, "We're gonna sweep the field towards you. We got two more possibles out there. Keep us covered."

At that he dropped down and crawled under the fence, Frost following shortly behind him. They crouched and surveyed the tall grass in front of them for a few seconds, then began slowly creeping forward, sweeping their guns slightly as they did. I saw Blue hold up his hand and drop, having reached the general vicinity of the guy I'd fired at first. I figured he had found his body and relaxed my tight grip on the pistol slightly.

I glanced towards the other two cops, still crouched behind trees some thirty yards down the fence from me. They suddenly dropped and switched sides of the trees they were behind, their backs now facing me. The silence of the still night was deafening, the beat of my heart pounding in my ears, as I feverishly looked and listened for anything to tell me why they'd changed their positions. I knew there were a lot more bad guys left, and that the three guys had probably told them all what happened and where we were.

A minute or so went by, the suddenly returning mating calls of frogs and crickets the only sounds, then I saw the cop closest to me go limp and heard the thwack of a bullet hitting flesh and bone in the same instant. I had heard the sound many times before deer hunting, and in the past two days, leaving no doubt as to its' meaning.

There was no sound for a few seconds as I again peeked over the tree root, having dropped down on realizing someone was firing. The other cop was now facing into the woods, his feet almost reaching the fence as he aimed his gun towards the stream. I still couldn't see or hear anything of our new assailants as the seconds ticked by.

I was clutching the pistol tightly and aiming into the woods, resting it on the root, when I heard the sound of a round hitting a tree. Looking towards the cop, he was crunched face down into the leaves, but slowly poked his head back up. As he began firing into the woods, bark, dirt and leaves began dancing around his tree, the differing sounds of impact sounding like a little orchestra playing unworldly music for a good five seconds.

No gunshots echoed through the valley from this fusillade, and I knew it was more than one gun firing from the whirlwind of debris generated. These new guys must have silencers and night scopes because their accuracy was dead on, his body jumping from the impacts numerous times before the 'music' stopped.

The distant thump of rotors permeated the air after a few seconds of silence. I ducked down again and tried to stop all sounds of my breathing as I wondered if I'd been seen. Hugging close to the tree and thinking once again, "Who are these guys?" I debated whether to stay or run, neither option offering much hope. I hadn't heard anything from Frost or Blue. Assuming they may have been seen and shot, I looked behind me and searched for the best way to run. After what I'd just seen, I knew my only glimmer of hope was getting away if reinforcements didn't arrive pronto.

From the direction in which the two now ostensibly dead cops had turned, I figured the new bunch of killers was coming in from the southwest. The thump of rotors grew steadily louder till the helicopter flew almost directly over me just above the treetops, a searchlight brightening up the slope of the pasture as it hovered for a few seconds then slipped sideways towards the top of the hill.

It began to descend near the peak of the sixty foot hill, looking like it was going to land there. A stream of fire came out of the woods, discernible whacking sounds hitting the chopper then a large whoosh sound and the trail of an RPG raced towards it. It had almost settled on the hilltop when it exploded in a spray of fire, crashing to the ground sideways as rounds began cooking off and shooting into the field. The night became like day for a few seconds as it completed a somersault and rolled down the hill towards me, flames shooting in every direction.

I decided right then that I had seen enough and began crawling away from the tree towards the meandering creek bank, about twenty feet behind me. Rolling over the edge, I slid down the mud bank and hit the gravel streambed, squeezing my lips together to keep from crying out. Gaining my feet quickly and trying to be as quiet as possible, I headed downstream, crossing the shallow brook a few times as my steadily throbbing left arm flopped.

Hunched over to keep my head below the bank, I had gone about two hundred yards when I heard the sounds of another chopper coming towards us. I hoped it didn't make the same mistake as the last one, but now felt my salvation could only come from distance and evasion.

As the stream turned towards the south, I climbed out of its' bed on a rocky shelf and headed up a hill into the woods. Figuring the enemy would expect me to head to the farmhouse I decided to go straight east.

Reaching the top of the hill, an uncontrollable coughing spell came over me. I doubled over and threw my right sleeve over my mouth, trying to smother the sounds. After being able to breathe somewhat normally again, I ran down the other side of the maturely forested hill, expecting to hear the sounds of running men closing on me any second

The rising half moon lit the forest enough for me to see most of the sparse saplings and brush coming as I frantically drove through the trees. I was almost at the bottom of the hill when another firefight began. I stopped and listened for a few seconds, briefly wondering if I should have stayed and tried to provide some kind of help to the cops with my pistol. The cacophony gradually subsided as I continued running to the east, away from the kill zone.

CHAPTER TWENTY THREE

Gray light coursed through the forest as I opened my eyes. I had run as far and fast as I could, always headed towards the rising moon, before pain and exhaustion had forced me to lie down between two large fallen trees and rest. I had only planned on a quick breather, but hours had gone by when I awoke to birds singing in the trees above me.

The throbbing of my shoulder and whole body brought me to instant alertness as I listened to the sounds of the early morning forest. I had crossed a few gravel roads and one paved road in my eastward trek, but decided the benefit of following them wasn't worth the danger. Moving steadily eastward through pastures and forest, an occasional house had beckoned, but always seemed too close to the scene for comfort.

I had always loved the sounds of the forest waking up, but on this particular morning it brought me no joy. Peeking over the top of the dead falls, I surveyed my surroundings from the shallow ravine. Tall yellow broom grass waved in a field about twenty yards to the south and solid woods extended as far as I could see in every other direction. Assuming it was about six from the sun's angle, still far below the treetops, I suddenly remembered the pistol, groping for it frantically in the thick leaf bed between the trees. I had carried it throughout my flight and upon finding it breathed a sigh of relief and began thinking of my next move.

Far away sounds of fast moving trucks to the east convinced me I was close to Route 79 in the Mississippi river valley. Making a quick appraisal of my physical condition, I saw that the blood from my wrists had clotted in the night. I had wrapped shreds of my sweatshirt sleeves around them after a mile or so, but they had still been oozing. The stitches in my leg were also bleeding and I began wondering if I had left a trail to follow in my flight.

Slowly and painfully I rose from between the trees and looked towards the west. Only woods sounds and the faint hum of distant traffic were audible as I followed my trail through the trees. The kicked over leaves from my stumbling gait were apparent, but I could not find any blood spots in the first fifty yards or so.

I had never tracked myself really, at least not looking for my own blood trail, and it felt really strange to be doing so. Maybe I should have been thinking about other things, but I felt a sudden empathy for the animals I had pursued. Realizing that I was now the hunted, I imagined the pain and fear of my own quarry over the years. The quest for life burns strongly in all creatures, and perhaps the sudden transformation made me think of the innocence of all animals compared to man. Though there are many types of predator in nature, only man kills his own kind with regularity and out of sheer hatred.

After backtracking myself for a hundred yards or so, I lost the trail in a glade between thick cedar trees. I slowly scanned the rocky floor of the glade in every direction from my last noticeable track. The search seemed somewhat surreal as I concluded they couldn't have followed my tracks, because I had no doubt they would have found me sleeping if it was possible.

Turning around, I began walking towards the edge of the broom grass, deciding to stop at the first house I came to and ask for help. Always listening for the sounds of pursuit, I made my way much stealthier than the preceding night for a quarter mile or so before I saw the roof of a house peeking through the trees.

Lights were shining through the windows in the early morning gloom as I approached the neat one story brick house. A narrow lane led away from the house through thick forest and there was no road noise close by. A dozen or so white ducks swimming on the small pond beside the house quacked and stirred as I walked over the short dam, the pistol dangling from my right hand. I didn't want to put these people in jeopardy, but knew I needed some bandages, food and water at the very least, having drained the small flask during my escape.

Reaching the end of the dam, I froze in position as the front door opened and a middle-aged lady stepped out on the front porch, a large mug in her hand. She didn't seem alarmed at all as she stretched and yawned, then settled herself into a rocker on the porch. I was thinking, "Didn't you hear the shooting last night?" as she slowly glanced around then locked eyes on me.

I saw her face undergo a sudden, dramatic change as she saw my blood caked body and the pistol in my right hand. Her left hand flew to her mouth and she jumped up, her coffee spilling over her housecoat as she dropped the cup. I didn't know what to do, so I half pointed the gun at her and yelled, "STAY RIGHT THERE!"

I began to imagine a husband coming out with a shotgun as she ignored my demand and pulled open the screen door. I yelled, "STOP OR I'LL SHOOT YOU!" as I began rushing towards the porch. She pulled to a stop with the screen door open in her hand. Finishing the few strides left and jumping onto the low porch, I said as I came up behind her trembling body, "I'm not going to shoot you."

She spun around to face me, and I assumed she must be alone because she hadn't cried out to anybody. Her panicked eyes looked at my scratched, bloody and bandaged body and then dropped to the pistol. I had lowered it and said, "I need your help. I'm not a criminal but I have a lot of them looking for me. Can I use your phone?"

She just stared at me for a few seconds wide eyed, then stammered, "M . . . m . . . my phone?'

"Yeah, I need to use your phone. I promise I ain't gonna hurt you. I just need to use your phone."

She stood there for another few seconds, the panicked look in her eyes slowly subsiding, then shakily opened the front door and said, "It's this way."

I put the gun in the holster and said, "I promise I'm not going to hurt you. Just show me where the phone is and don't try to grab it or anything else yourself." I didn't want her to possibly do something that might cause me to react defensively, for my sake as well as hers.

As I followed her through the front door, I asked, "Did you hear all the shooting last night?" We were in a cute living room, the decor showing the mark of a fastidious person. She had reached the hallway that led off this room and turned to face me as she answered, "Wh . . . what shooting? Wh . . . What happened to you?" I said, "The phone" and gestured for her to keep walking.

We turned into an immaculate kitchen and I saw a cell phone hooked to a charger on the counter top. I said, "Please sit down and I'll tell you. I'm real sorry I scared you, but I needed to make sure you wasn't gonna do anything stupid. Is there anybody else here?"

She took a seat at the kitchen table and said, "No, ma . . . my husband leaves for work at six."

I opened up a cabinet door and pulled out a glass, keeping an eye on her the whole time. After chugging one glass from the faucet, I grabbed the cell phone and sat down across from her, saying, "My name is Mitch Cones." Comprehension suddenly spread from her eyes to her whole manner as her chin dropped and she mimed, "Oh My God!"

Rushing through the main points of my tale as quickly as possible to abate her fears, at least as to my intentions, her face went from being hard and scared, to astonished, to sympathetic, to scared again. I finished with, ". . . and then I saw you come out the door."

During the quick recital of my tale of death and misery, I had debated on whom I should call, my recent experiences making this a much tougher decision than it should have been. She said, "They said you were dead. The story has been all over the news. Do you think those guys could have followed you here?"

"No, I don't think so. We're at least four or five miles away from there, and I tried backtracking myself this morning to make sure they couldn't. What's your name?"

"Sally Evans."

"Sally, can I trust you? I'll even let you hold the gun if it makes you feel better."

Taken back a bit by my first query, but recognizing my sincerity, she waved her hand and said, "I recognize you now from the news. You keep the gun. I wouldn't want to shoot it anyways."

"Thank you. The problem I got now is I don't know who to call. I'm going to see if there's any news about last night." There was a small TV on the bakers rack. Grabbing the remote from next to it, I began surfing through all the news broadcasts and then back again, but strangely could find no story about the previous evening's events. Having assumed that every channel would be broadcasting continuous coverage about it, this fact only increased my anxiety as I pondered its' meaning.

After a couple minutes of watching with me and noting my preoccupation as I fervidly continued my search for news she said, "I'm going to get you some bandages and get dressed. Can I get up now?"

Snapping out of my fixation on the TV, I looked over at her and said, "Sure you can. Just don't try to call anybody. I know you might have other phones."

"I won't, I promise."

Figuring I might as well push my luck I asked, "Can I get something to eat too?"

"Let me get the bandages and fix you up, then I'll cook you some breakfast." She got up and went down the hall, coming back in a few minutes fully dressed. Walking to the table with a pile of linens and a first aid kit she asked, “What’s wrong with your left arm?” She must have noted the way I’d been grunting every time I had to move it, and the fact that I wasn’t using it for anything.

“I think I separated my shoulder when the four wheeler wrecked.”

“Do you think you can take off your sweatshirt?”

I tried pulling up on it, but raising my arm proved too painful for me to finish. The sweatshirt was a tattered bloody mess and she said, “I’m going to cut it off you” as she pulled some kitchen shears out of a butchers block on the counter top.

I had imagined the possibility of her grabbing something for a weapon as we’d come into the kitchen, but her calm and caring attitude made me feel only a blip of trepidation as she walked towards me with the scissors. She inserted them at a shred and carefully snipped all the way up to the collar, then cut up the side and pulled it over my right arm. As it came off, she gasped as she saw the plethora of bruises, scrapes, scratches and cuts covering my torso. My left shoulder and upper arm were swollen to twice their normal size, and seeing it made me a little nauseous myself.

“You need a hospital. I think your arm is broken.”

I had debated calling an ambulance myself but didn’t want to give any clues to my pursuers, thinking they may be listening to those types of frequencies in an attempt to relocate me. I wasn’t sure if I wanted the cops to find me either, their involvement certainly not having kept me safe up to this point.

Thinking of what Andrea might be doing at this moment and ruing the fact that I hadn't even asked Frost about her, my only consolation was that since he'd shown up, she must have been left with other people who could help her. Strangely, her rejection had not hardened me against her at all, because I now knew she had made the only sensible choice.

Sally spent a half hour or so toweling dried blood off, bandaging and wrapping strips of a sheet she cut up around my chest and upper left arm to keep it immobilized. She pulled off my tattered boots, gasping once again as she saw the dark bruises running up my legs and lacerations on my ankles from the zip ties. Blood was soaking my pants from the stitches being jarred and she cut off the leg, rewrapping the cut there also.

The distant sound of helicopters could be heard during her nursing. She asked me all sorts of questions and I tried to answer them all as succinctly as possible. By the time she finished her fear of me had evaporated.

She got one of her husband's sweatshirts and pulled it over me, saying, "This is a triple x. My husband Paul is a big guy. Can I call him? I think he can help you a lot more than me. He knows the woods around here real good and I'm worried about them guys that are after you."

"What are you going to say to him?"

"I'm just going to tell him to come home and I won't say nothing about you being here."

"What do you think he'll do if he comes home?"

"I'll explain it all to him before he comes in the house. He's a gentle giant and he won't do anything wrong, I promise."

I knew I needed some help, but after all the people that had been killed helping me I was already feeling guilty about getting Sally involved. I also knew I couldn't just walk out of here and down the road, because any car that saw me could be the bad guys. To go from not even worrying about locking my car most times to thinking anyone could be a threat to my life showed me how much my faith in humanity had changed in the past few days. Even so, I decided to gamble on Paul, figuring this angel of mercy couldn't be married to a mean guy. I said, "Yeah, go ahead and call him. Just tell him that you can't get your car started or something like that. How far away is his work?"

"He's the manager at Kroger in Winfield. He could be here in about fifteen minutes once I call him." She called him and said, scared like, "I need you to come home. We got a pack of coyotes after all the ducks." She listened for awhile and said, "I'm not going out there. There's a whole bunch of 'em." After another bit, she said, "Hurry up, they're making an awful ruckus out there." After listening to his rant about her learning to use a gun, which I could plainly hear, she hung up after saying, "I will. Just come home now."

After hanging up, she looked at me and said, "I think that's the first outright lie I've ever told him. He knows I don't have to go anywhere, and he would have said my car could wait till he got home." Seeming ashamed, she began pulling stuff out of the fridge. Turning towards me as she shut the refrigerator door she asked, "What do you think your wife was thinking when they took you away?"

Omitting Andrea's rejection and contempt, I told her more detail about the attack at the farmhouse to help her, and perhaps myself, better comprehend the import of Andrea's vacant stare as I'd stepped out the door. As she whipped the pancake batter, she went on about how she couldn't imagine the horror and finality Andrea must have been feeling. Her compassion for Andrea seemed somehow more real than her sympathy for me as she said, "I imagine she's never gonna have another minute of peace in her life. I don't think I would if something like that happened to Paul."

CHAPTER TWENTY FOUR

About ten minutes later, the sound of a vehicle racing towards the house and then slamming to a halt on the gravel caused Sally to rush outside. After only a minute or so, Paul stormed into the kitchen and glared at me with obvious suspicion. Sally was trailing him, saying, "He didn't hurt me. I promised him you wouldn't do nothin' crazy, so calm down." He was at least six foot eight and three hundred pounds, so I sure didn't want him thinking I meant them any harm. I slowly stood up and held out my hand, his gaze straying to the pistol I'd left lying on the table as I approached him.

"Mitch Cones", I said to him after I'd walked around the table. He rather reluctantly held out his hand saying, "Paul Evans" as his gaze fell back upon me. Sally rushed back to the stove to take the eggs off on seeing this, perhaps thinking her statement had defrayed his apparent hostility. Locking on my eyes, he grabbed my hand and squeezed it hard, not letting go while he said, "My wife says you're the guy who saved that woman from the Cuivre the other night. The news said you were killed in a car wreck."

"Can't believe everything you see on the news."

Finally letting up on his vise like grip, he said, "I guess you can't." He had maneuvered himself towards the table during this introduction. Grabbing the pistol, he backed around to the stove side of the table and sat down saying, "Why don't you sit down and tell me what really happened."

Sally turned around, seeing Paul holding the pistol steadily pointed at my chest. As if scolding him, she said, "Paul, you don't have to point the pistol at him. I think he's been through enough already without that."

He glanced towards her, trying to assess the honesty of her indignation, then set the pistol down on the table. Sally turned back around and heaped pancakes, eggs and bacon on my plate, then carried it around to my side of the table and set it down, saying, "You want some more coffee?" as she glared at Paul.

Realizing Sally had no fear of me, he shook his head, seeming exasperated as he said, "Well, what'd you expect me to think. You never told me he had a gun!"

"You never gave me a chance!"

I'd already began wolfing down my breakfast, this being my first real meal since Andrea and I had breakfast at the hotel nearly two days ago. Silently watching me, his amazement at the speed the food was going down coupled with a dawning comprehension of my haggard condition had deflated his animosity by the time I'd polished off the first heaping plate. Past the point of feeling starved finally, I pushed back to take a break as Sally grabbed my plate and filled it up again. Saying, "This is what really happened," I began telling him of the chain of incidents that led me to be eating breakfast in his kitchen.

The gruesome, horrific scenes I'd witnessed were painstakingly revealed, each episode of my experience being told in vivid detail during the hour long, two sided conversation. As I finished my fairly complete, forthright tale, I omitted the empty threat I'd yelled at Sally as she'd prepared to flee into the house. I know she noticed, but thankfully, she didn't tell him either.

Paul rightfully seemed very concerned as he said, "What's the chances those guys could have followed you here? It seems like they'd try to do that if they could."

Explaining to him about my inability to find sign as I'd tried backtracking myself, including the empathy I'd felt with my own prey over the years, he begrudgingly shook his head.

"Yeah, I've felt that way a few times too. You didn't find any blood at all?"

"Not a drop."

By the end of my tale of woe, he seemed to have gained a sense of respect for me, and I felt as though he could finally be trusted not to shoot me or call the cops. He seemed earnestly wanting to help me, at least without putting either of them in more jeopardy, as he said, "I'm gonna go get a shotgun anyways, before we figure out what you should do next." He got up and headed into the basement, leaving the pistol on the table.

Sally had given me some Vicodin before she began her bandaging session, and the pain was down to a medium throb. I knew I needed more doctoring than Sally had been able to do, but was in a quandary as to how to get it. Barring Paul's initial and understandable reactions, the time here had been the most peaceful I'd had in awhile, but I couldn't stay here indefinitely.

Huffing as he hurried back upstairs, Paul moved quickly from window to window with the scoped shotgun, peering through cracks in the mini blinds without opening them. Completing his round of the house, and apparently satisfied that no one was lurking outside, he came back in the kitchen. He set the shotgun down on the kitchen counter, saying, seemingly apologetically, "I just had to make sure."

Appreciating his justifiable concern, I said, "I'm glad you did. Them guys may be a lot better trackers than me." Sitting back down with a cup of coffee, Paul pulled his phone out and called his assistant manager, telling him he might not be able to make it back today because Sally was so upset about their pet ducks being killed.

After Paul hung up, I told the Evans I'd decided to call O'Brien. The fairly complete story I'd told having given them some idea of his character, they agreed with me on my decision. Using Sally's cell phone, I dialed his number. He picked up on the second ring and said, "O'Brien here."

"Can anyone else hear you? Don't say my name out loud if they can."

"Mitch?"

"Yeah, it's me."

"I'm in my car so nobody can hear me. Where are you?"

"I'm at a house in the country. Is she okay?"

"Your wife? Isn't she with you?"

I realized he didn't know anything that had happened. "No, I'm by myself. You really don't know anything?"

"No, I just left my house. What the hell happened?"

"Well, the feds must have put a lid on it, because there wasn't anything on the news about it, even though it was like fucking D-day. Have you talked to your station or anybody else this morning?"

"No, I haven't. What do you mean it was like D-day? Did they try to get you again?"

"They had me, but I killed the dudes that were hauling me away, then a bunch more showed up and shot down a helicopter."

He didn't respond for a while, finally saying, "Fuck, why are you calling me?"

"I didn't know who to call. I'm pretty messed up, but I think everybody that was protecting me is dead. Can you keep this conversation to yourself? I need to know you can do that or I'm gonna hang up."

He didn't say anything for a moment. My finger was on the button when I heard him say, "'Till I tell you otherwise, this is just between me and you."

"That's not good enough. It has to be till I tell YOU otherwise. Can you do that or not?"

This time the silence lasted even longer. I actually took that as a good sign, because if he were going to bullshit me he'd probably have just said okay immediately. Besides that, almost everyone else that had tried to help and protect me was either dead or in the hospital. He probably knew I was putting his life on the line by asking him for help, considering my recent track record. Keeping this a secret could possibly cost him his job to boot, although I guess dead is worse.

After fifteen seconds or so he said, "What the hell. You got my word on that. Where exactly are you?"

I knew the general area pretty well, but had no idea of my exact location. I also didn't want to give my location over the phone, because I'd seen last night what underestimating these guys could cost. "What kind of car are you driving?"

"An '08 tan Impala."

"Go to the corner of W and YY and keep driving by there every fifteen minutes hanging your hand down the side of the car. I'll get there when I can." He said, "Okay" then I hung up.

Paul looked at me somberly and said, "Mitch, I wish you all the luck." Holding out his meaty palm to shake mine again, he then surprisingly grabbed me in a brief gentle bear hug. Somewhat startled and uncomfortable with this gesture, I just stood there and said, "Uh . . . thanks a lot." as he let go of me. I guess Sally knew her husband pretty well after all.

CHAPTER TWENTY FIVE

I had kind of dreaded finding out exactly where I was for some reason. Usually I always want to know, and prided myself on my navigational skills. Somehow though, it seemed like if I didn't even know where I was then the bad guys couldn't.

Maybe they had all been killed last night, but I sure wasn't going to bet my life on it. The numbers, firepower, dedication and professionalism of my adversaries led me to believe that they were just the tip of some huge iceberg of conspiracy. If many of them had been killed, that meant there must be many more by my way of thinking. Only the sheer luck of a strap breaking or coming undone had kept them from pulling off a nearly flawless op against an entrenched enemy. Their information, communication and execution would only perhaps be rivaled by the most elite troops in the world. And I got one cop in a sedan picking me up? What the hell was I thinking?

I turned to Paul and said, "You got any camouflage clothes? I can't let you drive me out of here. I need a map or some good directions on how to get to W and YY too. You got a computer?"

"I'll print you out a Google earth picture and you can follow that. And I got lots of camo and such, but I don't think it's going to fit you very good."

I'm five ten and about one eighty, and his sweatshirt was like a tent on me, even with my whole arm and shoulder inside and the sleeve flopping.

Sally spoke up and said, "I'll just tighten them up for you. It'll only take a minute." With that she went like a whir down the hall and within a couple minutes I could hear a sewing machine clicking as Paul and I went into an efficient looking office in the basement. Sitting down behind his desk Paul said, "I also have lots of guns, but I don't know if you could fire a long gun with your shoulder busted up like that."

He fired up his computer, and quickly was on Google earth and showing me where I was. From that I traced my route back to the firefight and the farmhouse. Straight line distance, I was roughly six and a half miles from both, so I had run farther than I thought and curved south.

The intersection of W and YY was only about two miles away. There were strips of forest the whole way, but the intersection itself stood in the middle of fairly open ground. I figured I should try to intercept O'Brien somewhere away from that intersection, if I intercepted him at all. Hell, these guys had me thinking like a commando. I talked to Paul as a newfound friend as I pointed out my route options, him pointing out hidden houses and other pertinent facts that might aid my decision. His interest had me telling him my many jumbled thoughts as we perused the screen.

I wasn't a couch potato, but age, being married and the aches and pains of my profession had made me more sedate in recent years. Until recently, I had watched very little television, preferring more active ways to spend my spare time. Wanting to spend my limited free time with Andrea, I'd begun watching many of 'her' programs, at least if they were on the DVR.

Andrea liked mostly cop shows and horror movies. I found most horror movies to be totally unbelievable because the victims almost always do the exact opposite of what reason would dictate. I thought my situation was closer to a war movie than a horror movie, but, even in fairly good war flicks, the characters, well usually just the bad guys, do so many things contrary to reason that the stories often seem tainted in their veracity.

The insulated and secure lives of 'typical' Americans have surely not been the norm throughout the centuries. In truth, I feared for the future of mankind since many people seem totally out of touch with the 'big picture', content to play Wii or live vicariously through the lives of their reality show TV heroes. Maybe I wasn't so far away from that, but the events of the past few days had me thinking about things I'd never had cause to before.

I vowed to not make the same mistakes I'd seen countless times on film as I traced the possible paths I could take, the exact nuances of cover and topography seeming paramount to my survival. "Paranoia will destroy ya" was thrown out the window as we discussed the various routes that would get me to the intersection of W and YY.

Paul proved to be the best possible source of information about the area I could have hoped for. After agreeing on the best route I asked, "How would they think?" Paul shrugged, not adding words, for he surely didn't know either.

Suddenly remembering my outburst in the hospital, the feeling of needing revenge came over me again. The men I'd killed last night were merely tools. I felt no remorse for killing them, but no sense of pride either. The only way I might feel that would be if I could make those responsible pay. That would take me staying alive until I could exact due vengeance for all the lives shattered by those truly at fault.

As Paul finished printing, I said, "Getting away won't be enough . . . What kind of guns do you got?"

Eyeing my steel face for a second he said, "Let me show you."

He led me through a TV room and into his trophy room. Head and antler mounts of whitetail deer, turkey fans and various mounted fish adorned the walls of his 'man' room. Noticing me eyeing his trophies, he opened a large gun safe with eight various long guns inside. He gently pulled them out one by one and gave me a quick rundown on each. This man loved his guns.

I felt a real kinship with him as he relayed brief snippets of his hunts. He told me that most of the bucks and gobblers had been taken on his own hundred and sixty acres. I was impressed by his obvious hunting skills but certainly had more pressing thoughts, eyeing his guns only from a practical standpoint.

I explained I wanted one good shooting rifle, hopefully with not too much kick, and he pulled out the Remington .270. "I think you can probably fire this one the easiest. It's a semi auto and holds ten shells after I pull out the plug. I'd give you the twenty two, but I think you need a little more kick for the game you're hunting."

Surprised by his seeming enthusiasm and acceptance of the fact that I might use his gun to kill another human, I debated asking him why. The thought that he might change his mind kept me from asking the question as he went to a workbench and pulled out the plug in a minute, handing the .270 to me as he finished. I had to know. "You do know I WILL use this if I have to."

Paul gave me a quick frown then said, very seriously, "I hope you do. Any group that would do all those things isn't just a problem for you. I kind of feel like you're doing the country a service, and maybe I am too by giving you the gun." Feeling a bit of relief that he had no qualms about its' intended use, I hefted the .270 in my right hand and pointed it one handed towards the clean window, taking in the view on the scope. "Feel alright?" he asked.

"It'll do just fine."

He loaded it up fully and asked, "How many more shells you want?"

"All you got."

The cartridges he gave me were all hollow points, or more generically called hunting ammo. The mushrooming effect of a hollow point is designed to kill big game as quickly and humanely as possible.

By international law, hunting ammo is forbidden in war zones or for any type of combat. Soldiers hit by such ammo will die far more frequently due to the massive internal damage caused by the expansion of the bullet as it contacts flesh. For this reason, only full metal jacket ammo is sanctioned for human conflicts.

He loaded up a box with about twenty more shells, maps, compass, binoculars, camo face paint, backpack, gloves and hat then said, "Let's see how Sally's doing with those clothes."

We walked back upstairs and Sally had a full set of camo lying on the table. She said, somewhat beaming, "Try these on for size."

Paul said, "Let's get these jeans off first."

With his help, in about ten minutes I was suited up in almost better fitting camo pants and t-shirt than my own. Sally had cut a hole in the sides of a lightweight camo jacket for my left forearm and stitched around the opening, pinning the left sleeve over the back. She said, "When your arm's better, you can just unpin the sleeve and use it." She put two bagged sandwiches, granola, a couple apples and two bottled waters in the copious pockets of the obviously expensive hunting jacket then said, "I hope this fits you." After Paul helped me put it on, he put three pairs of socks on my feet, then a size thirteen pair of camouflage rubber boots. I stood up and looked at my make over, using a mirror in the hall.

Staring at my reflection, the graciousness of these people in the wake of my recent experiences suddenly overwhelmed me. Walking back to the kitchen table, I sat down and began softly sobbing into my right hand. Realizing I had seen the breadth of human character in the past twelve hours, the obvious inequities made my anger at the world in general dissipate for a minute as I contemplated the kindness and generosity of the Evans. Paul put his big hand on my right shoulder and said, "You can stay here as long as you need to."

This brought me out of my jag, wanting to distance myself once again, for their sake, from people I cared about. Perhaps all of my pursuers had been killed in the firefight I'd heard. Perhaps if some were still alive, their resolve had disappeared in their flight from apprehension. Perhaps I was in the free and clear, and all my tactics were only the product of an over active imagination. Perhaps, but I didn't believe it, and knew I couldn't afford to think like that even if it was the case.

With a deep sigh I stood up and said, "Can I pay you for all this?" They had seen the roll, and knew where it came from. Both seemed, to say the least, surprised by my question.

Sally especially seemed genuinely hurt that I'd even ask, scoffing, "We wouldn't take that money if we were dying. You just keep yourself alive and come back and see us when you don't have terrorists chasing you."

"I sure didn't mean to offend you. Just I . . . I don't know how I can thank you enough and I just thought . . . ."

Paul cut me off, saying, "Don't think nothing about it. You got enough to worry about. I don't know how you're going to get yourself out of this mess, but I got a feeling if there's a way, you'll figure it out."

"Thanks for the vote of confidence . . . . and for everything else. You know not to tell anyone, I mean . . . ANYONE, I was here."

Paul shook his head, eyeing me gravely as he said, "Believe me, we know. Mum's the word."

"Well I . . . hope I'll see you again some time."

"Just keep yourself alive and go hunting with me this fall."

Hoping to allay their anxieties, even as I thought about my own, I said, "You can bet on it."

With his help, I filled the pockets and pack with the contents of the box. Thinking of how long it had been since I'd talked to O'Brien, and having no good reason to delay the next phase of my odyssey, I said, "Well, I guess I better get going if I want to hook up with O'Brien."

They both walked out on the front porch with me, seeming actually sorry to see me leaving. Sally and Paul both gave me a brief hug, wishing me good luck and making me promise to let them know what happened when and if I could.

The improbability, nay, sheer luck, of having stopped at this particular house gave me hope that maybe my ordeal was almost over, but the tenacity of my pursuers didn't allow me to fully believe this. I walked off the porch and felt like my whole life was beginning again, my brief hiatus into a world of comfort and understanding coming to an abrupt halt. I turned and waved at the Evans from the end of the pond, trying to put on a game face. Stepping into the woods, I suddenly thought unwillingly, "I'll never see them again."

CHAPTER TWENTY SIX

The May woods were alive with the sounds of birds and other creatures. I slowly and stealthily followed the Google earth printout, ever alert for the sounds of people. My garb wouldn't be given a second glance at some times around here, but it wasn't hunting season. I also didn't want anyone to see me carrying a rifle across their land, or even being on it, for that would surely cause a confrontation. As long as nobody saw me, I would be safe.

A few dogs barked and I narrowly missed being seen by a passing car as I crossed a paved road, but arrived seemingly undetected at a copse of woods about two hundred yards from the intersection in an hour and a half or so of slinking. Scanning through the binoculars, I had a good view of W across a newly sprouting soybean field for the first hundred yards north of the intersection. I was on the west side of it, and settled myself into a thicket at the edge of the woods, looking at each car that made the turn off YY onto W. In between cars, I scanned the perimeter of my vision with my binoculars, trying to pick out any possible movement that might indicate the presence of other 'watchers'.

After about ten minutes I saw a car come slowly around the corner, a hand hanging down. I could tell it was O'Brien through the binoculars as he slowly headed north on W, speeding up a bit after he got a ways from the intersection.

There was a narrow woods leading towards W about a quarter mile north of YY abutting the back yards of four fairly new houses. I slowly made my way through the trees till I came to the drainage ditch next to W. A small dip in the road would hide me from the houses as I intercepted O'Brien. Hidden in brush beside the ditch, I waited for his tan Impala to appear. Debating about how best to approach the road during the agonizing wait, I decided to just stand up at the edge of the ditch and hope he saw me.

Twenty minutes went by before a car looking like his, from the grill at least, came over the rise to the south. When it was fifty yards away I still wasn't sure, but I stood up and pushed through sumac saplings as the car neared the ditch and he slammed to a halt as he spotted me.

I heard another car coming at us from the north. I waved him away then quickly dropped back down into the brush. He pulled to the side of the road fifty yards ahead of me and stopped. Getting out of the car, he looked towards me and held up his hand in a wait signal. Another two cars went by before he waved me forward. I ran across the road and up the ditch on the other side then jumped into his back seat and sprawled out.

He got back in and waited for a car to pass, then turned on his blinker and pulled back out onto W saying loudly, "What the hell happened last night?"

"Don't move your lips like you're talking to someone."

After a few seconds he mumbled, "Okay."

"A whole bunch of them attacked the safe house. Take a left on C and pull into Kessler conservation area. I'll tell you all about it there."

The transformation from average citizen to armed fugitive, at least of sorts, wasn't even mentioned. Showing great restraint, he didn't ask anything further during the five minute ride. We pulled into the parking lot, empty, as I had hoped it would be, and he finally turned around and looked at me lying across the back seat. "Did you find out anything at all?' I asked.

He began telling me everything he'd learned about the previous night since I'd talked to him. I stayed down on the back seat as I pumped him for details, most of which he didn't know. Obviously frustrated, he finally said, "Why don't you tell ME what happened. This is a lot deeper than the shit I'm used to dealing with. Why did you call me of all people?"

"Call it a sixth sense or something, but I figured you were the only cop I could trust not to tell anybody else. Was I right about that?"

"We're sitting here alone, aren't we?"

The parking lot was hidden from the road by a single row of brushy trees. Hearing no noise from the road, I finally sat up. The pain from the effort caused me to grunt loudly.

After gazing around I said, "I guess we are. Let's walk into the woods over there and I'll tell you what happened."

"Why don't we just stay here. There isn't anybody around."

"I can't use the rifle from here, and if they show up we're gonna be sitting ducks."

Without further explanation, I got out of the back seat with the rifle. He followed me to a small hill a hundred yards from the parking lot, intrigued enough to not question my paranoia. Coming to the top of the knoll, I lowered myself down and gazed back towards his car. From this vantage point the parking lot and the road leading to it were in partial view.

Paranoid I was, but he seemed to agree with my precautions as I told him everything that had transpired in the roughly eighteen hours since I'd seen him. He didn't interrupt me through the whole story, even when I quit talking and peered through the binoculars at cars going by on C. He just pulled his pistol out and became as vigilant as I. After forty minutes of silently kneeling in muddy leaf clutter in a suit he finally said, "What's your next move?"

I knew right then I had made a good decision. In a nutshell, I told him my thoughts had been to disappear from the face of the earth, yet I couldn't do that without an informed outlet about by family. Perhaps if I never resurfaced into the Big Brother World, they would assume I had died. If I was a millionaire with offshore accounts I could have just left the country, but I didn't even have a passport.

They obviously hadn't bought the tales of my demise in the car crash. Whether this was because the guys in the van had seen me, or whatever, didn't matter now. They had been waiting for me to show up at a supposedly safe house, and this, by itself, could point to levels of conspiracy that I couldn't even begin to imagine. The only other logical assumption was that it pointed to levels of efficacy, and I wasn't sure which was scarier.

He listened very patiently through my discourse. I finished with, "I am going to disappear. First off, I need to know you won't try to find the people who helped me this morning. They don't want or need to be involved. Second, I need a doctor you can trust. Do you know anybody like that?"

I'd told him about my various injuries, at least the worst of them, in my fragmented story and he said, "I really think you need a hospital, but I'll take you to Hannibal and see if I can get you fixed up. I have an old friend up there that's a general practitioner. I haven't talked to him in a while, but we're still pretty tight. If I tell him about the situation, I'm sure I can get him to do it without telling anybody, and he's good."

"Can you find out before we head up there? I don't want to be sitting there and have a bunch of FBI or whatever show up."

"Give me a bit to think about how to approach this with him. Assuming he'll do it, where are you going to go from there?"

I'd been mulling that question over since leaving the Evans' and a vague plan had started forming in my mind. I said to him "Someplace where nobody will see me."

He shook his head slowly as he said, "I can see why you feel that way . . . . I promise I won't trace the call and involve them folks. They should get a medal, but he'd probably get in trouble for giving you the gun instead. I'll get you some cash, cause you sure can't use any cards."

I pulled out the wad of bills I'd taken off Jay.

"Shit, where'd you get that?"

As I counted out 67 hundreds and 17 twenties plus a few smaller bills I said, “It was in the pocket of the guy that stalked me after the truck left. I assume its’ partial pay for finding me, and it won’t bother ME none to spend it. He sure wasn’t going to be spending it. All’s fair in love and war, don’t they say?”

“Well, these guys sure aren’t hurting for cash. Where are you planning on going?”

CHAPTER TWENTY SEVEN

When I'd called him, O'Brien had been off work and planning on going to my funeral at noon. Part of his reasoning for going was to help with the deception, but he said mostly he wanted to be there to help console, and, if possible, alleviate the fears of my family.

The hour plus drive to Hannibal went by quickly, O'Brien spending most of the time on the phone. Arranging things with the doctor seemed to go smoothly. O'Brien gave me a thumbs up sign as Dr. Long agreed to do as he was asking. He called a couple more people and told them he was having car trouble and wouldn't be able to make the appointments he'd set up for after the funeral. Having eaten two more of the Vicodin that Sally had given me as we'd talked in the woods, I almost fell asleep. Each time I started to drift off, vivid, grisly scenes raced through my mind and quickly woke me.

Just west of downtown Hannibal, we pulled around the back of a new strip mall and pulled up by the back door to one of the units. We had no sooner stopped than a white frocked doctor came out the back door, waving his hand at O'Brien to come in after looking around. O'Brien helped me out and we hustled into the door, the doctor eying my getup as he said, "I'm Jeff Long, and I guess you're Mitch." He waved his hand forward and said, "You don't look dead but you look like hell, so let's get you checked out."

He led the way into an examination room where a nurse was standing. I had thought we were only going to have contact with him, but he quickly said, "This is my daughter Stephanie. She won't tell anyone you were here."

Stephanie said, "I promise. Dad told me a little about what's already happened to you, and I won't tell a soul."

My worries were allayed somewhat, but I knew that every person that even knew I was alive could be in danger. I looked at her somberly and said, "I don't mean to scare you, but your life may depend on it."

They carefully took off my hunting jacket and t-shirt then unwrapped the strips of sheet from my chest and upper arm. As soon as the arm was exposed Jeff said, "Let's get an x-ray of that." After he'd perused the x-rays, he told me the shoulder wasn't broken. The only thing he could do, besides telling me not to use it and giving me painkillers and muscle relaxers, was to put it in a cast, and that the cast should stay on for six weeks or more. The muscles and tendons that had popped out of place took longer to heal than bone, and some may be torn. This didn't seem too practical to me but I knew it had to heal. Not using it certainly wasn't an option.

After making sure my shoulder was back in place and taking more x-rays, he fixed me up with a plastic cast that allowed me to move the lower arm and changed all of Sallies' bandages, complimenting her work. He put three new stitches in my knee and about eight on each wrist and seemed amazed by the variety of lesser injuries I had, but he hadn't mentioned a hospital once when we made our way to the back door.

O'Brien carried a travel bag filled with bandages, antiseptics and a multitude of meds and paraphernalia. Jeff had seen the wad of cash, but held his hand up and said with a smile, "I'll send you the bill in ten years. Good luck!" as I pulled it out to pay him. I thanked him profusely and got in the back seat of O'Brien's car, waving at the two of them as O'Brien shut the door.

I'd left my guns in the car, and said to O'Brien as we pulled onto southbound 61, "He was as good as you said. How far are you willing to help me?"

He'd been on the phone with Courtouis and other cops for the duration of my doctoring, trying to get as much information as possible without seeming more nosey than his job would dictate. Pondering his answer for a minute, he said, "Well, I'd probably at least get canned for keeping this a secret so long already. In a way, you're one of America's most wanted. They're using bloodhounds to search for you, but they got access to the farmhouse locked tight from us locals. Homeland Security and FBI have damn near set up an air base there, but the fact that they even stifled the news means this shit is fucking scary . . . . But I wouldn't want to go back in protection if I was you either . . . . What do you want me to do?"

"Buy me ammo, get me a shotgun, buy all the crap I need and drive me down to the Current River country. Help me set up a camp that only you know about. Supply me at least every two weeks with a prearranged drop of food. Keep me informed as to what's going on. I think that's about it, but I'll let you know when we get there."

I waited as he mulled my blunt request over, but he didn't scoff or seem too surprised. "Shit Mitch, if you've managed to stay alive this long, I guess you can probably handle that, but are you sure that's what you want to do? You're still pretty beat up."

I just said, "That's it. If you don't help me, I'll just have to find another way to do it, but the less people that know I'm alive the better. It's already up to five, and I don't want it to go any higher. I'll pay for all the shit of course."

O'Brien let out a snort then said, "It ain't the money and you should know that by now. I just don't know if I can keep all that a secret from my wife and the job, even if I try. You caught me on one of the few days I could even do this without a major investigation into where I'd been. I can get you down there, maybe, but getting away for even a day every two weeks may be a problem from the secrecy side, because I sure wouldn't want either to find out. I know my wife would freak out, even though she thinks she's seen it all. Do you know anybody else you can trust that would do that?"

I told him I'd already ruled out all my friends and family. Of course they would agree to do it. Well, some would anyways. My enemies had all their numbers and addresses, and might assume I would contact someone off the list. One of my family or friends getting followed and killed perhaps if my pursuers got an inkling of proof I was alive didn't allow me to consider them. That left people I didn't know very well, and who would do something like that for somebody they didn't know well AND keep it a secret. Nobody I could think of. I sure couldn't just start calling people without being sure of the answer, because that would only drag more people into this.

I thought I could live off the land with a few basic staples, and had often wondered what it would really be like. This was my chance to try, although I'd rather have done it with a planned exit date. I'd never imagined having to do it with the stakes involved here.

Andrea and I rarely went to crowded campgrounds, preferring to rough camp on the rivers or at least at primitive campgrounds. Well, I did anyways. The abundant wildlife and solitude at our secluded camps had always seemed preferable to large campgrounds with the sights and sounds of more humanity than I dealt with at home. To watch a bald eagle eying me from a perch only sixty feet away while I cleaned my fish, a group of deer crossing the river a hundred yards from our tent in the early morning mist, or a three pound smallmouth shooting out of the water as I tried to land him brought me my own special peace.

The longest we went out was about a week and I was never ready to go home, but of course I'd had to. I had floated the Current many times and knew I could feed myself with fish, at least in the more remote stretches, without much chance of detection if I fished at night. The area is as remote as it gets in Missouri, with what I perceived as the best possibility of living undetected by people.

Survival in the wild, barring some accident, didn't really concern me as much when thinking of my plan as the loss of contact with the outside world. If this all ended, I didn't want to be like one of those Japanese soldiers coming out of a cave on Guadalcanal twenty years later, or even twenty days. I also needed to know that my family was okay or I wouldn't be able to stand it, though I was convinced that my disappearance was the best way to ensure their safety, at least besides my death. They may be mad at me later, but if I went back into the world now I sure wouldn't want them standing next to me.

Taking a break from my reflective reasoning, O'Brien said, "What about me? These fuckers seem to be aware of everything and scared of nothing. If they found out I knew where you were they might even grab me or my wife . . . . No, THEY WOULD. That doesn't mean I'm not going to help you, but it sure is shit to consider."

"I know that better than you, but you got a better idea, I'm willing to hear it."

After a minute or more he said, "Well . . . . if I put myself in your shoes . . . . seeing as how you don't seem to mind camping, I can't think of a better way to disappear . . . . I tell you what, I'll get you down there and get you set up. I'll get you a disposable cell phone and we'll try to find a camping spot with some reception. I may have to involve somebody else, but I can make sure you get food at least for a while. We can talk and figure something else out if that doesn't work. How's that sound?"

What could I say? I'd expected him to refuse me, but he seemed willing to go damn near all the way. "That sounds damn good. Let's stop at the Walmart in Bowling Green. We can get most of the stuff I need there."

CHAPTER TWENTY EIGHT

I recited a list to him after we parked in an empty section of the lot then settled down to wait, leaning against the door so I could peek out occasionally. An hour later as he approached the car with a very full cart, a lot attendant must have seen his load because all of sudden he was walking into my view through the side window. "Would you like some help with . . ." was all he got out before he glanced into the seat and locked eyes on me.

His eyes froze in position, his pimpled jaw dropping, till I finally saw O'Brien coming around the back of the car and pulling out his badge. I didn't know whether it was the cast and obvious injuries, my expression, or the rifle leaning against the door, but he looked like he'd seen a ghost as O'Brien glanced at his name tag then gave him a low voiced admonition.

"Terry, if you tell anybody about what you just saw you may be a dead man and I'm not shitting you, you got that? Now turn around and act like nothing happened and nothing will . . . . Shit, for Christ's sake quit crying . . . . Okay, just stay out here and get your shit together before you go back in there, okay, Terry. Here, help me load this stuff in the trunk."

As they walked around the back and opened the trunk, O'Brien said, "Nothing's going to happen to you as long as you keep your mouth shut, understand?"

He wiped his eyes a bit and said, "I know who that dude is and I ain't tellin' nobody, I swear. He's already dead."

"Keep that in mind and don't think nothing else. I'm trusting you on this one Terry. I don't want to find out you let me down."

"I won't tell and nobody can make me, okay?"

They loaded up the trunk then Terry turned towards me and stared at me briefly, then turned and looked around the parking lot.

He sure didn't know who he might have to deal with if he did talk, I thought, as he glanced back in the window and saw me giving him the quiet sign. He shook himself a bit, but tried to straighten up and act normal as he left my view.

The list I'd given O'Brien was pretty large and he hadn't been able to get a number of the more specialized survival items. As he explained this, I realized we couldn't chance another parking lot encounter, and of course, he couldn't take anything out of my house that would indicate I was alive to anybody. I also hadn't told him to buy me any clothes, the list already being two pages long, other than hiking boots and socks.

We headed down 61 and I said, "Let's get somewhere you can drop me off before you get the rest of it. You're probably going to have to go to Cabela's or Bass Pro."

I thought about the bag of wet clothes in the back of Andrea's car suddenly. "Where is Andrea's car?" I asked.

"Probably in the impound lot in Orion, but I don't know for sure. I could probably find out. Why you wanna know?"

"I just thought about the wet clothes I left in the back seat from Monday night and it made me wonder."

"You mean you haven't checked them since that night? I'm not sure whether they searched your wife's car or not, but you may have missed something the woman gave you. Did you check everywhere?"

I thought about that night, remembering that I hadn't checked my back left pocket. I never put anything in there and didn't ever check it as a result. Maybe she had slipped something in there but I sure hadn't felt it, either at the time or until taking my jeans off in Andrea's car. If I was sitting on something, I surely would have felt it. Nah, 'it' couldn't be there.

"I didn't look in my back left pocket that night, but I don't think there's anything there or I'd have felt it."

"Maybe not if it was small enough . . . . I think I need to find out where her car is. Maybe I can search it if nobody else has thought to do that yet. I should probably call this in, but they'd wonder what gave me the idea since I'm not on the case anymore. The feds have taken the whole thing. Maybe if I act like I'm just getting something for your wife they'll let me in the car, but I'd have to visit her first to cover that one. I'm not sure if I can even do that."

Even the small possibility that I may have had 'it' all along made me furious with myself. It also made everything that had happened since make a lot more sense. Assuming she had given me something, I might have a way to get out of all this, but that would require bargaining with the very people that were trying to get me. They had already exhibited such callousness towards human life that the thought of negotiation with them was unconscionable. Not going to happen. Still, I at least wanted to know what could have caused the furor.

"If you find something, I want to at least know what it was. That might be the only thing that can keep me alive."

"Let's worry about that if I find something. I don't even know if I'll be able to talk to Andrea or search her car yet."

He went to Kessler again and he carried a sleeping bag, a camo tarp and enough food and water to last me a day or so into the woods. He would try to get in to see Andrea, agreeing to only tell her I was alive if he was alone with her and she seemed ready to handle hearing about my plan to disappear. Without causing suspicion of his true purpose, he'd find out all he could about everything then search her car if he could figure out a way to do it. A lot of 'ifs'. Settling into a long, anxious wait, my thoughts drifted to my funeral. I wondered if it had been called off, a highly unlikely thing for a funeral.

Bow hunting had taught me patience and stillness over the years, but that night seemed like the longest of my life. As darkness fell I drifted into sleep after eating a couple peanut butter sandwiches and oxycodones, but woke up around ten with a shooting throb. I hitched myself to sitting position behind a large log at the edge of my enclave, looking out towards the parking lot.

Near total darkness, especially combined with painkillers and heightened paranoia, plays tricks on the human mind. Panting with pain in the honeysuckle thicket, I began to see shadowy forms of men materializing out of the dark. My imagination ran wild, and every sound of creatures stirring in the night brought me to full alert. The pistol never left my hand, and I aimed it at the figments of my imagination more than once.

After what seemed like days, the sun finally began to rise. My hiding spot was near perfect, thick invasive honeysuckle providing a tangled curtain of foliage no average hiker would have reason to explore. I felt silly, no, angry at myself for being 'afraid' of the dark, and vowed to never be so again. Even a campfire at night could cost me, and the comfort of light surely wasn't worth my life. After eating two granola bars, an apple and two more oxycodones, I carefully stretched out on the sleeping bag and was quickly asleep.

This being a Saturday, two groups walked within fifty yards of me along the trail. A family with four kids came by about ten o'clock, bringing me out of my disturbed sleep with a jolt. I could hear their chatter as they made their way into the forest, the parents calling to the older children to stay in sight as they scampered down the trail ahead. The sounds soothed me and I started feeling like maybe someday I could get back to that feeling of normalcy, of taking Willy on another 'walkie' as their sounds drifted into the distance.

As a young couple walked by an hour later, I began to make out their words. I heard the girl say, "What about ticks? They can kill you, you know." The man said, "If we stay on the trail, you're not going to get any ticks, but I'll be happy to check you for them." She laughed then said in a coy voice, "I think we better head back. I might have one crawling up my leg already." He stopped and faced her, grabbing her thigh and saying, "Oh, let me find that big, bad tick!" as she let out a feigned shriek. As they began necking, I began feeling like a voyeur, peeping unwanted into their private life.

Turning my head, I suddenly remembered similar scenes of Andrea's usual protests at being dragged out into the woods. She had always put up with my desire to be away from the sounds and sights of man, but going into the full on forest was where her humoring ended.

While her friends and family went on tropical vacations and stayed at nice hotels, we had spent the majority of our vacation time camping. Though she enjoyed the peace and quiet and certain other aspects of our trips, she probably would have rather been elsewhere. I thought of the many sacrifices she'd made so I could follow my passion for nature over the past six years. Though she'd certainly never rebuked me for my stubborn independence so vociferously, the crushing words she'd said at the farmhouse had probably been fermenting in her mind for some time.

In return for her willingness to venture into the wilderness, I had always gone to the myriad functions that her large family was constantly asking us to attend. I'd figured it was a fair trade, but if her words last night were any indication of her true feelings she obviously hadn't agreed. The complete rejection and obvious loathing of me had caught me by surprise, but thinking back on our time together, I probably had seen signs that I chose to ignore.

Perhaps this incident really was just the straw, not the mighty sequoia I'd assumed it would take for her to want to be rid of me. Either way, her desire would be fulfilled. In my mind, there was little chance I would ever see her again. Even with me gone, I figured there was a good chance they would still put her in witness protection, and she probably wouldn't agree to see me even if the whole thing went away. A feeling of being utterly alone in the world began to permeate my thoughts. After a while of lamenting everything and venting the desolation I felt as quietly as possible, I tried to concentrate on the more immediate problem of survival.

First, I began a mental checklist of things I may have forgotten on O'Brien's shopping list. One was a headset CD player and a few CD's, the lack of radio reception in the hills around the Current coming to mind. I started thinking about the five CD's I would want with me if they were going to be the only music I heard for the rest of my life, if only as a way to keep my mind active without reverting to despair. Every time I thought about my family, my resolve to disappear lessened a bit, picturing their anxiety as they were told whatever story the FBI, or whoever, fed to them this morning. I started thinking about ways to tell them I was alive, but figured that very knowledge alone could cost them their own.

Wavering between total dejection at times and feeling ludicrous for it at others, my mind bounced around all the possible ways I could 'play' this. After hours my mind was made up. Go with the gut. Many times in life I hadn't, trying to out think the problem, and it usually cost me.

Become invisible in the human spectrum. My first instinct had been that, and that is what I was going to do. No half measures. No wavering. No self pity. I could do this. With proper gear and precautions, I could disappear from humanity in the wild hills of southern Missouri, at least until deer season.

Many people use the forest during the summer, but their use is concentrated on the rivers and trails that interlace the many watersheds. Over two hundred thousand acres of mostly contiguous public land surround the Current and Jacks Fork river valleys, and I sure wasn't going to worry about trespassing if I had to. I knew the most remote areas from the roads, trails and rivers get almost no visitors until deer season, and very few even then. In this day and age disappearing is nearly an impossible thing, yet I felt it could be done, and certainly had the motivation.

Though not strictly a survivalist type, like most people I was becoming increasingly worried about the many problems of the world and humanity. The possibility that the world as we know it might change abruptly for the worse had been slowly cemented into my consciousness in the past few years. Our camping trips had been for fun, but many nights I had sat around the fire and wondered what it would be like to have to live off the land and my own wits without the benefits of civilization. Native Americans and the first settlers had done it and thrived, or at least survived. With the wealth of knowledge and equipment available today, it technically should be easier I figured.

Vowing to myself to stick to my plan unless I heard compelling evidence to do otherwise, I began to try and imagine a solitary life in the wild. Camping out in remote places didn't really count as roughing it, at least not compared to the venture I was envisioning. We brought nearly every modern convenience, including a camp kitchen with a sink and a DVR on our excursions. Andrea cooked wonderful meals for us as I hunted and fished. We sat around the fire at night and enjoyed the night sounds in comfort, and were always able to go to a store for anything we may have forgotten or ran out of. Firewood, grilling, water, washing dishes and camp setup and breakdown were my only real responsibilities on our excursions into the idyllic 'wild' once we got there.

We never camped for less than three days. I set up three tents; a huge main tent, a screened dining tent, and our bathroom tent with porta potty and hot showers. I always, well almost always, caught fish or scored on game. It had felt like paradise to me, but, remembering many of her comments, Andrea had not felt quite the same about it.

In April I had gone pig hunting for the first time, killing a two hundred fifty pound boar on the first day of the hunt in Mark Twain National Forest as he'd run towards me with a herd of sows and piglets running away. Dropping him at thirty yards with one shot, I pumped my 1952, Model 760 30.06 to reload for a follow up shot if necessary. The strange sound made me take a quick look, and I discovered that I had lost my clip somehow.

I'd shuddered a bit as I stood over the wild and fearless black boar and checked out his five inch tusks and solid frame, but that had only increased the excitement I'd felt. I butchered all my own kills and made my own jerky and sausage. I had always used a dehydrator or the oven, but it could be made over a slow fire.

In my mind, I had no home or wife to go back to. She had made that pretty clear, and though it pained me greatly to contemplate her reasoning, her rejection actually helped validate my goal of obscurity.

I had become a thorn in my enemies' side, and a thorn I hoped to stay. Thinking about all I'd seen on film and read about these types of people, I pictured some guy puffing a Cuban cigar and saying, "Just take care of the problem." Even before the attack at the farmhouse I'd known my life was wrapped up in this, so why not make it my life's ambition to somehow thwart them. The challenge ahead of me began to seem almost like an opportunity, if only to prove I could somehow outsmart or at least outlast the evil forces arrayed against me. If I stayed alive, I won. They would never be easy in their minds, their resolve to find me leaving no doubts about that, and that gave me a singular purpose. Revenge would have to wait.

The self pity and inner turmoil began to ease as my objective became firmly implanted. I resisted the urge to do some scouting, if only as a chance to stretch my legs. The normal weekend hikers would stick to the trails and there was little chance of an encounter, but the episode at Walmart made me realize the risk wasn't worth it. After getting up and stretching in my little enclave instead, I heard a car pull up in the parking lot, followed shortly by another.

Finally getting in a position to gaze through the foliage towards the parking lot, I couldn't see either car as I heard two doors open and close. It was about six and I was expecting O'Brien back, but the second car made me hope it wasn't him. He had said he may have to involve someone else, but certainly hadn't told me he would do that this quickly. The disposable phone he'd bought me at Walmart hadn't vibrated, but I'd told him not to call unless he wasn't going to make it back before dark. Someone began whistling the Armour hot dog song, our prearranged signal, and I anxiously waited to see who was with him.

CHAPTER TWENTY NINE

A few minutes later O'Brien and Pollitt crept on hands and knees under the overhanging honeysuckle and emerged into my six by six clearing. Pointing my pistol down as they crawled in, they stood up right next to me, having only cleared a small amount of headroom under the honeysuckle. Pollitt looked around my little hideout and said, "Well I guess this is better than dead. How you holding up, Mitch?" as he held out his hand.

As I shook his hand, I felt a surge of relief that it was him and not someone I didn't know at all. He had highly visible effects of the wreck, most noticeably stitches running across his left cheek in three different lines and a cauliflower left ear, and he seemed to be limping. I shook his hand and said, "Well, it ain't the Hilton. How are you doing?"

Feeling the stitches on his cheek, he said, "Well, they say scars add character, so I'm gonna have a lot of that . . . . All things considered, I'd have to say not too bad."

"How is Sanchez doing?'

"The first day was kind of rough, but he's getting better by the day. He's got more stitches than me, but he seems to be holding up pretty well. He's getting around on crutches already and joking with me about my ugly mug, so at least his spirits are up."

"I'm damn glad to hear that. I thought he was dead right after the wreck, so that's actually the first good news I've gotten in a while . . . . A lot of people died on Thursday and I've been feeling like shit about it."

"Well, as far as me and Joe are concerned, we sure aren't blaming you for any of this. Truth is, Joe's mostly pissed off at himself for taking you back to your house. I'd like to tell him about you being alive, but I'll let you decide about that."

Turning towards O'Brien, I asked, "Is Andrea okay? Where is she?"

"They took her to Orion General. She's in damn near catatonic shock from what I heard, but she's not physically hurt. I asked if I could see her, but they have her under heavy guard and she's under sedation anyways. I'll keep trying, but I'm not sure when I'll get in to see her."

"What about my pants pocket? Did you get in Andrea's car?"

They looked at each other kind of weirdly and Pollitt said, "Yeah, I found what they're looking for. You had it all along." as he pulled out a plastic evidence bag with a miniature CD in it from his jacket pocket. My jaw dropped as I realized I'd been literally sitting on the evidence.

"I don't know what's on it. Not turning it in yet was about the toughest career decision I've ever had to make, but till I find out I'm not turning it over to the feds. They got your wife quarantined like a plague victim, and if I give it to them, we'd probably NEVER know what this was all about. I tried pulling up the disc but I couldn't, and I haven't quite decided who to take it to that might be able to crack it."

"Where was Andrea's car? How did you get a hold of that?"

"They took her car to the impound garage before the feds came and got her. They got your van somewhere else, but we didn't think to search her car, and I guess nobody else had yet either. It's part of my job to search cars that get impounded for evidence, so Bill, the clerk there, didn't think nothing about it when I told him I was there to search your wife's car. It was in your back left pocket, just like you said. I guess it isn't too surprising you didn't feel it, seeing as how it's only big as a silver dollar and a lot thinner. I told Bill I didn't find anything, and he didn't even look up from his paperwork as I was leaving with it."

"Don't get me wrong, I'm glad it's you here, but how did you two hook up?"

"I ran into James here while visiting Joe at the hospital. He was sitting in the waiting room, looking like a man with the world on his shoulders. After we talked for a bit, he tried to bullshit me when I asked him why he was really waiting for a chance to see your wife."

James shook his head in affirmation of that fact, seeming somewhat ashamed he'd been busted as he said, "You can't fool a detective. I could tell you knew I was lying. Anyways, we're all in this together now, so let's go from here."

George said, "Yeah, let's. Mitch, I'm here to help you and nothing else. I want to see these bastards fry, but I promised James I'd follow all your terms already, so don't worry about me telling anybody."

"Thanks. I've been thinking it over a lot, but I haven't come up with a better plan. I guess you're going to take me down to the Current then, huh?"

George said, "I'm on medical leave for at least another week, so I can help you get set up without anybody wondering where I'm at. I'm not married, and as far as anyone knows, I'll just be off trout fishing, which is what I do in my spare time anyways."

Turning towards James I said, "You think having the disc now should make a difference? I mean, maybe I should rethink the whole thing. What do you guys think?"

James looked at me dolefully before he said, "We already talked about that. Even having the disc now doesn't keep you safe. They still searched your house and tried to get you, though you could well have turned it over the night of the rescue and have no idea what's on it. That's the part that I really can't figure out. Maybe that woman you rescued thought you heard some kind of warning from her about not doing that. Even so, it seems pretty fucking strange for them to come after you like that."

"Well, George, what do you actually think about my plan? Did James tell you about Thursday night?"

"Yeah, he told me." Seeming to stare off for a few seconds, he turned back to me and said, "We're dealing with some heavy hitters here. I knew that Wednesday, but the shit they did Thursday night puts them in another league from what I was even thinking about them. I think you probably got a better chance of staying alive if you disappear than if you come in. No matter what's on the disc, these fuckers want you for something real bad, and it can't be just to get the disc back. There's almost got to be a rat somewhere for them to be set up like that when you showed up at the farmhouse. If they find out you're still alive, no doubt they'll try to grab you again . . . . or maybe just kill you out of spite."

"They sure seem to want to take me alive, but I got no doubts that'd be short lived."

"We can talk about all this stuff on the ride. I got almost all the things from your list in my Blazer and a few other things I thought you could use. If you're ready to leave, we can get going."

They carried all the stuff to the car, then O'Brien came back and got me while Pollitt kept watch. Pollitt had an air mattress laid out with the back seat gone. They got me situated and O'Brien said, "I'll be working with George to keep you updated and all. Wish I coulda helped you get down there, but I think George knows a lot more about the woods than me. I'll be visiting your wife if I can and keeping you up on how she's doing. Just make sure you stay alive, because I don't want to be the one to tell her you're really dead."

I was thinking, "I'm not sure she'd care" as he held his hand into the car. Trying to force a smile, I said as I grabbed it, "I'll give you a guided tour of the Current when this is all over . . . . I'd try to thank you, but I don't think I got the words for it."

"Thank me when you take me on that tour."

CHAPTER THIRTY

As we headed out of the parking lot with O'Brien following, George said, "I been going to the Current River since I was a kid. If you want to get lost in Missouri, there's no better place to do it. We went hunting down there six years ago, me and three other guys. My buddy Bill got so turned around he spent the night in the woods. Do you got a specific place in mind? All the maps are in that folder, and there's a pen light in the tray above you."

I grabbed a hefty folder that I'd moved on getting in. As I began pulling out topographical maps and Google Earth photos I realized that many of them had been used extensively, with cryptic notations and spots circled. "I was thinking somewhere in the Sunklands. It's about the wildest place I've been, in Missouri anyway, and it borders on the Current. I see you've done some hiking around there yourself."

"Yeah, I've taken some nice bucks out of there over the years. It's a little more used than some of the other areas, but there's some pretty remote spots."

"If I want to fish, I'm going to have to be somewhere near the Current. I was thinking maybe a mile or so away."

"I guess a mile would probably do it. Not many people get that far off the river except on the trails. Why don't you tell me why this is the way you wanted to go with this. When O'Brien told me what you were planning on doing, I was a little puzzled why you'd choose this route instead of something else."

For the next couple hours, I tried to answer his query as I told him all about my past and my reasoning that had led me to this course of action. He probably hadn't assumed he was going to hear my life story, but he didn't interrupt me through my monologue.

My dad has always been an avid camper, hunter, and fisherman. Having camped close to a thousand nights in my life, starting in my early childhood, the woods were my favorite place to be. Having six kids, those were the only vacations my father could afford. As a child, that was fine with me.

He had grown up in the mountains of central Pennsylvania where, at the time, school was let out for the week of deer season, since none of the boys would have shown up anyways. When I was ten I began hunting with him and his hunting buddies, and on turning twelve he gave me my first shotgun, an Ithaca twenty gauge pump.

My dad has always been the semi official 'captain of the hunt' when we hunted with large groups, driving the cornfields and woods of central Illinois for deer, pheasants and other small game. He taught me how to track and read sign in the woods and ever since, I had tried to perfect my hunting skills.

The people that knew me, including my family, had always considered me an adventurer of sorts. In truth, I had never considered myself a really brave person, always feeling an inner fear of some great unknown calamity. Though my life had certainly not been without many, none had ever struck me as the one. Maybe that's just a normal fear of death but try as I might, I could never quite shake it.

Many people never get, or at least want to get, beyond their comfort zone. I'd always been willing to push that envelope. The thrill of new adventures and being on the 'edge' somehow made me feel more alive. As I'd aged, I started to realize that maybe I'd done a lot of things just to prove to myself that I wasn't a coward.

Since childhood I'd been a nature buff, many times preferring roaming the woods or picking blackberries alone to socializing with the other kids my age. This self imposed seclusion, I'd come to realize in my late teens, was perhaps my way of sometimes avoiding the decidedly more complicated task of dealing with other humans.

Having lived my whole adult life in major cities' suburbs, making a living precluded the possibility of isolation and I had tried to conform to the human social scene. Tiring of it in my late thirties after another breakup, I'd become increasingly more reclusive and outdoor oriented outside of my job and family till meeting Andrea. Her outgoing nature had brought me somewhat back into the scene six years ago, but I still preferred the wild to throngs of humanity.

Trying to select everything with an eye to mobility, my gear took up surprisingly little room compared to the van full of gear we usually took on camping trips. I didn't assume that these guys would be traipsing every acre of Missouri, but anyone I ran into might have seen my picture and the story on the news, and they might talk about it. The incongruity of a large camp in the middle of nothing would be sure to cause notice if someone came across it, but most people that might happen to come across a small tent probably would not think twice about it, assuming it to be just another backpacker. If I ran into anybody, I wanted to be able to pack up and move far and fast.

I would have to be gone from camp at least some of the time to secure provisions, fish and probably to get cell phone reception. Though I'd left isolated camps to hunt and fish for long stretches, the only times I'd ever gotten ripped off were at crowded campgrounds, so this possibility did not bother me. A person that is willing to walk miles into the wilderness for the experience is not likely to be a thief, at least by my way of thinking.

As a further precaution I could always try to totally hide my camp, but the best bet would be to find a place as secluded as possible. The daily routine of trying to hide my camp might be doable, even with my injuries, but there are places that no man ever ventures, even today. To somehow survive this, my best chance was to find a small area I could move about imperiously. Finally getting winded, I said, "The fact is, if it wasn't for the circumstances, I might actually be looking forward to this as an adventure."

After my lengthy, and certainly melancholy, explanation of my thought processes, Pollitt said, "You sure you can handle this? You seem like you like to talk."

"Hey man, I'm sorry about that. My wife always says I'm a rambler when I get going. Since this shit started my mind's been going a mile a minute, and I guess I needed to get it all out."

George chuckled then said, "Hey, it's no problem. I enjoyed the stories. Your dad sounds a lot like mine. We've been coming down to the Current since I was five . . . . I gave you my copy of

'Edible plants of Missouri'. I've never tried many of them, but there sure is a lot. If you find any they say are good in the book, you might want to try them."

"I always wanted to try some more of the wild stuff, but mostly I've just picked mushrooms and berries. What have you tried besides them?"

"Aw, one time we had a dandelion, wild onion and sponge mushroom concoction at turkey camp and it was real good, but other than that, not many of the plants in that book."

"To tell you the truth, I always meant to get that book. Where's it at?"

"It's in one them bins but I wouldn't try to dig it out. Let's get you set up and worry about what you might eat after. I think you're probably better off somewhere further downriver than the Sunklands. The fishing is better below Round Spring, especially night fishing because there isn't many catfish that far up. It gets a lot less canoe traffic too, at least till you get to Two Rivers. Did you ever float that stretch?"

"Naw, that's about the only stretch from Montauk to Van Buren that I haven't floated. I guess you've been on it before?"

"Yeah, but it's been about ten years. If we can get you near Big Creek on the east side you'll be in some of the wildest country I've ever seen. It's fifteen miles on shitty gravel roads to get back to the Current on that side . . . . Have you ever been alone for days on end before? Most people can't handle it too well."

"I've spent lots of two and three day stretches without seeing anyone else on hunting and fishing trips into the boonies, but I think three days is probably as long as I've ever gone without talking to anybody. I work by myself and hunt by myself most of the time so I'm pretty used to not having people around. After the other night, I think the peace and quiet will be a welcome relief. I still can't quit thinking about it, and I probably never will. I'm either the unluckiest or the luckiest man alive, and I'm really not sure which."

"Well, between the wreck and the shit you went through Thursday, you being alive could only mean you're lucky. I don't know how many guys died that night, but O'Brien told me everything you told him and I'd guess it's at least twenty and maybe thirty. That makes it about the biggest battle fought on American soil since Attu, at least that I know of.

The bitch of it is nobody, including the feds, seems to have any idea of what kind of threat we're dealing with here. We're going to have to turn in the disc if we don't get it decrypted pretty quick. How that woman got a hold of that important of a disc is beyond me, but it must be. And the real kicker is they still tried to grab you. James told me you killed at least three of them and maybe more. You feel like telling me about it?"

CHAPTER THIRTY ONE

As we continued south, I told him the whole story from the time I got put in the other ambulance till now. It seemed to help to talk about it. My thoughts seemed a lot more focused than they had been when I arrived at the farmhouse. The future then had been only an enigma, no plan, goal or idea of my self will in it apparent. My situation had gotten much worse since then, by any normal standards, but strangely, I felt more in control of my own destiny than I had then. The very purpose of my life had coalesced into a single, basic tenet—stay alive.

I told him in detail not only the actual events but my thinking, at least as I remembered it, of the past couple days. In that short span of time, I'd felt a life's worth of emotion. Love, hate, elation, dejection, gratitude, guilt, hope and despair had all played their parts in rapid succession. This swirling menagerie of acute sentiments had nearly broken my spirit, but as its' final act had somehow left me feeling more vibrantly alive than I could ever remember feeling. Fear itself had been looked in the eye and if not totally vanquished, at least its' hold on my psyche was broken by the knowledge that I had nothing left to lose, for what is fear but fear of loss. My life was over, at least as far as a continuation of relationships with my loved ones was concerned, so they couldn't even take that from me anymore.

Interjecting comments only occasionally throughout my soul searching dissertation, he finally asked, "Where do you see this ending for you. What if they don't ever figure this out, or at least figure out why they still wanted you. You can't just stay in the woods forever."

"Well, till this is resolved, I can't really surface again and have anybody I know anywhere around me. No matter what happens, it's gotta be better than the last five days."

"Yeah, even if we figure this out quickly they may still be looking for you. With a little fish and maybe some wild foods mixed in, there's enough food to last you at least a month in here. It's mostly freeze dried crap and it don't taste that great, but you can live on it. I'm still not sure that you have to go to this extreme, but it sure beats getting shot at."

After stopping in Salem for gas with me hidden under sleeping bags, Pollitt said, "I grabbed us some pizza at the gas station. I think you can get up now and eat." I sat up and slowly ate the pizza, savoring it with the knowledge it was likely to be the last food not cooked by me for awhile.

An hour later we were bouncing over gravel roads, ruts from the recent heavy rains making the road passable only with four wheel drive. After almost another hour of jolting we stopped at literally the end of the road, deep within the forest. It was after one and George said, "Let's get some shut eye and pack all your stuff in the morning. Nobody's going to be coming out here at this time of night anyways."

The sun was well up when he woke me the next morning. He opened up his door and stretched then said, "I didn't think I'd sleep that long. Its' nine twenty so we better get going if we want to get you all set up today."

We ate some bagels and cold sandwiches then got busy packing. Even with him filling a large camo backpack and me carrying my three guns, the ammo, and the medicine bag, there was still a large amount of mostly food in the Bronco. He said, "I'll come back and get the rest of it after we set up camp."

We were about two miles from the Current, and there was a little used trail leading to it that followed Big Creek for the last mile according to the map. As we came to the top of the hill above the creek we veered off, following the ridge top for a half mile or so before descending along the edge of a steep hillside next to the start of a rocky bluff.

A little past the midpoint of the three hundred vertical foot seventy degree slope we found a small bench littered with fallen slabs and boulders. We began checking it out and found two enormous slabs rested against each other creating a fairly dry ten foot deep by eight foot wide triangular shaped cave with the large opening facing the cliff behind us. Walking to the front edge of the bench the waters of Big Creek could be seen glittering in the sunlight through the trees, about a hundred yards away and a hundred feet below us. The steep slope continued towards the Current after the bench ended, its' curving edge disappearing from sight in the trees. There was no sign of humans on the bench and I said, "This looks like as good a spot as any."

We walked back to the cave and George cleared out the leaf and stick debris. We then made a tent under the slabs, using poles from the forest floor then draping a camo tarp over them and tying off the rivets to the improvised frame. I gathered firewood off the bench as he built a fire pit at the back end of the cave and a crude bench and table out of rocks and slabs. A four foot gap between the back of the slabs and the bluff would allow smoke to escape.

In this gap we dug a foot deep pit in gravel and soil between two coffee table sized slabs for a privy. After a couple hours of work I had a fairly dry and comfortable abode, all things considered.

George said, "I almost wish I could stay here with you. I don't think we could have found a better spot."

"It's a lot better than I was picturing. You think there's any fish in the creek?"

"Nah, I don't think they make it this far up from the Current. During the summer this creek's pretty shallow, at least down by the mouth. I've never been this far up it before."

Soon after, he headed back to the truck to get the rest of the provisions. I busied myself trying to camouflage the cave in case someone should wander onto the bench. I covered the narrow front opening with brush, leaving just enough space for me to wiggle through, and making it inconspicuous from anywhere on the bench.

After emptying the backpack, I grabbed the folding saw. Cutting down a cedar at the ground, I trimmed the boughs down to size and after checking for ticks built a bed on one side of the cave, throwing the leftover pieces of cedar bough out back to cover my privy. I covered my cedar bed with a tarp and two self inflating mattresses, checking it out and adjusting the boughs after I scrunched it down. Satisfied, I inspected the remaining contents of the backpack.

A quart sized water purification bottle and two gallon sized collapsible containers would allow me to drink water from the creek or collect it from the numerous seeps coming through the rocks from the recent rains. After filling it from one of these trickles I took a long drink, and the filtered water was better tasting than my water at home. After assembling the five section backpackers' fishing rod, I hooked it up with a jig in anticipation of heading to the river tonight. Munching on freeze dried banana chips I loaded the twelve gauge semi-auto shotgun with buck shot. It had a pistol grip and folding stock. Holding it pointed towards the cliff, I practiced aiming it one handed.

The sound of jet boats on the Current were much more frequent than I'd figured, echoing along the face of the bluff and sounding much closer than they really were. I began to question my campsite decision and walked along the perimeter of the bench looking for access to it.

The south end of the bench fell steeply away in a jumble of rock extending all the way down to the creek. A narrow erosion chute, carved by thousands of years of runoff from the bench, created a gap in the façade about fifty yards up the valley from my cave. Beyond this chasm to the north, a forty foot tall vertical rock face ran up the valley as far as I could see. The steep slopes below this cliff were covered with loose rock, the few trees clinging tenuously and sticking out at all angles. The downhill traverse along the north edge of the bluff had been fairly treacherous, but certainly doable for anyone who might try it. To climb straight up here from the creek bottom would be much harder, the narrow chute offering the only likely route.

After a thorough perusal of my hideout, I concluded that the only way anyone might just stumble across it was by coming down along the same route we had taken or traversing along the cliff top from far up the valley. Feeling a bit better about my chances of remaining undetected, the distant sounds of jet boats, paddles hitting aluminum canoes and occasional indistinct hollers of people calling from one canoe to another calmed me instead of worrying me. At least I won't be totally cut off from the sounds of humanity, I was thinking, as I heard the Armour hot dog song being whistled softly once again.

Pollitt emerged from behind the boulders carrying a large backpack and I asked, "Was there anyone at the parking spot?"

"No, haven't seen a soul except folks on the river since I left here. I tried both of our cells at a lot of spots, but the only place I got any reception was right at the top of the bluff close to the Current. You're going to have to climb up there to use your phone. I got some good news though. O'Brien got in to see Andrea. She's doing a lot better but there were other people around so he couldn't tell her about you being alive. The feds still think you got taken, since none of the first guys that came after you made it and I guess the dogs lost your trail at Silver Creek."

The slight thump of a paddle on an aluminum canoe reverberated down the bluff and after listening for a second he said, "I could see the river from the top of the bluff about a half mile down, but we're almost a mile away from the river here. Not too many people get out except at the gravel bars, and there's only the small one where Big Creek empties on this side of the river for a half mile or so in either direction. There's a big gravel bar across from the bluff that lots of people camp at, but most folks don't get off the gravel bars 'cause of all the poison ivy and stinging nettle. I doubt anybody ever comes up here."

I said, "It isn't easy to get on this bench either. The easiest way I've found was the way we came in, and that ain't all that easy. I looked hard for old campfires and didn't find any so I don't think anyone ever uses this as a camping spot. Long as I'm quiet, I don't think anybody will know I'm here."

We decided to have me try to call him at seven o'clock every other night starting tomorrow. If I couldn't get reception or he couldn't answer I would try again at eight the next morning. If he didn't get that call, he would head down here as quick as he could after trying to call me. It was an imperfect system, but we figured the best we could do without a risk of him getting caught talking to me by somebody. Two full spare batteries for the phone and a small charging unit that cranked by hand would insure I'd at least always have juice. We debated making my calls later at night so he would have less chance of being eavesdropped on, but I didn't want to be climbing down in the dark or using a flashlight.

Popping one of the four propane canisters to use with the single burner stove, we cooked up some freeze dried beef stew. Having never been impressed with the dried food I'd taken on canoe trips into the Boundary Waters, surprisingly it wasn't too bad. After going over all the details of our communication and resupply, he headed back to his truck.

CHAPTER THIRTY TWO

For an hour after he left I just sat at the edge of the south 'rampart' and listened for the sounds of people as I thought of my new reality. Thinking of Andrea's rejection and the rest of my family brought me to tears a couple times, but at the end of this reverie I got up and got busy. Stewing about it was futile, but I had to find a way to keep my mind busy if I wanted to avoid it.

Though there was little chance of a person wandering into my camp, I strung fishing line around trees along the perimeter six inches off the ground and terminated it at both ends at the back of my cave. I tied a rifle shell on each end, painstakingly adjusting the placement and tension until the slightest pull anywhere on the line would make at least one of the cartridges dink against a rock. The sound wasn't loud, but I didn't want someone tripping it to be able to zero in on it. I thought about rigging up more deadly traps, but decided the risk of hurting innocent people would be too great to chance them. I began to feel there was little chance anyone was even still looking for me and that I was safe here even if they were.

I stacked all the firewood I could find at the back of the cave. As the day waned the sounds of floaters and jet boats diminished. Around seven I packed my pole and the worms and grubs I'd found, hoping George had been wrong about the prospects of there being catchable fish in Big Creek. I hadn't heard any people noises all day coming from that direction. This gave me hope that no one floated it even when it was high enough, which it appeared to be through my binoculars, and certainly a big enough stream to at least have some fish.

After scrambling down the first ten feet of the chute I slipped and came down hard on my ass. The pain from my shoulder, just being jarred, shot through me. Laying out as I waited for the pain to subside, my foothold on a rock was the only thing keeping me from sliding further down the chute.

Panting and swearing under my breath, I decided the climb back up the chute would be a 'little' too tough in my present condition. The only other option was a long journey up the valley along the ledge top in a search for an easier way down. Following that route certainly carried no guarantee against a possible mishap either. I reluctantly came to the conclusion that until I was hungry the risk wouldn't be worth it. We had found a perfect hiding spot, but like all burrowing animals I wanted a back door, an escape route.

I slowly climbed back up, the reality of my condition settling in. I needed to rest and recuperate. I had enough food and provisions within easy reach to last me a month. With rains as frequent as they'd been lately, the steady trickles off the cliff would provide ample water. In short, I had no need to leave the bench, other than cell phone reception.

Resigned to the necessity of catering to my infirmities, I went in my cave and began organizing my few current possessions. As the light began to fade, I made a small fire in my pit and cooked up a packet of corned beef hash. Glancing through 'Edible plants of Missouri' as I waited for my dinner to heat up, I could only see the pictures of the numerous sources of food that grow wildly in the "Show Me" state. Finishing my first meal alone, the essence of my complete seclusion from humanity tugged at my conscience, but failed to dishearten me. I sighed deeply as I put out the fire, arranged my mattresses and climbed into my bed. My exhaustion did the rest and I fell asleep almost instantly.

The next five days went by with mostly monotonous tedium, punctuated by brief fits of despair during the day and vivid nightmares at night. Many of these woke me up and I would lay there for hours, trying to get back to sleep as I listened to the night sounds. The plaintive crying of bobcats and the vocalizations of coyote packs on the hunt sound eerily human and sometimes sent shivers down my spine if I awoke to them. Though having heard both many times before, especially coyotes, my isolation and paranoia fed my imagination. The sounds of deer and other creatures walking through the forest at night convinced me a few times that my enemies were closing in. I would clutch the shotgun and point it towards the mouth of the cave, heart beating wildly.

On our camping trips into the wilderness, our dogs had always warned us of the approach of any animal or man. The bravado I'd felt on the planning of my disappearance waned and broke at times, the necessity of staying hidden being the only thing that kept me from trying to reconnect with civilization.

For the last fifteen years or so, I'd usually floated the upper stretches of the Current during early spring or in October. The better fishing, weather, scenery and lack of crowds made it more enjoyable than summertime floats. The first thirty miles of the Current below Montauk Spring gets comparatively little jet boat traffic due to its' smaller width and water flow. During that week, the sounds of thirty or so jet boats a day went by, though many might be the same boats going back and forth.

On Thursday afternoon I was doing my tenth check of the fishing line alert system when I heard the unmistakable sound of a rattlesnake below the south rampart.

In all my outdoor excursions I'd only previously seen one rattlesnake in Missouri, about fifteen years before. Walking up along the rough of the seventeenth green at Pevely golf course looking for my, as usual, badly hit ball, a rustle in the thick grass grabbed my attention.

A large timber rattlesnake was devouring a mole, the tip of the moles tail the only thing still protruding from the rattler's distended jaw. I didn't even know that their current range extended this far north, and was surprised and fascinated by the sight. The snake was trying to crawl back into the brush, but having little luck moving quickly with his cargo as I called my golfing buddy Steve over to check it out.

He wanted to kill the snake immediately upon seeing it. Raising his pitching wedge above his head to do so, I said, "Don't do that!" as I grabbed his arms and prevented his swing.

I don't know for sure why I felt so adamantly about not killing that snake. Maybe it was because he had a mole in his mouth and, moles being the bane of golf courses and homeowners alike, I realized his worth to human society. Maybe it was the novelty of seeing something so incongruous to my view of the natural order of things. Humans usually attempt to wipe out all other forms of nature that could possibly threaten, and a rattlesnake on a golf course certainly fell within those parameters. Maybe this snake was the last of its' kind in the area. But maybe it was because I realized even a poisonous snake has its' attributes. Where do you draw the line between good and bad?

I tried to recall my memories of that encounter as I grabbed my pistol from the cave. Even so, the sound made me contemplate once again my choice of camp site, the jumbled rocks being a perfect spot for them. The snake seemed to be no more than ten feet below me. I'd once eaten a Western Diamondback that had the misfortune of crawling into my campsite below the Mogollon Rim in Arizona. Having enjoyed the taste of that one, the chance for fresh meat, and to eliminate the potential threat, made me think about trying to kill this snake. After some thought, hunting him in the rocks didn't seem like such a good idea.

I spent a lot of my time that week reading my three books, 'Camping and Woodcraft', by Horace Kephart, and the King James Bible being the other two. Raised a Catholic, I had not professed to be one since doing a college research paper on the evolution of the main religions of the world. My faith in God was unshakable, but my faith in organized religion was tarnished by my findings. The historical hypocrisy, greed and vindictiveness of organized religions, and the ever changing mandates of the Vatican in particular that I uncovered were disquieting. My evidence was enough to make me realize that, along with their virtues, they had all the faults of humanity in general.

Believing that everyone has the right to worship in their own way and certainly not faulting anyone for their own beliefs, I had adopted my own form of reverence. I believed the planet itself, as opposed to the human species, was God's greatest creation and consideration. If anything, we had only been put here to allow us to appreciate the wondrous bounty of this planet as no other species could. In my estimation, I figured God might be disgusted with our misuse and abuse of this world and with humans' predilection for doing evil things. Why else would he enable us to acquire the means of planetary destruction? We are being tested for worth as a species, and I sometimes feel we are failing miserably.

Consequently, I since had never read much of the Bible. Feeling a need to better understand the vagaries of human spirit I had recently encountered, I delved into it with the aptitude of a scholar. Many of the passages spoke to my soul as if they had been written for me, giving me a peculiar sense of camaraderie with the characters. Mankind had not changed much in two thousand years it seemed, merits and flaws still unevenly distributed but present in all humans.

My scheduled calls to Pollitt went out with no trouble besides a couple skinned knees. From the top of the cliff above the Current the view was expansive, especially at its' eastern edge. At that point the Current was nearly a hundred feet directly below the outermost promontories. I also got the best reception from there. After discovering this on Monday, I had been leaving camp by five so I could sit and enjoy the view, the monotony of my bench being tedious. The only humans I saw that week were campers and boaters from this vantage point. Hidden behind cedars at the top, I was invisible to them as they floated and boated past. Though out of my sight, almost every word the canoeists spoke as they passed under the overhanging bluff was audible, echoing up the vertical cliff off the water.

The disc had been turned over to the feds on Monday after Pollitt went back to impound and acted like he'd just found it. I was a little mad on hearing that, but believed him that it was for the better good and all after he reminded me of the unknown possible consequences of a delay in its' decryption. The bad thing for me was that he'd had to act like I'd hidden it to cover his professed inability to find it the first time he'd searched. He explained the second search by telling everyone he'd done it at Sanchez's impetus, and had to tell Sanchez the truth in order to validate his story. I wasn't worried about Sanchez ratting me out, but the web had just gotten a little bigger.

On Wednesday a party of six canoes set up camp on the gravel bar. Envying their joviality and care free spirit, I watched them while waiting for seven o'clock to roll around. Memories of the many times I'd floated with family and friends only made me more despondent. At exactly seven I dialed George's number and the good news I received cheered me up. Andrea was 'released' into protective custody that day, but before she was O'Brien was able to tell her I was alive and that I was in a safe place. She had reacted with disbelief when he first told her, but when he told her about what kind of 'safe place' she knew he was telling the truth. O'Brien's admonition of secrecy wasn't needed, her experience at the farmhouse leaving her no doubt as to the peril of my continued existence. Pollitt told me that O'Brien said it was almost like a light brightened her face as she was told of my plan to disappear, blubbering out, "He finally might get enough of camping." before she began crying. I guessed she didn't hate me after all.

As of our Friday night call he still didn't know what was on the disc. Telling me he had little hope of ever finding out, my hope for the disc being a way out of my quandary seemed to vanish. My silence after this revelation must have given him an idea of my dejection because he said, "Maybe I should come down there tomorrow. I could use a little fishing trip anyways."

His next scheduled trip wasn't till the following weekend, but I longed for some companionship. "Well, if you really want to go fishing, I sure wouldn't mind the company. It's a little different than I figured it would be. I haven't even gone fishing yet."

"Well, that settles it. I'll head down there tomorrow morning. Think I could get a reservation for that site? I could stay till Monday if I can."

The talking of any other humans had only reached my hideout a few times from the Current since Sunday, weekday floaters and jet boaters tending to be much less raucous and numerous than the weekend crowd. The isolation from all human contact and basically imprisonment on my bench was having a much more drastic effect on me than I'd figured. I relished the chance for some normal conversation, having thought about walking down to the Current a few times and acting like just another person enjoying the river so I could at least talk to somebody. Besides my vow to stay out of sight, the slowly moldering cast and the perils of getting to the river or someone recognizing me had kept me from trying.

I had tried to keep my cast dry, but the frequent showers and two big storms had made the forest drip nearly constantly. The stench from it had been slowly building and though the pain had almost gone away, the smell took its' place in a more constant reminder of my infirmity. I had tried a few times to take it off, always quitting when the pain of my attempts reminded me I still needed it. I said "I'll set you up in the presidential suite if you can help me change the padding on my cast."

"You got a deal. I'll try and get down there by noon or one at the latest."

The relief I felt on hearing this must have been palpable over the phone because after a couple seconds of silence he said, "I told you people can't handle being alone too well."

"Hate to admit it, but you were right about that."

"Well, the sooner I let you go, the quicker I can get my stuff together and get down there. I'll see you tomorrow."

"Thanks. I'll get the suite ready. See you tomorrow."

CHAPTER THIRTY THREE

Deciding to see how hard it would be to get to the river from there in the hope of fishing with George tomorrow, I followed a game trail leading away from my camp. A narrow canyon fell towards the river after I'd gone a few hundred yards. I made my way down through this ravine and the gurgling intermittent stream that had formed the valley emptied into the Current at a break in the bluff. Coming close to the river, I began hearing people talking and turned around. The trek wasn't that difficult, and I saw this route as my best option for fishing in the river provided no one was on the gravel bar.

I made the trek back to my 'home' in a lot better spirits than I'd had in a while. Darkness was falling but a nearly full moon was breaking through the trees as I started the descent along my trail to the cave. My mind was preoccupied with the prospects of fishing soon. Only yards from completing the descent, some loose rock caused me to slide a bit then tumble onto the level of the bench shouting, "SSSon of a BITCH!" as I sprawled out.

A couple seconds later I heard a woman say, "Did you hear that?"

"Yeah . . . . WHO'S UP THERE?"

The fall had jolted my shoulder and pain was shooting through me as I clenched my teeth and cursed myself for my carelessness. I lay there debating whether to answer, not trusting my voice to be steady through my pain. If I didn't answer they may figure me for being dangerous and just leave, but might report my presence to the rangers or some other authority. If I did answer, what should I say?

After thirty seconds or so the man shouted, "I have a gun down here so don't try nothing."

His voice wavered as he said it so I figured he really didn't or at least wasn't prepared to use it. I had calmed down enough to trust my voice and decided to answer. After picking myself up slowly I choked out a yell.

"Hey . . . . I just fell down the damn hill . . . . give me a second, okay."

The pain must have been still evident because he yelled, "Are you hurt bad?"

"No . . . . I be fine. Just . . . . got a little turned around on my hike today and I'm trying to get back to my car." I sure didn't want them to think I was camping up here, since no normal camper would choose this location to set up.

He answered, "We got some good maps. Where did you park?"

I tried to remember the names, well, numbers, of the roads coming in, something I figure anybody that drove in would remember but couldn't. I had to answer soon to keep his suspicions down so I said, "I think I'm up at the top of this valley. I thought going down to the creek would lead me back to the trail." Even as I finished I knew I'd slipped up. If they were parked there and no one else was they would know I was lying.

I breathed a sigh of relief as he yelled, "We floated down to here. Let me check my map and see where the road is up there . . . . You got a flashlight? It's pretty hard to get down here."

I figured that gave me a way out of this so I yelled, "No. Could you just tell me how to get back up to the end of the road closest to here. I'm pretty sure that's where I'm parked at. I don't think I can get down there." They had a small campfire going, which I hadn't seen till reaching the edge of the bench. I saw him turn on a battery powered lantern and powerful flashlight as he walked to the edge of the stream.

He yelled up, "I got a lantern. I can get up to where you are and help you get down here. The trail crosses the creek a couple hundred yards upstream from here. I don't think you want to be trying that cliff in the dark."

Damn, how was I going to argue with that logic and not sound suspicious? Let alone my cast, I hadn't shaved or really bathed in over a week and was beginning to look like a mountain man, so my story of getting lost hiking wouldn't fly if he saw me.

"Hey, I think I can just climb back up and find it if you point me in the right direction."

He was crossing the creek already as he answered, "I'll be up there in a minute. Just hold tight there."

Damn, damn, damn!

As I watched him survey the bottom of the precipitous slope some hundred feet below he said, "Let me see you so I know where to come up at."

He shined his flashlight up the hill towards me and I stepped back from the edge, trying to decide how to play this. The woman's scared voice and his wavering statement of having a gun had quickly convinced me that these people were not looking for me and therefore probably no threat. I stepped back towards the edge of the escarpment and said, "I'm up here, but I don't think you can get up here from there."

His flashlight shined up on my face but he couldn't see my body as he answered, "I think I see a way over here. I'll be up there in a second."

Damn. He began heading a bit up the valley, then the light started flickering in and out as he crawled up the narrow chasm I'd seen as my best route down to the stream. Within a couple minutes he was stepping into the bench. I quickly saw he really did have a gun and it was leveled right at me.

He said, "Just put your hands up and stay there!" not wavering a bit. "What the hell you doing up here and don't tell me you was just hiking."

I had carried the pistol with me the first two times I'd made the climb to the top of the hill but the need for it hadn't seemed as great as the week wore on so I hadn't bothered today. Suddenly not sure if he was a threat or just protecting his woman and himself, I wished I'd gotten a gun out of my cave before he got there.

As he stepped closer I said, "I can only put one up. I'm kinda fucked up."

He had gotten close enough by then to see me fully, saying, "What the . . . .", as his flashlight allowed him to see my shabby and impaired state. I was glad at that moment that I'd taken care to conceal my cave and cover up any sign of my being there throughout the week.

"I ain't got a gun so would you mind not pointing that thing at me."

He took another step and I heard the slight dink of my alarm system. "What was that?' he demanded, his beam shining down on the fishing line. His light shined back at me quickly, his voice gaining in pitch just a bit as he ordered, "Step over here and let me see you better."

I took a few steps towards him and he asked, "What the fuck is this fishing line for?"

Some great system you got there Mitch I thought as I said, "Well, it was supposed to be an early warning signal."

"An early warning of what?"

I sighed deeply then said, "Of people coming into my camp."

He glanced around the bench then said, "What camp?"

The irony of it struck me as I said, "You gonna shoot me or not? If you're not, I'll show you if you put that gun down. I got enough people trying to kill me already."

His voice went up another octave as he said, "Just fucking show me and I'll decide whether I'm gonna shoot ya'!" Between the powerful flashlight he was holding in his left hand and shining at me and my steady eye on his gun, I hadn't seen his face yet. He gingerly stepped over the fishing line as if it was the trigger to a bomb and I saw a typical Southern Missouri country boy. His grizzled chin, faded jean shorts, Harley t-shirt and camouflage hat actually calmed me a bit, figuring he at least wasn't after me.

"I'll show you. I ain't gonna do nothing to you, so just be careful with that gun. I just been trying to hide out here and I didn't want to even see anybody. I got some real bad mother fuckers trying to kill me already. That line's just got a rifle shell hooked to it so's I could hear somebody coming if they tried to sneak into my camp during the night."

He obviously still expected a trap of some sort. Waving the pistol at me, he said, "You just get about five feet in front of me and show me your 'camp'."

I did as he asked and soon reached the brush covering the cave entrance. I said, "It's right in here. I do have guns in there so if I go in first you might shoot me if you see 'em." He didn't say anything for a second and I was hesitant to turn around, so I said, "You wanna go in first or not?"

"How do I know you ain't got a booby trap in there already?"

I sighed and said, "Well, then I'll go in first." I felt the barrel of his pistol poke me in the back of the neck and said, "Damn it dude, can't you see I'm no threat to you."

"I ain't takin' that chance. Pull some of that brush away so's I can see in there before we go in."

He poked me again and I began pulling brush to the side. My guns were lying on the bed and my books were on the stone table. The whole cave was about as neat as it could be as he shined his flashlight around and checked it out. I thought, "This fucker may just kill me to rip me off" and wasn't prepared for his next statement. "Put your hands down and sit on that bench. I'm not going to shoot you."

Remembering saying the exact same thing to Sally I took a seat at the bench, hoping he meant it as much as I had. He set his pistol and the flashlight down on the bed, then took the lantern out of the crook of his left elbow and set it on the floor. Picking up the shotgun off the bed he checked to see if it was loaded, then stuck his revolver in the holster on his belt. He sat down on the bed and held the shotgun but didn't point it at me, saying, "Suppose you just tell me what the hell you're doing up here. I guess you ain't cooking meth like I figured."

The rampant use of this drug had spread rapidly, invading small town America and southern Missouri especially in the past twenty years. It's production being detectable by the smell of the chemicals used to make it, many 'cooks' had reverted to setting up as far away from humans as possible.

Figuring he couldn't be blamed for that suspicion I answered, "No, I'm sure not. The reason I'm here is a lot worse than that. There's some kind of terrorists or something trying to find me and that's why I'm hiding out here. Believe me when I say you can't tell anybody about seeing me up here."

He said, "Terrorists, huh?" with kind of a smirk, like I was kidding him or lying. Shaking his head back and forth and half chuckling, he said, "Let me see what those books are." as he held out his left hand. I turned and grabbed them one by one, handing them to him. He read the covers and set them down on the bed, then turned back towards me and asked, "How long you been here?"

"About a week"

The smirk had been replaced with a dour look, his curiosity evident as he said, "Well, why don't you tell me your story then. I got a feeling this is gonna be a good one."

He had all the cards, well the guns anyway, so I figured the best thing I could do was tell him the truth hoping he would have some sympathy for my plight. Telling him in a rush of my odyssey and the reasons for my self-imposed hermitage, he only interjected a few comments like, "NO SHIT?" throughout my dialogue.

He certainly didn't watch the news much because he hadn't recognized me and didn't react on hearing my name. Fully believing me after I relayed tales of the events of the previous two weeks, mocking was replaced with wide eyed fascination. At the end of it, I told him that Pollitt would be coming down tomorrow and could verify everything I'd said.

"There was some dude talking about you at the bar last week, but I didn't pay no attention. My name's Dan Strauss."

He held out his hand with a friendly look. I took it and he didn't shake mine, just held on to it and looked me in the eye, saying, "I hope you got no hard feelings about the way I roughed you up a bit. Ain't no telling what them crank heads might do and I figured you might be one."

Returning his steadfast gaze I said, “If I had my wife with me out in the woods I’d be as cautious as you were. No hard feelings,” finally shaking his hand up and down.

After another five seconds of holding my hand and looking me in the eye he said, “Beth’s probably scared shitless down there. I’m gonna let her know everything’s okay.”

He got up and walked to the front of the bench, yelling down, “Honey, everything’s fine. I’ll be back down in a few minutes.” I heard her reply in an angry, scared voice, but couldn’t make out the words then he yelled, “I’ll tell you why when I get down there. I’m bringing this guy with me, so don’t be scared when we get there. He ain’t gonna hurt us.”

He came back in the cave where I was still sitting on the bench, having made no move to arm myself. He said, “I’ll help you get down and you can have some supper with us and we’ll patch you up a bit. I think you’re gonna have to tell her the story too, cause she sounded really scared down there.”

CHAPTER THIRTY FOUR

A couple hours later I had a full belly of pork steak, baked potato and broccoli and had told a more complete version of my tale. She seemed more incredulous than he had been, but never in a mocking way. After my tale and a bunch of questions about it, I asked, "How well do you know this area?" Dan proceeded to tell me about them and their somewhat intimate knowledge of the surrounding forest.

Both in their early forties, they lived in Eminence, the closest town to us as the crow flies. Childhood sweethearts, they'd used the surrounding woods for all types of activities since they were teenagers. Becoming diehard outdoor adventure buffs, they'd utilized the vast assortment of public lands in the area for most of their vacations. With a few exceptions for trips to the Smokies and Colorado, to this day, hiking, camping, fishing, hunting and floating the surrounding wilderness was their main form of recreation. They took a canoe trip down Big Creek at least once every year when it had enough water to float in, camping here the first night and on the Current the rest.

Dan drove a logging truck, at least when they were harvesting the prime hardwoods Missouri is noted for, and worked at a barrel stave mill part time for a friend in the off season. Beth was a part owner and full time employee of a craft boutique. Eminence being very much a tourist town catering to outdoor and rustic enthusiasts, her income helped them through Dan's slow income months.

They had always appreciated the rugged isolation of Big Creek valley. Unlike the Current, Big Creek hardly ever got floated even with adequate water because you had to put in on private land in order to do so easily. The previous year they had smelled a strong chemical odor about a mile upstream and figured it for a meth lab. Though they had been coming here for twenty years, they had debated coming back because of Beth's fears of running into meth cooks.

Standing up after telling me all this, Dan said, "Let's see what we can do to get you patched up now."

My camo pants were torn at the knee and blood was slowly seeping into the remaining fabric. Pulling up my pant legs, Beth wiped up my scraped knees then they carefully took off my shirt and the plastic cast.

The swelling had gone down dramatically, but the putrid stench that emanated from the cast, and me, as they removed it made them both gag. I must have kind of gotten used to it, because it didn't seem as bad as their reaction. Looking at my arm and shoulder the skin was pruned and leathery looking, small sores oozing at places where the cast had rubbed.

Beth said, "First I'm gonna heat up some water and we'll get you cleaned up. You smell worse than a pig. Dan, get the rest of them smelly clothes off him." She headed to the fire and put a pot of water on.

Dan looked at me kind of funny then said, "You heard the woman."

After he helped disrobe me down to my underwear, Beth came back over and said "My God! I've never seen anybody as beat up as you!" Both helped me scrub as well as possible, taking care not to jar stitches or cause more pain than necessary. After my half hour sponge bath I couldn't smell myself anymore but apparently she could because she said, "Take off them shorts and finish the job in the creek."

She turned around after her order, busying herself with cleaning up the supper dishes. Looking at Dan again he only shrugged, holding his arms out sideways as he said, "I guess you better do it."

He handed me a bar of soap and a dish cloth. Walking into the clear stream to 'finish the job' the water was freezing, but I pulled off my stinking skivvies underwater and tried to clean the rest of myself up. Coming out naked and shivering, Dan held a towel up and dried me off a bit then wrapped it around my waist. Beth came over and both finished drying me off and helped me put on Dan's swimming suit.

It felt way embarrassing to have two strangers doing these things, but I was feeling much better as they began doctoring me up. Dan had carried my duffle bag of bandages and medicines down with him, and they bandaged the worst of my sores and cuts and put Neosporin on the rest. Beth said, "You're going to have to leave that cast off for a while. Let's get you hooked up with a sling."

At about midnight they finished with the first aid and she asked, "You got more clothes up there?"

"Yeah, a few, but they're all about as dirty as them."

They put a pair of sweat pants and a Mizzou sweatshirt on me and I sat down in a bag chair by the fire. Dan went back to my cave and brought down my dirty clothes, sleeping bag and one mattress, setting them up in the now very crowded small tent. Having dozed off in front of the fire, he woke me saying, "I'll help you get in the tent."

I was asleep again immediately, and must not have dreamed much because I didn't wake up till nine the next morning. Feeling way more refreshed than in nearly two weeks, I listened to the sizzle of a frying pan and other camp noises outside. The comfort of the sounds and smells seemed totally foreign to my recent experiences. Even my shoulder wasn't hurting much as I lay there for ten minutes or so just basking in the serenity of the moment.

Nature called, and I carefully crawled through the tent flap and stood up. Beth said, "We was beginning to think you might sleep all day. Hope I didn't wake you up."

"Nah, I think it was the smell of that bacon. It sure smells better than the crap I been eating this past week."

"Dan's down at the creek fishing. You want some coffee?"

"I'd love some. Give me a minute first."

After relieving myself in the woods, I heard the slap of a fish hitting the water as I grabbed the proffered cup. I walked to the edge of the stream and looked in the direction of the sound. Seeing Dan net a nice smallmouth he said, "Now, that's what I'm talkin' 'bout." as he glanced up and saw me.

He threw the fish in a fish basket and waded through the creek carrying it and his fishing pole. “Not a bad morning” he said as he opened up the basket lid and showed me the contents, eight or so decent sized goggle eyes and smallmouths inside.

“This hole under the bluff holds the fish until the water starts going back down. They come up here to spawn every year, and I have a lot better luck here than in the river this time of year. I usually just keep enough for us to have a fish fry tonight, but I thought you might want a little change in your diet.”

After a hearty breakfast of pancakes, eggs, bacon and camp toast, I felt way more human than I had in over a week. As Beth cleaned up and Dan filleted fish, I heard the thunk of a canoe hitting rocks upstream and got in the tent as fast as I could. A couple minutes later, Dan boomed out, “How you folks doin’ this morning?” as the noise of multiple canoes carried up from the stream.

“Great morning to be alive, isn’t it?” a hearty voice replied. I thought, “It sure is” as the otherwise silent flotilla faded from hearing momentarily. Within a bit, the sounds of gravel and rock scraping the bottom of canoes, laughter and shouts of “Paddle on the left!” rang out. After a few more minutes, Dan poked his head in the tent and said, “You can come out now. They’re gone.”

Neither said a word as I emerged, both eyeing me with solemn faces. After standing up I said, “I’m still pretty jumpy. What did those folks look like?”

Dan said, “They looked like normal folks to me, an older couple and four teenage kids. I guess we better get you back up top. This is the last gravel bar above water now till you hit the

Current, and we've had people get out and jabber a few times when we been here."

After carrying my bedding and bandage bag up the hill, he came back to help me get up the chute with no further injuries. Beth was scrubbing my cast and clothes off in the stream, the sun nearing it's zenith as she said, "When the detective gets here I'll come up there and help put this back on. I'm going to try and reline it with something if I can."

"Thanks . . . . I sure appreciate you guys helping me out."

She waved her hand at me in a dismissive gesture, saying, "I sure never ran into nobody that needed it as much as you before. I'm glad we could help."

CHAPTER THIRTY FIVE

Within ten minutes we completed the short but arduous, at least for me, climb with Dan staying right behind me in case I slipped. After heading into the cave, Dan picked up the Bible and said, "You know Mitch, if it wasn't for this, and the fact you never grabbed a gun while I was climbing up the first time, I probably wouldn't have believed you."

He set up my bed and grabbed the bag of garbage I'd accumulated. Walking back outside he said, "Give me a whistle when the cop shows up and we'll bring your cast and clothes up. I better get back down to Beth till then. We already decided we're going to stay here another night."

Holding out my hand, he grabbed it and I pumped his up and down saying, "You can't know how much this meant to me. I hope when all my shit's over we can get together and go fishing or something."

There was no smirk on his face as he stared at me and said, "We will. Get some rest and we'll be back up in a few hours." As he headed down I checked my alarm system then started putting the brush back in front of my cave.

A couple hours later as I was re-reading, 'Edible plants of Missouri' I heard the Armour signal, getting up off my bed and stepping out of the cave. Soon after, Pollitt rounded the last clump of boulders and walked into view as Dan began whistling the same song at the bottom of the hill. George pulled out his pistol and looked at me inquisitively, realizing I had clothes on that we hadn't brought. I whistled back to Dan then said, "It's alright. It's just a guy that helped me out last night. He's bringing my cast back up and he wants to meet you."

"How'd you meet this guy?" George asked as he stepped over my alarm and holstered the pistol.

"Well, that's kind of a long story, but he's okay. Him and his wife fed me and patched me up."

George headed into the cave and took his backpack off, coming back out quickly. He asked, "You sure about this guy?" as he reached me waiting for Dan at the top of the chute.

"Yeah, he's a pretty good dude."

George was still stretching out the kinks as Dan finished the climb. He went straight up to George and held out his hand saying, "I'm Dan Strauss. Glad to meet you, detective Pollitt."

As George somewhat warily shook his hand he said, "I hear you helped Mitch out. Thanks."

I hadn't told him that Dan knew the whole story, and realized he was being cautious as to letting it out himself. I said, "Dan already knows about everything so you don't have to worry about letting something slip."

I then told him of our 'introduction'. He kind of laughed about the story of the alarm system, saying, "So that's what that is."

A while later as we all debated the pros and cons of my wilderness exile, we heard Beth yell up from below, "Hey Dan, I got lunch ready. Come down here and help me get up there."

George and Dan went down bringing up Beth, a mess of fried fish, potatoes and coleslaw, washed clothes, and my cast, dried out, relined and smelling much better. We decided to eat in the cave and kept our talking to loud whispers. They heard the whole story from George's perspective and I added commentary.

Beth and George put my cast back on and she added bits of flannel fabric from a shirt of Dan's where I felt it still rubbing. After the cast felt as comfortable as I thought it could be, they were dressing me in the still slightly damp camo as Dan said, "I can help Mitch out and bring him food a couple times a week anyway. It's a lot closer for us than for you to come down here."

After pondering Dan's statement George said, "Well, since you already know he's here and all that might help a lot. I'm going back on duty on Tuesday and this is probably the last time I'm gonna have a few days to spend here for awhile. Mitch sounded awful damn lonely when I talked to him yesterday. I'm sure he'd appreciate the company." He was watching me as he said this, but I had no argument for his insight.

Dan said, "I'll be happy to do it. Give me your number and I'll let you know when I do so Mitch doesn't have to call you from the top of the bluff so often."

George pulled out a card and handed it to Dan, saying, "I just heard from Joe on the way down here what's on the disc, and maybe Mitch can come out of the woods sooner than we thought. It's got some kind of algorithm on it but they're not sure what it's meant to do. The variables in it aren't named . . . . I guess without that they can't tell. It's about twenty pages worth of mathematical mumbo jumbo to the average person and they got experts trying to figure out its purpose. Obviously it's worth a fortune to somebody . . . . they're just not sure who."

This knowledge made the attempts to grab me even more preposterous. Decent at numbers but certainly no mathematical genius, if experts couldn't figure out what the math really meant, I wouldn't have been able to. I sincerely wished, and not for the first time, that I had tried to pay attention to what the woman had been saying to me as we'd escaped the flood.

I knew what algorithms were, but certainly hadn't ever thought of them as being worth dying for. The secret of the whole thing must lie in something she'd told me and thought I understood during that ten minutes, some kind of clue to the algorithm's purpose or use, or perhaps some missing part of the equation vital to its' function. Try as I had no recollection of anything vaguely resembling a clue had come to mind.

As we discussed all this the sound of a jet boat echoed down the cliff. It was running fast upriver and none of us paid it any attention until it slowed and began coming up the creek. At the same time, two boats that had stopped at the creek mouth gravel bar earlier started up and quickly headed downstream.

The necessity of being able to negotiate rocky shoals made this the only type of motor feasible on the rocky streams of Missouri, but even jet boats have limits. For a few hundred yards below the gravel bar, Big Creek dropped quickly in a series of steps down to the level of the Current. After winding its' way up the creek slowly, the boat began trying to gun it up this rocky chasm but couldn't get past the first step.

Dan said, "That dude's gonna tear his lower unit out if he keeps trying that. Everybody 'round here knows you can't get up here in a jet boat."

We listened to the sounds of the jets straining to gulp water and the keel scraping against rock, the boat now only four or five hundred yards away. After a couple of attempts, the boat's motor shut off and the distant sound of another coming upriver was instantly heard in the sudden silence. Pollitt stood up and held his finger to his lips as the second boat's engine sounds died off, sounding to me like they had probably stopped near the small stream's mouth I'd checked out the day before.

I whispered, "There's been a lot more of them here than we thought. I've kind of gotten used to 'em, but none have tried to come up the creek all week."

Walking towards the entrance to the cave George whispered, "Let's see what them guys are doing."

CHAPTER THIRTY SIX

I wasn't alarmed, figuring it just to be some yahoos that didn't know the river well. We all walked to the front edge of the bench, George, Dan and I quietly and carefully peering through the rocks. No sight or sound of the boat could be heard as we waited for a good five minutes without anybody saying a word. The fact that we couldn't hear any voices began to seem ominous of itself, certainly different than the average boaters' boisterous nature. I carefully went back in the cave and grabbed my binoculars.

Returning to the south parapet, I began scanning the creek bottom. Seeing a flash of movement finally, I trained on the area and saw a fleeting glimpse of a man. Trailing the flickers of movement, he stopped at a spot I could see him more clearly through the foliage. Decked in camo, he surveyed the forest around him intently for a good two minutes before moving on.

He was walking quietly and stopping every few yards or so, carrying a rifle of some type. His actions reminded me of my own deer and pig, as of this year, hunting tactics. I'd always liked to stalk more than stand hunt, though I'd used both tactics with success.

Wild pigs are legal to shoot by any method and at any time of year in Missouri. Knowing this area has a few pigs but not nearly as many as some other public grounds in Missouri, the possibility this guy was pig hunting was slim but still plausible.

I handed the binoculars to George and said, "You see the guy about two hundred yards out by the creek? I think he's looking for me."

He raised them and perused the bottom. A few seconds later he locked on the guy, saying after watching him for awhile, "Maybe he's just hunting."

"Yeah, hunting me!"

George handed the binoculars back to me. Focusing on the guy again, he suddenly waved his arm forward. I knew what that gesture meant and trained the binoculars behind him. I made out three more guys stalking up the trail along the bank in camo and carrying guns through my binoculars. They were still a couple hundred yards away but my heart leapt in my throat as I recognized Hakim amongst them, his face plastered in my memory ever since he'd nearly brained me.

I shrank back involuntarily on seeing him, my face contorting into a grimace. The scene where Paul Newman and Robert Redford jumped off the cliff flashed through my mind as I whispered, "The second guy is the fuckin' dude that busted me with his gun at the farmhouse."

Handing the binoculars to Pollitt, he carefully peeked over the rocks and then looked back towards me. Beth was standing back a bit but had heard my statement, her hand flying to her mouth to stifle the cry coming out. Dan and George both looked at me wide eyed and George whispered, "Are you sure?" handing me back the binoculars.

Peering back through them, I slowly raised above the rocks for another look. Before I could put my binoculars back on 'Hakim', I ducked down as I saw the point guy looking up towards us. He had stopped a hundred fifty yards away and about fifty yards downstream from Dan's camp. The leaves only allowed a partial view of him, but in my brief glimpse it looked like he was trying to figure out how best to come uphill or maybe even had heard us.

Beth had gone back into the cave. Her attempts to choke off her crying weren't working altogether as Dan hurried in to hopefully shut her up. A few seconds later the sounds had disappeared. Hunkering behind the rocks I whispered, "I'm pretty damn sure. Even if it ain't him I know these dudes are lookin' for me. I think they know I'm up here."

As Dan tiptoed back next to us Pollitt said, "They must have followed me here somehow. That other boat we heard might be more of them trying to cut us off from the top."

We had three pistols, a shotgun and the .270, far less firepower than these guys were bound to be carrying. The even chance that it was Hakim down there and the fact they'd been looking up at my 'hideout' was enough evidence for me. I whispered, "Let's just take these mother fuckers out and worry about them later. I'm not gonna be able to outrun these guys."

In my mind shooting them right now was no foul.

Pollitt damn near mimed, "What if you're wrong?"

Dan whispered, "I don't think he's wrong. Ain't nobody that knows this water gonna try to get up the creek. Them guys didn't come up here hunting pigs or they wouldn't have made so much damn noise. I'll shoot the mother fuckers myself if you don't want to."

To take out even a couple of them was going to take good shooting. We had the height advantage, at least for a while, against the guys in the creek and should take advantage of it. I had no doubt as to their intentions but firing the first shot is taboo in a cop's mind. Dan appeared much more willing to do that and I knew it shouldn't be me shooting, the .270 being our only long range weapon.

The first shot would count the most, being the only one to catch them unawares and in the open. I might be able to make that one, being a put 'em down with one shot kind when it came to deer hunting. The shot or two after that might catch the remainder in the open and I might not be able to recover quickly enough from the first one to be effective on these. Firing a rifle accurately off a rest is easy compared to firing freehand, no matter the rifle or the shooter.

"Get the guns." I said to no one in particular. Moving to the right, I got behind the outermost edge of the bench. A minute later as I was peering through the rocks again, Dan tapped my shoulder and handed me the .270. I looked at Dan as he mimed, "I ain't never shot no one." He quickly ran over in a crouch and handed the shotgun to George as I realized the play was up to me.

Well, I had shot men, and like they say, it gets easier after the first one. Peering through the rocks, I caught sight of them. By now they had crossed the creek and were almost in Dan's camp. I figured they knew I was close, but weren't sure exactly where I was.

Slowly resting the rifle on a boulder top, I scoped them out as they stalked onto the gravel bar. I expected George to say either, "Don't" or, "I'll take it", as I lined up a shot at Hakim, but he said neither.

CHAPTER THIRTY SEVEN

As I focused on Hakim he disappeared behind leaves and went in the tent. A few seconds later he came into view again holding the bag of bloody padding and bandages. He began pulling them out and showing them to the others, total confirmation of his identity as I saw it.

I plugged him right through his skull, quickly focusing on the guy standing next to him and firing again. I thought I'd hit him in the left side but he moved sideways out of my view. Moving the scope looking for him or the other two, I caught a bit of movement through the leaves and fired three quick shots. Pivoting the gun on the rock again, I coolly looked for another target as a salvo of automatic rounds started hitting just left of me. Quickly dropping back behind the rocks, a split second later they found my vacated perch. The shooters clip emptied as a few more wasted rounds hit the rocks above us.

Dan was closest to me and I said, "Did you grab the ammo bag?"

He was looking a lot more freaked out than I expected, finally shaking his head no as I looked towards George. He was down behind the rocks about ten feet to my left, a little blood oozing through his shirt on his right shoulder but no tears in the fabric that I could see. Feeling his upper right arm he looked at me saying rather loudly, "It's just from a rock chip I think. Did you hit anybody?"

The need for whispering was long gone but I still did, saying, "I got at least two of them. If that other boat was more of them we need to get out of here before they can get above us."

Dan had gotten up and was already moving quickly towards the cave. George and I both got on our feet and began running crouched over towards the chute. Reaching it, he looked around an oak that over hung the hill and back at me, whispering, "There's nobody in sight. I think you're right about getting out of here. You take the rifle and them and I'll keep the shotgun here. You can cover me when you get up there. If one of them gets to here we'll be screwed."

I knew he was right about that. From the creek the steep hill and bench hid the first hundred feet of the climb, but if somebody got here while we were climbing they'd have us dead to rights. There was no time to debate and Dan and Beth were already heading up the hill carrying the ammo bag and my gun belt. I followed quickly behind them, slinging the rifle over my shoulder.

Gazing up from the creek this morning, I'd noted the last seventy feet to the top could be barely seen through the trees. I called up to Dan and Beth scrambling forty feet above me, "Go as fast as you can till you get to the top. Don't stop."

They had just about made the summit with me still forty or fifty feet behind them when another fusillade of fire began coming up from the creek bottom. The distance was a couple hundred yards but the bullets were chipping rocks just below them as they disappeared from sight over the top of the hill.

When the firing started I'd scooted to the side, slinking down behind a tree before the firing stopped. Laying there panting and groaning I knew I couldn't follow their path.

After about thirty seconds I pulled up the binoculars and slowly peeked around the tree, half expecting the shooting to start again. It didn't, and taking a quick scan through the binoculars I saw Pollitt still in position but no sign of anybody else. Looking quickly around, I decided to try to make it thirty feet to the side where a trio of boulders would give me more cover than this foot and a half wide tree.

After scanning the route I crouched behind the tree and told myself to move, but after five seconds I still hadn't. If they had seen me from the bottom they may be waiting for me to do just that. I got back down behind the tree and felt really scared for the first time since seeing Hakim. After a bit, I quit hyper ventilating and tried to calm my nerves, scanning the hill to the side and above me.

There were only a few scrub trees between me and the boulders and I felt like I would be running a gauntlet. Peeking around the tree again, Pollitt was disappearing from view as he began the climb. I wouldn't be able to cover him from here and wanted to steer him away from Dan's path. Crouching again, this time I didn't wait.

The boulders were about five feet away when the firing started and I felt sand and rock chips spraying me as I jumped behind the first one, banging the gun on a rock as I quickly scooted to the middle of the six foot wide boulder. Taking a few deep breaths, I unslung the rifle and looked up hill through the scope to make sure it was still functional. It looked fine and keeping down I made my way to the third boulder.

There was a small tree growing next to the boulder and I looked through the leaves trying to see Pollitt. He had stopped about fifty feet downhill from me behind a tree next to the trail and was looking up, but hadn't seen me. I whistled just loud enough for him to hear and he quickly looked towards my position.

"Come over to the side before you come any higher." I whispered loudly.

He shook his head and began traversing sideways on the slope. Pointing the rifle back downhill, I leaned it on the bottom branch of the tree, panning the creek bottom as fast as I could. I caught a flash of movement and pulled the trigger, seeing a guy get up and start running towards the base of the ledge as I focused again. I moved the rifle quickly and fired two more times, but he reached the safety of the hill.

Not waiting this time, I slung the rifle again and headed straight uphill from my position since I couldn't see the top of the chute from there. Grabbing at saplings with my good arm I crested the hill and got down, looking for Dan and Beth. I couldn't see them and didn't want to yell, so I ran about twenty feet towards the trail and then crawled to the edge. Picking my head up slowly, I looked down and saw Pollitt behind the same boulders I'd used for cover, seventy feet away. Figuring I only had two shots left, I debated whether to call out or look for Dan, but decided to stay and try to cover George's final ascent.

I whistled and he looked up. Waving my hand for him to come on, he began chugging up the hill. Peering through the scope towards the chute, I caught the sight of a man clearing it and scooting behind rocks before I could line up. As I began frantically panning back and forth searching for him he began firing up the hill. A second later I picked out his gun barrel sticking beyond a rock, heard George cry out, steadied my aim on the barrel, and pulled the trigger.

The barrel disappeared from sight as George cleared the top then sprawled down, rolling onto his right side with a moan. Dan was crawling towards him as I took another look through the scope, seeing no target. I yelled, "Throw me the ammo bag!" as Dan began pulling up George's shirt. He tossed it over to me and I fumbled through it spilling shotgun shells, finally grasping cartridges and feverishly trying to feed them into the magazine. I figured four would have to be enough as I dropped five and six.

Throwing the rifle up I caught sight of another guy coming through the top of the chute. I had an extra couple seconds this time and picked my shot, seeing him stagger back towards the chute as I lined up and fired again. This shot caused him to damn near cartwheel down the steep chasm, his gun flying out of his hands and clattering loudly as he disappeared.

I panned quickly without seeing any movement then scooted away from the edge. Picking myself up, I ran in a crouch towards George. Dan was pressing on his back and blood was oozing out between his fingers as I knelt down and said, "Did it go through?" George was clenching his teeth and moaning loudly as Dan rolled him up a bit and found the exit wound. The bullet had passed through his left side about five inches above his belt and three inches from his side. The hole in his back was barely oozing compared to the front.

"Did you grab the bandage bag?" Dan asked.

Shaking my head at this incongruous question, I said, “There’s still one down there and them other guys could be here any second. Take the rifle and let’s get him up if we can.”

Dan slung the rifle and we both pulled up on George, him trying to help but moaning loudly as we got him erect. We half carried him about twenty feet to a cleft between large boulders and set him down in the three foot deep gash. I said, “I gotta make sure that other guy ain’t coming up.” as Dan ripped off his t-shirt and began pressing it against George’s side.

As I grabbed the rifle George was looking at me and I said, “I’m sorry”, trying to think of something better to say for a second. I couldn’t and ran over to the cliff top thinking if I had been covering him right I’d have caught the first guy through the chute. Sticking the barrel over the edge, I had just started looking through the scope when the differing sound of a pistol barked, the bullet chipping the rock just below my barrel rest. I pulled the barrel back as two more rounds whizzed above me. They were being fired from way closer than the chute, maybe sixty feet away.

Dropping the rifle, I made a dash towards the shotgun we’d left lying on moving George. I had never fired it but had practiced aiming it one handed from many positions during the week, imagining not unrealistic enemies trying to get the drop on me. The pain I had figured for worth the practice and had gotten to the point that I could at least make the motions.

I grabbed it and spun around, heading for the spot I figured the guy was coming up. As I cleared sight of the hill he saw me at the same time I saw him trying to race up the last twenty feet of hill. He tried to react quickly but I had the shotgun pointed towards him and just pulled the trigger.

The recoil made me lose my uncertain footing and fall backwards, the shotgun clattering a couple feet away as his shot flew so close to my nose I felt the wind. As I reached out and grabbed the shotgun a gun went off behind me and I spun my head around searching for a target. No one was in sight and after another second I heard the sounds of a tumbling body. I looked behind me and Dan was still holding his pistol pointed towards the cliff. He said, "I nailed that dude." in kind of a daze as I picked myself up and headed that way.

"Where's Beth?" I asked as he lowered his pistol.

"I gave her your pistol and told her to start running for the truck and don't stop."

CHAPTER THIRTY EIGHT

After seeing the shots being fired at them, I'd thought one or both of them might be hit. Looking down and seeing George holding the shirt against his side, I was trying to do the math on when the other boat's guys could be here. It had taken me about twenty minutes to make it from here to the end of the cliff, moving slowly to avoid a misstep. Adding in the time to climb up from the river I figured the guys in the other boat could be here any minute, assuming it was more of them. George sat up slowly and choked out, "Any more still comin'?"

"I think that was the last one from that boat. We need to get back down to the cave. Do you think you can make it?"

Dan said, "My truck's only three or four miles from here. Why don't we head there?"

"Does Beth have the keys?"

He looked at me for a second like I was daft then said, "Shit, we always leave 'em by the truck an' I didn't tell her to wait for me . . . what about his truck?"

George was looking more woozy by the second, but he groaned then stammered out, "M . . . my keys er in ma backpack. I ca . . . c'n make it." Make it where was the question.

"We got bandages and shit down in the cave. I think we got all the guys from that boat, three outta four for sure. If we try to run them other guys might catch up to us in the open forest and we wouldn't have a chance. An' if it ain't more of 'em, we'll probably kill George trying to run."

Only height advantage and taking the initiative had enabled us to survive this. They had known where I was within a few hundred yards. I had been almost aching for revenge as the week had progressed, even many of my vivid dreams being tuned in on that. The thought seemed to come naturally.

I hadn't heard the slight beeps and sounds of talking over walkie-talkies like I'd heard in the pasture, but that was no guarantee that the other boat sounds weren't more of them. The whole why of it, something I'd agonized over, was thrown away in the split second I thought of it. The main thing now was to get the bleeding stopped, and the only way we could do that quickly was down at my cave.

"Can you make it to the cave?" I asked George.

He choked out, "I guess we'll see."

I ran and grabbed the ammo bag, picking up the spilt shotgun shells and pulling out two ten cartridge sleeves and stuffing them in my pocket. After hurrying back, I handed the whole bag to Dan and picked up the rifle, handing it to him. Before I could ask, he began pulling out cartridges and loading the rifle back up as I said, "I'll stay here with the rifle until you get George down. I won't be much of a help with him anyways."

Dan looked at me for a second like he wanted to say something, then just handed me the full rifle and grabbed the shotgun and ammo bag. Helping George up without a word, they headed towards the 'trail' to get down. As they disappeared over the edge, I began looking for the best place to defend their downhill trek. I quickly saw that a rocky point seventy feet away along the crest of the slopes face would give anyone a clear shot at them as they headed downhill, and it commanded a great view of the top of the trail.

Weaving my way along the slope and almost stopping at a couple of other spots, I remembered my rant to myself about instincts. Continuing along the cliff top, I reached the outcrop and scooted quickly into the cleft I'd chosen. Looking over top of the boulders towards Dan and George, I saw they were almost halfway to the cave.

Watching them as Dan slowly helped George down the steep hill, I felt responsible for all this, cursing myself once again. After seeing them round the boulders towards the cave, I was about to get up and head back towards the trail when I heard rocks clicking. My senses went into overdrive and I strained to hear any other sounds. Though very slight, the direction of the sound left me no doubt it was the men from the other boat.

I looked down, trying to see if anything might give away the location of the cave. The few trees on the precipitous hill giving me a fairly clear view, a yellow patch of Dan's tent was visible but no sign of human stuff on the bench could be seen.

I began scoping the top, wondering if I should shoot immediately on seeing anyone or waiting till they crossed in front of me and trying to get as many of them as possible in the first few seconds. The rage I'd felt towards myself I directed to my real enemies as I carefully looked and listened for the approaching men. The seconds ticked away slowly till I heard slight sounds some thirty yards away.

They were just over the curve of the hill from me, the slope starting to level off ten feet above me. Peering through some brush I couldn't see any of them. I heard slight gravel sounds then clearly heard, though it was only whispered loudly, "Rock, check out the cliff."

It sounded like a command and soon I could hear the sound of a man coming straight towards me. The brush and trees hid him for a few seconds as he veered towards the cliff between me and the trail, then I saw a giant of a man appear on the top about twenty feet away. I ducked down before he saw me, thinking, "I hope they're not all like him."

My heart was pounding in my chest loud enough for me to actually hear, and hunkering there I tried to get the nerve up to look again, but couldn't. The sight of this goliath had shaken me and though I felt I should pop up and try to take him out of the equation, the thought and actions didn't come together. After another minute I heard the murmur of a whispered conversation between 'Rock' and the unseen voice over the edge of the hill talking over some sort of radio.

Though I knew where they were, I couldn't take them all out from here. The only way I might have that possibility was if they all were on the trail headed down to the cave. Not knowing how many of them there were that would be a gamble either way, but no matter what I couldn't let them get on the bench. The guilt, rage and hatred eroded my fear, retribution and focus replacing it quickly. The recent fighting and many situations I'd imagined over the previous week helped, never having pictured myself shirking from the fray. These guys may be 'rocks', but a well placed bullet would kill them as quick as it did any other man.

Soon a few light sounds of footsteps began coming down the hill on the same track that Rock had followed. The sounds faded and I didn't hear another for a few minutes. I dared not move a muscle, and was trying hard to control the sounds of my breathing as I crouched there with the rifle pointed uphill. If any of them came straight over the hill they couldn't miss seeing me.

Almost ready to stand up and look for them, I heard one whisper, "Where you think they are?"

The voice was coming from the next limestone outcrop over, maybe twenty feet away. I thought he was talking about us, but a second later I heard another say, "Shit, you know as much as me. They haven't called in since the first shot."

That statement made me realize they had no clue as to what had transpired in the last half hour. The splattering of Hakim's head must have shaken even those ostensibly seasoned veterans of violence if they had felt the need to remain radio silent. They must be human after all.

The nearby voices sounded wary, if not scared. Well why not? Their whole other team had vanished, and then again maybe they also knew I'd somehow taken out at least three of their guys a week ago. There was no sign of people from where they were, but if they reached the top of the trail they would be sure to see George's blood. Would they be able to trail it down the hill? How would they even know who's blood it was?

I decided to stay down and listen for the sounds of them going downhill. Only then would I go into action. If I opened the ball now, I was as good as dead. There was no place to run, and if they had grenades they could take me out without risking themselves. Once again I felt the urge to damn near pray my pursuers away.

"Frog one, can you read me?"

Silence for twenty seconds, then, in a more subdued whisper, another said, "What the hell's going on. I can't see nothin' but a tent down there. You think that's Chase's?"

"Hakim seemed to think so when he found the bandages. After that we got nothing."

For the first time, I began to feel like I somehow had the upper hand. I knew where they were and the extent of their current knowledge of the situation, yet they were in the dark. From the tone of their voices I knew they were worried about their own skins, something I hadn't figured any of them for until just now. I had heard three separate voices, but that sure didn't mean that was all of them.

"Frog one, come in."

A few seconds later I heard sounds coming from farther away then a muffled conversation I couldn't make out. A minute later I heard one coming back, then another flurry of indistinguishable words. After that more loudly one said, "I'm heading down. Shoot anything that moves."

It sounded like Rock to me and I said 'shit' under my breath.

"Just hold up there Rock. Is that blood trail coming up the hill or going down?"

"Looks like its going down, and there's .270 casings over there. That's got to be Chase."

A fourth voice spoke up and said, "Where the hell are them guys? This was supposed to be a cake walk."

"Well it ain't, so just shut up and keep your eyes open. The signal is still coming from right below us."

Signal? My heart skipped a beat as I heard this. How they had found me had been constantly nagging me since seeing the first group headed up the valley.

"Why aren't they answering?"

Whew!

"Maybe they can't."

"You think they coulda' got 'em all?"

"They're not talkin' and nobody's shooting. What you think?"

"It wouldn't surprise me. This has been nothin' but a clusterfuck from the get go. You gonna send Rock down?"

Don't do that! Don't do that!

"Rock, head on down. We got you covered."

Shit! I looked behind me and tried to figure out how to turn around as quietly as possible. The crack was about two feet wide where I was crouching, widening to about three feet before the sloping rock floor petered out. There was only space below the outermost two foot of protruding fissured limestone as the slope fell nearly vertically.

Moving with the care but certainly not the dexterity of a tight rope walker, I switched directions without making a sound. Without standing up I couldn't see the top of the trail, but I could see the last forty feet or so above the bench. My whole body was throbbing as I slowly settled the end of the barrel on the side of the eroded limestone to my right. If Rock reached the ledge, I would have a clear shot at him as he rounded the last boulders. I picked my spot carefully, knowing the shot was likely to be the last thing I ever did.

In my climbing and descending of the hill over the past week, I had never been able to make a trip without making some noise, try as I had to avoid it. The areas between the larger boulders were covered with millennia of eroded rock, which many times cascaded down without warning. The trips up and down had slowly caused less noise as I'd cleared the looser detritus purposefully and inadvertently, but I was sure nobody could make the trip without some noise.

Listening intently and peering through the scope, the telltale sounds of a man heading down the trail made me increase my concentration on the shot window I'd chosen. The beating pulse in my brain anticipated the view of a man walking into this window, but after thirty seconds he hadn't appeared.

The temps were pushing into the nineties and every pore on my body was pouring sweat, the sun beating on me and becoming yet another nemesis. Taking my eye off the scope to look for Rock, the prodigious sweat from my forehead ran straight into my eyes. I heard a little sliding rock and tried to shake the sweat off my face, but it just caused more to sting my eyes. Trying to wipe the sweat out with my right sleeve, I heard the sounds of multiple boats at the same time coming from both directions on the Current. They were probably a couple miles or so away, but they sounded like they were coming fast.

CHAPTER THIRTY NINE

I thought, "How many of these fuckers can there be?" then almost immediately figured they were probably Conservation agents. Their jet boats were the only law enforcement watercraft I'd ever seen on the many small rivers I'd floated in Missouri, and then only rarely. They had all the powers of the police as many floaters had found out to their chagrin, but would probably be totally unprepared for the threat they were nearing. I couldn't imagine anyone else heading towards what had to sound like a battle as the gun shots had certainly echoed loudly down the cliff face and into the river valley.

Many people had to have heard the firefight. The automatic weapons and sheer volume of shots wasn't normal, even in an area which allowed hunting. In all my days on the Current I'd only heard the sporadic fire of hunters and very occasional target shooters, the difference always being apparent after the first few shots. Target shooting is actually illegal in the National Scenic Riverways, so anyone familiar with the river would know this was far from normal.

It was a beautiful Saturday afternoon, the week before Memorial day, and there had to be a ton of canoeists and boaters on the river within earshot. They had cell phones, mostly useless in the riverbed but there were some spots you could get reception. Hell, the more well heeled or cautious floaters could have sat phones. About twenty minutes had gone by since my first shot and somebody must have gotten a call out about this by now.

Finally getting enough of the sweat out of my eyes to see, I peered back through the scope and put my finger back on the trigger because it really didn't matter who was coming.

No movement appeared as the next minute ticked by, the nearing boats being the only sounds. After refocusing and scanning the slope, I couldn't see a thing moving, wondering if I'd missed Rock as he'd cleared the boulders. I was thinking, "He probably hasn't made it that far." when a shotgun blast echoed from directly below me. I couldn't see my cave from here, but it sounded like it had come from there.

In my brief glimpse of Rock I'd seen an assault rifle but no shotgun. "Dan must have blown him away" I thought as no other shots rang out. Another few seconds ticked by as I panned the partial view I had of the bench but couldn't see anything.

"Rock"

If I didn't know his name already, I wouldn't have understood it. Another ten seconds went by, during which the downriver boat faded as it stopped about where I figured these guys' boat had stopped.

"Sound like we got company at the boat. What's the call? Chase or the cop musta gotten Rock."

The barely audible words amazingly seemed to have no sense of urgency or worry in them. There was no answer for awhile, the sounds of the boat coming from upriver getting suddenly much louder as it rounded the bend and headed up the creek. The leader sounded surprisingly calm as he said, "Three, what's your twenty?"

After listening for a bit he said, "Negative. He's holed up in rocks below us. We lost team one and he just got Rock and we got company coming, probably rangers." Another pause, then he said, "Roger that. We'll keep him pinned."

Another guy said, "Who the fuck is this guy?"

"A slippery son of a bitch."

"Enough of the fuckin' chit chat. Kono, make sure they don't get out of them rocks. We're gonna cover three after they check out the boat from the creek. John, head down the bluff and check out our boat, then cover the trail up here till you hear from three. I'm gonna be over there."

I heard the sounds of men moving as I finished my slow turn around again. Having just gotten the rifle pointed back uphill, I heard the faint sounds of John on the opposite side of the crest following their route in. I breathed a silent sigh as I realized he hadn't followed the cliff edge. As that thought elapsed the next was, "What do I do now?"

One of them was in the next cleft over, twenty feet away. I assumed the leader had pointed at the spot he was going to be in. Where would that be? I thought about the layout of the slope and figured he would pick the boulders at the top of the chute. They were hidden from my cliff side view by the outcrop and I wouldn't have a shot at him from here. I figured John would check out their boat from the end of the bluff next to the side stream's valley. That put him a good ten minutes from here even if he hustled.

The boat from the creek shut off its motor and silence fell. Crouching in the cleft I realized I couldn't stay in that awkward position much longer, my body starting to shake already. If the boat was conservation agents or any other curious boaters for that matter, they were in for a world of trouble. I had to do something.

About five minutes had gone by since John left before I slowly stood up and pointed the gun towards the rocks I thought Kono was in. Had he been standing he would have seen me immediately, but gaining full height I couldn't see him at all. If I could get him to stick his head up I would have him dead to rights.

After carefully resting the rifle on top of the rock, I lowered my eye to the sights below the scope. A flicker of movement to my left caught the corner of my eye and I swung the rifle towards it, seeing a gun swing around the top of a boulder twenty feet further down the slope than the rocks I'd assumed Kono was in. As soon as I was on him I fired, the bullet chipping the top of the outcrop hiding his body from the chest down. He seemed to continue swinging his gun around and began firing as he flew backwards, disappearing from view and quitting firing only when the sounds of his body bouncing off rocks commenced.

It didn't even look like I'd hit him to me. Not stopping to ponder my good fortune I came straight up the cleft and began running towards the top of the trail. My only thought was to take out their leader as quick as possible before John showed back up. The familiar feeling of the thrill of the hunt, though never in this context, hit me full force. Be better than my quarry. Moving quietly and swinging the rifle around looking for any sign of the others, I passed the top of the trail and snuck a peek over the hill. No one was in sight as the far off sounds of men talking excitedly carried up from the creek.

There was no good cover close by so I headed up the ridge away from John's possible return. As I did, a motor started up in the creek and quickly headed downriver after entering the Current.

Fifty yards further up the ridge, I carefully peered back over the edge from behind a large tree. After thirty seconds of panning the hillside I caught a movement and saw a man behind some boulders halfway up the hill. He was facing away from me, pointing his gun towards the spot where I'd been. As I lined up the seventy five yard shot at the back of his head I briefly thought, "Is this murder?" before pulling the trigger. A second after seeing my shot was true I swung the gun around to face the cliff top.

Minutes ticked away with no sight or sound of John returning, eerie quiet enveloping the forest. I could see the front part of the bench and the top of the chute from my position and figured this was as good a spot as any to keep team three from approaching the cave. If nothing else these guys were tenacious, and I had no reason to believe the rest would just give up their quest.

Another twenty minutes slowly dragged by, the decision to stay put and not go check on George and Dan nagging at me. As my anxiety built, my patience for inaction started wearing thin. Preparing to descend the hill, I gazed all around for movement. The windless forest was as still as a morgue, even the ever present birds seemingly having vacated the area.

CHAPTER FORTY

Choosing my route down to the ledge, I picked my first stop and headed towards it. As I used this new vantage point to scope out the valley the sound of helicopters began to pulse the air, a few seconds later reverberating loudly off the cliff face as two flew past the mouth of the creek. They grew more distant for a moment then came back. One flew quickly up the creek valley level with me and then came back down the ridge top, slowing as it neared me.

Gazing up at it approaching I wondered if I should let it see me, not sure whose side it was on. I crouched down and debated this but the decision was taken from me as rotor wind began buffeting me and a loudspeaker blared, "Lay down your weapon or we will commence firing."

I set the rifle down and raised my hands as much I could, gazing up at the gunship hovering twenty feet over the sparse treetops almost directly above me. After seeing the helicopter get shot down in the pasture, my biggest fear right then was this one crashing down on top of me. Four zip lines came over the edge. Within mere seconds four camoed and face painted warriors were pointing their guns at me and approaching as another four zipped to the ground. The first to reach me kept his gun pointed at my head as he said, "Who are you and what the fuck's goin' on here."

Before I could answer, the second one grabbed my arms from behind and tried to pull both behind my back. The pain of my left shoulder being wrenched caused me to cry out as he realized

I had a cast on it and it sure wasn't going behind my back. The sudden pain and jerk caused my knees to buckle. I fell backwards as the second released me and said, "What the fuck?" jumping back so I wouldn't hit him as I fell. I landed on my ass and rolled over, crying out loudly.

The first one quickly patted me down and took everything out as I lay there moaning then repeated, "Who are you?"

Clenching my teeth to talk through the pain, I forced out, "One of the good guys. My name's Mitch Cones."

The second guy had been pointing his gun at my head as I was being roughly frisked. His eyes got big as he said, "You gotta be shittin' me."

The first guy stood back and just stared at me for a few seconds then said, "Where you from?"

"Orion, Missouri and there's still some bad mother fuckers looking for me out there, so you better start worryin' about them more than me."

"They the ones been doing all the shooting?"

"Not all of it. We shot six or seven of 'em already. They got another team around here somewhere and one of 'em headed down that way a half hour ago." I pointed my right index finger down the cliff then said, "If you don't mind, I'd like to take cover before we talk anymore."

They quickly but much more gently helped me up and we got behind the tree I'd been using for cover. The first one said into his headset, "We got bogies out there. This guy says he's Mitch Cones and they are looking for him right now. Says he shot six or seven already."

"Not just me. There's a couple guys down there that are with me," pointing at the cave.

He waved me off like I was bothering him. After a moment he said, "Yeah, that Mitch Cones." Another pause. "No, he doesn't have Id, but I think it's him." Still listening, he looked back at me and asked, "Where you think the rest of them are at?"

"I'd guess down in the valley, but I ain't heard or seen any of 'em. I just heard that dude talking to them." I pointed at the sprawled body of the last guy I'd shot as he was being checked out by two of the soldiers. "There's a cop and another guy in a cave down on that bench. The cop's a detective from Orion named George Pollitt and he's been shot. Could you send somebody down there to help him? Tell 'em to whistle the Armour hot dog song or they might get shot at."

"Five and six, we got a wounded friendly down on the bench. Go see and whistle the Armour hot dog song as you approach." "Yeah, that one." "Bird one and two, advise precaution. These guys might have RPGs. What's the twenty on bird three and four?" "Roger. Tell them to deploy on west side of Big creek."

The arrival of the gunships may have scared the rest of them off but they were still certainly in the area. The second boat taking off I had assumed to be rangers leaving once they heard the firing from Kono as he'd fallen, perhaps even seeing the body bounce down the steep hill face. I asked, "How'd you guys get here so fast."

He held up his hand as he listened to his headset. "Roger" He turned towards me and asked, "What's your date of birth and mothers maiden name." I realized the reason for his inquiry and quickly answered him. "Social security and children's middle names?" I said their whole names and he said, "It's him." As I wondered how they would have such quick access to those facts he listened for a lot longer then answered, "Roger that" before turning his attention back to me. "Mr. Cones, we need to get you out of here ASAP. Can you walk?"

The sudden change in address and demeanor towards me took me off guard. These guys had no insignia or anything on them to give me a clue as to their identity or even branch of service. The helicopter had been totally devoid of inscriptions, and only on recognizing it as a gunship had I meekly laid down my arms. I wanted a couple of answers myself before I trusted my life to these guys, no fault intended. "What's your name?" I asked.

He held up his hand again and listened. "Roger that. Extraction point A. Over and out. Five, what's the status of the cop?" He listened for a minute then said, "We are going to extract Chase. Squad two will be here anytime now. I'll send them down to give you a hand." He looked back at me and said, "Call me Adam. We need to move, NOW."

"What about George?" I'd seen the two guys approaching the cave but I couldn't just leave here without at least knowing how he was. The sounds of more choppers began to fill the air as he pocketed my shells, slung my rifle and said, "He's alive and we got a medivac coming in for him. Let's move." Grabbing my right arm, he began guiding me as we climbed to the top of the bluff, then turned us towards the Current River in the direction John had gone.

Remembering Sanchez grabbing me in the same way and what happened afterwards, I said, "Didn't you hear me? At least one of 'em headed this way a while ago and I think there's another one that was up here, but he could be anywhere. These fuckers are a lot more dangerous than you seem to think."

"We got another team coming from that way and they'll cover us. We're going to get you in a chopper and outta here."

Though the circumstances now were totally different I realized that was the exact opposite of what I'd wanted when I'd planned my disappearance. I pulled to a stop with Adam slipping, letting go of my arm as he regained his footing. Sitting down behind a large tree I said, "Gimme' my rifle back."

Adam looked at me and said, "Sir, I know you've been through a lot, but we got this."

"You ever been shot at?"

The question seemed to fluster him as he said more loudly, "I can drag you outta here but I'd rather not."

"How the fuck'd you guys get here so fast?" The arrival of gun ships so soon after the beginning of the firefight had me questioning the motives and affiliation of these guys, no matter how legitimate they seemed.

"We've been code red all week. We're stationed at the Wood and it's only fifty miles from here." Fort Leonard Wood, a major Army training center, was about that far as the crow flies.

"You got some credentials?"

Through his camo painted face the incredulity that I would even ask was apparent. "Mr. Cones, I understand your fears, but you are the reason why we were code red and why we were able to get here so fast. We'll get you out of here and safe."

Safe? What does that mean? My definition of that had certainly changed in the past couple weeks. Knowing there was a whole other team, plus John and maybe a fifth voice I'd heard still out there didn't allow me the luxury of feeling safe. These soldiers may be fully capable, but I knew he didn't quite comprehend the danger they were in. Maybe he was underestimating these guys by the mere fact we'd been lucky enough to eliminate some of them. "Where's extraction point A?"

"Down on the gravel bar below the bluff."

"No fucking way am I going down there. Any one with a scope would have an easy time picking me off from anywhere along the bluff. This is the third time these guys have tried to kill or capture me, case you didn't know. There's at least six more out there unless you guys have found 'em. Have you found 'em?"

No shots had sounded since they'd landed and I sure couldn't picture my adversaries surrendering. Adam looked at me and said, "We'll have a hundred men on the ground in the next half hour. If there's more of them out there we'll get 'em. I have orders to get you outta here, and that means I'm going to. We got the top of the bluff covered. Now, let's move."

He tried to grab my arm again but I pulled back and said, "Give me my rifle back and I'll go with you. Otherwise you're gonna have to drag me."

The three other soldiers that had approached me with him were spread out around us, intently surveying the forest for threats. One chortled briefly at my statement, Adam flashing a look of anger in his direction then saying, “Mr. Cones, I’m not authorized to allow civilians to carry weapons.”

“Civilian? What the fuck you think I been doin’? Ain’t your buddies even found the fuckin’ corpses all over this damn hillside?”

Adam was starting to steam but I didn’t give a damn. Two weeks ago I certainly would have followed his orders out of respect for his training and authority alone. Without the rifle I felt vulnerable and helpless, even with these soldiers around me. I’d been through more actual fighting, at least recently, than these guys and figured I’d done alright considering everything. George, Dan and Beth had put themselves in harms way because of me, and I decided right then that there was no way I was going to jump on a helicopter and fly out of here without at least finding out how they were.

CHAPTER FORTY ONE

"The guy's wife that's down there headed up the valley back to their truck. I think the third team came in from that direction. I'll go with you if we head that way."

"You'll go where we say." At that he reached down and grabbed my right arm again, pulling on it with more force than he'd used the last time. As I pulled back from him two shots echoed down the valley, sounding like they came from about where I'd first seen the party stalking up the bank. He dropped me back down, the sound of the second set of choppers nearing the other side of the creek filling the shots void quickly. The much louder sound of two explosions took away the choppers sound momentarily, then a burst of automatic fire from several guns erupted.

The firing died off quickly, Adam saying, "Seven, come in." as he scooted towards a firing position overlooking the hillside. "Five, what are you seeing?" He listened for a few seconds, then said, "Charlie, what's your position."

I could no longer see any of his team, they seeming to have evaporated within seconds after the first shot. I pushed myself up and slowly worked my way, mostly sliding on my butt, downhill towards Adam. He heard me and turned around from his almost prone position, trying to gesture me to stay put. One more shot rang out as I stopped my slide with my foot on the barely protruding outcrop Adam was hunkered behind. I looked all around not paying attention to his glare before I finished my ten second sweep of the hillside.

He had taken my rifle off his shoulder and set it down on the other side of the boulder. As I gazed back at him after finishing my sweep, I started saying, "Give me . . .", but he was already grabbing it. He was facing downhill so he swept it around his back with his left arm to hand it to me. My left arm wasn't working too well, and after grabbing the barrel I kind of clonked him in the head with the stock. He didn't flinch, much, as I said, "What's the word?"

He glanced back over his right shoulder at me with a weird look, anger part of it, but perhaps affirmation and respect mixed in. He whispered, "We got two down," handed me my spare cartridge sleeves, then turned his attention back downhill.

I whispered, "Binoculars" and he handed me his. The steepness of the slope allowed me a nearly 180 degree field of view above my bench, blocked only by the few trees. After panning the hillside and valley floor I handed the binoculars back whispering, "Can't see anybody. Where's the guys from the second chopper?"

Pointing with his fingers, he gestured that they were coming from the river along the bluff, then held up two fingers and pointed them towards the cave. Getting myself ready to move I said, "I'm gonna see if I c'n help George. I'm heading down."

Adam said, "Stay here!" but I didn't stop. I half slid and half walked down to the next outcrop hearing Adam order the other soldiers to cover us as he followed me. Trying to use the trees and boulders as cover, we made it to the top of the ledge about fifty yards from the chute. After scooting to the front edge, Adam began glassing the bottom and I headed towards the cave.

At the boulders above the chute I stopped and glanced down, seeing a body sprawled at the bottom. Faintly whistling I began approaching the cave and saw the body of Rock laying across my fishing line, his head a bloody mass. A soldier was at the south end of the bench behind the parapet watching me as I got close and whispered, "It's Cones," before entering the cave. Pollitt was laying on the bed with a soldier working on him, and Dan was peering out the back of the cave, the shotgun pointed uphill.

He looked at me, jaw set and eyes hard, saying, "How many of 'em were there?"

"Four or five in that group but there's another bunch that musta come in from the road. I heard the leader talking to 'em before I shot him and another one."

"One of 'em fell down to right above here. I thought it was you till I heard that last shot you took. I was takin' a peek out front when I heard the alarm go off and that big dude was looking down at it when I damn near blew his head off."

The soldier turned towards me and said, "I've done all I can to stop the bleeding and gave him some morphine. Did you get any idea how many more of them there might be?"

"I don't know . . . . maybe I'd guess five or six but there was twenty or so last week. Makes it kinda hard to guess."

Bloody bandages and wrappers littered the floor in front of the bed and George looked deathly white, his body twitching as I stepped closer. Dan got up and headed towards us as Adam, whistling softly, poked his head in. “Marco, can he be moved?” he asked the other soldier.

“Not till we get some plasma in him. He’s lost a lot of blood.”

“Charlie’s comin’ down the hill now and D is gonna stay up top. Me and Alpha’re headin’ down when they get here. Stay here with Nathan. We’ll have an evac team here in ten.”

Adam backed up and turned around without another word. I looked at Marco expecting some kind of order or something, but he just turned back towards George. I figured until the immediate situation was resolved I wasn’t a civilian, at least in their minds anymore, and I sure wasn’t Army, but the sudden change from protected to ignored caught my attention. Adam’s orders must certainly have been altered for him to not even say a word to me in the exchange. I said softly, “There was maybe a couple of ’em that were still up top. Did your other team run into them guys?”

Marco said, “We got four guys up top right now. Ain’t nobody gonna get to this cave.”

The bravado and assurances were starting to wear thin. “Did they fucking find them or not?” I just wanted a straight answer.

“No, they didn’t”

I looked at Dan, his face a mask of stoic determination as he looked back towards me and said, “I gotta find Beth!”

Marco turned around and said, "We have three companies enroute. One of them is landing about where you put in. If the truck is still there, they'll find her. We'll task a bird for that if it isn't."

Marco got up and put his hand on Dan's bare shoulder as he finished, the blood from George leaving a faint handprint as Dan pulled away. Turning and staring at Marco he said, "I'll meet 'em. Tell them I'm coming."

Dan turned and after a quick glance at me, his face showing no change, headed out onto the bench. I followed him to the entrance saying, "They'll find her" and reaching out to grab his arm but he was already moving. As I quickly slung the rifle and ammo bag, Marco grabbed my arm and said, "Stay right here. Nathan will get him."

"That guy saved my life less than an hour ago. Let go of me. I'll try to get him back."

Marco gave me a resigned look, then let go of my arm saying, "Hold your fire. Cones and Strauss are heading up the valley." as I headed after Dan.

Nathan got up from his perch and began following us saying, "Stay there. Hold it. Hold up."

Not turning around or paying any attention to Nathan I tried to catch up with Dan, already past the chute and following the back edge of the ledge top at a quick pace. I hoarsely yelled, "WAIT UP."

Dan stopped and turned around, his arms swinging the shotgun back and forth and eyes wild as he impatiently waited for me to catch up. As I did he said, "I shoulda gone with her. I was running away with her till I remembered I had all your ammo."

I sure couldn't have blamed him. He'd saved my life because he hadn't run away, and I wasn't going to abandon him now.

"I'll help you find her. Let's get our shit together first."

Reaching into the bag, I started handing him shotgun shells as Nathan caught up and took cover behind the ledge. After glancing around he said, "Mr. Strauss, we'll find your wife. You're going to make it a lot harder on us if we gotta hold fire cause it might be you."

Eyes still wild, Dan seemed torn between that logic and fear for his wife's safety. I guess fear won out because after a few seconds he abruptly turned and headed away. Nathan said, "Shit." and stood up from behind the ledge. He hadn't taken a step before he began falling and the report of a shot echoed. I had been turning to follow Dan and just kind of froze as blood began spurting from the side of Nathan's neck.

CHAPTER FORTY TWO

After a moment of vacillation and shock I slid down the ten feet to Nathan and pressed my hand over the large furrow in his skin, looking for Dan as Nathan's blood welled between my fingers. A fusillade of automatic weapon fire from above us began shredding the leaf canopy. The whiz of rounds directly over my head made me flatten out as I tried to stem the flow from Nathan's neck.

A chatter of fire rang out from close by and turning towards it I saw Marco aiming over the edge forty feet away. He quickly ran in a crouch towards us after firing, sliding rock from above announcing the arrival of two other soldiers as Marco flung him self down and tore a pouch off Nathan's web belt. After pulling out bandages, he grabbed my bloody hand and raised it off Nathan's neck. Wiping away the spurting blood to get a quick look at the wound he said, "SHIT!" as he saw the damage.

After quickly sprinkling some powder then placing a large gauze pad over the furrow and pressing down hard he yelled, "HOLD THIS" to me as he got a gauze roll ready. I pressed down for a few seconds then he began quickly wrapping rolled gauze around Nathan's neck, the shattering sounds of grenades thrown by the new arrivals not seeming to affect him as he completed the job.

One of them asked, "How bad is it?" the instantly soaked gauze answering his question as he looked towards us. I wiped my right hand off on a bed of moss, congealing blood already making my fingers sticky. Dan had stopped during the firing, but looking up I saw him scrambling uphill as I grabbed the rifle and prepared to follow him.

The violence of media images can never prepare the mind for the actuality of combat. Till now I'd been running on adrenaline, the carnage I'd caused and witnessed seemingly having little effect on my conscience or ability to act. I made two scrambling steps uphill before Marco grabbed my foot and pulled me back down next to Nathan. "STAY THE FUCK RIGHT THERE!" he screamed as a flurry of shots erupted from the valley below. Looking up, I saw Dan disappearing over the top of the hill, shirtless, blood stained and charging like a linebacker.

The history of humanity has largely been written about the conflicts of man versus man. The power struggles of the groups and nations of the world have always thrust their people into the fray, usually touting god or country as being just cause for average citizens to lay down their lives. Every civilization has extolled the virtues of its' warriors and perpetrated the thought in the mind of the average man that war is a necessary evil in human relationships. Glorification of war over the centuries has allowed the human psyche to accept this as the norm.

We all are made to believe from an early age that it's 'Us' against the 'World', the 'World' being the world of humans outside our 'Circle'. Though the teachings of all major religions espouse war and hatred, more wars have been fought in the name of religion than for any other reason. We, as humans, are our own worst enemies and by far the Earth's worst if viewed in the collective eyes of all its' millions of other species.

Shows about dangerous wildlife, the never ceasing climactic shifts of the earth and other natural calamities allow us to view other entities of the planet as more serious threats to our safety and well being. Truthful as accounts of these dangers are, historically they are almost insignificant compared to the proven ability and willingness of man to exterminate his own kind. To what end?

The daily scrabblings of humans leave little time to ponder the perpetuity of mankind beyond their own circle. Even in this age of democracy and knowledge we elect leaders largely based upon their perceived ability to provide us with the most immediate comfort, not their ability to perhaps make the world a better place for generations to come. Egotism, self advancement and prejudice rule our minds, even most of the 'enlightened' of the centuries exhibiting traces in their teachings.

Only in recent times has the welfare of the planet as a whole even been considered in our never ending battle for dominance of its resources. The squandering of these myriad resources through war and greed, human lives and potential included, has deprived every civilization of minds and materials. These resources, put to better use, certainly would have advanced the cause of humanity far more than the rusting machines of war littering parts of the world to this day. Maybe that's just the way it is and always will be.

Looking into Nathan's eyes as he clung to life while the warriors around me slugged it out for no good reason, I suddenly decided my own life wasn't worth the cost. I was just another man, another cog in the ever spinning wheel of life and death. Better men than I had already died to protect me, and I didn't even know why I was still alive. Maybe this was the bottom, the time to get sucked into the vortex of fate. Maybe that would end all this. Maybe.

A chopper mounted Gatling Gun began tearing up the valley floor though no other shots had been fired for thirty seconds or so. The crescendo of sound brought me out of my stupor. I grabbed Nathan's suddenly outstretched hand as Marco scooted back down beside us and said, "Hang in there buddy. We're gonna get you outta here."

Nathan's eyes were wide open and looking right at me as his grip went slack. Marco began CPR almost immediately, but I'd seen the life go out and knew he was just going through the motions. I held on for another few seconds then gently placed Nathan's hand on his chest. Had I not followed Dan, he would still be alive. I killed him. I killed them all, good and bad. Had I just let the woman drown nobody else would have died.

CHAPTER FORTY THREE

The other two soldiers began heading into the valley as more zipped down from choppers at the top of the hill. The air was alive with the sounds of helicopters coming from every direction. Marco gently closed Nathan's eyes and stood up as a cadre of soldiers advanced down the hill towards us. A group of four headed towards the cave as a much older officer and twenty or so soldiers reached our level. Everyone but the officer spread out along the ledge top. He looked at me and asked, "Are you Mitch Cones?"

I looked back at him, his chastising expression reminding me of my recent like thoughts about myself.

"Yeah"

Glaring at me he said, "You sure have caused a mess. What the hell you doing way out here?"

"Just trying to stay alive."

Looking down at the body of Nathan he asked, "Is he gone?" Marco just shook his head, then the officer turned back to me and said, "Well at least YOU succeeded at that. hmph."

As if I wasn't feeling guilty enough already.

He turned to Marco and said, "Go see if you can give them a hand with the detective. I need to talk to Mr. Cones here for a minute before we evac him." Marco wagged his two fingers in a brief acknowledgment of the order then headed towards the cave.

The emotions running through my brain at that time were so conflicting that I didn't know what was going to come out of my mouth next. The greater part of me was still totally remorseful but part of me was thinking, "How dare you!"

He turned to the closest soldier and said, "Sergeant, take your squad on down. C company's in the bottom already." The soldier complied, waving his hand down at the other men spread out farther up the valley. He then turned to the guy closest to us in the other direction and said, "Go set up a perimeter around the cave till they are ready to move the detective." The men with him began moving towards the bench as the officer looked back at me, his face now impassive.

After scrutinizing me for a few seconds he finally said, "Did you really think you could just hide out here and everything would go away? Nah . . . never mind. What do you know about the disc? Why'd you hide it?"

Ah. Now his enmity was making sense. "I didn't hide it. I never knew I had it till George found it in my back pocket. He just said I hid it to give him an excuse to search my wife's car again and act like he'd just found it."

I immediately regretted saying that, since it could get George, O'Brien and even Sanchez in lots of trouble, assuming George lived through this to face it.

"You telling me you never had your hands on it and don't know anything about it? That's kind of hard to believe. Why have these guys gone to such great lengths to find you then?"

"They think I was told some kind of password or something about it by the woman I pulled out of the river. What the hell is so damn important about that disc anyway? Do you know?"

He was staring at the ground shaking his head, seemingly deflated by my professed ignorance of the contents of the disc. "What a waste. If you'd just come in none of this shit would have happened and that boy there and a bunch of others like him wouldn't have even been here." He looked back up at me with nothing but contempt saying, "If I didn't have strict orders to get you out of here, I'd just let you stay here and rot."

Taken aback for a second by his statement, I finally blew up and shouted, "You know what, FUCK YOU! You don't have any fucking idea what I've gone through and you ain't got no right to talk to me like that, I don't care who the fuck you think you are. Leave me here. I don't give a shit anymore. Take your fucking troops and get the hell out of here."

I didn't see the punch coming but it knocked me down. I fell towards the steep uphill side on my back and he stood over my feet, putting his hand on his holster as his eyes bulged with fury. I guess he never got talked to that way and sure didn't know how to handle it. He made a motion to pull the pistol out, his hand grasping the butt. I was so pissed I just cocked my right foot back and drove it with all my might towards his crotch, catching him square in the gonads. The slope of the hill helped launch him towards the flat ledge five feet below, his head glancing off a rock as he sprawled out in an inert heap.

Shit, what have I done now! I looked around quickly wondering what the other soldiers would do but none were still in sight. After sliding down to him, I pulled his face out of the dirt. His hat had flown off and a large bloody welt was running across the left side of his close cropped head. He was unconscious but still breathing as my once again churning brain tried to figure out what the hell to do now.

I'd figured he was going to shoot me and knew I'd acted in self defense, but that probably wouldn't be the story he told when and if he came to. Who were they going to believe? Should I call the other soldiers to help or just try to get the hell out of here?

CHAPTER FORTY FOUR

The sound of moving men took the second option away as two ghillie suited soldiers suddenly appeared next to me. Both looked grim and determined as they pulled me up and away from the prostrate officer. I figured they were just going to let me have it. Instead, they let go of me and one grabbed the officer's head, tearing out bandages then pressing them to the wound. The other began pulling him to a less awkward position as the first one turned to me and said, "We saw and heard the whole thing but that probably won't help you much when this spook wakes up. I do believe he was getting ready to shoot your ass."

The other soldier was nodding his head in agreement. They both had scoped and camouflaged rifles so I figured they probably had gotten a clear view of the episode.

"Is he gonna live?"

"Aw, hard headed as this dick is he'll probably be waking up any time now. We don't even know who he is but we've had to listen to his crap ever since he showed up at the base. We just were told to call him Mr. Smith."

The somewhat flippant salute that Marco had given him came to mind as I realized that these soldiers had no love for 'Mr. Smith'.

"You guys willing to tell everybody what you saw? I didn't want none of this shit to happen and you guys are the only ones who knows I was just protecting myself."

They both looked at each other for a bit then the second said, "It probably won't matter. This guy had full rights to you. You'd have been out of here and long gone in another twenty minutes."

The mike on Mr. Smith began chirping. They looked at it and the first one held his hand up in a hold everything kind of gesture as its' incessant beep continued. Finally he picked it up and said, "Mr. Smith has had an accident."

He listened for a while then said, "No, he was gone when we found Mr. Smith."

The expletives were easy to understand as the guy on the other end of the com ranted for thirty seconds. The soldier held the earpiece away a bit as he listened to the diatribe, finally saying, "This is lance corporal Sheldon Breathwaite. Roger. Will try to reacquire Cones."

Huh? After listening for a while longer he said, "Yes, acknowledge, over and out." Sheldon turned towards me and putting his fingers to his lips first in a keep it quiet kind of sign whispered, "Was all that stuff you told Mr. Smith true? I mean about you not knowing shit about what was on the disc or why all this shit has been happening?"

"Swear to god, I ain't got no idea what's on the disc besides what George told me about it being some kind of algorithm. I just been trying to keep them fuckers from killing me or my family and I figured disappearing was the best way."

"How do you think they found you?"

"Shit, I don't really know, but I think they probably bugged George's phone or somehow followed him here. They showed up real soon after he did this afternoon, maybe too soon. They had the boats and everything so they must have been waiting close by already and were trying to catch us both. I heard one of them say something about a signal so maybe they planted a tracking device on George and used that."

The possibilities were damn near endless but I knew now I had once again seriously underestimated their ingenuity and resolve. Mr. Smith had seemed ready to execute me, whether because I just pissed him off or because he had orders to. Which was it? I had to believe it was sanctioned even if his anger had only caused him to expedite those orders. Those same orders were obviously not given to the rest of the soldiers. Whoever he worked for must have decided that in the event I was useless to the deciphering of the disc, my existence became a liability to them.

Sheldon said, "They'll have this area satellite tasked in awhile. Then yours and our options will be gone. I couldn't tell them we saw everything because we would've had to hold you till another spook gets here or Mr. Smith wakes up. What you think, Stew?"

Stew looked at me and said, "Whether he wakes up or don't, I wouldn't give two cents for your chances right now. You think you can get away if we give you a head start?"

"From you guys? I doubt it, but I'll take my chances. How long do I get?"

"Till Mr. Smith wakes up or another spook gets here." Sheldon handed me a couple MRE's and his canteen, then bent down and picked up my rifle. Handing it to me he said, "Don't shoot any soldiers or we WILL hunt your ass down. Get going and head that way." He pointed northeast towards the top of the ridge behind us. "If you get caught, we never saw you and don't try to say we did. Or, you can stay here and we'll say you came back on your own, take your pick."

I said, "Thanks," throwing the rifle on my shoulder. I glanced down at Mr. Smith to be sure he was still out then began hurrying along the top of the ledge. After a hundred yards I looked back towards the snipers, half thinking they may just plug me when I got far enough away to cover their lie to Mr. Smith's cohorts. I couldn't see them and kept moving as quickly as possible up the valley, hoping I didn't run into any other soldiers.

CHAPTER FORTY FIVE

A steep but shallow draw led to the top of the hill after a couple hundred yards. I headed up it, trying to walk as quietly as possible now that I was pretty sure Sheldon and Stew hadn't just jerked me around. Topping out along the ridge, I spent thirty seconds or so catching my breath and looking for any sign of other people. Seeing no one and hearing no sounds other than helicopters and the indistinct shouting of men in the far below valley, I began running away from Big Creek.

Following the contours of the hills and crossing a few valleys, after miles without stopping a much deeper and wider valley loomed below. I was beyond played out, my lungs hurting and my body shaking as I stopped for a breather behind some rocks. The complexity of my new predicament was too hard to even ponder, but resting there I gave it a shot anyway.

How hard would the Army or the CIA or whoever Mr. Smith worked for try to find me? As hard as the bad guys? Probably. Or were they in fact the same or at least in cahoots with each other? Maybe. How long could I last out here without the benefit of any other help or a cache of supplies and equipment? I guess I'll see.

My hastily arrived at conclusion was that only by not being found by either group did I stand a chance of continuing living. The fact that I'd given up momentarily the burning desire to do so after seeing Nathan die was ignored. Take it from the here and now. First off, get as far away as possible. Planning on running all night I headed up the side valley along the hill top.

It was about five o'clock and the suns rays were already behind the hill above me as I stopped at an outcrop a couple miles up the valley and scoped the creek bottom below. Only the gurgling stream and distant thrum of helicopters broke the stillness as I slowly headed downhill. I'd long ago finished the canteen of Gatorade Sheldon had given me. Bending over the swift stream filling it back up a splash directed my gaze downstream.

After getting behind a clump of willows growing out into the gravel, I peered through the thick foliage. A man suddenly appeared, coming around the bend of the stream about eighty yards away. Clutching an assault rifle in the ready position he was looking intently all around as he ran through the shallow water of the rocky streambed.

No other sounds or movements indicated the presence of other men. His camo didn't match anything the soldiers had been wearing, so this must be John or the other guy I'd heard at the top of the cliff. He would be ten feet away from me in less than a minute. I pointed the rifle at the spot where he'd round the willow clump, ruing the timing of my trip to the stream. Having no choice but to shoot him as I saw it, I somewhat shakily tried to hold the gun steady with both hands.

The rapidly nearing splashes allowed me to judge his distance. At the first instant he cleared the willows, I fired. The bullet hit him just above his left elbow, smashing into his rifle after it passed through. His rifle flew into the stream as he spun away from me.

Holding my rifle on him I walked towards him. Eyes flashing back and forth as his mouth opened in spasmodic grimaces, he looked towards me and down at his assault rifle laying five feet away underwater. His right hand was clasped over his left arm, the angle of it indicating the bone had been shattered as blood dripped steadily into the stream. He let go of his left arm trying to grab his pistol, but slipped and collapsed into the water instead. I had been a split second away from pulling the trigger again but as he landed on his face hard I just kept the rifle pointed and ready.

I walked around him as he lay there trying to push his face above the eight inch deep water. his hand slipping on the mossy rock. Reaching the assault rifle I stood there and watched as he struggled to push himself up with his right hand. His injury was different and worse but it immediately reminded me of my own attempts to rise after falling on top of the four wheeler driver. I thought he might just drown and I was going to let him. He kept trying and finally pushed himself up with his feet and good hand after a couple of stabs at it. Trying to stand he slipped again, but was able to roll onto his back, gasping for air.

The swift, shallow water was carrying him slowly downstream as I walked closer to him. He made a clumsy move towards the holster on his belt. Seeing this I attempted to stomp my boot down on his right hand, saying, "Oh, no you don't!" He tried to grab my foot, still having some fight left. Evading his grasp I drove my boot into his right side, then stomped it again and again onto his right hand and forearm. On about the sixth stomp I heard the wrist snap as it passed over a high spot in the bedrock.

Stepping back I pointed the rifle at him. I could have easily shot him again before this, but was trying to avoid the sound that would make. In rolling hills one sudden shot is hard to get a vector on, but the second allows the ear to determine direction much more assuredly. I didn't want to give any more help to my possible pursuers than I already had.

He hadn't said anything resembling a word yet but as he pulled his shattered hand in he blubbered out, "Fer crissake just kill me."

His plea had the opposite effect on me. I realized I needed him to stay alive, at least till I could get some information from him. His right hand was folded over and touching his forearm and his left arm was leaving a large v shape of pink water as his blood mingled with the current. He was no longer any threat to me.

Setting my rifle down on the bank, I waded back out to him and grabbing him by the collar of his jacket dragged him up onto the gravel. After getting him out of the water I stood over him and said, "You want me to kill you, huh?"

He might have been one tough dude five minutes ago but now he was cringing and pathetic. Reaching down to pull the pistol out of his holster, he made an instinctive move to stop me with his right hand. The pain from the attempt as the shattered wrist made only slight contact with my forearm caused him to finally let out a loud gargled AAAGGH of pain. I grabbed his pistol out of the holster, pointing it at his head.

"I'll be happy to oblige ya' but first you're going to answer some questions."

His body spasmed with pain and his teeth were chattering from his immersion in the cold stream. He actually looked quite pitiful, but I felt no mercy towards him.

"Who do you work for? Why have you and your buddies been trying to get me?"

His eyes opened wide at that, because he only right then realized who I was. "Ya . . . ya . . . ya . . . you ca . . . ca . . . Cones?"

"That's right. I'm the guy you was sent to kill. Why?"

He leaned his head back onto the gravel, closing his eyes as he began half laughing then proceeded to coughing. As he quit coughing, he said, "Na . . not kill. They ne. need ya. you alive."

"Who is they?"

He closed his eyes and shook his head slightly as if to say, "I'm not going to tell you."

While he stewed it over I began taking all his equipment off him and searching his pockets for clues. He had a lighter, a few bills and a small folded piece of paper in his pocket. Unfolding it I saw four series of eight numbers written in pencil.

He was carrying a small backpack. Ignoring his obvious pain, I rolled him over and pulled it off his destroyed arms. I emptied it on the gravel next to the rest of his stuff and checked out its' contents. Between his belt and backpack there were laminated contour maps of the area, spare clips for his pistol and assault rifle, a six inch K-bar knife, high quality binoculars, a GPS device, a quart sized water bottle, a compass, five juice boxes, nine energy bars, a half pound of beef jerky, a packaged lightweight camo poncho, headset and a spare battery, a small flashlight, waterproof matches, a small fold up first aid kit, a packet of various pills, some rolled up twine and rope, eight zip ties and a space blanket. Quite a score for me.

Whether I killed him or not I needed all his stuff to give me a better chance of living through this myself. After checking it all out I said, "You ready to answer me or not?" He shook his head no as defiantly as he could muster. I put my foot on his left elbow and began twisting it and he finally howled with pain. Taking my boot away I said, "Dude, I'll fuckin' tie you up and let the damn coyotes or bears eat you alive if you don't start talking."

The sudden fear apparent in his eyes showed I'd hit a weak spot in his macho facade. He was looking at me as if to determine my sincerity and I just shook my head up and down to confirm it. I said, "You ain't never gonna be even found, so why don't you save yourself a lot of pain and tell me what you know. And if you want to live, I'll even patch you up a bit and let you go if I think you're telling me the truth."

His teeth had stopped chattering and he seemed to be weighing his options as I started repacking the backpack. "Ban'age up my arms an' give me some of them pink pills and I'll tell ya'."

He knew he couldn't help himself once I left. Maybe the thought of being eaten didn't sit well with him, though I'd never heard of humans being eaten by either bears or coyotes in Missouri. Whatever his reasoning for talking didn't matter to me anyways.

"Okay, but you better make it quick. I need to be gone in five minutes." I opened up the pill packet and asked, "What are these?" There were eight of them in the packet, too many to believe they were poison or something designed to kill.

In much more gargled words he said, "They're pain killers mixed with an antibiotic."

"How many you want?"

"Ta . . . two now . . . . and two more to keep."

I wondered how he'd manage to take the second two but didn't really care. Pulling two out, I put them in his mouth and held the canteen to his lips to wash them down. After sticking the second two in the poncho case and then tucking them in his jacket pocket I started opening the first aid kit saying, "So, who's after me?"

After coughing a few times he said in barely understandable words, "That woman you saved is a mathematical genius from Bulgaria. Her name is Marlene Kasmarov. She was developing an algorithm for a German company. I don't know what it was supposed to do, but they snatched her a year ago and made her keep working on it."

Thinking back on her garbled words and my inability to understand them, I realized it could have been only because of her accent. The few things I had understood had come out clipped, the sign of a second language, or in her case, maybe third or tenth language.

Using the razor sharp K-bar I cut off his left jacket and shirt sleeves at the shoulder, then pulled them down over the arm. He quit talking and gritted his teeth, groaning at the pain of moving his arm around. After exposing it I looked at his mangled upper arm. The fibula was shattered two inches above his elbow. Blood was still flowing freely from the wound and small pieces of bone were stuck to the inside of his sleeve next to the exit hole of the bullet. I stopped and said, "I ain't got all day."

He coughed a couple times, then haltingly choked out, "She's one smart bitch, cause she fooled them into thinking she would finish it willingly for a hefty price or wouldn't finish it at all. They agreed, but when it was done, I imagine she would have just disappeared. Well, somehow she encrypted it then killed her guard and his girlfriend that were holding her. I was one of the guys that found the mess she left. She stabbed Hank in the eye with a pen and it was still in him, buried all the way. She must have left with Sarah, but we got word she'd been found in the river."

I shook my a head a bit at this and said, "Damn, I knew she was trouble. I've been having nightmares about that bitch ever since."

"She took us all by surprise. I was watching her the week before and I thought she was just a bookworm. She was always so polite, we just had to make sure she kept working. She even seemed happy about it."

Grabbing a handful of moss from a crevasse of the rocks by the stream, I wiped the worst of the blood off and packed the moss around the wound, wrapping gauze around it to hold it in place. He didn't question my doctoring, just watched me amazingly quietly as I tied the shirt sleeve over the gauze then looked at his right arm. Both bones were broken, the ulna barely piercing the skin and revealing a jagged edge after I cut off the sleeves. Leaving him lying, I cut off two foot and a half long by inch thick willow splints. He endured the pain better than I would have as I tried to straighten out his arm, bandaged the puncture wound then wrapped his arm with gauze and the shirt sleeve. I finished by putting the splints on and binding them with pieces of twine from the pack. I hadn't expected him to be very talkative during this quick, painful and improvisational fix, but thirty seconds later I asked, "Who is them?"

"Shit, I don't know any names, just that they are a group of rich and powerful bastards that call themselves the 'Inner Circle'."

"Why in the hell do they need me? I don't know shit about that kinda stuff."

"The encryption code to the disc was protected by a Fibonacci sequence. She gave you the disc and the key to the sequence, at least that's what she told them. She thought she'd managed to delete all other traces of the finished algorithm but the computer she worked on it from had an undetectable mole built in. They have the algorithm but without the key it'll take them years to break the encryption, if ever. You're never gonna be able to quit running."

"Why don't they just make her tell them the key? You guys got her, don't you?"

"I told you she's one smart bitch. She gave them a wrong key and while they were checking it out she either bribed or fooled the four guys who grabbed her they'd be better off if they got her away, at least that's what it looks like. I guess they figured they'd rather not share because we haven't found any of them yet. Grabbing you became the only way to get the key."

"What the hell's a Fibonacci sequence."

"It's a mathematical progression that goes forwards or backwards or both, the turn around points being the only important numbers."

"And what would a key to one of them look or sound like. I didn't understand shit that she was saying when I was pulling her out of the river."

"It could be anything. You don't think she tried to tell you something like that?"

"I think she did, but it was so noisy I didn't hear her. She asked me if I had it and I said yes but I sure didn't know what she was talking about."

"Fucking figures. I told them we were probably on a wild goose chase but the money they were putting out was too much to pass up."

"Was it worth it?"

"Not now. Even if you don't kill me, I'm probably gonna be a fucking cripple for life, and at the beginning I thought this job was easy money."

I was almost beginning to like this guy, but not enough to trust him or help him any further. Everybody's gotta pay the piper. "How'd you guys find me?"

"We bugged the phones of everybody on your family list and all the cops you'd been with that we could. We heard George talking to you and got a rough fix on your location from that on Wednesday. When he told you he was coming down here today we put a tracking device on his truck."

"How many more of you guys are there?"

"Shit, I don't even know. The only thing I do know is that the 'Inner Circle' has been doing this kind of shit all over the world for decades now. We were just one of their cells that were paid to always be ready for anything they threw our way. The pay for this job was a quarter million per man, but each cell divides up the total between the guys that live to collect after the job is done. I guess they figure that'll keep the rest of us at it if the shit hits the fan."

"You still want me to kill you?"

He snorted a laugh out, pretty impressive considering his condition, and said, "No thanks, I'll take my chances elsewhere. You mind answering a question for me?"

"Depends what it is."

"Why you out here by yourself? I was watching when the choppers came in. Another five minutes and I'd have had you."

"Or maybe I'd have had you. Seems maybe some of your Inner circle guys have somebody helping them on the inside. Some fucking CIA dude or something like that was gonna waste my ass right after they showed up. That's why I took off . . . . Can't trust fucking nobody these days . . . . What's your name?"

He looked at me for a few seconds then said, “John Shaw.”

“Well, John Shaw, I’d shake your hand for the info but I doubt you want me doing that. If you ever get back with the ‘Inner circle gang’, do me a favor and tell them I don’t know shit.”

The five minutes had stretched into twenty five and getting out of there become my next mission. I stood up and started arranging all his stuff to carry then walked over and picked up the assault rifle out of the stream, debating whether to keep it or the .270. The .270 won out if only because of the bullet ding above the trigger guard on his A-15.

I knew he wouldn’t be able to use the assault rifle, even if it still worked, but wondered if I should disable it anyway. That might take noise I really didn’t want to make, so I carried it into the woods a few yards and buried it and the clips under a rotting fallen tree. Coming back out into the stream bed, I threw the pack and my rifle on my right shoulder and glanced at John. He was watching me with a resigned look, maybe thinking I was the last human he would ever see or talk to.

He said, “Can you help me stand up?”

Suddenly thinking about the numbers on the slip of paper in his pocket I said, “I will if you tell me what these numbers are for.”

I dug out the slip and showed it to him. “Them’s the coordinates of our extraction points if we had you and if we didn’t.”

“Which ones are which?”

"The first ones for if we got you and you were alive. The rest are if we didn't"

"You think anybody'll be there considering how this shit went down?"

"I kind of doubt it, but that's where I was headed."

"Show me where they are on this map."

I took the pack off and dug the map out. Realizing he wasn't going to be able to point at them, I pointed at the map and said, "Tell me which way to move my finger." The first was a few miles behind us and the others were by Route B and Route 21 north of Ellington, about five and ten miles to the east of our position.

I still didn't figure I really owed him anything but got behind him and helped pull him onto his feet anyway. He groaned a bit but didn't say another word as I turned around and headed upstream. When I was about fifty yards away I heard him say, "Good luck" but I just kept walking into the unknown.

CHAPTER FORTY SIX

Twilight had long ago turned to darkness as I climbed out of the creek bottom and angled up the hillside. Thinking about everything John had said as I'd furtively followed the valley floor, I'd completed another three or four miles of distancing myself from the day's action. Climbing a set of rocky steps I slipped and came down hard, my knees hitting the rocks. Beat and bedraggled, and not wanting to injure myself further stumbling in the dark, I found a level mossy spot and set down my pack and rifle, digging out the space blanket. After drinking a juice box and eating some jerky the longest day of my life concluded within seconds after laying down on the surprisingly soft bed of reindeer moss.

I awoke the next morning to the sounds of people calling my name from the valley below. It was just getting faintly light and the still far off voices were yelling, "CONES, MITCH CONES" every fifteen seconds or so. I folded up the space blanket, not wanting it's reflective glare to give my location away. My shoulder was aching from sleeping on it. Taking a calculated chance I ate one of the pink pills, washing it down with a juice box. Quietly I got my pack situated and prepared to continue my flight.

The rocky forest floor seemed impossible to track across, for I had been careful about my foot placement throughout my flight from Big Creek, but it seemed whoever was in the valley had somehow managed to do so. Or maybe they had people scouring the whole area for me. I surmised it was probably the latter since if they could track me they wouldn't need to be yelling my name. That meant there were probably soldiers spread throughout the area. Marco had said they were bringing in three companies but many more could be called upon. At least three hundred people then.

If they were calling for me it meant they probably weren't going to shoot on sight or at all. The big question was whether I'd be given straight to the likes of Mr. Smith after they got me out of the woods, and if so, would that be worse than not being found at all. The voices were drawing nearer and I had to make a decision quick, at least if I still wanted to remain on the loose. If the old saying, 'between a rock and a hard place' had ever applied to a decision in my life it was right then. I was so far over my head in this already that I knew there was no way to be sure which was the right course of action.

"Should I stay or should I go now," the old song by 'The Clash,' popped into my head. I'd always had a weird habit of pertinent lyrics doing that. "If I go there will be trouble, but if I stay it will be double." The next line actually made up my mind for me. No less sure than flipping a coin, and I'd used that method countless times when the choice between options had been too close to call. Maybe song lyrics weren't the best way to arrive at so important of a decision but it was certainly the clincher in this case.

Taking one last look down the valley floor to make sure nobody was in sight, I headed to the top of the ridge and took a compass bearing. As I'd shown John the topographic map I'd figured out about where I was. The valley ran almost due north and I continued along the top of the ridge through open forest moving with as much speed as possible.

After a mile I came to a forest road. Digging the map back out, I figured this was forest road P-232. I could no longer hear anyone yelling my name, although I'd heard it faintly from the valley on the east as I'd been running up the ridge top. Maybe I'd gone far enough to get out of their search grid.

I'd been questioning my decision to remain on the lamb mostly because I was just tired of running in both senses of the word. The information I'd gotten from John, assuming as I did that it was all true, might be enough to keep Mr. Smith's faction from killing me. Unfortunately it also might be enough to ensure my death if in fact members of his faction were also members of the 'Inner Circle'. The actions of Mr. Smith convinced me there was only one person I could really rely on. Keep running.

Wearily picking myself back up I crossed the road and continued my flight. After making it about a hundred yards into the woods I heard the sounds of vehicles nearing. As I ran down the hill away from the road they stopped and I heard multiple doors slamming. Slowing my pace as I headed down a steep ravine I heard the faint sound of my name being called again.

I ran that whole day out and the next, till I figured I had to be far enough away to be outside of any search grid they could possibly have tried. For the next week, I never stayed in the same spot for more than one night, moving three to five miles a day and always bearing east. Eating minnows, crawdads and small fish out of the streams and any edible plants I could be sure of from my reading 'Edible plants of Missouri', I grew steadily hungrier and more morose.

Coming to a secluded and seemingly undisturbed shallow cave in mid afternoon on the ninth day after shooting John I decided I'd run far enough. Worn out, starving and almost delirious, I plopped down in the leaf pile at the entrance and tried to go to sleep, basically wondering if anybody would ever find my body if I didn't wake up.

The sun was setting as I awoke, the crunching of leaves nearby bringing me to full alert. Believing someone had trailed me my heart was beating wildly as the footsteps drew closer. I pointed the rifle towards the approaching sound and as the doe stepped into view, oblivious to my presence, I let out my breath. She was twenty feet below me and looked up with sudden fear a second before I poached my first deer.

CHAPTER FORTY SEVEN

The thrashing squirrel was quickly dispatched with the K-bar and I stuck it in my backpack with the other one I'd snared. While deer hunting in my previous life I'd always found squirrels to be annoying, their scampering sounding like deer approaching at times. Now I appreciated their abundance. Stopping to grab the sock I'd found next to the Black River, half full of shelled acorns, out of the stream, I made my way back to the cave as darkness was falling.

After skinning and deboning the squirrels I put the meat in the coffee can and started the fire. It took me a little longer than usual and I reminded myself to find a better piece of chert tomorrow. When the squirrel meat had browned enough I added the nettles, Queen Anne's lace seeds, acorns and water. Acorns taste like shit and have to be leached to get the worst of the bitterness out of them, but I'd found this concoction to make them at least palatable. It's amazing how few acorns are left by the end of the summer considering the billions that fall each autumn, and I'd had to search hard for this bunch. Never thought I'd be competing with squirrels and deer for food.

As the stew simmered, I notched the map and said out loud, "Tomorrow is Sunday, October first. Bath day." At least I was pretty sure of that. The daily ritual hadn't started for a couple weeks after the escape, as I liked to think of my decision, and I might be a day off. So what.

I scraped the little meat that was left on the squirrel skins off and put them in the hollowed oak stump with the others, adding more oak chips and water and stirring it up. The tannic acid in the oak cured the skins, making them pliable and hairless after about a week of soaking. After they dried, I hung them in the smoke for a couple fires and they didn't stink too bad. I still hadn't figured out how to stitch my cured collection of forty or so together into something usable as clothing, but didn't want to throw them out either. The nights were already getting nippy and my clothes were in tatters.

Taking the stew off I set it on my bark table to cool. The shoulder was acting up again, and I decided to just take tomorrow off after my bath in the stream. I had plenty of jerky, or pemmican as the Sioux had called it, the difference being that no chemical cure, only smoke, was used in the making. The trudge to check my ever widening circle of snares could wait until Monday. Most times the critters were still alive anyway when I reached them. I ate the stew, my best batch yet I thought, then boiled water in the canteen and scrubbed it with sandstone.

After stepping outside to pitch the rinse water I decided to leave the fire going, sensing it would be unseasonably cold that night. The willow slats of my bed creaked as I hit the sack. Thinking, "You better get some more tomorrow" I promptly fell asleep.

The next morning was the coldest yet, my breath billowing in plumes for the first time as I lay under my space blanket and deer skins deciding I couldn't afford a day off. The shoulder was stiff and throbbing more than it had in a month, but winter would be here soon if this morning was any indication of it's early arrival. "Maybe I'll just use the sinews to stitch the skins together today."

I thought, trying to envision the process that had been used by primitive humans.

The red nylon of the onion bags I'd found along the Black River would be a better thread substitute, but I had cured and saved all the possibly usable sinews from the last two deer I'd killed with my 'home made' crossbow. I hadn't fired either of my guns since that first life saving doe, wanting to save my ammo for self defense and worried the sound may cause me to be found.

With that always in mind I'd crafted a functional crossbow after numerous attempts out of a split hickory sapling and outer bands of split willow, using the stout twine from John's pack as bindings and string. Half inch thick, straight oak shafts with turkey or hawk feathered fletching and rudimentary metal points served as arrows. Rusty metal implements, containers, clothes, bags and other human debris had been utilized and converted, always paring the burgeoning collection of potentially usable garbage down to what I could carry when moving.

Daylight finally brightened enough to see by. A light rain was falling, the constant patter of drops in the forest outside drowning out the usual bird sounds of early morning. Rising from my improvised cot I stretched my gaunt frame, careful to not move the left shoulder too much. Thinking, "I'm probably down to one fifty two," my high school wrestling weight, I added kindling to the slight embers in my fire pit. I'd kept the fire going throughout the night for the first time. Adding kindling then blowing until a flicker began to rise, I pondered the day's agenda.

Since childhood I'd marveled at early mans' ability to survive. The constant longing for human contact that I'd felt in the first month of my indoctrination into their ways had slowly been replaced with a reverent awe for their perseverance. "Just another day in paradise." I said out loud, grabbing larger sticks to throw on the fire.

The heat was glorious as I huddled over the fire and added water to the coffee can. I pulled out my rapidly dwindling bag of chicory root thinking there was another trip I needed to make soon. The only place I usually found it was along roadsides and the collection was always risky. I hadn't been seen by anybody as far as I knew for four months now, and I wanted to keep it that way.

I was maybe seventy miles east of the Current. Staying by the Black river during the third week I'd tried to use fishing for basic sustenance. The many close encounters I'd had with people had forced me to abandon that strategy, perceiving all people as potential threats. Seeing the less used areas of the forest as my only chance of remaining undetected, from then on I'd set up my camps with total separation from humanity as my goal.

The necessity of finding game and edible plants had forced me to move five miles or more every few weeks or so. Each month it had gotten a bit easier as I'd figured more ingenious ways to survive and healed more. This cave was the most comfortable yet, but I knew I'd have to move soon. I added a smaller amount of chicory root to the pot than normal, wanting to preserve my stash a little longer.

CHAPTER FORTY EIGHT

"What the hell you doing here?"

The sound of a human voice startled me more than the words. Turning to face the entrance to the cave I saw a gray haired man in camo holding a bow. He said, "Oh my lord!," his eyes widening as he took in my appearance. He had a pistol and quickly dug it out of his holster after dropping the bow. My beard was getting long and unkempt, my clothes were literally rags and my skin was dark and burnished by constant exposure to the sun and weather. He was as shocked as I, not seeming to be able to say anything as he looked at me for another ten seconds.

Though I talked to myself often the words just wouldn't come out. "Uh . . . . Uh." was all I managed before he finally stammered out, "Who . . . who are you. You're on my land."

Trying to think quickly of what to say I blurted out, "I'll be moving today."

He dug a phone out and said, "You just come on out here. I'm calling the sheriff."

Assuming his cell phone wouldn't work here but realizing I couldn't take that chance, I blurted out, "You can't do that. Let me tell you why I'm here before you do that."

I guess his curiosity got the better of him. He quit dialing and stared at me saying, "Well, go ahead."

I got out, “My name is Mitch Cones and . . .”

“Oh my lord it is you ain’t it. Ever’body in the world was lookin’ for you a few months ago. How’d you get all the way over here?”

“I walked. I’m sorry ’bout being on your land but if you call the sheriff I’ll be dead in a few days or maybe less.” I still honestly believed that.

“Why would the sheriff kill you? He probably will want to shake your hand.”

Huh? “What? No, not the sheriff, the CIA or the gangsters that was chasing me. That’s why I’ve been living out in the woods for the last four months.”

“You been here for four months?”

“Nah, I only been here for about a month. I’ve been moving every month or so.”

“I thought I smelled smoke a couple times before but I really started smelling it as I was coming up the creek this morning. My names Earl Watkins. Glad to meet you, Mr. Cones.” He holstered his pistol and held his hand out, stepping towards me to shake mine.

Surprised by his sudden geniality all I could say was, “Glad to meet you Earl.” as he clasped mine firmly and pumped it up and down, looking all around my cave at first and then staring at me in a real peculiar way, even considering everything.

Letting go, he said excitedly, “I’m gonna go get my son Jack. He was gonna hunt the lower field this morning. He ain’t gonna believe this. I’ll be back in twenty minutes or so. I ain’t gonna call the sheriff or anybody else, okay, so don’t take off.”

“Tell ya the truth Earl, it’s kind of a relief that you found me. I ain’t gonna take off.”

He said, “Please don’t. I’ll be back in awhile,” then abruptly turned and headed down the hill towards the creek. Blowing out my breath in a long sigh I turned towards my coffeepot and stirred it, smelling the pungent chicory brewing.

The waiting minutes were a whirlwind of thought, my desire to pick up and run tugging at me but not winning. As promised Earl was back in about twenty minutes with his forty something year old son.

Jack walked up to me and held his hand out saying, “It’s awful nice to meet you Mitch. You’re about as famous a character round here as it gets. They had a thousand folks looking for you back in May and there’s been all kinds of talk about what happened to you since. It’s died down a lot lately but everybody round here . . . . and probably cross the country knows your name at least.”

“Why was a thousand folks looking for me?” What he’d said made no sense to me.

He continued, “Well you’re a damn folk hero, didn’t you know that?”

A folk hero? “No, what do you mean?”

"Well, most folks think you just died and they couldn't find your body, but Dan Strauss and that John Shaw guy always said you were still alive."

"John Shaw? How'd he get to talkin' to people? He's the last guy I shot. I figured he was probably gonna die or get caught by the Army and never be heard from again."

"You really don't know, do ya? Well that ain't the way it went down. He managed fucked up as he was to walk out to B highway that night. This guy named Tom Lawson found him and Shaw talked him into taking him straight to the TV station in Poplar Bluff, still bleeding and all. They put him straight in front of the camera after cleaning him up a bit, and everybody in probably the whole world has seen that interview.

He told the whole story about how you'd outfoxed and killed some of the baddest dudes in the world and 'bout the Inner Circle and how you'd saved his life, even though you was the one that shot him. Showed the whole world the moss and bandages and splint you'd put on his arms. Said he'd have died otherwise and he owed you at least that. Even told about all the shit he'd done around the world fucking with folks for this inner circle bunch, saying he knew they would kill him for it. The stories he told were the kind of shit you just can't make up.

Then he faced the camera and said, and I remember the exact words, "This is to the members of the Inner Circle. Mitch Cones does not, I repeat, does not, know the key to the Fibonacci sequence. Leave him alone." He didn't really want nothing except to get it all off his chest it seemed, cause he knew everything he said could get him in more trouble with the law and obviously this inner circle bunch. By the end of his story there was truckloads of folks heading to the area he said you was in trying to find you, but obviously they never did. How the hell did you manage to not get found and stay alive all this time?"

The implications of what I'd just heard hit me like a ton of bricks. I started laughing and crying at the same time, and they just stood there looking at me like they were wondering if I really was crazy.

"You gonna be okay?" Earl asked after I'd gone on for a few minutes.

Finally able to settle down enough to talk and believing that my long ordeal was almost over I said, "I never been better!" I looked at my bag of chicory root saying, "I guess I won't have to dig any more of this after all." I dumped the remainder of the roots in the pot and added water, insisting, "You have to try some of my chicory coffee."

Looking dubiously at my coffee pot Earl said, "I think you're going to have to prepare yourself for all the press, and maybe we do too. You feel like telling us your story? It might help all of us get ready for the storm of reporters that's gonna be here."

"It sure's been awhile since I talked to anybody. I'd like to tell you what happened to me, but do you know what happened to my wife, Detective Pollitt, and Dan Strauss and his wife?"

Earl said, "Yeah, they're about as famous as you. Your wife came to Eminence and thanked everyone at the first big meeting Dan and Beth set up to organize the search. What I saw, looked like she was pretty messed up about the whole thing but she held herself together pretty good. They all been in the news a lot since, and they even interviewed Dan on 'The Today Show'. A lot of your family was down here looking too and Dan and some of them are still spending time looking for you or your body, far as I know. There's a few others that spend time looking too, but not nearly like right after. Detective Pollitt was damn near dead when they got him out of there, but he made a full recovery from what he says. Last I heard he was talking about writing a book about the whole thing."

They willingly, if somewhat reluctantly, tried my coffee and pemmican as I told them the whole story. When I got to the part about my time in the woods, they seemed amazed by the bow and other gadgets I'd crafted as I gave them the grand tour of my, well really, Earl's cave. Stretched skins of three squirrels, a groundhog and a deer hung from circles of willow branches bound with cast off fishing line. Racks for sun drying my different smoked meats, now holding drying Queen Anne's lace flower heads, sumac berries and Cattail roots sat on slabs of sloughed bark that made for shelves and tabletop, supported by sturdy cross membered pole frames. An Adirondack style chair and my willow slatted frame bed drew the most inquiries about their making, but they seemed to be impressed by it all as Earl said, "Looks like you could have stayed out here forever if I hadn't found you. You been carrying all this stuff with you every time you move?"

"Nah, I burn it and make new ones at my next camp. This is by far the best set I made yet."

Jack sat down on the chair and said, "Don't burn this one. How'd you know how to make all this stuff?"

"I was a pretty handy guy before this happened and while I was hiding out I read a book about it and remembered some of the plans. When you ain't got nothing but time really, it's amazing what you can come up with."

Leaning back in the comfortable chair Jack said, "I guess it is. How you want to handle us bringing you out of here. You feel like you're up to talking to all the press? Believe me, there's gonna be a lot once they find out you're alive."

What might occur upon my reintroduction into society made me suddenly fear it. My elation at hearing what John Shaw had said was being quickly tempered by uncertainty of the unknown factors that might come into play. I needed more time to think it through.

The thought of letting all my adversaries know I was still alive was so incongruent with my post 'escape' mind set that it had touched off a barrage of doubts about the wisdom of it. The Inner Circle, Marlene, and maybe even Mr. Smith might still be holding a grudge, to say the least. Even though John Shaw had told the world I didn't know any key they might still believe I did. Even barring that, the very act of being thrust into a spotlight after my prolonged isolation scared the hell out of me.

Wondering about the possible chances I was still not out of the woods, literally and figuratively, I asked, "Did you ever hear what the algorithm was supposed to do or anything about it on the news?"

Jack said, "There was lots of speculation about it, but I'm pretty sure it's never been made public if they did actually figure it out. There's been a big investigation into the allegations John Shaw made but I don't think anybody's been arrested or anything like that. You think you might still be in danger if they find out you're alive?"

"Well, I certainly pissed a lot of people off and folks like that don't forget. Do you think you could get a hold of Andrea first and only tell her about this for now?"

Eyeing me with a strange look Earl said, "Mitch, whatever you want us to do will be fine. I'm not sure if we can get in touch with her, but we can try. I don't want us finding you to end up being a bad thing. You think they might still be bugging phones or whatnot in case you happen to turn up?"

"If the press finds out they won't have to. Can we just go to your house for awhile and not tell anybody else till I figure this out?"

Earl said, "Like I said, whatever you want. Let's grab your guns and such and we'll head there. I imagine you wouldn't mind taking a hot shower and getting some real food in you."

Looking at him with mock indignation I retorted, "What do you call my pemmican?"

CHAPTER FORTY NINE

We gathered my weapons and made our way to his truck, parked a mile or so away at the start of the last pasture before the up thrust of hills became solidly wooded. Bouncing along rutted dirt racks for the majority of the two mile trip to Earl's farmhouse, we passed cattle grazing in pastoral meadows and two large cornfields as we neared the house. My ability to remain undetected was explained as he told me about his use of his property. I'd been living on his land for four weeks but he rarely went into the twelve hundred acres of woods abutting the National Forest on the north end of his property till deer season. As we neared the barn my uneasiness about the situation began to get hold of me.

"You sure you're wife is gonna be okay with this?"

He didn't answer me for a while as he pulled the truck in front of the barn. After putting it in park he said, "Tell you what, I better go in first and tell her about finding you. She might be a bit taken if I just come a walkin' in with you. Why don't you and Jack just wait here till I come out."

Earl headed down the barnyard driveway towards the house. Jack motioned for me to follow him into the barn saying, "You want a soda or a water or something?' as we came to a refrigerator and he opened it. Glancing in, I saw a twelve pack of beer.

"I'll take a beer. I guess considering the circumstances I can be excused for drinking at nine o'clock in the morning."

Jack handed me one, grabbing himself a bottled water, then said, “I think I’d agree with that.” as he tipped his water bottle on my beer can.

I popped the beer open and took a long drag. After I finished my swig I said, “It’s been a long time between these.”

After draining the rest he said, “I been thinking about what you said about them folks holding a grudge and maybe we need to think this over before we go rushing in. Can you think of anybody that might relay the message to your wife? I don’t think we should call her or even try to from one of our phones.”

“I’m with you on that one. John Shaw told me they’d even bugged the cops’ phones. There ain’t no telling what they might be doing now. Maybe one of her friends or somebody like that should call her first.”

Throughout my time in the wild, though certainly more so in the first month, I’d been in a constant state of depression. At many bleak moments the thought that I might be reunited with my wife and family was the only thing that had kept me going. My isolation was even more complete, but like a convict I’d thought of the people I would reunite with on my first day of ‘freedom’ if that day ever came to pass.

Many times I’d thought of walking into town at night and just calling somebody, anybody, that I knew. I’d tried to force that yearning out of my brain but I’d spent time each day memorizing the phone numbers of my family and friends, albeit with little hope of their use arising. Now that it might be here, my cloud of doubts about further vengeance against me wouldn't allow my conscience even that respite from my loneliness.

My family had been put through a grueling ordeal, including a funeral and a subsequent fruitless, protracted search. I'd often agonizingly wondered how they were faring as a result of this. Especially after some of the more vivid nightmares I'd been plagued with I had many times pictured dismal scenes.

The more worn out I was at night the less these incarnations of horror afflicted me. I noted this after a month and from then on had tried to physically push myself each day to the point of exhaustion in order avoid them as much as possible. They didn't totally end but the side benefits of constant movement from sun up to sun down were myriad. My focus on productive activities, honed by fear of the night sweats as much as by the necessity, had enabled me to build things, experiment with and utilize new gadgets and procure enough food to at least not starve. Perhaps most importantly, it had enabled me to maintain my sanity by keeping my mind busy enough for the depression to not consume me.

Jack asked me, "Do you remember any numbers of people like that?"

"I sure do. Why don't you take these numbers down so's you have a copy." Reciting names and numbers out to him I got to twelve and started trailing off, the less crucial ones not being as firmly embedded.

Earl and Eileen walked into the barn, a dumbstruck look crossing her face as her eyes riveted on me. She looked back at Earl and said, "You didn't tell me he was near starving to death." Turning back towards me she held her strong looking hand out and said, “I’m Eileen. Let’s get you into the house and get something besides beer into you.”

I set the half full second beer down on a workbench and after a quick shake of her hand said, “I have been kind of on a diet, but I sure could use some real food for a change.

CHAPTER FIFTY

After more questions about my condition to which I basically told her I was not as close to starving to death as she seemed to think, we went inside. After eating a banana and an apple, the tastes seeming heavenly, Eileen gave me a full set of clothes, scissors, razor and a pair of tennis shoes saying, "The bathroom's right at the top of the stairs. I'll have breakfast ready by the time you're done."

Forty five minutes later, showered, shaved and feeling strange for the sensation of being truly clean, I came back downstairs to see a virtual banquet laid out. They all seemed as amazed by my transformation as I'd been.

During the hearty meal of fresh eggs, ham, fried potatoes, rye toast with wonderful homemade strawberry preserves, real coffee and orange juice, I told them of the various plants and animals I'd eaten in the past four months, including a large black snake. To relieve mainly Eileen's preoccupation with my gaunt condition I maintained that I'd had enough food to live on, and had never really feared of starving to death. I'd had plenty of deer meat since the first doe but none of my food had much fat and that was the main reason I'd steadily lost weight. All in all, after the excellent breakfast I felt sicker than I had in at least the past two months, if only because I'd eaten too much.

After breakfast we discussed my options. Earl's assumption that I would want to be reunited with my family and come out into the public world again as soon as possible didn't hold true as I pondered the best way to proceed. My fears were far from erased. Thinking of another indirect way of notifying Andrea I asked, "Do you think my wife might still keep in contact with Dan?"

Earl said, "He probably at least knows how to get a hold of her, I'd think. He probably got tons of calls from people offering to help with the search, so a call to him from here wouldn't be too suspicious even if his phones are bugged. Jack, go in the office and look up that web site him and Mitch's sister set up."

Five minutes later as Eileen was filling me in on the publicity regarding my case and the search being done to root out the members of the 'Inner Circle', Jack walked back in with a perplexed look on his face. Staring at me he said, "The web site is down. Maybe the big search for you was over, but it still seems kind of strange for it to be taken down so quick. I tried looking up the phone number and called information for it but it's been disconnected. He was giving that number out the whole summer on TV in case anybody had any information."

Feeling a sudden anxiety but not wanting to voice the thoughts that were forming, I said, "Maybe he got tired of living in the spotlight and just wanted to put the whole thing behind him."

"Maybe, but him and your wife and family never had given up hope from what I gathered." I didn't respond to this, and after a few seconds he said, "Who do you think we should try next?"

I thought about it for awhile then said, "His wife Beth's shop was called 'The Crusty Crawdad'. I think I'd like to try and find out about her and Dan before we start calling anybody else. See if you can find the number for that."

A couple minutes later he came back and said, “I got that number. You want me to call it?”

“Yeah, but don’t say anything about me. Just see if you can get her on the phone.”

He dialed, and a second later said, “Hello, is Beth Strauss in?” He listened for a few seconds, a look of worry crossing his face, then said, “No, I don’t know her, I was just trying to reach Dan about a job and found out their phone’s not working.” He listened for a bit then said, “When was that?” My anxiety was kicking up in strides as he listened for a longer while before saying, “Have they ever done something like that before?” Another minute, then, “I’m very sorry to hear that. If you don’t mind, I’d like to talk to you about this further. I’ll just come into the shop when I’m in Eminence.” “I will. Thank you very much, goodbye.”

He seemed to be digesting the information as he looked at the floor for a second before saying to me, “Beth and Dan disappeared on Friday. That was her partner, Debbie, at the store, and she sounded worried. Said Beth didn’t come in on Friday, and she doesn’t know where they’re at. We haven’t seen anything on the news about it and I would think that would be getting all kinds of coverage.”

I said, “Even if they were trying to avoid publicity or left on their own for some reason, you’d think she would tell her partner about it. Did she say anything about police involvement or anything like that?”

“Said she went to their house yesterday. Dan’s truck was gone and it looked they’d packed in a hurry, but other than that, there wasn't any sign of mischief. She doesn't know what to think right now."

What did this all mean? My brain churning once again with the resurrection of my conundrum, I tried to outline my thoughts in a virtual lecture to the Watkins.

The web site being down I could see as a logical conclusion to what had to seem like a pointless exercise. The phone being disconnected implied they'd done it themselves for if they'd been snatched, I couldn't imagine their captors doing that. Also, they'd been very much in the public eye for four months and if the Inner Circle or one of the other factions had wanted them for information, revenge, or any other reason they wouldn't have waited so long to kidnap them.

On the other hand, firmly ensconced in Eminence, the chances they'd decided voluntarily to just up and move were almost nil. The only logical assumption was that they'd felt scared enough by something to see that as their only option.

Finally exhausted by the mental exercise of trying to figure the answer to a paradox, I hung my head and closed my eyes.

"Just when I think I've uncovered the secret to peace and tranquility, that lonely, sinking feeling, creeps up on me." The line from a 'Cowboy Junkies' song popped unbidden into my brain, the import of the words being dead on to my recent change in outlook. Aghast at the thought that Dan and Beth might be just the latest victims of my decisions I began heaving great sighs of exasperation, tears rolling down my clean shaven cheeks.

It wasn't over. Remembering Andrea's ominous prediction, "Them people aren't ever going to leave us alone." my recent elation seemed like nothing more than a cruel mockery. The Watkins seemed nearly as astonished and reflective as I, Eileen gnashing her hands together as they stared at me.

Earl finally broke the silence. "We can't read too much into this just yet but till we find out about them, I think you're just going to have to stay here Mitch. Jack, I want you to drive to Eminence and talk to Beth's partner and the cops about this. Tell them we were looking for a driver to haul logs off our property. I think that should be a good enough cover in case they check you out. Eileen, let's me and you clean out that room in the attic. Can't have anybody seeing Mitch."

Turning towards me he said, "We got twelve grandchildren and they tear around here on a regular basis. Fact, my daughter Jesse's supposed to be here this afternoon for Sunday dinner."

"Did you think you could just hide out here and everything would go away?" Mr. Smith's face as he said those words burned itself into my consciousness. It wasn't going to go away on it's own. That much at least seemed certain to me now. The time for that delusion was over. The coincidence of me being found and Dan and Beth vanishing at roughly the same time I saw as the oft times cruel hand of fate dealing me a pat hand. No choice but to stay in the game.

My hair had been salt and pepper when this started, mostly pepper, but now it was solid gray. I'd lost pushing thirty pounds and hadn't even recognized myself in the mirror as I'd stared at the sunken eyes, weathered face and wild hair looking back at me. I said, "Jack, you think you could find some pictures of me from the news or something on the Internet?"

He looked at me with some puzzlement, so I said, "I don't think I really look anything like pictures they may have shown anymore. I want to go to Eminence with you, and I want to see if there is any chance people might recognize me."

"I know they had lots of pictures of you at one time or another. That shouldn't be too hard."

Coming back with six prints of different shots, we all studied them. Eileen said, "I don't think I'd recognize you from these. You look a lot older and almost like a holocaust victim now."

Though not entirely agreeing with that assessment of my condition I said, "Thanks, but I think you're right about that. With a little more disguise I doubt anybody but maybe my family would even come close to recognizing me. I appreciate the offer but I can't just hide out in your attic, and I can't go back to the woods either. Time to put an end to this, one way or the other."

Eileen had offered to give me a haircut during breakfast, but I decided to leave it long and unruly. Wearing a beat up cowboy hat and clothes to match, hopefully to make my wizened face seem more natural, and sunglasses to cover my eyes, easily the most recognizable part of the face, I walked to Jack's truck with all of them. Noting the empty rifle rack in his cab window I said, "If you don't mind, I'd like to bring my guns with us."

They all raised their eyebrows, perhaps still not getting the true gist of my continuing predicament. Seeing their apprehension I said, "It's not like I'm gonna have to use them . . . . well . . . I don't know . . . . I'd just feel a lot better . . . . I've kept 'em close for so long, I guess I'd feel kind of naked without them."

Seeming to understand Earl said, "Yeah, I guess you still have good reason for that. Jack, go grab my cleaning kit. I think his guns could use one."

As Jack and Eileen went into the house, Earl and I headed into the barn. My guns were lying on the workbench. Looking closely at them he said, "They don't look too bad. How'd you keep them from rusting up?"

"I rubbed em down with boiled animal fat. Haven't ever even fired that pistol, but I tried to keep them in good shape . . . . Never knew when I might have to use them."

Seeming to ponder this for awhile before replying, his eyes took on a distant look.

"I hope you don't have to use them today, but might as well make sure they still work."

As we began cleaning the guns, I said, "Earl, I don't know what's going to happen, but I doubt these guys are even still looking for me. I hope I didn't scare your wife by wanting to bring the guns."

He said, "I think she'll be fine. Soon as we get these cleaned up we'll take them behind the barn and see how they shoot." After test firing two shells out of each gun, we headed back to the barnyard and Jack and I climbed into his truck.

Earl put his hands on top of the cab and looked in, saying to Jack, “Just don’t get too nosy and be careful when you get there. Call me and let me know when you’re coming back so we can make sure Jesse and the kids are gone.” Tapping his palms on the cab then stepping back he said, “Good luck” then turned towards the house.

Those being the last words spoken to me before my ‘escape’ my mood only deepened. Jack started up the truck, saying, “Had no idea I’d be involved in espionage when I woke up this morning. You ready for this?”

CHAPTER FIFTY ONE

Ready for what? I didn't have a clue about what might happen today. The enormous contrast between today and yesterday, or a hundred yesterdays for that matter, already had me bewildered before I'd found out Dan and Beth were gone. Not ready but determined to find out what had happened to them I said, "No, but like they say, if not now, when?"

Only shaking his head in agreement we turned out of the driveway. Somber, reflective and not wanting to speculate openly about my dreadful thoughts I spent the first half hour of the trip without saying much. Jack seemed very edgy as he drove his F-250 west, lighting up a chain of cigarettes and looking over at me frequently but not saying much either. Seemingly aware of my need for introspection he didn't press me for lengthy replies to his few queries.

After another five minute silence he glanced at me briefly for the hundredth time as we entered Ellington. "The more I look at you the better I feel about you not getting recognized, but I don't think you should go to the police station with me. What are you really hoping for by coming along?"

Finally having the realization that no amount of thinking about it was going to solve my problem I said, "I'm not sure, just felt like I couldn't just wait around anymore. If something happened to Dan and Beth because of this then I have to assume it could happen to my family. Hell, they might think somebody really knows where I am and are going to kidnap them all just to be sure. I just don't know and that's been the damn problem since this whole fucking thing started. Maybe I never will, but if it means turning myself in or whatever I gotta do this is going to end soon."

"I hope you're not right about that for your sake, and maybe mine too. Let's hope they just took a sudden vacation and didn't bother telling anyone."

Fat chance! Positive that wasn't what had happened I replied, "Wish I could believe that, but I can't. Why don't you drop me off downtown when we get there and I'll wander into Beth's shop. I'd like to see it anyway. When you get done at the police station I'll meet you on the street out front."

"I was thinking I'd want to go to the shop first. If you want we can both go in there together and you can kind of hang back and listen. I don't think you should be really talking to anybody, and probably not Beth's partner for sure. She's bound to have seen lots of pictures of you, and if she recognizes you she might really lose it."

"Yeah, no telling what she might do. Sounds like a plan."

A half hour later we parked on the side of the street in downtown Eminence. Comprised of the bulk of commercial establishments in this mainly summer town, the three block long stretch of Route 19 was bustling with activity. A banner hanging across the street proclaimed, 'Welcome to the one hundred forty second Eminence Oktoberfest'. An Oompah band was playing in the park, the distant strains of accordion and bass beat of drums keeping time with the festive flow of shoppers and early revelers in this German tradition.

Thinking this actually might be a good thing, Jack and I found 'The Crusty Crawdad' and walked separately into the shop to the tinkle of a bell hung over the door. The odors of scented soaps and candles, potpourri and other fragrant smells assailed me as I glanced around the crowded boutique.

A stout, fifty something woman was standing behind the cash register, thanking the couple she'd waited on as they grabbed their bag and headed to the door. I kept my face mostly turned as she walked around to another lady customer standing close to me, saying, "We get a lot of people that come in just for that maple syrup. Have you tried it before?"

It took another few minutes before it was Jacks turn, Debbie flitting and ringing up sales but seeming to be looking at me more often than necessary. I tried to act like just another shopper, but then again, she probably didn't get a lot of old cowboys in here.

The crowd had thinned out as Jack said to her, "Debbie, my name is Jack Watkins. I talked to you this morning about trying to find Dan Strauss for a logging job. I know this might be a delicate subject, but I was wondering if you have heard anything since then about them or have any other ways I might get in contact with him."

I thought it was said pretty diplomatically but as she turned to him her smile became a scowl and she said vehemently, "What makes you think I'd be able to get in contact with him? Didn't I tell you this morning I couldn't do that?"

Recoiling away from her noticeably, Jack said, "I'm sorry. I didn't mean to upset you. I was just trying to get in touch with Dan."

"Are you a reporter? If you are, get the hell out of my shop!"

The other customers all had turned and stared but I dare not, turning towards the door instead. I had grabbed the handle when she demanded, "Cowboy, stay right there!"

I ignored her order and pulled the door open, trying to casually step into the street as if she hadn't been talking to me. I got two steps out the door before I felt her hand clenching my shoulder and surmised my disguise hadn't been good enough. Stopping and turning around with the intent of playing it to the hilt anyways I said, "Ma'm, I didn't think you could be talking to me. What's the problem?"

She stared at me for a few seconds, seemingly unsure of herself momentarily, but the recognition becoming clear in her expression quickly. Expecting her to yell out something like, "You're Mitch Cones, aren't you?" instead she surprisingly said, "I'm sorry. I thought you were someone else. I hope my outburst didn't scare you out my shop. Please come back in and I'll be able to help you momentarily."

I still assumed she'd recognized me, appreciating her quick thinking as I said, "Well, I did see a few things my wife would like. I'll just wait till you get done with your other customers."

She beamed a fake smile and said, "Oh, I'm sure I have lots of things you might be interested in. I'll be with you as soon as I can."

Shrugging my shoulders slightly in Jack's direction as I walked back into the shop, he headed out the door seemingly at a loss as to what he could help me with at this point. Fiddling with the merchandise, I tried to think of what to say to her when she finally 'helped' me.

Some of the astonished patrons, probably not locals, had left the shop at her outburst. The ones who'd stayed eyed me unnervingly as I tried to act nonchalant for the next five minutes. Debbie finally came up next to me holding a jar of apricot preserves and said, "Those are excellent, but that's only the display jar. Is your wife not here with you?"

Suddenly thinking I may have overestimated her perception I said, "No, she stayed at home today. Just thought I'd bring her something special."

"I just got a new batch in. Could you come back at five? I'll have them out by then."

I'd noticed the sign on the door stating the hours as ten to five on Sundays and knew the ruse was up. Finally looking fully into her eyes I said, "I'll be back then, if you're sure it isn't a problem."

"Oh, no problem at all. I'll be happy to help you." She turned towards another customer standing in front of the register and said, "If you're ready, I can ring you right up."

Heading out the door I saw Jack standing in front of the next store. I walked right past him and headed for the truck, not sure how to feel about this unexpected development. Hearing the click of the unlocking door, I climbed inside as Jack made his way to the driver's side. After getting in, he blew out his breath then said, "So much for our espionage skills. What did she say to you after I left?"

"She said to come back at five and she'd be happy to help me. I think she kind of recognized me right away and probably was sure when I bolted for the door. She sure played it pretty cool though, I gotta give her that."

"Well, she doesn't seem to like reporters much. Are you going back to meet her?"

"She said she had things I'd be interested in and I don't think she was talking about the apricot preserves. Can you stay here till then? I know I'm already putting you out doing this."

"Mitch, don't you worry about me. I don't have to be anywhere and I'm as curious as you. This is starting to seem like a real adventure."

"I appreciate you helping me and all, but lots of people have died since this adventure started. You sure about me maybe even being in your truck now? If she recognized me, other people might be able to. Shit, they might even have somebody watching the shop for all I know."

Starting up the truck he said, "Maybe we should get out of Eminence till five. Did you notice anybody else looking at you funny?"

"Only all the other customers. None of em looked suspicious, I guess, but they probably wouldn't use a jarhead to stake out the shop."

I began looking all around for anybody that might be eyeing us too closely, regretting my decision to come along. Turning onto 106, no cars followed us and I hadn't seen any indication of too much attention coming from the sidewalk crowds.

Shortly after crossing over the Current a few miles out of town, Jack turned down a gravel road leading into the National Scenic Riverways. After a couple miles he pulled onto a dilapidated logging road, stopping once we'd gotten out of sight of the main road. As I grabbed my rifle off the rack, Jack said, "I don't think anybody followed us."

I didn't think so either, but I said, "It won't hurt to be ready." as I opened the door and stepped outside with the .270. As I began loading up the rifle Jack looked at me sorrowfully, pursing his lips and shaking his head back and forth but not saying anything.

Once the rifle was fully loaded, I looked at Jack and said, "I'll be back in a few minutes." After walking back towards the gravel road, I took up a defensive position where I could see anybody coming.

The look that Jack had given me played through my mind while I began waiting. He obviously had been thinking I was over reacting and that we were in no danger, but he hadn't tried to stop me. Maybe I WAS over reacting, but my perspective was way different from his, and he just didn't, and in no way could, understand mine. During the first five minutes of the vigil I was convinced of the prudence of my actions, keeping the rifle pointed towards the road.

After ten minutes no other vehicles had come down the gravel road. Assured that no one had followed us out of Eminence I began walking back to the truck, slightly less sure of the necessity of my precautions.

Jack was standing outside and smoking a cigarette as he watched me approach, his steadfast gaze devoid of castigation. Reaching the truck I climbed back in the passenger seat with the loaded rifle, leaving the door open. Jack stubbed his cigarette out in the ashtray as he climbed back in and shut his door. Looking at me with a grim smile, he said, "Mitch, I . . . . well . . . . I guess I just don't know what to say. You been through so much shit I can't say you're thinking wrong, but I don't think you need to think everybody's trying to kill you either."

My thoughts had been roughly the same as I'd walked back to the truck. I said, "Can I bum a smoke off you?" I hadn't smoked a cigarette in nearly a year but I felt like what could it hurt. It sure wouldn't kill me instantly anyways.

CHAPTER FIFTY TWO

During the two hour wait Jack told me a lot about himself, seemingly to reassure me that he was up to the task at hand. He had two kids, a fifteen year old daughter and a twelve year old son. They lived with his ex-wife in Poplar Bluff, still in the house he'd lost in the divorce two years ago.

Soon afterwards, perhaps because of his despondence over the divorce, his dad had asked him to come help him on the farm. Using the reason that the daunting task of raising four to five hundred head of cattle a year along with the many other responsibilities of having over three thousand acres to maintain was becoming more than he could handle after he'd reached seventy, Earl had compelled him to go back to his roots.

Since then he had immersed himself in the work, not only to help his dad but because the farm would be passed to him. It's substantial income would be his but the land itself was sacrosanct. The living will stipulated that the farm could not be sold or divided, only passed down through the family. He would only be able to spend the rest of his life there and it was his passion to do so.

His great great great grandfather, Clarence Watkins, had purchased the two hundred twenty acres surrounding the farmhouse in 1852 for eighty cents an acre. After clearing the first forty acres and building a log cabin and barn he'd begun raising cattle, pigs, corn and vegetables. A hard working, Bible toting man, Clarence had diligently spent the next four years clearing pastures and potential crop land. Soon he began to prosper, using all his extra money to purchase more tracts adjoining his land.

Immediately after his purchase of the tract encompassing the cave the Civil War broke out. He'd spent the next four years alternately fighting bushwhackers, Confederate and Federal troops as they'd all attempted to plunder his farm. The cave I'd been living in had been his home for six months after the Federals burned his house and barn in 1864 on the unfounded suspicion he was helping the rebels, a common occurrence in southern Missouri during the war. Since then five generations of Watkins had grown up in the house he'd built after the war's end, all hearing the stories of Clarence's unyielding perseverance in retaining his land.

He found it especially poignant that I had been living in the cave in somewhat similar circumstances as Clarence. My furniture and rudimentary implements might bear a great resemblance to the provisions he'd used during his stay there. Coupled with that, the praise that John Shaw, Dan Strauss and others had heaped on me for character and spirit made him somehow think of me as a reincarnation of Clarence. He knew his dad felt the same way, though Earl had never mentioned Clarence to me.

The fact that this trip could actually be dangerous had only occurred to him when I'd asked to bring my guns, but that had only instigated a greater desire in him to help me see this through.

As four thirty rolled around, we headed back towards Eminence. The town was still buzzing with activity on this now brilliant Indian Summer afternoon. Turning off 106, the traffic forced us to creep south on 19 through the throngs of people enjoying this beautiful day. Many of the pedestrians walked casually across the road between the slowly moving traffic, some of them seeming to eye me as we inched our way through town. By the time we parked at the south edge of town in a large lot for the grocery store and overflow parking from the street, the crowds had me feeling nearly claustrophobic.

Putting his truck in park, Jack looked over at me slouched down somewhat on the seat and said, "You sure you want to go in there?"

The outside temperature was only about seventy but I was sweating profusely and breathing hard. Unaccustomed to being around so many people, or any for that matter, my heart had raced wildly with the thought that any one of them could be a sentry for the Inner Circle. Only the possible import of the information I was about to receive from Debbie kept me from saying, "GET THE HELL OUT OF HERE!"

I looked at Jack as I tried to get my hyper ventilating in check and stammered out instead, "Na . . . no, but . . . but I need to know. I have to do this. Could you . . . would you just wait here for me. This might take a while."

Jack gave me a doleful look again then said, "Mitch, I'll be right here. Go talk to her."

Taking a big breath and blowing it out forcefully, I opened the door and climbed out of the truck eyeing all the people as if they may pull a gun suddenly. Nobody seemed to be even looking our way as I looked back at Jack and said, "Thanks . . . . for everything. Well, here I go." Shutting the door slowly, I saw Jack give me a thumbs up as I began the three block journey. Uncertain of anything my apprehension steadily mounted and the walk seemed to take forever.

At exactly five o'clock I knocked on the back door to the shop after carefully inspecting the area for possible prying eyes. Soon it opened and Debbie stood there staring at me for a while before saying, "Well, come on in, Mitch." After shutting the door she faced me and said softly, "Where the hell you been for the last four months?"

She seemed angry and wondering why I said, "That's kind of a long story. I been . . ."

A bell rang, and she pointed to the door to the office and said, "Wait in there while I close up." At a total loss I sat down in the desk chair, debating running back to Jack's truck.

After taking care of her last few customers she came in and said, "Was that Jack guy with you?"

"Yeah, him and his dad just found me this morning."

"Found you? Where'd they find you?"

"I've been living in the woods for the last four months and I was living on their property in a cave for the last month of it. His dad smelled the smoke from my fire this morning and surprised the hell out of me when he showed up. What about Dan and Beth? Do you really not know where they are? I've been worried sick about them since Jack called you this morning."

Ignoring my question, she somewhat harshly demanded, "Why didn't anybody else find you? They had whole caravans of people looking for you."

"Because I was thirty miles away by the time the search got organized by Dan and I been doing my best NOT to get found. I never heard what John Shaw said till this morning and I figured the Inner Circle guys were still looking for me. And I doubt this was on the news, but some CIA guy acted like he was going to shoot me right after Dan left to find Beth. Didn't seem like I had much choice but to disappear."

Raising her eyebrows, her glare softened as she said, "No . . . . that sure wasn't on the news. I guess that explains why you really didn't want to get found . . . . Did Jack tell you about all the time Beth and Dan spent not only looking for you, but organizing everything and running the web site and all?"

"Yeah, they told me. I guess this has been some kind of media circus, but even though John Shaw said what he did I still don't feel like this is over. What do you think Dan and Beth left for?"

Looking practically stricken, she hung her head and slowly shook it back and forth. After an agonizing few seconds, she finally said, "This whole thing, the publicity, the interviews and all, have been pretty hard on Beth. Seems like it made her just keep reliving that day . . . . You can't know how much that day at Big Creek messed her up. Poor girl's had nightmares ever since. I've found her crying many a time right here in the office."

This protracted answer to a simple question was becoming agonizing, but the welling tears made me realize this had affected her drastically also. Trying to control my impatience, I asked softly, "Have they ever just taken off before?"

After eyeing me over for a minute as if trying to make up her mind if I was friend or foe, she finally said, "I didn't say they just took off."

"Do you know where they're at or not?" I asked loudly, my exasperation evident.

She stared at me with eyes hard once again, then said ruefully, "Fact is, she and Dan felt like they needed to get away from all of it for awhile and they sure haven't been able to do that around here. Both of them have been wondering whether they could ever get past all this. I've never seen them so depressed. I think it's because they finally gave up any hope of finding you . . . . Yeah, I know where they're at."

As she'd informed me of the miserable state of their minds and outlook I'd hung my head, but her last statement made me snap my head back up. This overdue admission made me want to cuss her and hug her at the same time. Realizing that in her roundabout way she'd just told me the best news I could have heard at this moment, my elation won out. I grabbed her unexpectedly by the shoulders, Debbie shrinking back as I nearly shouted, "Do you know what this means?"

The sudden, ambiguous query seemed to baffle her for an instant. Her focus on her friend and partner's happiness hadn't allowed her to appreciate the importance of her statement to me. She stared at me as if she didn't know the answer before I grabbed her briefly in a hug and kissed her cheek. Leaning back but still grasping her shoulders, I implored, "Where are they?"

She seemed to suddenly get it, her face lighting up as she said, "They're pretty close. I'll take you there."

Grabbing her in a real bear hug this time, after ten seconds I let go and began whooping with cries of joy. Debbie apparently was getting caught up in my mirth as she gleefully said, “I can’t wait to see the look on their faces. They’re camping at Bay Creek on the Jacks Fork. We can head out there as soon as I close up.”

All the implications began flooding my brain. I could be reunited with my family. I could maybe begin life anew without overwhelming trepidation, although I’d never be able to forget. My ordeal had changed me a lot, and only time would tell if the nightmares would end and a somewhat normal resumption of my life was still attainable.

Though borrowing Debbie’s phone was my first inclination, sudden reservations made me think that before I began calling my family I needed to talk to Dan. He would know perhaps more than anybody if I was truly out of the woods. He’d probably also have Andrea’s new number and I wanted to call her first.

Debbie was doing a few last minute things as I said, “I need to go tell Jack about this. He’s parked on the south end of town next to the grocery store. You want to meet me there or should I come back here?”

Her mood seemed positively animated as she said, “I’ll drive over there when I get done here. Shouldn’t be more than a few minutes.”

Itching to share the good news with Jack I said, “He’s got a blue Ford F-250. I’ll see you over there,” as I left the office with a newfound spring in my step. I headed out the back door, the strains of country music having replaced the Oompah band.

The somewhat beat up Nike tennis shoes I had on felt like Hermes' slippers compared to the broken down boots I'd had on this morning. Hitting the street the urge to run became overwhelming as I felt the springiness in my step, and in my heart. Jogging at first and then running, I was going full speed down the middle of the empty street behind the shops as I raced to tell Jack the good news.

Seeing me coming from more than a block away he started up the truck and threw it in drive, squealing his tires as he accelerated quickly through the parking lot and bounced out onto the street coming off Route 19. I realized he thought something must be wrong because of my pace. I slowed and then stopped at the corner fifty yards down, trying to gesture for him to slow down as he sped towards me.

A patrol car squealed around the corner off 19, it's siren and lights activating as it did. Jack was already hitting the brakes hard to stop in front of me and the patrol car slammed to a halt directly behind him, the officer quickly getting out of his car. He was only thirty feet away from me and I was looking right at him as he walked towards the side of Jack's truck. I had taken my sunglasses off in the shop and never put them back on. The young officer had been looking at the truck as he'd exited his vehicle, but as he neared it he began looking straight at me.

Jack had stopped directly across the street from the corner I was standing on. He was looking at me for a clue as to how to proceed as the officer veered towards me, pointing at Jack with a motion to stay right where he was. Crossing the street towards me standing there wide eyed at this sudden development, the officer took off his sunglasses as he stopped in front of me. Not saying anything for a good ten seconds, he finally said, "You . . . you're Mitch Cones, aren't you?"

I debated trying to deny it for a second as I thought of all the possible ways I might be able to succeed in fooling him. I had no I.D. or wallet, and that alone would be hard to explain away. Feeling trapped, I knew his recognition was complete as he said, "Damn, it is you, isn't it?"

Seeing no hope of successfully denying it I said, "Yeah, that's me" as I wondered what his reaction would be.

"Well I'll be a son of a bitch!" he said as his eyes seemed to grow, probing mine as his surprise overtook him.

Pointing at Jack he asked, "Is he with you?"

I looked towards Jack and he held his hands up and mimed, "I'm sorry," as Officer Tillman waved at him to get out of his truck and come over to us without a reply from me. Seeming embarrassed, Jack opened the door and walked towards us as Officer Tillman turned back towards me and asked, "Where the hell have you been? Damn near everybody in this town has been looking for you since May."

I had given him the gist of my recent whereabouts as Debbie pulled up right next to us and quickly got out of her car. Looking at Jack for a second first and then turning to the officer she said, "Brian, we don't need the whole town knowing about this already," obviously having surmised up the situation pretty well at first glance.

He turned to face her and kindly said, "Debbie, you know I can't just ignore this. I need to take him down to the station right now."

She put her hands on her hips and said, "You're not going to do any such thing. We were just heading out to Bay Creek to find Dan and Beth and tell them about this. I'm sure Mitch will be happy to come down to the station later, but you aren't taking him anywhere right now."

Appreciating that they knew each other well or otherwise she surely wouldn't be talking to him like that, I said, "I'm not wanted for anything, am I?"

He seemed very unsure of himself as he admitted, "Well . . . no, not technically anyway, but . . ."

Debbie interrupted him and said, "There you have it then. Brian, keep this under your hat for right now. I'll call you and let you know when Mitch is going to come and tell you about everything but please don't tell anybody else just yet, okay?"

Blowing out his breath between his teeth, Brian turned to Jack and said, "I guess it's you're lucky day."

Turning back to me he said, "Mr. Cones, if I don't hear from you in a day I'm going to have to turn in this information. Maybe you don't know what the folks in this town have done for you but I think they have a right to know you're alive at least. I'll be waiting to hear from you."

He handed me his card and with a very earnest look said, "Call me before you get here. I think I'd like to talk to you first."

He looked back at Debbie and said, “You make sure he doesn’t just disappear again!”, then he turned and headed back to his patrol car, shaking his head back and forth like he didn’t know what had just hit him. Debbie waved at him as he opened his door and looked back towards us, seeming very unsure that he’d made the right decision as he climbed in his car.

Facing back towards Jack and I, Debbie said, “That’s my sister’s kid. He won’t tell anybody or he knows he’ll have to deal with me. Jack, you mind driving us out there? The road in is pretty rough and I’m sure your truck can make it a lot better than my car.”

Jack had been standing there seemingly flabbergasted at the turn of events, but he quickly said, “I don’t know what just happened here, but I’m glad you showed up when you did. Sure, let’s take my truck. How far away are they?”

“It’s about twenty miles from here.”

CHAPTER FIFTY THREE

On the ride to Bay Creek Debbie told us both in detail of the search for me, the reporters that had been in the shop almost daily, at least for the first month, and the rallying of the town in general around the cause.

A number of the town's residents had been on the river that day and remembered seeing the two boats and men as they'd camped a half mile down from Big Creek Bluff. Most said they'd known there was something fishy about them, but had no reason to be alarmed until the shooting started. The gunfire and explosions had echoed for miles down the valley, and everybody that was within earshot said they'd known some kind of battle was going on.

Many of these boaters had been the first to begin the search, and they had recruited the help of their friends and neighbors. Hundreds of people had been combing the woods by the third day after my escape, each having at least seen a photo of me. In all likelihood, many of the people in the shop and on the street had actually recognized me but, due to my drastically changed appearance, hadn't been quite sure enough to approach me.

As we begin winding down into the Jack's Fork river valley my excitement at seeing Dan and Beth again, coupled with an uneasiness about explaining to them why I hadn't tried to contact them, had me fidgeting in the back seat of Jack's truck. Coming down the final stretch of rutted road before the first of the widespread primitive camp sites at Bay Creek a lump was forming in my throat as I thought of everything this couple who'd known me for less than a day had done on my behalf. It was surely a debt I would have little chance of ever repaying.

Debbie said, “That’s their camp,” pointing towards camp site 108 as we neared it. Jack drove down the short side road and pulled in behind their truck. He had just stopped when Dan appeared, walking quickly up the trail from the river to see who was at their camp. By the look on his face, he was apparently not too happy about being disturbed as he saw the unfamiliar truck.

Striding towards us he saw Debbie first as she exited the truck, slowing and giving her an inquisitive look, then he saw me as I climbed out of the back. His eyes growing large he stopped suddenly, dropping the can of beer he’d been holding. Shouting, “Beth, get up here!” he began running towards us, his face breaking into an ear to ear grin as he stopped in front of me. After my worries during the trip out there, I was struck speechless by the apparent joy he felt at seeing me again. Looking me over for a bit and seeming to understand my reticence, he just grabbed me and began thumping my back saying, “Damn, Mitch, you don’t know how glad I am to see you!”

Seeing Beth approaching with the same type of expression a flood gate of unusual emotions, for me at least, just kind of opened, my arms wrapping around Dan in a man hug as my exuberance overwhelmed me. I began thumping his back and crying, saying, “Man, I didn’t think I was ever gonna see you guys again.” Beth wrapped her arms around the both of us and we pivoted around a bit in a big group hug, tears streaming down all of our cheeks.

The emotions I felt were in many ways more intense than any I’d felt throughout my ordeal, and that was surely saying a lot.

In that moment I realized we'd been bonded together for life by that day at Big Creek, and no amount of time or distance would ever break that bond. Only the three of us would ever know what it was really like, no matter how we tried to explain it to others.

Debbie was standing a few feet away, crying loudly also as she watched the display of heartfelt emotion coursing through our circle. I waved my left arm at her to join us and she wrapped her arms around Dan and Beth as they began to get their emotions in check.

Finally leaning back a bit, Dan said, "Where . . . how . . ." then just stared at me as if he could tell the answers by my appearance. He looked over at Jack and I stuttered out, "Tha . . . tha . . . this is Jack."

Jack had been standing there watching us with a look of amazement, perhaps, as he'd recognized the depth of our feelings. Walking towards us, Jack held out his hand towards Dan and said, "Jack Watkins. It's awful good to meet you Dan!"

Obviously wondering who Jack was, or at least how he fit into the picture, Dan shook his hand and looked at me for further explanation even as he said, "Dan Strauss."

Taking a cue from this, Debbie said, "Jack and his dad came across Mitch just this morning. He hasn't come out of the woods since Big Creek."

CHAPTER FIFTY FOUR

The emotions and exuberance of our reunion turned to a steady stream of queries about what had transpired since Dan disappeared over the hill. After a few moments of confusion caused by all of us asking questions at the same time, Dan said, "Time out! Let's grab some chairs and go down to the river. This is going to take a while, and I think we might all want to be sitting down."

Jack and I grabbed the lawn chairs from around the fire and Dan carried a large cooler down the short trail to the gravel bar. Emerging from the trees, the Jack's Fork was twinkling in the rays of the setting sun. The ripples in the quickly flowing water distorted the reflection of the massive bluff a quarter mile upstream, the scope of its grandeur not discernible in the kaleidoscopic image.

Like the ripples in the water, we all held only a part of this saga in our own memories and experiences. I thought of all the people my ordeal had affected, of all the ripples it would take to piece the whole thing together into one clear picture. Staring at the waves, I knew that the whole of it would never be discernible to me or anyone else. All the little waves would never stop, never come together into a cohesive portrait. Just as the molecules of water in a flowing river are forever intermingling, the wide array of people that had played a part in what I had considered mostly my own dilemma would never come together again in the same arrangement.

How I could even begin to somehow make amends to the families of the men killed and thank all those who had tried to help was totally beyond me. The tears began anew, and Dan finally grabbed the chair out of my hand and set it up on the gravel. Putting his hand on my shoulder he said, "Mitch, why don't you sit down. Before we hear your story, there's something you need to know, and I think you should sit down for it."

Looking at him and seeing his concern, I tried to stem my tears with a few swipes across my eyes. Dan opened the cooler and pulled out three beers and a water bottle. After handing a beer to Jack and I and the water to Debbie, he sat down on the cooler as the rest of us took the chairs.

Looking me in the eye for a second, he said, "I haven't even told Beth this yet, but Andrea called me the other day."

Beth looked puzzled, and I felt a premonition of what he said next.

"She's living with another man, a reporter she met when she came down here. I've been wondering why she wasn't calling lately, but I didn't expect that from her. She has filed a request to have you declared as deceased so she can get a divorce."

Taking this in, I strangely felt no anger, surprise, or shock. Instead, a sense of relief and an unexpected calmness washed over me. My own fears of reprisals were certainly not over and to subject her to them again wouldn't be fair. She had obviously been telling the truth at the farmhouse and had planned on getting away from me even then. Though it had only been four months, the chance I was still alive must seem miniscule to her considering the situation. The only thing that really bugged me about it was that she was living with a reporter she'd met because of my disappearance. Suddenly, staying 'dead' seemed like the best course of action I could take. I said, "Maybe that's not such a bad idea."

They had all given me a moment to ponder this news, looking at me with varying degrees of concern and, in Beth's case, apparently disgust. She said, "To tell you the truth, Mitch, me and her never really hit it off. She told me the first time she was here, right before the meeting with the search volunteers, that she felt in her heart that you were dead. After that she never seemed to give it much chance that you weren't. Oh, she acted concerned and put up a front for the news and all, but she almost seemed . . . well . . . . anxious . . . for it all to be over with. She didn't even talk to your family much, like she was trying to distance herself from them. It almost was like she thought you got what you deserved."

I tried to picture how she would react if I showed up on her doorstep, but couldn't quite imagine the scene. The desire to even see her again vanished, for no matter what I would never be able to forget her rejection. It was time to put her in the past and think about my real family.

"Have you kept in touch with the rest of my family? Jack said they spent a lot of time looking for me."

Dan said, "Yeah, I think I've met them all. About twenty of them were here for the first week of the search. A lot of people called and said they'd seen you, some from all over the country. Your mom and dad stayed for the first month and manned the phones and such. I finally had to convince them to go home because I could see their spirits sinking as the days went by.

You have a lot of people who love you, Mitch, even if your wife doesn't. I hope you know that."

"Do you know if Morgan and Patricia are still in the states?"

"Morgan went back to Uganda after a couple weeks, but Patricia has been transferred to New York. They both still call me every week or two. You sure have two wonderful daughters. Patricia stayed with your parents for the first three weeks and she was a real inspiration to all the searchers. Said you were capable of living in the woods forever and that you were trying not to be found. She still acts like you're just away for a while and expects you to come back anytime. Her and Andrea had a few . . . disagreements . . . about that and didn't seem to like each other much."

"They never really did. Patricia's got a heart of gold and she never appreciated Andreas' sarcasm and snide remarks. She even told me not to marry her. Said I couldn't trust her to not run off with another man. I guess she knew her better than I did."

"Well, she obviously knows you pretty well too. What happened after I left? Why were you even where you were when you shot John Shaw? The official report says you left when the fighting was going on, and nobody there knew why. What really happened?"

I proceeded to tell them the whole story of Mr. Smith, my encounter with John Shaw, and my reasoning for disappearing.

Over the last four months I had purposely fostered a steady conviction in the wisdom of my decision. Only my belief that remaining unfound was mine and my family's best option had enabled me to justify and tolerate my seclusion. Coupled with what Dan and Beth had experienced that day at Big Creek, the tale of Mr. Smith's actions had them nodding in agreement with my assessment.

". . . well, after Nathan died I was about ready to . . . . chuck myself over the ledge . . . . the whole thing was just . . . I don't know . . . too hard to take. Then Mr. Smith shows up and starts telling me it's all my fault and that I don't even deserve to be around and that I got Nathan and all the other soldiers killed. I kind of lost it and told him to fuck off, then he sucker punches me and acts like he's going to shoot me . . . . so I kicked him in the balls. He hits his head on a rock and looks like he might die and then these two snipers show up and they basically told me to run away."

I expected them to be somewhat miffed at me, but when Dan spoke I knew my apprehension was unwarranted. He said, "That guy gave me the creeps. He wanted to be informed the minute you were found and gave me a satellite phone to call him if you were. So you actually gave him that lump?"

"Yeah, and I don't think he'll forget. I was unarmed and on my back and he was pulling out his pistol. Even the two snipers thought he was about ready to cap me. They must have stuck to their word if they never said anything about seeing me. Tell the truth, I've been more worried about running into him again than the guys from the Inner Circle."

"That explains a lot. How many other people know about you besides us here?"

Debbie spoke up and said, "Mitch came into the shop today and I recognized him pretty quick. I think maybe a few of the customers did also, but Brian really recognized him right before we headed out here. He expects Mitch to come down to the station by tomorrow. He promised me he'd keep it under his hat till then."

Jack added, "My folks know too, but you don't have to worry 'bout them saying anything."

Dan thought about this for a moment before saying, "I think if I talk to Brian we can get him to keep quiet about it. The other thing I need to tell you Mitch is that I know I've had someone watching me the whole time. I've never seen anyone that I could be sure of or anything, but the feeling just won't go away. We had round the clock protection for the first month and nothing happened, so they said we didn't need it anymore and finally left. I was glad when they did, but started feeling a little anxious about everything pretty soon afterwards . . . Maybe it's just a feeling . . . . I don't know. I just know in my heart that you shouldn't assume everything is over."

Even in the dwindling light, the familiar jaw set reminded me instantly of the last time I'd seen him. He truly had as foreboding a sense of the future as I, his earnest expression conveying this clearly.

So many questions remained to be asked that I didn't know where to start. If even Dan felt some sort of premonition still then my own should not be ignored.

The distant sound of vehicles crunching gravel on the entrance road broke the thoughtful silence. Everyone turned their heads towards the quickly loudening crescendo of multiple cars approaching at a much faster pace than the road would normally dictate. A collective grimace formed on our faces, for we all knew it wasn't more campers.

Debbie broke the tension by saying, "I really thought he'd wait!"

As blue strobe lights began dancing off the river downstream I stood up and felt an urge to run across the river and disappear into the woods once again. "Better the devil you know" flashed through my conscience. A Styx chorus followed quickly, taunting me even further to run away.

"The jig is up, the news is out, they finally found me. You renegade, you had it made, retrieved for a bounty."

Dan seemed to read my thoughts as he said, "We can tell them you left a half hour ago."

My vacillation ended with those words. I would not run again. My resolve to end this, one way or the other, cemented itself in my thoughts. As the lights stopped on the road behind Jack's truck I said, "I can't do that. Let's go see what they want."

The rocky trail from the river was well lit in blue as I headed towards the road. Topping out on the small rise I saw three police cruisers and a huddle of officers conferring. I half expected them to draw their weapons and begin firing as they turned in my direction.

As I closed the distance they all stared at me, but didn't draw.

About the Author

Countless treks into the wild have given me unique moments of retrospection about the natural world and man's interaction with it. Over time, I have come to realize that the diversity of human relationships is as complex as the planet we live on. I am a contractor and currently reside in Grover, Missouri, utilizing the many pristine public areas of southern Missouri for nearly all of my outdoor adventures.